MILLENNIAL RITES

DOCTOR WHO – THE MISSING ADVENTURES

Also available:

GOTH OPERA by Paul Cornell
EVOLUTION by John Peel
VENUSIAN LULLABY by Paul Leonard
THE CRYSTAL BUCEPHALUS by Craig Hinton
STATE OF CHANGE by Christopher Bulis
THE ROMANCE OF CRIME by Gareth Roberts
THE GHOSTS OF N-SPACE by Barry Letts
TIME OF YOUR LIFE by Steve Lyons
DANCING THE CODE by Paul Leonard
THE MENAGERIE by Martin Day
SYSTEM SHOCK by Justin Richards
THE SORCERER'S APPRENTICE by Christopher Bulis
INVASION OF THE CAT-PEOPLE by Gary Russell
MANAGRA by Stephen Marley

MILLENNIAL RITES

Craig Hinton

DOCTOR WHO
THE MISSING ADVENTURES

First published in Great Britain in 1995 by
Doctor Who Books
an imprint of Virgin Publishing Ltd
332 Ladbroke Grove
London W10 5AH

Copyright © Craig Hinton 1995

The right of Craig Hinton to be identified as the Author of
this Work has been asserted by him in accordance with the
Copyright, Designs and Patents Act 1988.

'Doctor Who' series copyright © British Broadcasting
Corporation 1995

ISBN 0 426 20455 7

Cover illustration by Alister Pearson

Typeset by Galleon Typesetting, Ipswich
Printed and bound in Great Britain by
Mackays of Chatham Ltd

*All characters in this publication are fictitious and any resemblance
to real persons, living or dead, is purely coincidental.*

This book is sold subject to the condition that it shall
not, by way of trade or otherwise, be lent, resold, hired
out or otherwise circulated without the publisher's prior
written consent in any form of binding or cover other
than that in which it is published and without a similar
condition including this condition being imposed on the
subsequent purchaser.

This book is dedicated
to the memory of my dear friend,
Ian Mitchell Clarke

Wer mit Ungeheuern kämpft, mag zusehn, daß er nicht dabei zum Ungeheuer wird. Und wenn du lange in einen Abgrund blickst, blickt der Abgrund auch in dich hinein.
He who fights with monsters might take care lest he thereby become a monster. And if you gaze for long into an abyss, the abyss gazes also into you.
*Nietzsche – Jenseits von Gut und Böse
(Beyond Good and Evil)*

A sad tale's best for winter.
I have one of sprites and goblins.
Shakespeare – The Winter's Tale

Prologue

In the Beginning Was the Word

Yeti, Cybermen, Daleks. Ashley Chapel stared at the images on the three television screens in fascination. On the first, unstoppable silver figures strode through the deserted streets of London. The second showed huge furry creatures patrolling the silent London Underground, while the final video displayed squat, metallic monsters with their ape-like servants, engaging army troops outside a country house.

Chapel paused all three recordings and frowned. Thanks to his sources, he now had all the proof he needed that the Earth was prey to all manner of alien invasions, and it was only a matter of time before the planet's valiant defenders – Dame Anne Travers's precious UNIT – met their match. He sighed. The Earth needed a man of vision, a man of strength, to unify and protect.

He thought of his late lamented employer, Tobias Vaughn, and shook his head. During the five years that he had been Vaughn's personal assistant, Chapel had bought into his dreams of unity and direction. The people of Earth were weak and directionless, and Vaughn had known that he was the only one who could lead humanity and protect it from conquest.

But Vaughn had made a single mistake: his allies were ill chosen. The Cybermen had betrayed him, and Vaughn's life had been the cost of that betrayal.

Chapel stood up and walked over to the window. Outside, night was falling over London, but he could still make out the reconstruction work going on at Canary Wharf. He smiled. When Cesar Pelli's Tower was complete, Chapel fully intended to occupy it with his portfolio of companies. But there were more pressing matters to attend to that evening.

Opening a cupboard, he pulled out a metal tray holding a complex assembly of electronic circuits. Very special electronic circuits.

Vaughn may have died, but his legacy lived on: the micro-monolithic circuit, invention of the Cybermen, was Chapel's; he now owned the patent, and despite its inclusion in virtually every piece of electronic household equipment, only Chapel knew of its hidden nature.

For the last five years, he had been experimenting with the circuit. Vaughn's notes — and Chapel's genius — indicated that the circuits could be used to boost the latent telepathic potential of the human mind, and his experiments up till now validated that idea. But experiments on animals could only reveal so much; the time had come for the final test of the circuit's abilities.

Placing the thin metal circlet over his head, Chapel switched on the device. As a faint humming rose from the assembly, he concentrated, reaching out with his mind.

Vaughn had first contacted the Cybermen through the clumsy medium of radio. But radio could lie, radio could hide the truth. Anybody who heard Chapel's pleas would see the conviction in his heart, and would be incapable of lying in return. Chapel would choose his allies wisely, unlike Vaughn, and those allies would give him the backing he needed to set the Earth straight once more.

For the briefest of moments, Chapel was convinced that he could hear Vaughn's mocking laughter, but that was impossible, wasn't it? And then his mind touched something — someone. An intellect that burnt more brightly than the sun, an incandescence of genius that radiated inside Chapel's skull.

Saraquazel.

It wasn't just a name, it was a word of power, of glory, of majesty. A word that resonated with possibilities, all of which could now be achieved.

Chapel had found his ally.

Dawn was breaking when Chapel finally severed the link. Not that he would ever need the device again; he and Saraquazel were bonded. And together, they would usher in a new age of harmony and prosperity.

A new millennium.

Part One

Fin de Siècle

One

'Melanie Bush, you really are a sanctimonious old prude,' snapped Chantal Edwards. 'We're in the nineteen-nineties, not the eighteen-nineties.' The attractive brunette shook her head. 'You haven't changed, have you?'

Mel's expression didn't waver. Morals were morals, whatever the century, and her old university friend's brazen revelation that she was having an affair with a married man deserved only one response.

'I stand by what I said, Chantal. What about this man's poor wife? Sitting at home, unaware that her husband's having yet another romantic tryst with you – how must she be feeling?' Mel was so indignant that she almost stamped her feet.

In an attempt to calm down, she looked around the large room, which was festooned with Christmas decorations and packed with her contemporaries. And sighed. What secrets were they hiding? In calendar terms, it had been ten years since she had last been in the Student Union of the University of West London; ten years in which her former classmates had married, had affairs, had babies. But for Melanie Bush, time traveller, it had only been a couple of years since she had sipped her orange juice and winced at the noise from the latest student band. Such were the vagaries of time travel, she decided, returning her attention to Chantal. 'Well?'

Chantal sighed. 'His wife happens to be doing exactly the same thing, Melanie,' she continued. 'Only last week, we had to leave a restaurant because she came in with her toyboy.'

Mel ran a hand through her cascade of red curls. 'Then you're all as bad as one another. Two wrongs don't make a right, you know.' But she was suddenly acutely aware that Chantal had gained an experience of life over the last decade that she had missed out on, and momentarily wondered whether she should try to temper her high moral stance. Her friend's next words made her mind up for her.

'So, how's your love life? Or, did you finally decide to become a professional virgin?' Chantal transfixed her with a cold stare.

Any response that Mel was composing – and she was having difficulty – was aborted by the arrival of Julia Prince. Plain and unremarkable when she had been a student, the last ten years had affirmed Julia's frumpiness. Mel couldn't understand why the woman didn't do something about her hair, her clothes, her make-up; but at least she and Julia had seen eye-to-eye on those delicate ethical issues.

'Julia!' she exclaimed, grasping her hand warmly. 'You look –' For a second, Mel's natural kindness was almost overridden by her desire to say something about her friend's appearance. But her sensitivity won out. 'You haven't changed a bit!' she gushed.

The woman with the mousy hair tied up in a bun and thick glasses smiled, revealing slab-like teeth. 'Nor have you, Melanie. Have you been in suspended animation for the last ten years?'

Mel smiled contritely. The computer science reunion at West London University was neither the time nor the place for her to admit that she had spent the last couple of years in the company of an eccentric time traveller. Nor could she explain to Chantal, Julia or any of the others that she had persuaded – although bullied might have been a better description – that same time traveller into nipping forward to 1999, so that she could attend the long-arranged reunion. She thought of a suitable reply that was both sufficiently evasive yet truthful. Naturally. She glared at Chantal. 'Healthy living and a clear conscience – much better than any pills or potions, or –' The next words were spoken as if blasphemous, and directed towards the unaware Leonor Pridge and her reshaped nose, '– or surgery.' Leonor's ears must have burned, because she looked directly at Mel and gave a tiny wave.

'So, what are you doing now?' asked Julia, enthusiastically. 'The lecturers reckoned you were the brightest one out of all of us.'

Already committed to a discussion on nose-jobs and breast enhancements, Mel was momentarily stuck for an answer. And again, she decided to fudge the issue. 'Oh, I've been travelling. All over, really.'

'I would have thought that you'd have been snapped up by one of the big computer companies. Or didn't you fancy being a corporate woman?' said Chantal, making the words 'corporate woman' sound like 'prostitute'.

Mel's perfectly accurate memory went back to her final year at West London, when the big companies had turned up to interview them as part of the so-called 'milkround'. Her qualifications had been impressive, and all the major computer companies, such as IBM, I^2 and Ashley Chapel Logistics, had offered her jobs.

She had already turned down the place at I^2; and after what the Doctor had told her recently about that particular company, she was quite relieved. She was as broad-minded as the next person, but working for a company whose director was a bionic snake seemed almost unpatriotic. And she clearly remembered her interview with David Harker, ACL's head of development; she had been very impressed by what he had to tell her about the company, and probably would have accepted the position he offered her as a junior programmer. If the Doctor hadn't intervened.

'I was going to work for ACL,' Mel replied.

'Then you'd have been looking for another job now,' Chantal pointed out. 'They're all being made redundant today. I thought you would have known.'

'It's funny that you should mention ACL,' said Julia, rescuing Mel from trying to come up with a response to Chantal. 'It's all thanks to Chapel that this place is here.' She gestured through a nearby window at the impressive library and computer block, ten storeys of polished aluminium. 'Ashley Chapel funds the university to the tune of millions. He baled out the university when it was having financial problems, and then pumped loads of hard cash into setting up the best compsci department in the country.' She smiled. 'Then again, I'm biased: I work here. Have done since I graduated.'

'That's right,' agreed Mel. 'I remember you applying for a place here.' But Julia's account of Ashley Chapel's generosity was puzzling. She could clearly remember that Chapel had been considered to be something of a philanthropist, but why fund West London University, she wondered. Surely it would have made more sense to go to one of the more prestigious universities, such as Oxford or Warwick? Before she could say anything, Julia continued.

'Actually, it's all a bit weird,' she whispered in conspiratorial tones, ushering Mel and Chantal closer with a furtive wave. 'One of the conditions of the funding was the setting up of a research team that reports directly to Chapel.'

'What's so weird about that?' asked Chantal, grabbing another glass of white wine from the nearest table. 'Most universities have direct links with industry – it's how they survive. The company I work for does a lot of work with Luton Uni's psychology department.'

'That's not what I meant,' said Julia. 'Chapel's team is working on some really odd stuff, new computer languages, that sort of thing.'

Mel shrugged. 'Isn't that what they're meant to do?'

But Julia smiled, and Mel got the feeling that she was about to deliver the *coup de grace*.

She wasn't wrong. With a drama-laden voice she announced: 'They've solved Fermat's Last Theorem, algebraically!'

Mel cocked an eyebrow. A large part of her degree had included mathematics, and the importance of such a discovery wasn't lost on her. The algebraic solution to Fermat's Last Theorem – which stated that equations of the form $y^n = x^n + z^n$ were insoluble if n was greater than 2 – had been a mathematical Holy Grail ever since the seventeenth century, when the French mathematician Pierre Fermat had indicated that he had proved it. Unfortunately for mathematics, he had neglected to write the proof down, claiming that the margin of his copy of Diophantes had been insufficiently wide to contain it. Others had been trying, and failing, to duplicate his work ever since. So, solving it was a key mathematical discovery.

'Fine,' said Chantal. 'So the university gets another award, and everyone's happy.' She leant over and grabbed another glass of wine. Mel couldn't help tutting: that made six glasses in the last hour.

'You only get awards if you let people know what you've done,' Julia stated. 'They proved the Theorem a year ago, but I haven't seen it published anywhere. Have you?'

This last question was aimed at Mel, who shook her head, but she was rather behind with her technical journals. Mainly because the sorts of journals the Doctor had lying around the TARDIS were a little too esoteric for her tastes, with titles such as *Abstract Meanderings in Theoretical Physics* and *Wormhole Monthly*.

'All I know is that they solved it, and then kept it quiet. All seems a bit suspicious to me.' Julia was really pressing her discovery.

And to me, decided Mel. Filing the information away in her photographic memory and tagging it so that she would mention it to the Doctor a little later, she changed the topic of conversation to fashion. And hair. And make-up. And how they would dramatically improve Julia's life.

The newly opened Chapel Suite of the Dorchester Hotel was packed. Surrounded by antique mahogany tables and Chippendale chairs, with unbelievably heavy crystal chandeliers hanging overhead, the Civil Service mandarins floated round the buffet with prim expressions and prissy small talk, while junior ministers from all four of the major parties made polite but pointed conversation amongst the wine and the canapés. And, sitting at the centre of the celebration, trying to make out that she was enjoying the whole shebang, was a woman whose expression made it embarrassingly clear that she wasn't.

Despite the fact that today was her fiftieth birthday, she was modestly aware that she had aged well: her high cheekbones and thin, arched eyebrows, coupled with good skin and doe-like eyes, definitely belied her five decades. And, although her once black hair was now shot through with grey, she looked ten years younger.

But Dame Anne Travers OBE, scientific advisor to the Cabinet and reason for the party, was well aware that she was in great danger of becoming a right party-pooper. All these people, here to celebrate the fact that she hadn't died yet, all eating and drinking and taking absolutely no real notice of her, save the odd 'hello' and 'how are you?' She shuddered at the hypocrisy of it all. And at the inappropriate choice of location.

She had risen through the ranks, from scientist to civil servant, before finally replacing Rachel Jensen as chief scientific advisor to the Cabinet. Anne had held that position for the last eighteen years, offering her advice and counsel to successive governments. Every aspect of British scientific policy had fallen under her remit, from the aborted attempt to tap geothermal energy early on in her tenure, to the British Space Programme of the nineteen-eighties. But her greatest professional success had been the UK branch of UNIT, the United Nations Intelligence Taskforce; under her, it had received enough funding to become an example to the rest of the UN of how to run a paramilitary organization, and repel alien invasions into the bargain.

But throughout that period, two subjects had been guaranteed to elicit strong emotions within her: one of UNIT's earliest enemies, and the man standing on the other side of the suite that he had paid for, the suite that bore his name. Ashley Chapel, philanthropist and genius. The man who had destroyed her father's life. And when she discovered which of her underlings had reckoned that the Chapel Suite at the Dorchester would make a perfect place to celebrate her birthday, she would bounce them around Whitehall and right out of the door.

'Care for a drink, Dame Anne?' The voice was charming yet forceful, and Anne couldn't help but look up from her reverie. The man addressing her was tall and heavily built, and dressed in the boringly ubiquitous dinner suit worn by all of the male attendees. His hair was curly and light brown, and his face was friendly, and obviously capable of deep passions. He was holding two glasses of white wine. Anne rose from her chair and took a glass.

'Thank you, but I don't believe I've had the pleasure,' she said, smiling. Falsely.

'I'm afraid you have, Dame Anne,' the man grinned. 'But it was a long, long time ago.' He squeezed her hand. 'I'm the Doctor.'

Anne stared at him as if he were mad. Which of course he was: the Doctor was a small man with a mop of dark hair and an impish expression, a man whose knowledge had helped both her and her father in their personal crises. A man who would have understood the problems that weighed so heavily on her mind. Not this imposing figure who brimmed with arrogance and bravado.

He stepped back and held up his hands. 'I admit, I'm

not your father's Doctor. But I am the genuine article, all the same. If you want proof . . .' He placed his glass on a nearby table and reached into his black jacket, producing an object which made Anne gasp as he held it on the flat of his left hand. 'Recognize it?' he whispered ominously, rolling the ball around on his palm.

It was all too familiar – and all too intimate. She grabbed the shiny silver sphere without asking and turned it over in her hands as if it burnt. The surface reflected her face and hair in pink swirls and grey loops of confusion, mirroring both her looks and feelings.

'Where did you get this?' she hissed. And then louder. 'Where!'

'Hush,' muttered the man, making her aware of the increasingly curious audience with an askance nod. 'If you need further proof, I retrieved it from a deactivated Yeti near the Goodge Street platform of the Northern Line about twenty-five years ago.' His tone changed to one of long-standing annoyance. 'After Jamie and Colonel Lethbridge-Stewart accidentally thwarted my plans to destroy the Great Intelligence, that is.'

Anne staggered back and grabbed the arm of her chair, ignoring the stares from the other guests, vaguely aware of the Doctor grabbing the falling sphere with an underhand catch and dropping it into her handbag. A small portion of her mind accepted the fact that the stranger was the same man who had helped her father against the Intelligence in the Tibetan mountains, who had then turned up forty years later – looking not a day older – to fight the same evil in a web-ensnared London. It was helped by the circumstantial evidence: Lethbridge-Stewart's mysterious scientific advisor, instrumental in the two Auton attacks, the Axon presence, the Zygon gambit with the Loch Ness Monster; wasn't that scientific advisor called 'the Doctor'? And a report that had arrived on her desk only a few months ago – from Brigadier Winifred Bambera, wasn't it? – had mentioned the invaluable help provided by UNIT's former scientific advisor in the

Carbury situation. And weren't there four totally different descriptions of this 'Doctor': a scruffy clown, a debonair dandy, a bohemian, and an imp with a Scots' burr? Why shouldn't this tall man with his fruity expression and cat-like manner be yet another version of the same person?

Glorious, glorious rationalization. But it didn't stand a chance against the deep-seated terror that preyed on her mind every second of the waking day, and in every corner of her nightmares. Her greatest fear, and it was intimately connected with the Doctor. She couldn't help the outburst that exploded from her.

'So why the hell have you come this time? Another visitation by the Intelligence?' She knew that she was shouting, but she didn't care. She didn't care about the mandarins with their holier-than-thou expressions. She wasn't worried about the Leader of the Opposition, all handbag and perm, raising her eyebrows in indignation. She ignored Prince William's alarmed look. She didn't even care about Ashley Chapel himself, who turned from his conversation with the Defence Minister and gave her a quizzical stare. All she cared about was that her greatest fears stood personified in front of her, greeting her like a long lost friend, his handshake the precursor to death and horror and alien invasion.

'No,' he said quietly, smiling with understanding. 'I've come to celebrate your birthday.'

She deflated, sinking her body into the chair and her face in her hands. 'I – I'm sorry.'

The Doctor knelt down next to her. 'That sounded like a heart-felt plea for help, Anne.' He grabbed her shaking hand. 'Would you like to tell me about it?'

Anne's feelings were in turmoil. This had been meant as a happy occasion, one where she could wallow in the plaudits and praise from her friends, rivals and outright enemies, while nibbling the odd vol-au-vent and passing an inconsequential few words with the Chief Whip or a minor Whitehall dignitary. And although things had started badly – the Chapel Suite, indeed – she hadn't really been prepared to enjoy herself anyway. But seeing the Doctor was making it unimaginably worse, bringing back all the dreadful memories that had haunted her over the last twenty-five years, since her first encounter with the Great Intelligence and its furry robot hordes.

She didn't move from the chair, aware that her whole body was shivering uncontrollably. 'I've kept it to myself for all these years,' she whispered, an admission and a plea in one.

'I think we need to talk,' said the Doctor reassuringly. 'At least, you need to talk.'

She dabbed at her eyes with a paper tissue, hurriedly retrieved from her handbag. And managed a weak smile. 'I – I'd like that.'

Barry Brown sauntered down the wide corridor, hands in suit pockets. Possibly not the demeanour expected from a professional, but he didn't really give a toss. Today was his last day of gainful employment, and if his bosses took offence at his casual manner, what difference would it make? Eventually, he would have to clear his desk of personal belongings, but that could wait. He was more concerned about the people he was going to miss than a few old journals and a couple of out-dated books.

He reached the double doors that led into the next section of the office area – in truth, the whole office was nothing more than a vast, open square, partitioned into smaller areas by yellow metal walls and glass doors – and caught his reflection in the glass: he knew that he was cursed with one of those permanently miserable-looking faces, but even he was surprised by exactly how dejected he seemed. He brushed his light brown fringe out of his eyes and tutted at his collar length hair; with all the recent upsets, he had totally forgotten to get it cut. It was time he got somebody to cheer him up. Or make them as miserable as he felt, he decided maliciously.

He reached the third bay in the area and crept round

the partition. Louise Mason was furiously typing at the keyboard of her Tablette computer, watching the words appear on the LCD screen with absolutely no enthusiasm – just desperation.

'Ciggie?' he whispered in her ear, smiling with satisfaction as she jumped in her seat.

'Oh, it's you,' she gasped, putting her hand on her chest. 'You half scared me to death.' She nodded at the slim black Tablette on her desk, before running a hand through her blonde hair.

'Well?' asked Barry.

'What? Oh, a cigarette.' She shrugged. 'Yeah, why not?' Although Louise didn't smoke, she was as much a regular in the smoking room as any of the twenty-a-day brigade.

Barry raised an eyebrow. 'Because Derek Peartree might be in there?' he laughed.

The rumours of redundancies had first started back in September, three months ago, and the ACL gossip network – infinitely more efficient than the Internet, and usually coordinated by himself and Louise from the depths of the smoking room, where most of the rumours originated – had gone into overdrive, especially given the mysterious circumstances surrounding the bankruptcy of the company's long-time rival, I^2. All manner of possibilities had been mooted, but the truth had come in the form of a terse e-mail message to all employees. With a few exceptions, everyone would be made redundant on 30 December.

Derek Peartree had been the person who had appeared to take it worst of all. The first reports of his behaviour in the smoking room had been greeted with disbelief by the gossip network. But, after a number of reliable witnesses had seen him crying openly, he became one of the few bits of entertainment to liven up the increasingly depressing atmosphere. Eventually, very few people in the company had failed to encounter the weeping programmer, boring everyone stupid with the same old anecdotes and the same old emotions.

Louise shook her head. 'No fear of that,' she said. 'He's off with the outplacement consultants.'

ACL's term for an up-market job club, Barry mused. He fiddled with her mouse. 'Then I hope they've stocked up with kleenex.' He pointed at the screen, where a table of schools, qualifications and experience stared back at him. 'Another CV?' he asked, rhetorically.

Louise stood up, smoothing down her ankle-length green skirt and adjusting her white blouse. And then she shrugged and gave a wry smile. 'Of course. Some of us have got to find new jobs.' There was venom in the statement, but it wasn't aimed at Barry. Rather, it was aimed down the corridor, where the advanced research group sat. The fifteen members of that particular team were the only survivors of the sweeping cuts in ACL headcount that Ashley Chapel had decreed, and, by six o'clock that night, they would be the only people still employed by the company.

'Calm down. It's not going to do any good if we upset Chapel's chosen few, is it?' Barry was well aware of the threat of 'retroactive dismissal' that senior management had leaked to the gossip network: if you displeased Chapel in any way, he was well within his rights to demand the generous redundancy payment back. Not something that either Barry or Louise could really afford, given the current Government's position on state benefits.

The flush faded from her cheeks. 'I suppose not. Anyway, how's your job search going?'

Barry looked up from correcting her spelling with a puzzled look. And then realized. 'I forgot to tell you: I've been accepted on that catering course. I'll be doing that for the next three months.' He grinned as he dreamt about a future of haute cuisine, far away from technical manuals and bad-tempered programmers. Food – both cooking it and eating it – was his greatest passion, as his waistline proclaimed, and the course promised a three-month respite from the dole queue.

She smiled. 'Well done. And there was me thinking that you were going to become an award-winning novelist.'

He pointed at the gold- and silver-jacketed book that lay on Louise's desk: *Programmer's Reference Guide to the ACL Probe Language*. 'That's hardly going to win me the Booker Prize, is it?'

Louise pulled Barry from the chair by his sleeve and pulled him towards the corridor. 'Given your last three work appraisals, I doubt it.'

With an ironic grunt, Barry followed her past the morbid people who were worrying about their future, and the few smug people who weren't. Well, someone had to keep her in check, didn't they? He still remembered narrowly preventing her from barging into Chapel's office and giving him a piece of her mind when the news of their imminent redundancy had been announced. 'I've got a good feeling about the future. I mean, the new millennium and all that? A new beginning for all of us.'

'Thanks for the platitudes,' said Louise, but she wasn't laughing. 'I'll remember that when I'm queuing up to collect my job-seekers' allowance after the redundancy money runs out. Then again, it's all right for you. You haven't got any responsibilities.'

Barry winced. 'Thank you for reminding me of my marital status, Lou. That's just what I need.'

'Oh, I'm sorry,' she said. 'I didn't mean it like that –'

He held up a hand to stop her. 'I know, I know. Cassie,' he stated.

'Who else? I'm a single parent and I'm about to be made redundant. What reason have I got to look forward to the year 2000?'

As the atmosphere grew ever more morbid, they reached the double doors that led from the office area to the toilets, lifts and smoking room, and Barry felt a slight moment of nausea in the pit of his stomach; David Harker, Chapel's head of programming development and right-hand man, was coming the other way. The atmosphere plummeted even further.

While Ashley Chapel's presence was mainly due to his charismatic personality, Harker's was a direct result of his physical appearance. He was large, in the way that brick walls are large. And grey, in the way that battleships are grey. This was reinforced by a couple of things: his never-changing grey suit (Barry suspected that Harker had a wardrobe full of them) and his never-changing expression: grumpy. Actually, that wasn't strictly true: he did smile, occasionally. And then everyone knew that it was time to run for cover. But the Harker pushing open the door was the grumpy version, so Barry relaxed, and hurried Louise forward before she could launch into yet another tirade. He reached into his suit jacket and felt for his cigarettes and lighter.

As soon as Louise opened the door of the smoking room, she realized her error. She should have peered through the frosted glass porthole in the door and checked before barging in. But it was too late now; Barry was pushing past her, and Louise tried to suppress a smirk at his horrified expression.

Derek Peartree was in the smoking room.

Barry sat down in one of the plastic chairs and lit up; Louise sat opposite and shrugged. At least Derek didn't seem to be crying.

'I thought you were supposed to be with the outplacement consultants?' asked Barry, politely.

Derek leaned back in his chair and smiled, revealing a mouthful of uneven and yellowing teeth. 'Well, that's where you're wrong, Mister Brown,' he said unctuously, and Louise shuddered. The man had no redeeming features. 'I don't need to go searching for another position, so I don't need those do-gooders tearing my CV apart and telling me that my skills aren't marketable any more.' He scratched at the scraggly beard that just about covered his pointed chin.

'You've got a job?' replied Barry. 'That's – that's great,'

he finished, trying to sound pleased for him. And failing.

'Indeed I have, young man.' He took another cigarette from the packet on the table and lit it. Oh God, thought Louise. If only we'd been five minutes later. 'I've taken up Mister Chapel's most generous offer –'

'You've taken the King's shilling? You're joining Chapel's private army?' Barry sounded both surprised and angry, and Louise could understand why; they were out on their ears, and someone like Derek was staying on? It just didn't seem fair.

'Doing what, exactly?' asked Louise.

Derek stopped trying to peer down her blouse and frowned. 'My dear young lady, I can't tell you that. As a member of Mister Chapel's advanced research team, I appreciate the need-to-know basis of the work that's going on. And since neither of you were considered suitable material for the team, it wouldn't be my place to speak out of turn, would it?'

Louise sighed. She wasn't sure what was worse: Derek as an emotional wreck, or Derek as a supercilious old fart. Deciding that the latter was by far the more disagreeable, she stubbed out her cigarette and indicated for Barry to do the same.

'Sorry, Derek, must dash. Things to do,' she muttered.

'Such as?' he whined. 'You're being made redundant, aren't you?'

She bit her lip. 'Packing, that sort of thing.' She followed Barry through the door, as Derek carried on talking. The fact that there was no audience any more didn't seem to slow him down. Then again, Derek Peartree had always been his own best audience.

'I have a meeting with Mister Chapel later on this evening, when he'll tell me the important role I'm going to play in his operation . . .'

As the droning voice faded in the distance, Barry shook his head. 'Member of the advanced research team? He's not even fit to be a member of the human race.'

* * *

'So, what was all that about?' asked the Doctor, handing Anne Travers a glass of Australian Chardonnay. He had led her to a private inglenook, well away from the fawning and inquisitive dignitaries, in a quieter room in the Dorchester: two leather armchairs, a low mahogany table, and a wonderful view of Hyde Park, covered in snow. Very festive, Anne decided.

She sipped the wine and smiled. A 1994 – a good vintage. After all these years of holding back, of bottling up her hidden horrors, the knowledge that she was just about to release it all was akin to the anticipation of having sex, and the wine was a perfect accompaniment. Indeed, this current incarnation of the Doctor wasn't that bad looking. But it was time to ease her conscience rather than fulfil her repressed libido. 'The Great Intelligence,' she stated.

The Doctor frowned. 'What about it? It was defeated almost thirty years ago. I repelled it from its human host and left it adrift in the void.'

'It came back four years ago, Doctor. Or didn't that particular invasion merit your attention?' she added spitefully.

He stroked his chin. 'As a matter of fact, no, it didn't. Earth's defenders – the defenders that you've devoted your career to supporting – managed to overcome its perfidy without my assistance.'

She had to admit that the Doctor was correct. The forces of UNIT, bolstered by some old friends, had proved victorious, but the cost had been in a coinage that she had not been prepared to pay. 'Whether it was defeated or not, Doctor, the fact remains that it returned.' She shook her head. 'It's all my fault, isn't it?' She stared at him, masochistically hoping for both blame and benediction. 'I brought the Intelligence to Earth, didn't I?'

The Doctor sighed. 'Would you like to hear a story about the Great Intelligence?' He reached out and grabbed her hand.

Anne squeezed it. 'I'd like that.' Facing up to your

demons, wasn't that what you were meant to do?

The Doctor took a deep breath and picked up one of the doilies that lay on the table, protecting the varnished surface from the bowl of complimentary nuts. 'Before this universe was created, there was another one. A totally different universe, with alien physical laws. The heavens were green, and the stars looked like –' He chuckled. 'Giant doughnuts, to be brutally frank. Very, very different. And, as in this universe, there were people who discovered the deeper mysteries of time and space. In this universe, they're my people, the Time Lords. In that universe, they were also Time Lords, but they were lords of a very strange version of time and space.' His gaze shifted to the window and the snowy wastes of Hyde Park, but Anne got the feeling his thoughts were much, much further away.

'As their universe reached the point of collapse, a group of these "Time Lords" shunted themselves into a parallel dimension which collapsed seconds after ours. Moments later, they erupted into our universe, and soon discovered that they were in possession of undreamt of powers.' He swigged from his glass. 'And I'm afraid that the power went to their heads – or what passed for heads given their new bodies. They decided that since they now had god-like powers, they should behave like gods. And the one called Yog-Sothoth, who had been the Time Lords' military strategist, decided to dedicate his new-found abilities into discovering whether his tactics and stratagems would have worked.' He held up the transformed doily: it now resembled a string of white Yeti.

Anne placed the glass on the table. 'Yog-Sothoth? Now why does that sound familiar?'

'It's the Intelligence's real name, and it crops up in certain arcane literature from time to time. Over the billennia, he mounted thousands – millions – of campaigns against inhabited planets, trying out the gambits and games that he had only played on computers in his previous existence. On Hiskith, he chose to use the Hisk version of koala bears to invade; on Danos, domestic animals – like dogs – were the vanguard. And on Earth, well, the Intelligence seemed to have a fondness for Tibet and the Yeti.' The Doctor held up his hands. 'Don't ask me why. Perhaps some childhood teddy-bear fetish.'

Anne pinched up her face. 'But why did the Intelligence use the Yeti on the other occasions? They're hardly in keeping with the London Underground, are they?'

He picked up his glass and savoured the bouquet. 'Because he was under pressure to keep up with the others. After his failure in Tibet, the other transient beings muscled in and embarrassed him. Lloigor had dominated Vortis, until I turned up, that is; Shub-Niggurath conquered the planet Polymos and colonized it with her offspring, the Nestene Consciousness –'

'As in the Autons?' Anne interrupted.

'As in the Autons, yes,' agreed the Doctor, with not a little impatience. 'Surrounded by the success of his peers, and shamed into continuing, Yog-Sothoth tried once again to control this planet. But he was desperate, short on time and resources, and he had a mountain in Tibet full of Yeti parts. Once he established a bridgehead, it was child's play for him to arrange transport to London.'

Anne remembered the cleaning-up operations that had followed the incursion in the Underground. 'The Yeti production plant that UNIT found in Wimbledon.'

'Exactly. And now there's no production plant, and no bridgehead. And after the splendid show that UNIT put on four years ago, no Intelligence.'

Anne rubbed her forehead. 'If only I could be so sure. It's hovering about me – I can feel it!' She waved her hand above her head. 'It's going to come back!'

'Anne, Anne, Anne,' he insisted. 'No, no, no! The Intelligence is dead, consumed by its own hatred and corruption.' He lifted the glass from the table.

She took a deep breath. 'So why do I still feel all of

this, this apprehension? Why am I so convinced that the Intelligence is going to return?'

The Doctor shrugged. 'The mind is a mysterious mixture of logic and intuition, Anne. Perhaps this rarefied atmosphere of political intrigue is a little too heady for you.' Steepling his fingers, he gave her a mischievous grin. 'How do you fancy getting away from all this? Let's leave the mandarins to their finger buffet and see out the last days of the millennium somewhere a little more . . . sybaritic?' His eyes sparkled.

Anne forced a faint smile, which grew broader as she remembered a certain restaurant that she had always favoured. Grabbing her handbag, she rose, feeling unimaginably relieved. 'And I know just the place.'

Barry pressed the enter key and watched with more than a little sadness as the last of his personal files were downloaded to floptical. Ten years of non-management approved activities were being written onto a single three-and-a-half inch optical disk in only seconds; years of Internet gossip, amusing e-mail notes and all manner of personal correspondence; megabytes of information that Barry doubted he would even look at once he left ACL. But his nostalgic streak demanded that it should be kept.

While the last few bytes trickled onto the floptical, he looked at his desk. The innumerable recipes, all culled from countless magazines by both himself and the less serious-minded of his colleagues, had all been removed, leaving bare grey partition walls enclosing a veneer desk bearing nothing but a telephone and the black packet of his Tablette. ACL's Tablette, he reminded himself. In a few hours, his personal computing power would be massively downgraded, as he lost the vast network of Ashley Chapel Logistics, a network which had given him access to the entire world.

Barry sighed and swivelled round on his chair; this pointed him in the direction of the advanced research team, or Chapel's Private Army, as they were less than affectionately known. Five of them were sitting around one of the circular tables, pointing and whispering at the image on a Tablette screen. Not for them the depressing task of packing up the possessions of one's working life; business carried on as usual for them, the sole survivors of the draconian job cuts. Barry caught the eye of James Campling, the most approachable of the generally high and mighty team, and gave him a little wave. Campling nodded and returned his attention to the screen.

Barry shrugged, and turned to his own Tablette. The downloading was complete, so he removed the floptical and shoved it in the carrier bag, squeezing it in with the posters, course notes and copies of manuals he had written. One carrier bag. Not much to show for ten years of loyal service, was it? No, he reminded himself, not quite ten years; the redundancy meant that he missed his ten-year clock by three months. But why was he bothered by a gilded carriage clock? Others might think it to be the least of his worries.

He knew why: the sense of acceptance that the clock represented. His life lacked the continuity that most people's had. Being adopted, he had grown up knowing that his origins were a complete mystery. Whereas other people had their parents to look to for some clue as to their appearance when older, Barry had only a vague description of his natural mother and no knowledge at all about his father. Although his adoptive parents had neither hidden the truth nor withheld their love from him, there was a deep-rooted feeling of insecurity that had caused so much trouble over the last fifteen years.

Of course, he had tried to find his natural parents; he had lost count of the number of adoption agencies and organizations dedicated to reuniting children with their families that he had contacted. But every one had drawn a blank, and Barry had finally resigned himself to never knowing the woman who had given birth to him.

'Ciggie?'

It was Barry's turn to jump. Louise was standing right

behind him, her hands on the back of his chair. He leaned his head back to look at her, and was just about to agree when he spotted out of the corner of his eye that the advanced research team had vanished – probably for one of their frequent summit meetings with Chapel. When Chapel snapped his fingers, his private army started marching. He shook his head. 'No, I'm not really in the mood.'

'Oh, come on,' she urged, pointing at the wall-mounted clock: 4.30. 'We'll be out of here in an hour.' Her tone softened. 'It could be our last visit to the smoking room.' She made a trip to the nicotine-stained cupboard sound like the search for the Holy Grail, Barry decided wryly.

'I'll be in in five minutes,' he said. 'Honestly. Just let me download the rest of my stuff.'

Louise shrugged. 'Okay. See you in a bit.'

Barry waited until he was certain that she was safely through the double doors before he stood up and strode over to the area in which the advanced research team shrouded their activities from the rest of ACL. Constantly aware of the people who would be walking down the corridor behind him, he tried to act with consummate calm and confidence, knowing full well that he was shaking like a leaf. He hurriedly scanned the desktops, covered with magazines, flopticals, mousemats and the rest of the detritus that comes with being a programmer – or a technical writer, he reminded himself, remembering his own desk before he had cleared it.

And then he saw what he was looking for, nestling innocently amongst the discarded beige towers of plastic coffee cups and piles of inch-thick periodicals: a single floptical with the word CODEX written on the label in thick green felt-tip. Barry knew – as did any visitor to the smoking room, thanks to garrulous Ivan Crystal's delight in telling everybody everything – that Codex was Chapel's mysterious secret project, the raison d'être of Chapel's Private Army. In seconds, stuttering fingers had prised open the clear plastic box and shoved the floptical in his jacket pocket before strolling nonchalantly towards the corridor. He looked around, making sure that no one had seen him. The only people he could see were Digby, the youth trainee, fussing over a broken Tablette, and Dave Richards, another of the survivors, strolling into the LAN room. But neither of them had seen him.

And then he set off for the smoking room – he deserved a cigarette. But as he pushed open the double doors, the reason for his theft bounced around his mind. ACL software was notorious throughout the computing industry for being 'too much, too late': excellent applications – with outstanding technical documentation, he reminded himself proudly – trying to make their mark in an already saturated niche. If Chapel had finally realized this, and was closing ACL down because of it, well, what the hell was his private army working on? What on Earth was Codex?

The reunion was coming to an end, a fact marked by the departure of most of the reunionees. But Mel remained – having switched from wine to orange juice after a single, sociable glass that had lasted her hours – and was staring into the yellowy dregs, trying to make some sense of Julia's piece of academic espionage. Fermat's Last Theorem, solved and then ignored like an unwashed teacup; it just didn't make sense! Why would a department dedicated to research not publish one of the greatest finds in mathematical history? The problem had been preying on her mind since Julia had told her, and she had almost missed Chantal's exit with Jimmy the stud, she had been that preoccupied. Then again, she had still been able to explain to Julia about the benefits of make-up, and how it was a woman's duty to make the most of her physical appearance. And, after Julia had vanished – rather hurriedly, Mel decided – she had spent twenty minutes asking Leonor pointed questions about liposuction and rhinoplasty, but Mel's attention had been firmly fixed out of the window at the computer science block and library.

'Mel?' It was Julia, she realized, and was pleased to see that she had let her hair down – literally – and applied a little lipstick and powder. Obviously she had seen the wisdom in Mel's words, and Mel knew with certainty that Julia would see a definite improvement in her life from now on. Although any change would be an improvement, Mel thought. And then chastized herself for her bitchiness.

'Julia! You look wonderful!' Mel gushed.

Julia shook her head urgently. 'Never mind that. It's about what I told you earlier –'

Mel held her hands up. 'Don't worry, I won't breathe a word. I'm the soul of discretion,' she insisted.

'I know that. I also know that you're the best computer programmer out of all of us. That's why I want you to have this.' She handed Mel a slip of paper, her hand shaking.

Mel unfolded it and looked up in bewilderment. 'What does Codex mean?'

'Codex is the codename of the research project I was telling you about – Chapel's project. And the rest of the stuff represents the protocols and directory chains that you'll need to get access.'

'And what am I supposed to do with this?' said Mel with not a little confusion. Julia leaned forward and whispered in her ear.

'Something strange is going on, Melanie. Something . . . evil. You're the best there is. You were always streets ahead of the rest of us. You know that!' Mel blinked rapidly with embarrassed modesty. 'Could you, could you hack into the Chapel computer net?' asked Julia.

Mel's eyes opened in amazement and horror. And then she smiled, an unfamiliar thrill stirring in her stomach. 'Sounds like quite a challenge,' she said, slipping the paper into her miniature handbag. 'If you can start wearing make-up, I suppose that hacking into a computer system is the least I can do.'

* * *

Half an hour later, the reunion was well and truly over. Some of the former students had decamped to other bars in the Student Union, while others had gone home while their legs still functioned. But Julia was still sitting amongst the dirty glasses and discarded paper plates, staring into her half-empty wine glass and lost in thought.

She started as a tuneful warbling came from her handbag. She reached into it and withdrew her mobile phone.

'Hello? I've been waiting for you to call. Yes, she did turn up. And yes, I did give her the information. But I don't see – All right, all right. Yes, I'm sure that she'll be able to hack in. But –' She groaned in annoyance as he ended the call, realizing that she was still as much in the dark as ever. Why the hell did David Harker want somebody to hack into his own computer system?

Two

Number One, Canada Square. In the early eighties, the area had been the derelict remains of London's once proud shipping trade; a rat-infested, dirty no-go zone that most Londoners ignored. And then the Prime Minister had decided – in her infinite wisdom – that the Government could win the next election by transforming the decaying banks of the River Thames into the nucleus of a new inner city: expensive housing, expensive office space.

The Government lost the election, and London's Docklands remained an embarrassing aluminium and glass white elephant. Until millionaire philanthropist and genius Ashley Chapel had urged his fellow captains of industry to flock to the area. And, in particular, to Number One, Canada Square, colloquially named Canary Wharf Tower.

The building was visible from most of South London; a fifty storey tower block of polished aluminium, its roof a squat pyramid which lit up the London skyline. Chapel had set the precedent: he had moved his fledgling software company – Ashley Chapel Logistics – into the top floor immediately, and many others had followed suit, apart from the notable exception of Lionel Stabfield, who expressed a desire to keep I^2 in the Central London offices that the software and hardware firm occupied.

A golden age for the UK's computing industry seemed assured; and then the collapse began. I^2 fell, amidst rumours of extra-terrestrial involvement, and Chapel had immediately moved in and bought out their hardware and software patents, as well as the little equipment and information that remained after it ceased trading. But even that hadn't been enough: Chapel's *Probe* product was excellent, outstanding, a market leader ... but it wasn't enough in the saturated software market. Ashley Chapel Logistics simply didn't have the momentum to carry on.

On 5 November 1999, Chapel delivered the biggest firework of them all: as of Thursday, December the thirtieth, ACL would cease trading as part of the Ashley Chapel Holding Corporation. A smaller company, FantasyLab Limited, would remain, but one hundred and eighty-five of the two hundred employees would be offered generous payments.

And fired.

And now it was 30 December. Louise walked through the red marble and onyx foyer which served as the reception for all the businesses housed in Canary Wharf Tower, carrying her possessions in two silver carrier bags emblazoned with the ACL logo – a rearing golden antelope – and wearing her anger quite openly. Barry trotted beside her with his solitary bag and a look of resignation.

'So,' he muttered grimly, 'that's that, then.' He nodded at Vincent, the large and balding security guard with the thick ginger moustache, and received a friendly smile back. Vincent was one more entry on the ACL payroll that would survive the redundancy, and Louise knew that he was definitely going to miss Barry. She grabbed Barry's arm affectionately. 'Come on, Baz. You're supposed to be the one putting on a brave face.'

He shrugged. 'I know. It's just that, well, this is it, isn't it?' He gestured towards one of the sets of glass double doors that led from Canary Wharf Tower. 'Once we leave here, that's the end.'

'Thank you, Mister Cheerful,' she groaned. 'What was all that stuff about the millennium and a new beginning, then?'

Barry swallowed, and Louise realized that it was about to begin. 'That was before I realized how wrenching this was going to be. I mean, every morning for the last ten years I've said "good morning" to Vincent over there.' He nodded at Vincent, who smiled rather too warmly for Louise's liking. 'As of tomorrow, the only thing I'll be saying good morning to is going to be my cats.' He stopped and bowed theatrically to the red marble floor. 'I'll say good morning, and then I'll discuss all my problems with them as I fork out their cat food.' He poked a finger over his shoulder at the doors to the ACL lifts that lay behind them. 'That place was more than a job – we were a family, Lou – we cared about each other.'

Louise had known that this was going to happen: it was just a matter of when. Barry had taken the news of their redundancy so calmly, so rationally, that the explosion was inevitable. She urgently beckoned Vincent over as Barry started to sob uncontrollably.

'You're worse than Derek,' she whispered. 'Can't you wait until you get home?'

'D'you want some help, Lou?' asked Vincent gruffly. Louise knew that he could be counted on to help; his feelings towards Barry were just one of the many running jokes amongst the ACLers that would now run out.

'Can you order us a taxi? I don't think Barry's up to the light railway at the moment.'

Vincent nodded, trying not to stare at – or ogle – Barry as he sat down on one of the marble benches, crying. 'I see what you mean. Where are you off to, his place or yours?'

Very arch, thought Louise. 'Battersea. I think he ought to come back to mine.' She ignored Vincent's bitter expression. 'I don't think he should be left on his own. Do you?' Desperately hoping that Vincent wouldn't offer his services, Louise was relieved when he wandered off towards the phones. She sat next to her best friend and threw her arm round him. 'Come on, Baz, please pull yourself together. We'll get a taxi back to my place. My mum's there with Cassie. When she goes, you can cook.'

Barry managed a half-hearted smile. 'How do you fancy tagliatelle carbonara?'

'I wouldn't have anything else,' she replied. 'It's your signature dish, isn't it?' If there was one thing guaranteed to cheer Barry up, it was giving him the chance to demonstrate his culinary prowess. And yes, he had definitely stopped crying. She pulled him up to a standing position – given his love of alcohol, this wasn't an unfamiliar exercise – and gave Rupert Russell, who was off to take up a very lucrative contract in California, a vague farewell wave as he passed by. 'Feeling better?' she muttered in Barry's ear.

He sniffed and rubbed his eyes, and then pointed towards the huge glass doors. 'Your kitchen awaits,' he said, with a forced grin. But Louise caught the look of absolute venom that went with it.

Outside the foyer, Ashley Chapel was climbing out of his Jaguar, laughing with his chauffeur.

'Bastard,' Barry hissed.

Hanway Street, a darkly lit lane connecting Tottenham Court Road and Oxford Street, contained one of Central London's best kept gastronomic secrets: La Bella Donna. Despite its less-than-wholesome name, the restaurant served the finest Italian cuisine outside of that country, but its reputation was jealously guarded by both its management and its patrons.

It wasn't featured in the *Michelin Guide*, nor had Egon Ronay ever given it a mention. Even Michael Winner's column in the *Sunday Times* had failed to review the establishment. But all who had visited La Bella Donna had returned again and again to sample the exquisite food, the friendly service, and the comfortable surroundings. They simply chose to take part in the cover-up which maintained the restaurant's exclusivity.

Dame Anne Travers was one such patron. And, sitting at the table which was laden with glasses for every occasion, staring at the wood-panelled walls with their tasteful prints, trying not to notice the rest of the cognoscenti who were doing their damnedest not to notice her, Anne was grateful for the secluded anonymity that La Bella Donna afforded. She sipped yet another glass of wine and transfixed her dinner companion through the cut glass.

'So, what did happen to Jamie?' she asked, placing the empty glass back on the green and white tablecloth. The house red was as wonderful as ever, but she was beginning to feel a little light-headed. Then again, she wasn't harking on about the Great Intelligence anymore. The Doctor's company was as intoxicating as the wine, and he had enchanted her with stories and anecdotes which had had her laughing so much that she had managed to place that particular worry back in its box – for the time being. Victoria was fine; Anne had seen her during the Intelligence's last incursion, four years ago. But Jamie, that fine, virile young Scotsman . . .

'Ah, now there's a story,' said the Doctor, draining his glass and indicating to the waiter for another bottle. 'A few months after that dreadful business with the Cybermen – when you and your father were in the United States – I was forced to contact my own people –'

'The Time Lords,' said Anne, demonstrating her familiarity with UNIT's files.

The Doctor nodded. 'That's right, the Time Lords. And then we were forced to part company –' He broke off as an insistent bleep forced itself from within his dinner jacket.

Anne giggled like a schoolgirl. 'A portable phone? From the man with the ultimate portable phonebox?'

The Doctor gave her a rueful look. 'Melanie's idea. And, very probably, Mel's call, since I'm ex-directory – I don't want the Daleks making obscene phone calls, if you please. Anyway, if you'll excuse me.' He withdrew the little black phone from his jacket and pressed a button. 'Mel?'

All Anne heard was a hurried and emotive screech. And then the Doctor replaced the phone in his inside pocket. 'After Victoria, Mel might prove a little lively.' At that moment the waiter arrived with the wine, and the Doctor asked him to set another place at the table.

As the waiter departed, the Doctor opened the leather-bound menu and studied its contents. 'The problem with Mel is that she doesn't appreciate the finer things in life, such as tagliatelle carbonara and a good burgundy.' He tapped the leather-bound menu in front of him. 'When she discovers what we're having this evening, she will not be happy.'

'Why on Earth not?' Anne had already decided that she was going to have the carbonara – the house speciality, no less – and felt a wave of irritation at the suggestion that she might have to choose something else. She leant forward and whispered into his ear. 'She is human, isn't she?'

The Doctor pouted. 'Mel is the sweetest person imaginable – and the most human. Unfortunately, she also has the most annoying idea that she always knows best. In this incarnation, I seem to be somewhat indulgent as far as the finer things in life are concerned.' He patted his stomach, just above the black cummerbund. 'Mel has decided that a diet of rabbit food and carrot juice is the best way to keep me in trim, as if a Time Lord has to worry about cholesterol levels!' he exploded. And then he subsided, and raised his glass. 'Here's to decadence, my dear Anne!'

She clinked her glass against his. 'To decadence, Doctor!' To hell with Melanie's health regime. The carbonara it was.

Chapel threw open the door of David Harker's office and hung his grey overcoat on the hatstand in the corner. 'Any problems while I've been away, David?'

Harker looked up from his Tablette, where he appeared to have been analysing the results of the latest

Codex compilation. At least that was what Chapel hoped he had been doing. As ACL had wound down, far too many people had been abusing his computing power playing adventure games. 'Nothing that we didn't expect, Ashley. A few people throwing their weight around, a few sad tossers sitting in corners crying.' He closed the lid of the Tablette and scratched his nose. 'As mass redundancies go, this was a doddle.' He smiled. 'Better than the closure of I^2: at least the photocopiers didn't start eating people.'

Chapel didn't crack a smile; I^2's catastrophic bankruptcy had provided ACL with a portfolio of patents and a wealth of hardware which had made certain aspects of their current project possible. But now was not the time for reminiscences. Now was the future.

He sat in the chair opposite Harker and ran his hands through his swept-back hair. He had started thinning and going grey when he had been in his thirties, but somehow it had only served to reinforce the debonair image that he had tried so hard to cultivate; the image that had graced a multitude of magazines, from *PC Week* to *Time*. 'Excellent. That's what I call goodness, David.'

'How did the do go, then? Did the old bag appreciate it?'

Chapel laughed. But he wasn't feeling very amused. 'Dame Anne Travers, scientific advisor to the government. Hah!' He slammed his fist on Harker's desk, making the photograph of a much younger Harker jump into the air. 'That woman is pathetic. They all run around, pretending to respect her; everybody knows that her pet project – UNIT – is now totally in the hands of the EC. God knows why she keeps recommending that the Government up their funding!' He narrowed his eyes. 'But I'm sure she's heard rumours about what we're doing here. I wanted to have a word with her, but somebody whisked her away. Probably the first and only time somebody of the opposite sex has shown any interest in her since her husband died.'

Harker made a valiant attempt to calm his boss. 'Come on, Ashley, don't get worked up about some stupid bitch's paranoid fantasies. She's spent the last twenty years devoting herself to UNIT: that's bound to make her a bit odd. And we both know why she hates you. But there's no reason why she should suspect anything about what we're doing. Besides, we're almost there.'

'Almost there?' snapped Chapel. 'Almost there? You're my head of development, David. Can't you be a bit more precise than that? Or can't you even handle project management software? What about rustling up a Gantt chart or something?' Chapel knew that he was overreacting, but there was so little time left, and still so much to do. It was time he supported Harker, rather than denigrating him. 'What exactly is our current status, then?'

Harker stood up and stared out of the window. 'According to the last program compilation, there are still bugs,' he muttered. Very quietly. And then Chapel's good intentions flew out of that same window.

'Bugs? Bugs?' Chapel span round, grabbing a marble paperweight from Harker's desk and thumping it down on the table. 'It's supposed to be ready tomorrow,' he hissed through gritted teeth. 'Or had you forgotten why it's called the Millennium Codex, David?'

Harker turned from the window. 'Of course I haven't. But if it isn't ready . . .' He looked at the floor. 'As long as it's midnight somewhere on Earth, it'll still work. I mean, you yourself said that the date and time were nothing more than theatrics.'

Chapel arched an eyebrow. 'Maybe so, but you're being paid handsomely so that I can indulge those theatrics.' He pulled his chair next to Harker's and opened the Tablette. 'Let me run through the bugs; perhaps I'll be able to spot something you missed?'

Harker grunted and sat down, placing his hand on the black mouse as he did so. 'The compilation reckons that the main problem lies within this subroutine, Ashley.' He clicked open a program file and pointed with the cursor. 'This branch keeps looping.'

Chapel tutted and cracked his knuckles. 'If you want a job doing properly, it's always best to do it yourself.'

Despite his sarcasm, Chapel appreciated the problems that the Codex presented to the advanced research team: they were writing modules and routines in a language that they barely understood, to a design that they couldn't possibly comprehend. And as for Harker: he hadn't even seen the designs. Indeed, Chapel was the only person who really knew what was going on, and – for the next twenty-four hours at least – it was going to stay that way.

He started typing, before a stray thought occurred to him. 'Did you remember to run the inventory scan?' The scan would ensure that all ACL hardware and software had remained ACL hardware and software after the exodus, and not an added bonus for ex-employees. Although he could personally afford for every member of his erstwhile staff to walk out of the building carrying Tablettes, printers, and box-loads of flopticals, it was the principle of the thing. And that was the other codex that governed Chapel's life.

Harker nodded. 'Should have the results in about half an hour. Although I doubt that anyone would be daft enough to walk out of here with the Codex.'

Chapel gave a sinister smile. 'They'd be very sorry if they did.'

'I feel a right prat,' admitted Barry, as he plonked himself down on Louise's sofa.

Her house in Battersea was just like the sofa: comfy and well worn. But the efforts that Louise had made to liven up the house for Christmas had worked to a certain degree: the tiny tree, decorated with little wooden figures and the shapeless plasticene lumps that Cassie had made created a bright corner to the room. Despite the impressive salaries offered by ACL, the impressive mortgages that Central London demanded, coupled with the high cost of child care, meant that Louise had precious little left to spend on hearth and home. Although his own flat in Catford was hardly Habitat crossed with Laura Ashley; more like Oxfam crossed with MFI, he decided. Then again, he had a liver to support.

'Don't worry about it,' said Louise as she returned from the hallway, having seen her mother off. 'You've just been made redundant. You've got a right to be upset. At least you saved your outburst until you were almost out of the door.' She adjusted the lights, taking the glare off the room. 'I was about to tackle Chapel in his office, remember?' And then she gave him an odd look. 'Vincent was quite worried, though.'

'Don't be funny,' he snapped. For the last ten years, Vincent had made his feelings towards Barry quite clear; and although Barry wasn't gay, he wouldn't ever hurt the man's feelings and had developed a very defensive attitude towards him. 'Vince is a decent bloke. I'm just not that way inclined.'

'Tell me about it!' she laughed, throwing herself into the armchair opposite him. 'Still, I know what you mean. It's all over. Ten years of the ACL support network, and now we're on our own.'

'Don't remind me.' Barry reached into his suit and plucked out a cigarette without extracting the packet. A trick he had learnt over countless years down the pub. 'Ashtray?'

Louise reached under the coffee table and retrieved a large pottery ashtray, which Barry grabbed. He lit the cigarette and sighed. 'Were you serious about the tagliatelle, or was it a ruse to get me away from ACL?'

'Of course I was.' She reached under the cushion next to her and pulled out a packet of cigarettes. 'Have you got a light?'

Barry leaned forward, his face skewed in surprise. 'You still smoke?' Horrible feelings began to grow in his stomach. Horrible feelings that he wanted to express, but knew the trouble that they could cause.

She frowned, obviously trying to decide whether to tell the truth. Knowing Louise as well as he did, Barry knew that she would. And she did.

'I never gave up. I just didn't smoke at work. And I never smoked when you came over.' Her conscience must have got the better of her. As always.

Barry expressed his feelings, and regretted it even as he spoke. 'So you kept on smoking while you were carrying Cassie?'

Louise stood up, the cigarette packet dropping from her lap and her face announcing that this was the last thing she wanted to hear, today of all days. 'Yes,' she muttered. 'I know it was wrong, I know I should have given up. But the doctors explained that her, her problems were environmental. Okay, the smoking didn't help. But it wasn't the reason.' She pointed out of the window at the light smog that hung over London like a comfortably lethal blanket. 'That caused it, not cigarettes, not anything else but that poison out there!' She started trembling, and Barry jumped up and hugged her. But he looked back through the window at the view: through the green clouds, he could just about make out the ziggurat of the Millennium Hall, the ugly shape which blighted the once perfect view from Louise's house.

'Come on, Lou,' he whispered, stroking her back, 'I wasn't accusing you. I just wondered why you hadn't told me.' Realizing that this was one conversation that neither he nor Louise wanted to get into, he pointed towards the kitchen, which led off the hall. 'Shall I start cooking?'

She nodded, although the confession had clearly shaken her. As Barry reached the doorway, he stopped and frowned. 'What about the ingredients?' Louise wasn't known for keeping her larder fully stocked, and he had lost count of the dinner invitations which had ended up as a lash-up of lentils and the odd onion which they had found languishing at the bottom of the fridge.

Almost back to her normal, happy-go-lucky self, she giggled. 'I applied a bit of amateur psychology. I guessed that you'd be upset today, and I knew that letting you cook would bring you out of it. So I went to Safeway's yesterday and bought everything you need. It's all in bags on the table.' And then, as if she'd read his mind, 'So no need to go rooting through the crisper for a mouldy onion.'

Barry laughed. 'Great. And I've got quite a dessert lined up.' He pointed towards his silver carrier bag, plonked in the corner next to the television. 'A little bonus from Ashley Chapel Logistics.'

'And then she gave me the protocols that I'd need to get into this Codex project –' Since arriving at La Bella Donna, Mel had rattled off her story like a red-headed machine gun, sparing only a second to say hello to Anne and to order a light salad. The Doctor had been right when he'd said that Melanie Bush was nothing like Victoria; that demure woman wouldn't have lasted a second against Mel's excited self-confidence. Then again, there was a sweetness, a goodness, that Mel exuded that made it very difficult to dislike her. Get irritated about, certainly, but nothing as strong as dislike. And then something Mel had said triggered those special memories.

'Did you say Ashley Chapel?' asked Anne.

'Yes,' replied Mel. 'Why, have you heard of him?'

If Anne hadn't known that Mel came from a decade earlier and had been travelling through time and space in a police box, she would have asked her where she'd been for the last few years. Instead, she trotted out Chapel's impressive credentials. 'He's a self-made multi-millionaire, a genius, a philanthropist, and one of the most arrogant, condescending men I have ever met.'

'Sounds like someone not a million miles away,' quipped Mel, giving the Time Lord a cheery smile before sipping her mineral water.

'He made his first million about twenty years ago. After the Cybermen shut down International Electromatics,

Chapel was recognized as the man behind the company's innovative computer circuitry.' She stopped as the Doctor almost choked on his wine.

'Really?' The Doctor said in surprise. 'And I thought dear old Tobias had built that company single-handed. It only goes to show that egomaniacal megalomaniacs often exaggerate.' He raised his glass to Mel. 'Remember that, the next time we meet the Master or the self-styled Queens of the Satanic Winding Sheet.' He frowned. 'Or the Terrible Zodin, come to that.'

Mel snorted. 'Please, Dame Anne, carry on.'

'When the company was dissolved, Chapel went to court and won the rights to the patent for the micro-monolithic circuit.'

'Didn't the Cybermen appeal?' interrupted the Doctor once more, before stopping under Anne and Mel's best stares. Anne was just as aware as the Doctor that Tobias Vaughn's cybernetic allies were the true patent owners, but now was neither the time nor the place for such discussions.

'From there, he started his own company, which rapidly grew into the Ashley Chapel Holdings Corporation. Ashley Chapel Logistics was a branch of that. That began by creating systems software, before finally branching out into the consumer market: graphics packages, spreadsheets, that sort of thing.'

Mel tapped the side of her glass with a long red fingernail. 'This must have happened after I left, and that market was pretty saturated even then. His products must have been extraordinary to have succeeded.'

Anne allowed herself a rather cruel smile. 'They were, but they didn't – apart from the Paradigm operating system, of course, but that's part of a different division now. Ashley Chapel Logistics closed today with the loss of nearly two hundred jobs. Rather tarnished poor Ashley's reputation. Not that it really matters to him. I always suspected that ACL was more of a hobby than a going business concern. Over the last ten years, his private portfolio of businesses has diversified, ranging from art collecting to real estate. Especially one particular piece of real estate.' Moments after delivering the meaningful line, she realized that neither the Doctor nor Mel could have the faintest idea what she was talking about. 'The Millennium Hall,' she explained.

'I assume that it has something to do with tomorrow evening?' inquired the Doctor. 'Although as a Time Lord, I should point out that the end of this particular Millennium actually takes place at midnight on 31 December next year. Still, any excuse for a celebration, I suppose.'

Anne nodded. 'I have to agree, Doctor. Things have started getting pretty grim in Britain. We've been well and truly stitched up by the European Union, and the increase in pollution has resulted in a horrifying rise in deaths and abnormal births. People have lost direction, purpose, faith. All manner of religious cults and new age philosophies have sprung up, half of them promising that the world will end at midnight tomorrow, the other half claiming that it will usher in a new age of paradise. In short, everybody in Britain has one eye firmly fixed on New Year's Eve.' Her voice became low. 'And what has the Government built to symbolize this momentous occasion? The Millennium Hall.' Suddenly it occurred to Anne that she hadn't explained herself very well after all – a feeling reinforced by the puzzled expressions on the Doctor and Mel's faces – so she started again.

'Back in 1993, the Government of the time suspected that people's feelings might run high as the century came to an end. And then some bright spark remembered the Festival of Britain, that fervour of jingoism in the Fifties, and decided that the best way to drum up patriotic feeling in this country – short of declaring war – would be a Millennial Festival, with a Millennium Hall as a permanent landmark.'

Mel shook her head. 'I'm sorry, Dame Anne, but I still don't follow. What's this got to do with Chapel?'

'The Government invested a lot of money in the Millennium Fund, both from taxation and the Lottery income, but it wasn't enough. So, like the white knight that he likes to think he is, Chapel rode in and donated millions from his own fortune to prop up the fund, but on one condition.' She paused and took a drink of wine.

'That he design and build the Millennium Hall?' suggested the Doctor, chewing on one of the After Eights that the waiter had just left along with the bill.

'Quite. Designed and built to his personal tastes. So now London has a four-hundred-foot-high ziggurat on the site of Battersea Power Station.'

The Doctor placed a hundred pound note on the plate and returned to the conversation. 'I could be mistaken, Anne, but I sense that your animosity towards Mister Chapel runs a lot deeper than architectural indignation.' He tugged at his bow tie. 'Although, I must admit that this ziggurat has fired my curiosity somewhat. Why are you so interested?'

She sighed. She owed it to the Doctor to tell the truth. 'It has to do with my father. Professor Edward Travers,' she added for Mel's benefit. 'Towards the end of his life, he became obsessed with certain myths – Tibetan myths, to be precise. And then one of his more eccentric acquaintances told him about a library which contained all manner of forbidden texts, including the original scrolls of the first Lama of Det Sen. Father was fascinated, and started making inquiries about this place. He even managed to obtain his own ticket.'

'The Library of Saint John the Beheaded in Holborn,' muttered the Doctor. 'Fascinating place.'

'You've heard of it?' exclaimed Anne with some surprise, before resigning herself to the fact that, if anyone had heard of the library, it would be the Doctor. 'Forget that, of course you have. You're probably a member as well, aren't you?' Taking in the Doctor's sage nod, she continued. 'Anyway, within weeks of visiting the library, all of father's Government funding was axed and his reputation was in ruins, the papers making him out to be some crackpot. They even made out that the second Yeti invasion was all his fault. Father never recovered,' she whispered. 'He was ridiculed by his colleagues, and was eventually forced to leave the country. He spent his few remaining years in Tibet. And then . . .' The image of her once proud father as a blind, shambling vagrant, animated by alien hatred during the Intelligence's third invasion, burnt in her mind and made her eyes mist with tears.

'And you think Chapel was responsible?' asked Mel. 'Why?'

Anne's voice hardened to diamond. 'I'm the most senior civil servant in the country – have been for years. I'm the scientific advisor to the Cabinet, Doctor.' She grinned. 'Who do you think paid for all those Japanese electronic components you pestered the Brigadier for, when you were working for UNIT?'

'Oh,' replied the Doctor, nodding with understanding. 'I wondered why my requisitions were cleared so easily.'

'Quite. Anyway, through my contacts, I discovered that Chapel threatened the Prime Minister and three other members of the Cabinet with some major scandal which would have brought the Government down, unless they, well, helped him out. My father had somehow crossed Chapel without realizing, and Chapel destroyed his life because of it.'

'I'm very sorry about your father, Dame Anne, but how does that apply to me?' asked Mel with a definite lack of tact, waving the slip of paper in the air.

Before she could react, the Doctor grabbed it from her and read it. Frowning, he handed it back. 'Why is Chapel using the university if he has an entire computer company at his disposal, I wonder? Then again, it closed down, didn't it? Unless . . .' He swigged back the last of his wine and leant forward, whispering conspiratorially. 'Is there anybody left at ACL, Anne?'

'A few people: Chapel and his right-hand man Harker, the advanced research team . . .' she trailed off as she understood the significance of her words. 'Another advanced research team?'

'Exactly!' announced the Doctor. 'We have two advanced computing teams, a ziggurat in Battersea, and an imminent Millennium. Add to this potent brew a millionaire philanthropist with an unhealthy interest in a library of the arcane and Mel's worried friend, and it has all the hallmarks of a first class mystery.'

Mel laughed. 'That sounded like the back cover blurb to a very bad paperback, Doctor,' but he quietened her with a dismissive wave of the hand. Anne was impressed.

The Doctor's voice became grim. 'There's a lot more to this, I can feel it. And the last thing I want is you to place yourself in danger, Mel.' He snatched the piece of paper from her, his eyes narrowing into slits. 'If there's any hacking to be done, I think I should be the one to do it, don't you?' He picked up his glass and swirled the contents round, gazing into the ruby contents with those catlike eyes. 'Anyway, Anne. How do you fancy a visit to what's left of ACL tomorrow?'

She nodded, but her attention was fixed on Mel. Somehow, Anne couldn't see her meekly following orders.

'That really was magnificent, Barry.' Louise placed the tray on the floor and sank back into the green dralon of the armchair. 'Ever thought of doing it professionally? I can just see you as the next Marco Pierre White.' She pointed at the discarded copy of last week's *Sunday Times*. 'Perhaps Michael Winner would give you a good review.'

Barry laughed raucously. 'You must be joking, Lou, running a restaurant?' But he had to admit that the idea had occurred to him. 'Then again, after ten years writing computer manuals, well, who knows?'

Louise's amateur psychology had worked perfectly, the cooking taking his mind off the loss of the comfortable network of friends that ACL had represented. That and the seven glasses of wine, he decided ruefully. He put his own tray down next to him on the sofa and stood up, feeling far less steady than he would have liked. 'Time for dessert?' He was pretty sure that he hadn't slurred, but he doubted that Lou would have noticed anyway.

'You mentioned this earlier.' Louise rose to her feet before collapsing back into the chair in a fit of giggles. 'What is it? A humorous mousemat? An amusing screensaver?'

Barry looked at the three empty bottles and laughed. 'Don't worry, I'll go and get it.' He walked over to the window, trying hard not to stagger. 'Power up your computer.'

Louise finally managed to achieve escape velocity from the sofa and weaved towards the table in the corner of the room, while Barry reached into the silver carrier bag. Recipes, folders, course notes; he pulled out a clear plastic block. 'Recognize this?' He definitely slurred that time. And realized that he didn't actually care.

'It's the award we all got when Probe sold its first thousand copies, isn't it?' said Louise, also slurring. 'The only thousand copies, come to that.' As she spoke, she managed to slide her backside into the chair next to the table. 'Is that it?'

'No!' snapped Barry, more annoyed with his body's inability to obey his brain than anything else. Then again, he was used to it. Barry and drink were very old friends. Unfortunately, it wasn't a friend that most of his other friends – or bosses – approved of very much. But on the day of his redundancy, he didn't give a toss. Throwing the perspex block over his shoulder – where it hit Louise's empty plate, which promptly cracked in half – he finally found what he was looking for. A floptical with a single word written on the label. He pulled it from the bag and waved it around in drunken triumph like a trophy. Which, in a way, it was. 'Here we go!'

'A floptical?' Louise turned away from the computer, the screen now showing the bright pink and yellow stripes of her customized desktop. 'What's so exciting about a bloody floptical? What is it? Chapel's research project?' she giggled.

Barry suddenly wasn't laughing. 'That's exactly what it is, Lou. Part of the Codex. I nicked it.'

Louise swallowed nervously, sobering instantly. 'I – I'm not sure we should be doing this, Baz. I mean –'

'That bastard screwed us, Lou,' he growled. 'He threw us out on the streets and kept his chosen few behind to work on his secret project.' Then he did stagger, over towards Louise at the computer. 'This is Chapel's precious Codex, Lou. Aren't you slightly interested in what they're working on? What was so important that they all got kept on and we got thrown out?' He presented the disk to her. 'Go on, insert it!' he ordered, and then tried to keep a straight face at his double entendre. And failed. Snorting, Louise grabbed the floptical from him and shoved it into the slot.

'There. Done it.' She pulled him over and forced him to kneel next to her. Under other circumstances, Barry would have taken advantage of the situation, but he was as fascinated by the contents of the floptical as she was. And then the floptical appeared as an icon on the pink and yellow desktop background, a blue icon with the word Codex written below. A second later, the icon expanded into a window showing the lone contents of the floptical: a single file named C-OSU5.EXE. And, according to the information that the computer could glean, it was enormous.

'I think we've hit the jackpot, Lou,' whispered Barry almost reverentially. 'Open it.' Obediently – clearly as transfixed as he was by Chapel's secret research – she moved the cursor over the file and gave it a double click.

Barry's eyes narrowed as the true nature of C-OSU5 was revealed. 'What the hell is that?' he exclaimed.

The opened file didn't look like anything that Barry had ever seen before. Before he had become a technical author, he had spent a few years as a programmer, and he was familiar with a number of computer languages. What stared out at him from the screen was like no computer language he had ever seen, although he wondered whether there were any similarities with some of the symbolic languages, such as APL or Monobase, which didn't depend on recognizable words. He tried to focus on one of the Louises that hovered in front of him. 'You're the programmer. What sort of language is that?'

Louise shook her head. 'I haven't the faintest idea. It looks like –'

'Magic,' Barry murmured. 'It – it looks like a spell.' Even as he said it, he knew that it sounded stupid, but that was what the program reminded him of. As an added touch, Louise's computer had somehow rendered the lines of programming in Gothic script, and Barry rationalized that the ornate lettering, combined with his alcohol-fired imagination, had planted the idea of magic in his mind. Even so, the first few lines leapt off the screen:

> V'nactu, Niai! Pluve etet trianel, en evenarah?
> Garof, iver niver Pluve? Sharom sharah, etstatis clute?
> Requin par aloran, et parune Saraquazel!
> Teffum ssim elttil – Knum, Knum!

'This is just, well, weird,' he said, shaking his head. 'What's the file format? Anything we know?'

Louise's fingers stumbled around the mouse for a second before she brought up more information about the nature of the file. 'It's definitely an executable program – at least, that's what the Paradigm thinks.'

Barry's mind went blank for a second as he tried to work out what Paradigm was. And then he remembered: it was the operating system that had knocked OS/2 and Microsoft Windows out of the market; the operating system that was on all the ACL Tablettes, and also on Louise's computer. The only piece of software that Ashley Chapel had ever successfully marketed.

'Although how you can execute a file like this . . .' muttered Louise.

A wicked grin crossed Barry's face. 'Paradigm thinks we can execute it, so who are we to argue?' He leaned over and made a few clicks with the mouse before rocking back on his haunches and waiting.

He didn't have long to wait.

The familiar whistle of the computer as it read the floptical suddenly changed into a raucous screeching, a chalk-down-the-blackboard noise that made Barry wince. But he was puzzled: the noise wasn't mechanical – it sounded like some nightmare bird had got itself trapped within the motherboard and was trying to get out. Then, as the squealing grew louder, Louise's yellow and pink desktop started to fragment, as if a virus had got into the system, before the random pixels turned into an image of purgatory: flames and pits of molten lava, depicted with terrifying reality and a very convincing sense of 3D, and screams that seemed to come from a far better sound chip than Louise's computer possessed.

Barry grabbed Louise's hand and pulled her away. Barry didn't really want a ringside view of hell. But he was transfixed; he could hear the damned souls screaming, he could see tiny little stick people burning alive in rivers of blood-red fire.

They both jumped even further back as the holographic flames suddenly erupted from the screen in a searing volcano. Barry watched in disbelief, as they burned up and around and actually seemed to flow around the computer, flowing over its black casing before being absorbed back into it with a sucking sound. And then a dark shadow, both bat-like and spiky, pulled itself from the screen – drawing the brilliant colours into itself and then hovering about the computer like a flapping, burning bird of prey.

And then the bird exploded in a soundless burst of scattered light, making both Barry and Louise shut their eyes.

Please God, let it be over, prayed Barry. And then he opened his eyes. The screen was black, the little green system light dark. Under other circumstances, he would have phoned up Dave Richards and asked him what to do, but Barry doubted that it would make the slightest sense to anybody else. And he refused to move anyway; he decided to allow his brain to try to make some sense out of what he thought he had just seen.

'What – what was that?' whispered Louise. 'It looked like some sort of hologram.' She shook her head. 'What the hell is Chapel up to?'

'Hell is the operative word, Lou.' He leaned over and gave the casing a tentative prod. Then he sighed as he pulled his finger away without suffering any ill effects. 'Whatever it was, it might have fused the transformer.' He grabbed a screwdriver from the cup of pens, pencils and other useful equipment that stood next to the computer. 'I'll take the back off and have a nose around.'

Half a minute later he had unscrewed all six screws, and carefully removed the back of the computer's flat system unit. And then stared at the interior in soundless surprise. It just wasn't possible.

Instead of the expected motherboard, printed circuitry and other assorted technology, the computer's system unit was filled – stuffed, even – with some kind of blue-black fabric, embroidered with circuit-like tracings of silver and gold. He poked it; it seemed harmless enough. But totally and utterly inexplicable.

Barry swallowed. 'Er, Lou, you might want to take a look at this.'

Three

David Harker replaced the receiver with an angry thump. The news was bad enough as it was; but having to relay it to Chapel, who was already in a foul mood because of that stupid bitch, Travers . . .

'That was the security sweep report, no doubt?' asked Chapel, expectantly.

Harker nodded. Chapel wasn't one for preamble or polite conversation, but, then again, neither was he. 'Something's missing.' Everything of value in ACL – from packets of printer paper to Tablettes and printers – was tagged electronically, and the security sweep compared its recorded inventory against what it scanned. And tonight it had discovered a discrepancy, and had phoned Harker to tell him – with all the welcome of a double-glazing salesman.

Chapel sighed and pushed himself out of the chair. 'This really isn't my day, is it? Let me guess: one of our ex-employees has decided to increase their severance payout and leave here with some of my fixtures and fittings.' He groaned and rubbed his high forehead. 'What's missing, then? A Tablette? A box of flopticals?'

'One floptical.' This is it, decided Harker. This is where everything goes pear-shaped.

Chapel's eyes sparked with restrained fury. 'Tell me I'm wrong, David. Tell me that this floptical was blank.'

Harker looked downwards and coughed before replying. 'No, Ashley, it wasn't.'

'For the love of God!' the other exploded. 'What sort of an operation are you running here, David? Why the hell did I install one of the most sophisticated security systems in the industry? What's the point of having that security guard on the door?' He sat down again and rubbed his eyes with his palms. 'What was on the diskette?' he asked quietly.

'C-OSU5,' Harker muttered, bracing himself for the reaction. It didn't take long.

'I can't believe I'm hearing this! C-OSU5 is one of the few parts of the Codex that can run standalone!' Harker was forced to agree; most of the Codex architecture was dependent upon being surrounded by a host of support programs. C-OSU5's design meant that it could run on any computer with Paradigm installed.

Chapel's anger continued. 'What if somebody does run it, and gets curious about the results?' And then he sank into the chair. 'What am I saying: if they run it, of course they'll get suspicious. How many other programs . . .' He trailed off and slammed the table, making the Tablette jump into the air. 'C-OSU5 is Campling's module, isn't it?'

Harker nodded, even though he knew that the question was rhetorical: Chapel knew every module, every subroutine, every line of code of the Millennium Codex, and he also knew exactly who was responsible for each one. 'But he's not likely to have nicked anything. He's sound.'

'I know that. I chose him to work on the Codex, didn't I?' The implication was clear: if Chapel employed them, they had to be okay.

Chapel continued. 'Let's just hope that my wonderful security system is worth all the inconvenience of its installation.' Turning to the Tablette, he clicked and typed with his usual prowess. Less than a minute later, a window had appeared.

'Let's assume that the floptical was stolen from Campling's desk, shall we?' Chapel continued typing; as Harker watched, he entered the day's date and two times — 9 a.m. and 6 p.m. — and then the location of Campling's desk in the shorthand used to specify any part of the ACL office complex. And then he pressed the enter key.

Another window expanded from nothing; this one was a video replay, showing Campling's desk. Chapel instructed the security system to fast-forward the mundane to-ings and fro-ings: Campling's arrival was there, as he unpacked his briefcase and powered up his Tablette; a few informal chats with colleagues who were leaving; the odd coffee break, all of this took place at an almost unwatchable speed, but Chapel seemed to absorb everything.

After a few minutes of frenetic video, Harker's attention was seriously wandering, but a satisfied 'There!' from Chapel brought him back to the screen. The freeze-framed image showed someone holding the diskette in question.

'Our guilty party, David. Do you recognize him? He's not one of my programmers.'

Although Chapel knew every single programmer in ACL – whether they worked on the Probe product or were members of his Private Army – the 'peripheral people', as Chapel called them, were a faceless mass. Testers, technical writers, support staff, to Chapel, they were as individual as cupboards or vending machines. A resource to be used. But Harker had made it his business to know everyone, however inconsequential.

'It's Barry Brown.'

'Brown?' Chapel stroked his chin, and raised a finger as he remembered. 'Ah yes, our resident alcoholic technical writer.'

Still feeling vulnerable after his phone call to Julia Prince, Harker automatically leapt to Brown's defence. 'He was very good at his job, Ashley.' And he'd always found him an entertaining companion in the smoking room.

Chapel shrugged dismissively. 'So? I've always found it very difficult to take someone seriously when they smell of alcohol at ten o'clock in the morning. But that's wholly irrelevant. He's stolen part of the Codex, David. And that is a crime beyond imagining.'

'But we have Campling's work in library storage –'

'That isn't the point! Someone out there' – he jerked a finger towards the window – 'has a copy of a computer program which could seriously incriminate us. If this Brown person runs C-OSU5, he will encounter something so far beyond his comprehension that he may very well call in people who might understand it. UNIT, for example. And wouldn't dear old Anne Travers like that, eh?'

Harker knew that Chapel had probably already formulated a solution, so he kept quiet. But he reckoned that Chapel was over-reacting: Brown may have once been a programmer, but he couldn't possibly understand what the module was designed to do. So he was hardly likely to call in UNIT, was he?

'Anyway, Brown can be dealt with quite easily,' continued Chapel, closing down the security application. 'By the time this evening is over, he'll be very sorry that he pried into my research.'

Harker shuddered. Despite his reputation as ACL's hard man, he hated unnecessary violence. But he could see Chapel's point: Barry Brown had to be shown that silence was the best policy. And he would act as the perfect smokescreen while Melanie Bush started hacking.

'Are you sure that you want to go home?' asked the Doctor. 'We're only a taxi ride away from the TARDIS, and there's plenty of room at the inn, I assure you.'

Anne was torn: if she had read the signals correctly, the Doctor's offer of a bed promised a lot more, and since her husband's death such comforts had been few and far between. But she had to sort something out, and that took precedence over her desperate needs. 'Honestly, Doctor, I appreciate the offer. But I really do need to get home. My cats will wonder where I am,' she added, with a forced laugh.

'It's your decision.' He grabbed her hand and gave it a very chivalrous kiss. 'I'll see you tomorrow as arranged, then?'

She nodded. 'Definitely. I'll look forward to it.' She turned to Mel and touched her on the shoulder. 'Very nice to meet you, Melanie. Will you be coming along tomorrow?'

Mel shook her head. 'No. I think I'll go shopping.' She smiled, but her tooth-and-curls bonhomie wasn't convincing. 'Best to stick to the things that I'm good at.' Anne couldn't be certain, but she was sure that she detected the slightest tinge of jealousy in the young woman's voice. Was there something going on between the Doctor and his latest travelling companion? But no. Surely the Doctor wouldn't be interested in this diminutive, hyperactive genius? She took her hand off Mel's shoulder and gestured behind her towards the entrance to the station.

'I'd better get going. I'll need a good night's sleep if we're going spying tomorrow.'

'So be it.' The Doctor put his hands at the lapels of his tuxedo. 'See you at eleven?'

'Eleven it is, Doctor,' she agreed, before giving a cheery wave and walking down the stairs into Tottenham Court Road tube. She was still wondering whether she should have stayed in the TARDIS that night when she eventually got off the tube at Holborn. And set off for the Library of Saint John the Beheaded.

Three mugs of black coffee later, Barry and Louise sat silently in the living room. She was curled up on the sofa with her legs tucked underneath her; he was sitting on the armchair, clasping the empty mug and staring into the brown-stained interior. Every few minutes, his eyes wandered to the black object on the table, before snapping back as his mind refused to comprehend it.

As far as conversation between he and Louise was concerned, the incident might never have happened.

Everything they talked about was so mind-numbingly normal – mortgages, Sainsbury's, the weather – as if they were both desperately trying to reassure themselves that their familiar world hadn't just flipped over to become a nightmare, where printed circuits were transformed into silk from a magician's pocket.

'We can't just ignore it, can we?' Louise's words broke his reverie. She untangled herself, rose, and walked over to the table. 'It happened, and no amount of small-talk is going to change that.'

Barry couldn't help laughing. Once again, Louise's thought processes were in parallel with his own. 'What do you suggest, then? Perhaps I should phone up Chapel and complain that his top secret software has blown up your computer.'

'Not Chapel, no.' She chewed a nail, and Barry knew that she was about to suggest yet another of her hair-brained schemes. 'James Campling.'

'Campling?' He jumped. 'Why the hell should he help us?' Guilt made his words harsher than they should have, guilt by association; the floptical was, after all, Campling's to begin with.

Louise gave a wicked smile, clearly unaware of his reaction. 'Because he fancies me.'

'Tart!' A humorous explosion of guilt, but Barry knew it was hiding his jealousy.

She shrugged innocently. 'If you've got it, flaunt it. That's what I say,' she said, coquettishly.

Barry suddenly remembered that they weren't alone. 'What about Cassie?'

'We'll leave her here,' muttered Louise, but she must have seen his horrified expression. She quickly added, 'Not on her own, you idiot. I'll give my mum a ring, get her to babysit. I'd drop Cassie off there, but it's in the opposite direction from James's house,' she added.

Barry raised an eyebrow. 'Oh yes? How do you know that, then?'

She sighed in exasperation. 'Don't be so suspicious.

He's invited me for dinner there enough times. And before you ask: no, I haven't ever taken him up on it. I just happen to remember the address.' She looked at the carriage clock on the mantelpiece, and a sinking feeling reminded Barry that it was her ten-year clock.

'Half-nine. I'll phone Mum and then a taxi. And then I'll give James a ring,' she said seductively. 'I know he won't refuse a visit.'

'God, ACL really was the wrong profession for you, wasn't it?' He didn't like the idea, but if they could get some answers, well, it was worth it. Probably.

Chapel's own office was exactly the same size and shape as Harker's, but considerably better furnished. While Chapel's head of development had to make do with standard office furniture, Chapel had surrounded himself with a small fortune in antique furnishings. Authentic old masters hung on the walls, which were themselves wood-panelling transplanted from one of Chapel's country mansions, vying for space with the exotic tapestries that he had picked up on his many visits to the Middle East. It was a home from home. Then again, with the hours that he always dedicated to his work, it might as well be home.

In truth, the trappings represented only the minutest fraction of his vast wealth, but they were sufficient to impress the plebeians he employed. Had employed, he reminded himself; even the advanced research team would be out of a job at the stroke of midnight the next day. Then again, things would be very different for everybody come midnight, and he very much doubted that unemployment would be high on most people's priorities.

His reason for returning to his office was simple: his computer set-up was more powerful than Harker's, with access to some extremely powerful – not to say unusual – software. One particular application interfaced with all the various telephone networks, and Chapel was currently finding it very useful. Especially the call from the foyer, when that hapless security guard had phoned for a taxi. Chapel cross-referenced the taxi's destination with the personnel files in seconds, and came up with the answer: Brown had gone to Louise Mason's house in Battersea.

He sighed. Brown was a technical writer, a profession that Chapel had very little time for – it was only a matter of time before software documented itself, making it a bit of a dinosaur as jobs went. But Mason, she was a programmer, that most glorious of roles. Her work had been brought to his attention on a number of occasions, and he had considered offering her a place with his advanced research team. But a cursory look at her circumstances had immediately ruled that out: she was a single parent, and, in Chapel's experience, that was incompatible with the dedication he demanded from all his people.

But her complicity in the matter of the stolen floptical vindicated Chapel's decision. She was untrustworthy, deceitful, and downright dangerous. Although there was only just over a day left until he was due to run the Codex, he couldn't afford to take the chance of the operation being shut down by Anne Travers's army thugs, should Brown or Mason go running to the authorities. Despite his dislike of Travers, he had to admit a grudging admiration for her professionalism, and if she suspected anything at all at ACL that might possibly fall under her remit, UNIT would come marching in immediately.

An information window suddenly popped up on his Tablette screen. He had released a tiny program into the phone system, one which would tell him if any calls were made either to or from Mason's number. And now it was doing just that. Even as he watched, two more calls were added to the list in the window: the first was to a taxi firm; the second was to her mother (more cross-referencing, this time to the next-of-kin field on Mason's records); and the third – Chapel didn't need to consult his records to check on that number. He had made it his business to memorize the home numbers of all his research team, in case he ever needed to call them at home. Which was quite often. Private lives took second place to ACL. With a twisting feeling in his stomach, he knew that it was Campling.

This put a whole new complexion on his problems. He would have sworn that Campling's loyalty was beyond question, but his upcoming tryst with Mason and Brown suggested otherwise. For one terrifying second, he wondered whether he could trust anybody at ACL, even David Harker. Then he re-established his equilibrium. With Campling implicated, time was now of the essence, and such a desperate situation demanded desperate measures. He sighed. Mason and Brown had no idea of the magnitude of their crime, and simply frightening them off would be sufficient. But Campling . . . His betrayal had sentenced him to a far more serious fate.

Chapel picked up the phone and dialled his secretary. 'Gill, is Derek Peartree still waiting? Excellent. Could you send him up, please?'

Replacing the receiver, he stood from his desk and strode over to the wall opposite the door. The wall was no different from the other three: wood-panelled, and hung with famous works of art. Chapel reached out his hand and tapped out a complex rhythm on one of the panels, then stepped back as a door-shaped section of tapestry simply blinked out of existence. Solid holography was still in its infancy as far as the scientific community was concerned, but that was mainly because Chapel had both bought all the patents and persuaded his friends in the Government to suppress any further research. There were thirteen such solid hologram doors in the ACL suite, but Chapel had only found a use for one – this one, in his office.

The room behind the illusory door was about the same size and dimensions as his office, but there the resemblance ended. The walls were hung with blue-black drapes, shot through with gold and silver filaments.

The only illumination came from the concealed lighting in the black ceiling: their pale amber glittered off the filaments making it look like a satanic fairy grotto. Chapel smiled at the imagery and walked towards the centrepiece of the room, a large black cone engraved with runes and symbols. The only other object in the private chamber was a large golden statue that would have been familiar to any of ACL's ex-employees, or those embarrassingly few people who had ever bought ACL software: a rearing antelope, the defunct company's logo.

Chapel laid both hands on the cone and closed his eyes in intense concentration. The result was striking. The cone flared with a blinding light that shot upwards in a pillar of ruby incandescence, hitting the ceiling and apparently passing straight through. An observer – not that anyone save Chapel had ever seen the phenomenon – might have considered it to be magic, but the truth was far less mystical, though no less impressive: underneath the runic trappings that Chapel enjoyed so much was the most complex micro-monolithic circuitry array ever constructed. As ever, he gave thanks to his ex-employer, Tobias Vaughn, and his Cybermen allies for designing the technology in the first place. The fact that he held the patent was simply the spoils of war, as far as he was concerned.

Linked in concert, the array became a psionic focusing device, feeding off the mental energies in the immediate vicinity and amplifying them. The more circuits, the greater the amplification, and Chapel's cone was the largest array ever built.

With every passing second, the pillar of light pulsed with constantly reamplified energies, until the blue-black tapestries themselves began to fluoresce. The psionic capacitors housed in the pyramidal summit of Canary Wharf Tower had reached the limits that Chapel had specified.

Now that he had sufficient psychic energy, it was time for a different sort of magic. People such as Anne Travers might know about micro-monolithic circuits, but they had no idea of the power of Saraquazel.

Then there was a knock at his door. He turned to see Derek Peartree entering his office and smiled. There was a very sad individual who was about to become very happy.

'I don't like her. I don't like her at all.'

The Doctor opened the door of the TARDIS, ushered Mel inside and closed the great doors before responding. 'Aren't you being a little premature?' he asked, removing his bow-tie with one hand and extracting himself from his dinner jacket with the other. With the legerdemain of a conjuror, he stored the tie in the jacket pocket and flung the jacket on the hatstand in one fluid movement.

'She means well, but she's a dried up old spinster with a vendetta against Ashley Chapel,' Mel pronounced, lying down on the red velvet chaise longue that the Doctor claimed was from a variant of the Roman Empire he had visited not so long ago. If it was good enough for Cleopatra, it was good enough for her, Mel decided.

'Dear, oh dear, oh dear,' said the Doctor, turning from the hexagonal control console. 'Who's rattled your cage?'

'Nobody,' she snapped. 'It's nothing.'

The Doctor perched himself on the wooden arm of the chaise longue and stared at her. 'Come on, Mel. What's the matter? It's not like you to be so – so bitter.'

She sighed. 'It was the reunion, Doctor. They were all ten years older, but for me it's only been a couple of years. A couple of years spent cooped up in here' – she waved a hand around the roundelled white walls of the TARDIS – 'while they've been living real lives.'

'Real lives? Real lives?' He leapt from the couch like an electrified cat. 'And what have we been doing, eh? Or have you forgotten the vicious Herecletes? Or the Stalagtrons, with their inhuman plans for mankind?' He span round with his arms outstretched. 'Or the Vervoids?' he proclaimed. 'Without my cunning scheme to use vionesium, Earth would have become a galactic compost heap!'

Mel smiled. 'We haven't met them yet. Remember?' For some strange reason, the Doctor seemed obsessed with the Vervoids. Apparently, they were some sort of nasty alien plant race. But every few weeks, he would start mentioning them. 'Or, are you about to tell me about them?'

'Ah, no. No, this is neither the time nor the, um, time. But the point is Mel, I can drop you back minutes after we left Pease Pottage. You can have the chance to live those years – nothing's been wasted.'

'But I've changed my own future!' she exclaimed, sitting up. 'If you drop me back, I'll end up meeting myself at my own college reunion!'

'Probably not,' muttered the Doctor, fussing over the console.

'And what is that supposed to mean?'

He shrugged. 'Time has a marvellous way of preventing those sorts of paradoxes, Mel.' He leant back against the console then stood up as a cacophony of bleeps issued from it. Mel tried very hard to suppress a giggle. And failed. 'Yes, well. Anyway,' he said, obviously trying to regain his composure. 'Let's say I do return you to 1989. And you carry on your life from the point at which you left it. The chances are, the night you set off for the reunion, something will happen. Perhaps you'll miss your bus, or your taxi doesn't turn up. Or you change your mind. The end result is that you don't turn up, your earlier self does, and the web of time retains its integrity.' He frowned and scratched his chin. 'Anyway, that's the way the First Law of Time is supposed to work. And don't be so rude about Anne. She's been through a lot.'

'Has she met the Vervoids yet?'

It was the Doctor's turn to laugh. 'Hopefully not. But she has had rather more than her fair share of encounters with the Great Intelligence, and that's enough to make anybody bitter. Especially since its agents killed her husband.' He shot her an arch look. 'So your comment about her spinsterhood was in error. The result is that all of that anger has been bottled up and directed at two people: myself and Ashley Chapel.'

'You?' Mel got up and prodded the Doctor in the chest. 'She was all over you like a bad case of measles!' Mel's voice became a mockery of Anne Travers. ' "Oh, Doctor, do you really think so?" "Oh, Doctor, you're so clever." She made my skin crawl. She's obsessed, Doctor – and I would have thought that somebody as clever as you would have seen right through her,' she added pointedly.

The Doctor frowned. 'She was just being friendly –'

'Friendly?' shrieked Mel, standing up. 'When you offered her a bed in the TARDIS, it was quite obvious whose bed she was thinking of!'

'You're not serious?' His brows knotted. 'You are serious.' He sighed. 'Oh dear, oh dear, oh dear. That wasn't my intention at all.'

'Then you should keep as far away from the old bat as possible.'

The Doctor placed his hands on her shoulders. 'Mel, please. Anne is very worried, and your own evidence does seem to corroborate her story, does it not? Ashley Chapel is obviously up to something suspicious, and it falls to me to investigate it. This is a very delicate time in Earth's development, and the fact that Chapel is responsible for the continued marketing of the micro-monolithic circuit – an alien invention – is more than enough to arouse my suspicions.' He held up his hands to ward off Mel's inevitable protest, and she bit back her words.

'There are too many variables in this equation, Mel. Which is why I don't want you snooping around the university.'

'But Doc,' she implored.

'Tor,' he completed. 'A good night's sleep; that's what's needed. Then we can all wake up refreshed and ready to sound out all that's left of Ashley Chapel Logistics. Agreed?'

Mel stretched, before pointing towards the door that led to the TARDIS interior. 'You're right. That reunion was more exhausting than I realized. Shall I give you a call in the morning? Six o'clock?'

The Doctor shook his head. 'I doubt that I shall sleep tonight, Mel. I have some research of my own to carry out before tomorrow's exertions. Perhaps a light breakfast? Grapefruit and a bowl of bran?'

She smiled broadly. 'That sounds wonderful.' She jogged towards the door. 'Goodnight, Doctor.'

'Goodnight, Mel.'

Closing the door to the console room behind her, Mel set off down the corridor – more roundelled white walls – towards her room. But sleep wasn't part of the agenda.

The soft, warm glow of the oil lamps sank into the beige carpet and the damask drapes that hung from the walls, but Anne's first impression of the vestibule of the Library of Saint John the Beheaded was that the place was frozen in time. Fabrics and furniture that must have been hundreds of years old looked brand new, as if age was holding itself at bay out of respect for the august institution. Anne breathed deeply, and detected a pot-pourri of scents and odours: musk, cinnamon, lavender; definitely not the stale smell that one usually associated with libraries.

'Madam?'

Anne turned in surprise to see a tall, thin man with a balding pate standing in the far doorway, the one that presumably led to the interior of the library. He was dressed in floor length black robes, and Anne would have laughed at the incongruity of his attire – except that it was anything but incongruous, given the surroundings. Indeed, it was becoming increasingly difficult to believe that the end of the twentieth century lay beyond the library's entrance.

'Do you have an appointment?' His voice was dry and paper-like; quite fitting for a librarian, Anne decided.

'Er, no. But I do have this.' She nervously reached inside her handbag and pulled out a light brown ticket. 'This – this was my father's. I understand that they can be passed down.'

The librarian took the ticket from her and peered at it intensely before handing it back. He gave her a respectful nod. 'You must be Dame Anne Travers.'

'That's right. I assume that I can use the library's facilities, Mr . . . ?'

'Atoz, Jeraboam Atoz,' he intoned with another nod. 'I am the Head Librarian of the Library of Saint John the Beheaded. And yes, of course you can.' He frowned momentarily. 'Or did you think that there might be some hindrance to your researches?'

Anne paused. Atoz had hit the nail on the head, but she was reticent to say anything in case he changed his mind. But her curiosity forced the words from her mouth. 'My father's researches here led to Ashley Chapel starting a smear campaign against him. I just thought that –'

'You wondered whether Mr Chapel's ownership of the library would preclude your use of it,' Atoz completed with consummate tact. 'Dame Anne, I can assure you that Mr Chapel has no say in the day-to-day running of our learned establishment. Indeed, if I might make so bold, I believe that the only reason he purchased the library from the Pontiff was to ensure himself a ticket. Under other circumstances, we would never have offered our services to a philistine such as Chapel.'

Anne giggled with relief. 'My thoughts exactly.'

'Good, I'm glad that's settled.' Atoz held his arm out to indicate the library proper. 'Now, let us withdraw to somewhere more comfortable, and you can tell me the nature of your inquiries. Would you care for a sweet sherry?'

* * *

Mel stood in the middle of the TARDIS library with her hands on her hips. Somewhere amongst the millions of books was the single one that she was looking for. But where to begin? The library was a single corridor, miles long, with bookshelves for walls. Brass ladders punctuated the shelves every few feet.

'Now, now, Melanie,' she muttered to herself. 'You've got an IQ of one hundred and sixty-two – think rationally.' Unlike a normal library, the information stored here wasn't catalogued according to any system Mel recognized, although she suspected it mapped perfectly onto the Doctor's chaotic thought processes. A quick glance at the nearest shelf confirmed the disorganization: a leatherbound copy of Kafka's *Metamorphosis* – in its original German – was squeezed between an Agatha Christie thriller and a book with golden squiggles on the spine.

And then her subconscious deposited the answer in her mind. The Doctor was always going on about the TARDIS being a sentient being, responsive to thoughts and emotions. Well, thoughts and emotions didn't come any clearer than hers.

She sat on the floor and forced herself into the lotus position. Then she began her breathing exercises, allowing the inhalations and exhalations to clear her mind of clutter. Within a matter of minutes, only one thought remained, shining with all her concentration. It was the title of a book that the Doctor had once mentioned. He had only meant it as a throwaway line, but Mel's eidetic memory had filed it away for future use. Such as now. Demeter Glauss's *Cybercrime: An Analysis of Hacking* was apparently the seminal work on breaking and entering computer systems; written in the early twenty-first century, it laid open every operating system ever created up to that point. Just the ticket for a rummage through Chapel's network.

Mel would have sworn that the chime rang only in her mind. She opened her eyes, and they were immediately drawn to the nearest shelf. But *Metamorphosis* had itself metamorphosed: a burgundy leather edition of Glauss's book had replaced it. She stood up and prised it from the shelf, but wasn't prepared for what happened next: Kafka's book rematerialized – with a tinny TARDIS noise – in its place. She shrugged – business as usual for the Doctor's time machine, she supposed – and opened the book in her hands. That was yet another surprise. The leather volume was hollow, like one of those pretentious video cassette cases her mother had favoured, with a paperback of Glauss contained within. Mel winced at the lurid cover, showing a busty blonde in a leather catsuit leaning provocatively over a stylized personal computer, but a glance at the contents confirmed the Doctor's opinion. There didn't seem to be a single operating system for which Glauss hadn't described a back door: Windows, OS/2, OffNet; there were even systems mentioned that Mel assumed hadn't been written yet, such as Amber, Gridstat and Multivac. But there was an entire chapter devoted to the system in which she had a vested interest: Paradigm, Ashley Chapel's only successful software invention.

Clutching the book tightly, Mel left the library. But as she reached the door, she turned back.

'Thank you!' she shouted. It always paid to be polite.

Louise paid the taxi driver, and waited for him to drive off before speaking. 'James lives over there. Number fifty-one.'

'James, is it? Very cosy.' Barry pulled his brown leather jacket closer around him to ward off the chill December night. 'Perhaps I should go. I'd hate to play gooseberry.'

She gave him a playful punch on the shoulder. 'Oh, very funny. I'm willing to prostitute myself to try to sort out your mess, and all you can do is crack jokes.'

Barry held up his hands. 'I'm sorry, I'm sorry. I promise I'll keep my mouth shut from now on.'

'That'll be a first.' She started walking towards Campling's house. And then stopped, before turning and urging Barry to hurry up.

'What is it?'

'Look.' She pointed at number fifty-one. The front door to the house was wide open, the hall lights spilling out across the front garden.

'My God, he must be eager,' quipped Barry.

'This isn't funny. I think something's wrong. Come on.'

Barry couldn't help but giggle as Louise tiptoed up the garden path, but his first glimpse inside the house confirmed that something was seriously amiss in the Campling household. A hall table had fallen across the doorway, leaving the phone – off the hook – upside down on the carpet. The remnants of the telephone directory were strewn across the hall.

'We should call the police,' advised Barry, but Louise shook her head.

'Listen,' she hissed. An irregular thumping was coming from upstairs.

'All the more reason to call the police.' But Louise had already clambered over the table and was heading up the stairs, and Barry had no choice but to follow her. As they reached the top, the thumping grew louder, accompanied by a furious scratching noise like a horde of rabid mice.

'Shouldn't we defend ourselves?' whispered Barry. 'They could be armed.'

'Don't be stupid,' she snapped, but he could see her looking around for a suitable weapon without success. They turned onto the landing, only to discover that it was in a worse state than the hallway. Pictures had been knocked off the walls, curtains ripped from the windows, and glass ornaments were smashed and ground into the carpet. And then Barry located the source of the disturbance. The bedroom door in front of them was ajar, and the thumping seemed to come from within. And now there was another noise, a gurgling.

Louise was first into the room, switching on the light as she did so. And then she screamed.

Barry followed her in, and could fully understand her reaction.

The gurgle must have been Campling's death-rattle, because he was most certainly dead. Live people's heads simply didn't hang at that angle. But his dead body wasn't the cause of Lou's horror; that honour went to the creature that had its claws round Campling's broken neck.

Five feet tall, its arms and legs ended in vicious curved talons that were no doubt responsible for the ripped wallpaper and shredded bed linen. Its face was cruel and inhuman, with slitted eyes, an almost unnoticeable nose, and two small curved horns.

But the most horrible aspect of the creature was its skin. Blue-black, and tattooed with gold and silver tracery that resembled circuitry. Barry swallowed as he recognized it.

'Louise,' he stammered. 'It's the same as the computer.'

Hearing Barry speak, the creature turned its face towards Louise and Barry and smiled; a smile full of tiny sharp teeth, surrounding two very nasty fangs. And then it spoke.

'Hello, Barry. Hello, Louise. Enjoying your redundancy?'

Despite the demon-like appearance, the droning, whining voice was instantly familiar.

It was Derek Peartree.

Four

Jeraboam Atoz stopped sharply and inclined his head towards the velvet-curtained doorway. It had taken them nearly twenty minutes — twenty minutes of lushly furnished corridors that twisted and turned and ascended and descended through the seemingly infinite interior of the library — to reach the room that she wanted.

'This entire section is devoted to the subject that you wish to research, Dame Anne. Do you need any further assistance?' Since entering the library from the vestibule, his voice had become reverential, sepulchral, even.

Anne was almost shivering with a combination of nerves and anticipation. Behind the burgundy drape lay the final answer to all her nightmares. She shook her head. 'No, that'll be fine.' She had had the means to do this for years, but had always put it off. Only her knowledge of the Doctor's support had given her the resolve to visit the library, all these years after she had inherited her father's ticket.

'Excellent, Dame Anne. If you do need anything, there is a bell-pull. Either myself or one of my colleagues will be only too happy to oblige.' He smiled briefly. 'And you will find a fully stocked drinks cabinet at your disposal as well.'

Anne returned the smile and put her hand on the drape. Atoz's discreet cough made her turn round.

'If I might make so bold, Dame Anne, this also happens to be the section of the library that Mister Chapel favours. Since any chance encounter might prove, erm, awkward, I shall inform you if he should enter the library.'

'Thank you, Mister Atoz.' As she opened the drape, she pondered Atoz's words. If Chapel was a regular visitor to this section, it suggested that his researches were heading in the same direction as her father's. And her father's researches were now hers by birthright. If Anne's spies and informants were correct, time was running out. She silently cursed herself for leaving these final, oh-so-critical inquiries until the last minute. If Chapel succeeded, he would be able to summon the Great Intelligence to Earth before she discovered a means to prevent it. And that was her greatest fear, a fear that she couldn't reveal to anybody, not even the Doctor.

Closing the curtain, she walked carefully down the three carpeted steps and looked around. The room was enormous, at least three hundred feet square, the walls nothing more than giant bookcases stuffed with books of every size, every colour, every form of binding. There were no windows in the room; the only illumination came from the ever present oil lamps, casting their sepia tint everywhere. Countless armchairs, soft brown leather with high arms and back, were dotted between the heavy mahogany tables and around the wonderfully inviting drinks cabinet, the polished wooden top crowded with cut crystal decanters containing every possible spirit and liqueur.

Anne immediately made her way to the cabinet, and even went so far as to take out a glass from within the glass-fronted cupboard and pick up the decanter full of scotch, definitely a single malt, before deciding that she was procrastinating. Having a drink was simply putting off the moment when she would extract her father's handwritten list of forbidden texts and commit herself. And besides, she was still feeling a little light-headed from the sherry she had shared with Mister Atoz. She swallowed dryly, before pulling the creased and folded piece of paper from her handbag. And then instinctively crushed it protectively in her palm. This represented her father's legacy to her, and her promise to him. Never again would anybody bear the guilt that she carried within her.

She unclasped her hand, unfolded the paper, and stared at the first entry in the list: *On the Cessation of Oracles*, by Plutarch.

Steeling herself with determination, she put down the decanter and the glass and started looking for the 'P's.

'Derek? Derek, is that you?' whispered Louise hoarsely. After the mysterious transformation of the computer, she had thought that she was prepared for anything. But this?

The midnight blue demon nodded like a mongrel, allowing two flails of drool to whip out from the grinning mouth. 'How do you like my new job?' He giggled, and stood upright, waggling his black talons and letting drops of James's blood hit the pale green carpet. 'You three have been very naughty boys and girls, very, very naughty. You've upset a special friend of mine, and he doesn't like that. Oh, no, no, no, I can tell you.'

Louise shivered. Despite his transformation, Derek Peartree still possessed the condescending, supercilious voice that had made so many visits to the smoking room such a living nightmare. And now he was a living nightmare, it made that droning, overbearing tone all the more terrifying.

'Oh no, Ms Mason and Mister Brown, you have been so very, very, naughty. So was Mister Campling, but he won't be a naughty boy any more, will he?'

Louise almost threw up as the Derek-demon licked the remaining few gobbets of James's blood from his talons. 'Ugh,' he complained. 'What a sad and dry little wine that turned out to be.' He looked up at Barry and Louise and grinned. 'Let's hope that you're of a better vintage. As they say, the longer they're laid, the better they taste.' He gave Louise a lascivious glance, before clawing at the air with his talons. 'You've been far too naughty to let you live.'

'What are we supposed to have done, Derek?' It was

Barry, his tone placatory. 'We came to visit our friend. Why have you killed him?' Louise couldn't understand why he was being so rational.

The Derek demon chuckled — at least, that's what Louise imagined the demon thought it was. To her, it sounded like somebody gargling with blood, which it probably was, she decided grimly. She glanced at Barry, and saw him watching the demon steadily. He was smiling, and Louise suddenly realized what he was doing; he was trying to reach the Derek part of the Derek-demon. Despite the fact that Derek himself was so vile.

She added her voice to Barry's. 'James hasn't done anything!'

'Hadn't, Louise dear, hadn't. Please, we can't have incorrect grammar, can we? Such things are so important.' Her memory chucked up a particularly gruesome memory of being stuck in the smoking room with Derek as he expounded the virtues of good English to her. And then an outburst from Barry made her turn round.

'As is getting out of here!' he shouted, impaling the demon with a straightened coathanger. Purple blood gushed from the wound, but all the creature did was look at Barry and then down at the blood with a perverse smile.

'How kind! A light snack!' He began to lick at the wound.

Louise stared at the scene in both disbelief and horror before she felt a hand grasp her wrist.

'Come on!' insisted Barry. 'We've got to get out of here. Now!' He pushed her through the doorway and slammed the door shut behind them, before taking the stairs two at a time.

When they reached the hallway, Louise grabbed his arm to stop him. 'What about James?' she shouted. 'We can't just leave him there.'

Barry twisted her round so that she was face to face. 'We haven't got any choice. James is dead and we aren't –

and I want to stay that way. If we go back up there that, that thing will tear us apart.'

Then she followed Barry's gaze into the living room, its contents as scattered and broken as the rest of the house. But there, there on the floor, was a very familiar object: the flat black shape of an ACL Tablette. Barry darted into the room and grabbed it, before virtually shoving her out of the front door and down the street, as if the brighter lights of the main road would somehow ward off the creature that Peartree had become. Then again, pondered Louise, why shouldn't it be true? It wasn't any more weird than computers and people turning blue. They stopped to grab their breath outside the bookmaker's, its green and red neons adding yet another nightmare touch to the evening's proceedings.

'The police, then,' said Louise breathlessly. 'Let's at least call them in.'

'And tell them what? That our mate James was murdered by another of our colleagues from ACL? Oh, and by the way, officer, that colleague had been transformed into a hideous demon.' He spat out a bitter laugh. 'I just don't fancy spending another night locked up for being drunk and disorderly.'

'But we can't just leave him there! What about that creature?'

'I doubt that the police are trained to arrest demons, Lou!' he shouted, calming down as he did so. 'Anyway, it's probably long gone by now.' He fingered his chin. 'We'll go in the morning. How's that?'

Louise shivered, not sure whether it was the cold or emerging shock. 'Okay. I think we'd better go home, now.' And then the shock really did hit her. 'Oh my God! What about Cassie?'

'Your mum's looking after her.'

That wasn't what she had meant, and her throat tightened as she tried to explain. 'But that thing – it was waiting for us! It knew where to find us!' she screamed.

Barry understood immediately, it seemed. He pointed

down the road. 'There's a taxi rank over there – we'll be at your place in ten minutes.'

Two yellow eyes watched them from behind a privet as they ran off towards the line of waiting black cabs. 'Naughty, naughty children,' hissed Derek Peartree, wiping the drool from his fangs with a talon. 'You should have taken more notice of what I had to say in the smoking room.'

Standing in the console room, Mel was sorely tempted to forgo the use of a taxi and try out her proficiency with the TARDIS.

After their recent, harrowing escapade with the Quarks and the giant wasps, the Doctor had finally relented to Mel's insistent requests and showed her the fundamentals of TARDIS operation. The lessons hadn't lasted long – the Doctor's impatience had seen to that – but Mel was sure that she could arrange a short hop to the university campus without too many problems. Then she remembered the Doctor's explosive grumbles when they started to materialize in London that morning; something about anomalous fluctuations in the quasion field and quite alarming quantum subharmonics. Besides, the Doctor would know exactly what she was up to, and that was the last thing she wanted.

No, she decided, tweaking her hair in the reflection from the time rotor, it was better for all concerned if she phoned for a taxi. For a brief moment, she also wondered whether the TARDIS systems could interface with the telephone network, but then decided that this was far too complicated and hardly worth the bother. She'd be better off phoning from the box that the TARDIS nestled next to, in the shadow of Nelson's Column.

She pulled up the door lever and waited as the great doors opened with their customary hum. As she waited, she made her final judgement as to her appearance: the dark blue leotard and red leggings, the heavy black woollen jumper, a perfect outfit for a winter's night.

Satisfied, she shoved the lever back and departed through the closing doors, ready to tackle anything that the world could throw at her.

Anne refilled her glass and sighed contentedly. After two hours, she had unearthed over half of the books that her father had indicated: huge, musty tomes with leather bindings and titles ranging from *The Gnostic Apocrypha of Nostradamus* to Joachim of Fiore's *Liber Inducens in Evangelium Aeternum*, taking in the *Eltdown Shards*, the *Pnakotic Manuscripts* and the *Book of Eibon* on the way.

The library had proved as enlightening as she had hoped, a veritable cornucopia of the mystic and the phantasmagorical, with a comprehensive index that was making her search far easier than she could ever have imagined. But her father's list was merely the beginning of her quest. He had died, a broken and disillusioned man thanks to Chapel, before he could interpret the cryptic puzzles that the two stacks of books had provided.

That was now Anne's legacy: to complete her father's work and prevent the Great Intelligence from corrupting the Earth with its evil ever again. 'The Great Intelligence, indeed!' she muttered, her fear abated by the protection that the library seemed to afford her. 'Such conceit.' She tried to remember what the Doctor had called it. Yoth– Yog– 'Yog-Sothoth!' she announced. And then a firefly memory lit up in her mind: Yog-Sothoth.

She prised herself from the armchair and came to a halt as waves of dizziness overcame her. Silently cursing the sherry and the whiskey, she waited for the room to come to a standstill before she retraced her quest along the bookshelves. After two or three minutes of twisting her neck to read the spines, she finally found the book that she had seen earlier: *The Many Eyes, Lies and Lives of Yog-Sothoth*, written by Count Alexei Mussomov. She slid the gold-coloured volume from the shelf and opened it. And gasped.

The frontispiece was an illustration, a shapeless mass

with hundreds of eyes and hundreds of mouths, all radiating pure evil. Thousands of extrusions, ranging from whip-like tentacles to thick pseudopods, seemed to writhe from the bloated body, their surfaces dripping with mucus. Anne read the description below the picture, although she already knew what it was going to say:

Yog-Sothoth, the key and the guardian of the gate.

Anne slammed the book shut and tried to calm herself. Her heart was racing, and she was breathing so heavily that she was in danger of hyperventilating. Somehow, she knew that this book held the answer, the ultimate goal of her legacy, and that knowledge helped her regain her composure. In a few hours, she could have the solution to her worst nightmare –

'Dame Anne?' Mister Atoz was standing in the doorway wearing a look of contrition.

She removed her hand from her breast. Atoz's interruption had almost been as shocking as the illustration in the book. 'I'm sorry, Mister Atoz, you startled me.'

'I apologize, Dame Anne, but in light of our earlier conversation, I thought you'd like to know that Mister Chapel has just entered the library.'

Anne had no choice; she had to leave immediately. But her eyes wandered to the gold volume she was still clutching under her arm. She knew that the library's rules prohibited the removal of books from the premises, but this really was a matter of life and death.

'I'm sure that I don't need to remind you that you must leave all books here, Dame Anne.'

She felt the flush of embarrassment on her cheeks, and placed the book on the pile of others she had located.

Handing Anne her coat, Atoz pointed towards the darkened rear of the room. 'There is a corridor hidden behind the far shelves which will take you directly to the St Giles Rookery.' She heard distant footsteps, but panic reminded her that the convoluted architecture of the library made a mockery of distance. As Atoz strode into the shadowed recess, Anne started after him. Then she stopped. If Chapel was coming here, into this room, he would immediately find her books, and, if her suspicions were correct, put them to very bad use. There wasn't time to hide all of them, but Mussomov's was the most important to her, and therefore to Chapel. She snatched it from the table and hurried to catch up with Atoz. Just before she reached him, she shoved the book in a convenient gap that was so far away from its proper position that she doubted that even the magnificent index of the Library of Saint John the Beheaded would be able to locate it.

Thirty seconds later, she was back in the chilly midnight of London, and the honk of a taxi was the final reminder she needed that she was back in the twentieth century. For the next twenty-four hours, anyway.

The console room was empty. As the Doctor had expected, Mel was gone. He should have guessed that the simple act of telling her no was woefully inadequate against her dogged determination and razor-sharp mind. He leant on the console and groaned. Mel had no idea of the danger she was placing herself in, but then again, neither did he – not really. Every one of his Time Lord instincts was telling him that something evil was brewing in the mind of Ashley Chapel, something so evil that the Doctor wondered whether the Earth would even see the next millennium.

He slumped into the chaise longue with an even more bitter sigh. Melanie Bush was one of life's innocents, a person who wandered into every situation looking for the best in everyone. But sadly, life – and the universe – wasn't like that. And the saddest thing of all was that he had never wanted to meet her at all. After his kangaroo court trial on board the Celestial Intervention Agency's space station – a trial arranged by the most corrupt members of his own race where the learned court prosecutor had been a dark and twisted version of himself – the Doctor had decided to give up his jackdaw meanderings and settle down. At least, that's what he had deluded himself into thinking. In truth, he had been trying to avoid the predestined future that the Valeyard – his dark side – had predicted. If he could avoid ever meeting the Melanie Bush that the Matrix predictions had foretold he would meet, he could shift time onto a different track, a track in which the Valeyard never came into being. In which he never succumbed to his dark side.

For a time, he thought that he had succeeded. His first attempt at a companion had been Angela, but that had ended quite tragically with that business with the Network. But then he had met Grant, and they had shared many adventures together before eventually parting company. Others followed, and he had felt certain that he had bucked destiny – until a random – and companionless – landing on Earth had once again brought him into conflict with his arch-nemesis, the Master.

The Master was hell-bent on yet another of his petty, spiteful conquests. This time, he was trying to undermine the Earth's stock markets in partnership with his latest allies, the Usurians. Obviously, he must have been very bored at the time, the Doctor mused. Only the assistance of a spirited, flame-haired computer programmer had foiled his plans; the Master had left the Earth with his tail between his legs, and the Doctor was confronted with one, final, problem. The computer programmer was Melanie Bush, the companion that the Matrix had prophesized. And she was the first step on the road to the Doctor's transformation into the corrupt, immoral Valeyard.

He had refused to let her travel with him. He had forbidden her to enter the TARDIS, and had sent her away. But she had tricked him, stowed away, and become his companion without his consent. So he told himself. Even then, he was convinced that he could divert the course of Time. The Matrix had foreseen that he and Mel would answer the distress call from the Hyperion III; all he had to do was ensure that that particular event never, ever occurred.

He was still waiting.

But he told himself that he could still do it, he could still avert his metamorphosis into the Valeyard. Never again would he place a companion in danger. He would protect them, ensure that the dangers that dogged his existence never touched them, never harmed them.

And now Mel was blundering around in Chapel's computer systems, and he hadn't even tried to stop her. What was wrong with simply locking the doors, for Omega's sake? He hadn't locked them, because he had wanted her to do it. And now, sitting on the chaise longue and reflecting on his actions, the Doctor realized that he had taken the second step. He had started to manipulate. A minor manipulation, it was true, but he had forbidden Mel to tackle the Chapel network on her own, in order to provoke her to do just that.

He slammed his fist on the carved wooden arm of the chaise longue. How long before he started using his companions as pawns in some cosmic chess game? And how long before he was prepared to sacrifice such a pawn to guarantee a checkmate?

The Doctor eased himself off the soft velvet and stared at his reflection in the time rotor with an inevitable thought. When would he wear the black and silver robes of a learned court prosecutor? When would the dark side that the Time Lords had taken advantage of finally come into existence?

He decided that a long walk through the endless corridors of the TARDIS was called for. He started to turn towards the interior door, before remembering the odd readings that he had seen as the TARDIS had materialized in London that morning. In truth, it could wait until morning, but such scientific curiosities had always piqued him, especially where the planet Earth was concerned. As he recalled, the anomalies were at the quantum subharmonic level, which automatically suggested a Fortean flicker, and they were usually nothing to bother about. But there wasn't any harm in checking it out, was there? He played the console with his usual finesse, watching with his cat-like attention as readouts and screens analysed and extrapolated the data that flooded into the TARDIS's sensors.

And then he froze. A burst of information suddenly erupted from the telepathic circuits – an overspill from her calculations, a design fault in Type 40s that the Doctor was aware of, but unprepared for – and a packet of knowledge ignited the Doctor's complex neurons, ganglions and superganglions with a terrible interpretation.

Familiar names – Mel, Anne Travers, Ashley Chapel – churned and curdled with images and words and a name that was unknown, Saraquazel. And, cackling above it all like some deranged and vindictive raven, was an all too recognizable figure.

The Valeyard.

Overcome by the vivid images that the TARDIS was pumping into his mind, the Doctor collapsed over the console, his hands desperately reaching for the telepathic circuits in an attempt to halt the flow. He failed, and lost consciousness in a multicoloured heap that slid indecorously onto the pristine white floor.

Even at midnight, the library and the adjoining computer block were remarkably busy, Mel mused. As she eased herself into the soft leather chair and switched on the top of the range Tablette – Julia Prince hadn't been joking about Ashley Chapel's benevolence – her mind wandered back to her own student days. Back then, the computer block had been a cramped and draughty room in one of the oldest parts of the university, where people like Julia and Chantal had stayed up all night, sustained by endless cups of coffee and packs of cigarettes, in a desperate attempt to meet some deadline or another. Naturally, Mel had never needed to cram like that. Her essays and reports had always been finished well ahead of schedule – such were the benefits of a good time management system.

The surroundings might have changed after ten years, but the behaviour of the people certainly hadn't. Mel recognized the desperate looks and heart-felt sighs from around her, as well as the endless stream of students back and forth to the coffee machine. And then her mask of superiority momentarily slipped, as she once again realized exactly what she was doing in the computer block. This wasn't a late assignment or an overdue report; she was about to illegally access a private research project belonging to a legend in the computer business. She reached into her handbag and retrieved a bottle of mineral water. As she swigged from it to assuage her drying mouth, she opened her copy of Glauss at the bookmarked page.

According to Glauss – who wouldn't even be born for another twenty-six years – the key to unlocking the Paradigm operating system was an insignificant file located in the monitor driver directory. For those in the know, the file was an open door that led straight into the system nucleus of Paradigm. And from there, Mel could surface anywhere in the local area network. Such as the private files of the Chapel research team.

Nimbly manoeuvring the mouse, Mel found the driver directory almost immediately. And, within seconds, was trespassing in Paradigm's system nucleus.

Ashley Chapel rubbed his hands in satisfaction. It had been a productive night. Apart from finally tracking down the last two books he needed from the Library of Saint John, Campling's betrayal had been dealt with in a permanent manner, and Brown and Mason should have been sufficiently frightened to forget all about what they had seen.

And, just to stress the point, they had quite a surprise awaiting them when they got home; since they weren't stupid – Chapel would never have employed either of them, had that been the case – he hoped that they would heed the obvious warning and cease prying into something beyond their comprehension. Campling had deserved his fate. As part of the advanced research team, Campling was expected to show unswerving loyalty, and his betrayal was a mortal wound to Chapel – but the other two . . . Their minor role in ACL required no such devotion, and their actions were no more than those of an ungrateful child.

His ponderings were halted by a sudden message that appeared on his Tablette screen: someone had broken into the Paradigm LAN through the back door.

Chapel smiled. He liked a challenge.

Mel was faintly surprised by her rate of progress through Paradigm's complex directory structure. When the Tablette screen had first displayed its rotating three-dimensional image of the structure, Mel had gasped at the intricate branches and knots that made it resemble the roots that grew below some ancient tree. But Glauss had cut through the complexities with a short paragraph of code that brushed the roots aside like a spade.

And now she had arrived: the system nucleus of the Paradigm local area network or LAN, which connected all the computers at both the library and ACL together. The screen showed it as a scintillating polyhedron of uncountable sides.

Each face represented some part of the complicated software which combined to make Paradigm one of the most powerful operating systems on the market – at least, that was what Demeter Glauss had written. She had also written that the chink in the nucleus's coded armour was the face of the polyhedron that belonged to the printer driver – the other end of the back door which had enabled Mel to get this far.

Chapel aimed a tiny jerk of his finger towards the screen of his Tablette, where the intruder was shown as a flickering blue diamond against the blue-black background.

'Clever little bugger,' muttered Harker, called in by Chapel to watch this unexpected display of breaking and entering. Unexpected, because Harker hadn't suspected that Chapel would be notified. 'How the hell did he get this far?' he asked, hoping that his surprise sounded sincere.

Chapel leant back in his armchair and raised an eyebrow. 'Did you know that there's a back door into the inner workings of Paradigm?'

Harker shook his head urgently. 'That's not possible. We took every precaution –' he bluffed.

'And so did I, David, so did I. I installed the back door.'

Harker frowned. Paradigm was arguably his boss's finest achievement: guaranteed to be one hundred per cent hack-proof, with ICE-traps and antibodies designed to destroy every known virus, and quite a few not created yet. Melanie Bush was probably the only person capable of cracking Paradigm, but even she would need help when she entered the Codex libraries. The last thing that Harker had expected was that she would have an audience when she did it.

And here was Chapel, calmly confessing that he had sabotaged his own creation. Not for the first time, Harker began to wonder whether the strain of the whole Codex operation was proving too much for the man. That was why he needed to know exactly what was going on in those heavily guarded program libraries that Chapel chose to hide from his head of development. He had to be ready to take over if Chapel cracked.

'I can see that the wisdom of my actions has escaped you,' he explained. 'As you know, I have never been over-impressed by the recruitment processes that we have always employed; they leave so much to chance. But someone with the chutzpah and skill to burgle my own, private LAN using one of my own machines, what an employee that would be, eh David?'

Harker could see the reasoning, but it still seemed

quite a risk to take. Especially for someone as security-conscious as Chapel.

Chapel continued. 'An employee like that would go far, maybe all the way to the top.' Harker felt an icy spasm in his stomach at the cold warning. Despite Chapel's positive response, Harker knew that he was directly responsible for computer security. For this to happen less than twenty-four hours before the Codex was due to run was a direct indictment of his abilities; and the last thing he wanted was for Chapel to start checking up on him.

'She's coming at us from the university library, by the way.' Chapel tapped the screen with the arm of his glasses. 'An ingenious route, but quite expected.'

'She? You know who it is?' If Chapel suspected anything . . .

Chapel snorted and peered at Harker over the top of his gold-rimmed glasses. 'I thought you would have realized by now, David: there's very little that I don't know. Her library card identifies her as Melanie Bush, a graduate of the computer science department at the university. She graduated about ten years ago –' He touched a finger to the bridge of his nose. 'Of course! Melanie Bush, I offered her a job. Don't you remember interviewing her?'

Of course Harker remembered, but he feigned a vagueness that he hoped would convince Chapel. 'Erm, spirited little red-head, wasn't she? But she never accepted the position, did she?'

'No, she didn't.' Chapel waved him quiet, his voice containing the barest hint of irritation. Nobody had ever turned down a position at ACL – except Melanie Bush. And now she was breaking and entering into their systems. 'A hacker of quite monumental nerve and knowledge, guilty of an almost undetectable fraud in the university's computers: a worthy opponent. Let's see what she makes of the systems nucleus, shall we?'

'You're not letting her in, are you? What about the deadline for the Codex?' If Chapel carried out a full investigation, there was a chance that Harker would be implicated. And he wasn't quite ready to show his hand.

'If she's as clever as she appears to be, there won't be much I can do about it, David,' Chapel sighed. 'I designed the back-door so that only a genius of my abilities could unlock it. And as much as it pains me to say it, I seem to have met my match.'

The sum total of Chapel's computing resources hung within easy reach, like software Christmas tree ornaments glittering in the firmament of cyberspace. Then Mel chastized herself for such a twee allegory, and referred back to Glauss for her next move. She could have read and memorized the entire chapter back in the TARDIS, but she had decided to make the situation more exciting by going through it step by step.

A typed password later, Mel was hurtling down a directory chain, the one that Julia Prince had indicated led to the mysterious Codex.

'She knows what she's looking for,' growled Harker, and then cursed himself for saying it. Chapel shot him a quizzical look.

'Indeed. Now how does she know that?'

Harker shrugged. 'Coincidence?'

'Quite a coincidence that she's heading straight towards the Codex, wouldn't you say?' He shook his head. 'When this display is over, I want you to conduct a full investigation into our security. Flopticals going missing, hackers in the system. I've never believed in coincidence, David, and neither should you.' But any further insinuations were cut short by the activity on the monitor; the intruder was cutting through the ice-traps and crippling the antibodies as if they weren't even there.

As the final layer of anti-intrusion software peeled away, Mel clapped her hands in glee. I'm in, she thought proudly, patting Glauss. Moments later, the protocols and passwords supplied by Julia went to work, and the Codex directory was wide open.

She peered at the contents of the directory: things that she assumed were programs floated past the screen like multicoloured balloons, with strange alpha-numeric labels hanging underneath them: C-V34, C-OSU5, C-664716, and none of them made the slightest sense to Mel. For the briefest of moments, panic gripped her, before she reassured herself that she had got this far without any help – apart from Glauss.

Everything she had done up till now had simply been preparation. Now that she was inside Ashley Chapel's secret treasure trove, Mel remembered that Julia Prince had been convinced that her sharp mind would instantly discern its secrets. She shrugged. With nothing else to go on, there was only one course of action. Picking one of the balloons at random, she opened it up for a closer look.

'She's opened up C-V34,' Harker observed, before realizing that Chapel wasn't doing anything to stop her. 'Aren't you going to do something?'

Chapel smiled. 'Why? C-V34 is one of the last three modules that need debugging. And given today's fiasco, why shouldn't we let our Ms Bush have a go? I mean, she can't do any worse than your developers, can she?'

Harker cast his eyes to the floor, more to hide his anger than out of any sense of embarrassment. It was funny that the advanced research team always belonged to him when anything went wrong, but to Chapel whenever there was a bit of glory in the offing. 'I suppose not, no.' And if he made too much of a fuss, it might make Chapel even more suspicious.

'Quite. She might even have the honour of becoming the last ever recruit to Ashley Chapel Logistics.'

Louise turned the corner into her street and stopped. Her house was dark. 'Barry, the lights are off!' she hissed.

'Perhaps your Mum's gone to bed.' He waved his wrist watch in her face. 'It is nearly one o'clock.'

Louise shook her head. 'No, Barry – she'd wait up. For God's sake, she's always waited up, you know that.'

Barry laughed nervously, remembering countless other nights when he had fallen foul of Mrs Mason's inability to accept that her daughter was an adult. 'Come on, then. There's no point in waiting around up here, it's freezing,' he complained, punctuating his words with little clouds of condensation. He walked towards the front door, its colour transformed from white into amber by the nearby streetlamp. And felt his stomach flip-flop as he noticed that the door was ajar.

Then Louise was beside him, noticing what he had noticed. She started screaming something – a name – that Barry could scarcely make out, before belting up the path and throwing open the door, revealing the same destruction that they had seen at Campling's house. Without hesitation she was inside, Barry right behind her. And when she next screamed, Barry did understand, and felt it, deep, deep inside.

Five

His heart pounding, Barry followed Louise through the hallway and into the living room. It was worse than he had dared imagine. The furniture had been thrown over, the empty wine bottles smashed, the drawers and cupboards opened and their contents vomited over the carpet. Clawmarks were gouged into the walls, deep grooves through the wallpaper and into the plaster.

For the tiniest of moments, Barry knew that there was something he should do but couldn't remember what it was. And then it hit him. Louise's mother, creature of habit that she was, would have left some sort of message. He bolted into the kitchen and skidded to a halt in front of the freezer, where little multicoloured magnets shaped like fish sandwiched all manner of notes and lists between them and the white metal surface. And there it was, a square of white paper with copybook handwriting in red biro:

Louise
   Your father isn't feeling well, so I've taken Cassie home for the night.
   Phone you tomorrow morning.
   Love Mum

'Lou!' he yelled, running into the living room, and then — seeing it empty — bounding up the stairs two at a time towards Cassie's bedroom. He found Louise sobbing on the landing, her hand squeezing the doorhandle so that her knuckles were white.

'I can't go in,' she managed to say.

'It's all right, Lou, it's all right.' He held the piece of paper up. 'Cassie's at your Mum's.'

She sighed and then started coughing. Barry gave her a soft pat on the back and made reassuring noises. But her elation didn't last long. 'What about Mum? What if they've gone to her house?'

As she started to panic, the phone rang downstairs. Vaulting the stairs three at a time, Barry stopped in the doorway to the living room and tried to locate the source of the sound. Whatever had thrown a wobbly in there hadn't been too particular as to where it had left anything. He found the socket and followed the wire behind the sofa and under a blue throw-cushion, and then picked up the receiver.

'Hello? Oh, Mrs Mason. Yes, yes, I'll just go and get her.'

Anne tried to sleep, but it hovered too far out of reach to embrace. Instead, her mind leapt and swooped around the day's events with a randomness and distortion that was addictive. The Doctor, the library, Ashley Chapel, and there, like a black cloud descending with the wrath of ancient gods, was the Great Intelligence. But she knew its name, and names were power over spirits and demons and devils like Yog-Sothoth. Just saying the name was a calming mantra, as she repeated it and repeated it, relishing the control that she now possessed.

And soon she was able to embrace sleep, her final thoughts aimed at the next midnight, the millennium. She would stop Chapel now. At last.

Barry came back into the living room carrying two mugs of very strong coffee, just as Louise put the phone down.

'And how was your charming mother?' he asked, handing her the blue mug. 'More parental guidance?'

'Don't be so nasty – at least I know Cassie's safe. And Mum won't answer the door at this time of night.'

'Tell me about it.' He could easily bring to mind the night when she had forgotten her key. He had hidden behind the hedge as Louise had tried to get her mother to open the front door, but to no avail. The following day, her mother had explained – in the middle of interrogating Louise as to her whereabouts the previous night – that she never answered the door after half-past-ten, because of what had happened to Mrs Keeble two doors down with the flasher.

'So, what do we do now?' he asked.

'We should call the police.' She blew on the coffee to cool it. 'What's going on, Barry? How did Derek turn into that, that thing?'

He stared into the swirling coffee. 'It's Chapel. Derek admitted as much. And it was Chapel's work that wrecked your computer, wasn't it? Unless "Insides turning into blue silk" is a known bug in the computer industry.' He sighed. 'You saw what Derek had turned into – the same colour, the same gold and silver – he was working for Chapel, Lou – he admitted it!'

She pondered, and then nodded. 'You're right. But what is Chapel doing?'

'Something . . . evil.'

'Evil?' she repeated. 'Aren't you over-reacting a bit?'

'Am I? When I looked into the eyes of what was left of Derek, well, that's what I saw. Evil.' He put down the coffee mug with a thump. 'You're right: we've got to go to the police. And then tomorrow we go to Chapel and get him to explain.'

'What?' snapped Louise. 'You stole part of his research project, remember? And it's gone a bit beyond petty theft. James is dead, and there's a bloodthirsty demon skulking around London! We're in over our heads, Barry. And even if we do go to the police, what are we going to tell them?'

Barry grabbed her hands. 'Don't worry. I'll have thought of something by the time we get to the station.' He reached over and grabbed the phone. 'I'll order a taxi.'

'The police station?'

He shook his head. 'First stop: my flat. I fancy a shower and a stiff drink before facing her majesty's constabulary.'

One hour after opening the file, Mel was pretty sure that she understood the peculiar language that the C-V34 program — if that's what it actually was — was written in. Having read the six thousand lines of code in the first ten minutes, she had then taken out a pad of paper and a propelling pencil from her handbag and proceeded to jot down random impressions, as both sides of her brain went into overdrive.

Twenty sheets of mind-maps and logic matrices later, she was able to write her first few lines of code.

Half an hour later, she spotted something in the program that concerned her. Everything in her logically deduced model of Chapel's language held together in a perfectly self-consistent way; this indicated that she had got it right. But if that was true, what she was seeing in C-V34 was a bug. She returned her attention to the pad next to her, and began copying out the lines that she suspected of being in error.

It struck her immediately: there was a minor syntax error, an absent exclamation mark. For a second, she pondered the wisdom of interfering; and then she decided that it wouldn't take a second to put it right, and it could be considered a sort of compensation to Chapel for her unlawful entry. With a decisive prod at the keyboard, she added the punctuation mark. And then she spotted another error.

Within minutes, she was totally engrossed in debugging.

'She corrected the syntax,' whispered Chapel in tones of near-reverence. And then his voice snapped back to normal. 'Assuming that Ms Bush had never encountered the Codex language before this evening, then her ability to spot an error in a piece of our code, in less than an hour, is nothing short of genius. At this rate, she'll debug the entire Millennium Codex in less than five hours.' He poured himself another cup of coffee from his silver cafétière. 'Perhaps we should give our research teams tomorrow off.' He looked at his watch. 'By tomorrow, I really mean today, of course.'

He turned to Harker. 'I intend to follow the progress of bright Ms Bush, David, but you appear to be surplus to requirements. Why don't you get a few hours' sleep? We've got a busy day ahead of us.'

Harker knew that a few hours' sleep didn't mean a trip home – not that that mattered much any more. It meant an uncomfortable night in his office, tossing and turning on the fold-up bed that he kept in a cupboard for such situations. But it was a respite from Chapel, and that was exactly what he needed at the moment. He held up his hand to say goodnight, but Chapel didn't even see him leave.

Chapel was too preoccupied with the way that Ms Bush was optimizing one of the sort routines – at a rough guess, she had just increased its sort rate by five hundred per cent. He scratched his nose and wondered how long it would have taken to complete the Codex with a team of Mels – even one Mel – to help him.

7 May 1994, he decided, settling down to his own version of breakfast television with a pot of hot coffee.

Barry wandered blindly into the living room of his flat, his vision obscured by the towel that hung down over his face as he dried his hair. Throwing the towel over his shoulder – where it expertly wrapped itself around the back of a chair – he grabbed the brandy bottle and poured himself an extremely generous measure. He was a lager drinker by preference, but he'd bought the brandy for some recipe or other that he had once wanted to try. It certainly wasn't Remy Martin, but it was drinkable. Then again, he reflected, after this evening's experiences he would have settled for a bottle of meths and a straw.

Louise was curled up in the corner of one of the two blue two-seater sofas, a large brandy glass cradled in her left hand, the drink swishing from side to side. Engulfed in the spare towelling dressing-gown, she looked calm and relaxed, but this cool demeanour was betrayed by the overflowing contents of the ashtray next to her. Even as Barry watched, she lit another cigarette and drew on it.

'Are the windows locked?'

Barry couldn't help laughing. 'Yes, Lou. The windows and the front door. Besides, our Derek-demon would have to know where to look.'

She stubbed out the half-smoked cigarette. 'If we're up against Chapel –'

'Which is a fairly safe bet,' he interrupted.

Louise wasn't impressed. She continued, stressing each word. 'If we're up against Chapel, he knows where to find all of us from our personnel files.'

'Not me,' he objected, winking as he did so.

'Sorry?'

Barry sipped his brandy. 'Not me. When I moved from the flat in Putney, I never bothered to let ACL know.'

'That's against company procedures –' She ground to a halt as she realized how ludicrous that sounded. 'Why did you do that?'

To Barry, it had been obvious, but his particular work ethic wasn't one widely shared by the rest of ACL. 'Work is, was, work, and home is home. As you – as well as every manager I've ever had – knows full well, when I come home, that's it. Look at John Greenstreet. In the office till eight every night, working weekends, putting ACL first every time –'

'And becoming the youngest manager in the company,' Louise pointed out, lighting two cigarettes and passing one to Barry. 'Seems like a pretty good trade-off to me,' she puffed.

'Before he was made redundant like the rest of us,' countered Barry smugly. 'At the end of the day, none of it made the slightest difference. To us, to Greenstreet. But it did to James,' he added quietly.

'That's what I don't understand,' said Louise. 'Where does James fit into it all? You stole a floptical and I'm guilty by association, but poor old James . . . How did he get tangled up in all this?' She trailed off, before staring at Barry with a mixture of horror and anger. 'Of course — it was his floptical!' She scrambled to her feet, knocking the ashtray and spraying dog-ends over the paisley sofa.

'You bastard! You absolute bastard! James is dead because of you! There's some demon out there who wants to kill us, kill James, kill Cassie!' She tried to punch him, but the attack was sufficiently telegraphed for Barry to grab her wrist.

'Please, Lou, calm down.' He gently sat her down onto the sofa. 'Do you really think I would have put all our lives at risk if I'd known what it would lead to? I took the floptical from James's desk because he was stupid enough to leave it in plain sight, and I was curious. You know how strict Chapel normally is about security.'

'There's one hell of a difference between a written warning and having your neck broken by a demon, Barry,' said Louise quietly.

'I know, I know,' he agreed. 'But you must believe me —'

She placed her hand on his. 'I do. I know you wouldn't do anything to hurt me or Cassie. It's just difficult to think rationally — demons, computers turning into windows into hell —' She shook her head. 'For God's sake, Barry, the world just doesn't work like that.'

He squeezed her hand in an attempt at reassurance. 'It does now.'

'Let me see if I've got this straight,' growled the policeman, a blond man with a cleft chin and halitosis. 'You arrived at Mister Campling's house about an hour ago, about midnight, and found the front door wide open.'

Louise shook her head. 'Not wide open, just open.' Over another brandy, she and Barry had hammered out their story, agreeing on the points and details that they needed to convince the police to investigate. The events of earlier that night – specifically the presence of a blue-black demon that had once been a colleague from ACL – had been, well, altered. Louise just hoped that their mutual story was both believable, and, just as importantly, consistent.

'And the interior of the house suggested a struggle of some sort?' The policeman chewed the end of his biro.

'The phone table had been knocked over –'

'Very conclusive, Mister Brown,' said the policeman sarcastically. 'Ever thought of a career in the force?'

Barry stepped closer to the desk. 'PC Chapman, we came here because we were worried about our friend.' Louise suppressed a shudder, knowing that James Campling would never have to worry about anything ever again. 'There's no need to be funny about it.'

Chapman shot Barry a look of disdain, but his tone was much more sympathetic as he continued. 'At this point, you and Ms Mason came straight here. Didn't you think about going in?'

'No, officer,' Barry replied wearily. 'Believe it or not, we were frightened. What if the person responsible was still inside?'

'I see your point, Mister Brown.' Chapman picked up the sheet of paper from the desk and thumbed towards the door behind him. 'I'll just go and have a word with my superiors and be right back. Take a seat in the waiting room.' With that, he was gone.

'Well?' asked Louise as she sat down on one of the plastic chairs. 'What do you think?'

Barry shrugged. 'We've done our best.'

'But what about Derek?' she hissed, the memory of his transformation vivid in her mind. 'He could still be out there!' The thought of that monster somehow finding her mother's house and threatening Cassie was more than she could bear.

Barry grabbed her hand and squeezed, a gesture of both support and of silence. 'For Christ's sake, Lou, what are we supposed to do? You saw what that little tosser was like. If I'd started going on about demons he would have thrown us out.'

She reached into her bag and withdrew a crushed packet of Benson and Hedges. 'Cigarette?'

He pulled one from the packet and straightened it, and then lit it as Louise proffered the flame from her lighter. 'Thanks,' he said through the blue cloud. 'At least this way, someone can deal with James's body, can't they?'

'But it leaves Chapel in the clear, Barry!'

'I know,' he said imploringly. 'But I don't know what else to do!'

They both fell into an awkward silence, and Louise passed the time by reading the trite and patronizing posters that covered the walls.

After what seemed like hours, a cough from the desk drew their attention. PC Chapman had returned, and his expression didn't give Louise a particularly warm feeling.

'Mister Brown, Ms Mason?'

They stood up and walked over to the desk, both holding their latest cigarettes behind their backs, like naughty schoolchildren caught behind the bikesheds. Chapman also stood with his hands behind his back, but this was probably his attempt to appear the perfect bobby.

'The area car took a look at Mister Campling's house,' he stated.

'And?' urged Barry. Louise knew that Barry hated it when people said things for effect, holding back the real information because it gave them a sense of power. It was one of the reasons why he had been such a lousy player in the game of office politics.

'And, Mister Brown,' continued the policeman with spiteful relish, 'there was absolutely nothing out of the ordinary. The front door was closed –'

'But the hallway!' protested Barry.

'Because of your concerns, Mister Brown, PCs Ventnor and Daffern entered the house.' Louise could feel his disdain. 'And everything was in perfect order. Including,' and the sarcasm simply dripped off this bit, 'including the hall. A nice, tidy hall, with a nice and tidy and upright phone table. There was no sign of Mister Campling.'

'Surely that should tell you something, officer?'

'Not exactly, no.' Chapman slid a piece of paper out from beneath the statement and waved it in front of them. 'Do you know what this is?'

Louise tried to make it out. It was a computer printout of some sort, but the precise words evaded her.

'No? Then I'll enlighten you. It's an e-mail message from a Mister James Richard Campling, of Fifty-one, Aspley Road, Chelsea. Informing his local police station that he will be on holiday, as of Thursday, 30 December, and asking whether we could keep an eye on his house while he's sunning himself in Lanzarote.' He crumpled the message in his fist before slamming it on the counter. 'And yet you claim that his front door was wide open, and the hallway wrecked.' He glared belligerently. 'Is this some kind of joke?'

Louise froze. Sending a message from Campling's e-mail address would be child's play to someone of Chapel's genius. And this was clear proof that Chapel was one step in front of them.

She could see the panic in Barry's face, she could feel the cogs turning in his mind as he tried to come up with another convincing story. 'But –' he began.

His objections were cut short when Louise wrapped her arm round his and dragged him out of the police station, leaving an irate PC Chapman open-mouthed.

'What are you doing, woman!' he shouted as they

pushed through the double doors.

'Saving our necks.' She grabbed and lit another cigarette to replace the one that she had dropped in the station. 'If you hadn't noticed, Barry we've been stitched up. Stitched up perfectly. Chapel knows exactly what we're doing – and he's not going to let us get away.' She took a long drag on the cigarette.

Barry plonked himself on the low wall which surrounded the police station and rubbed his face with his hands. 'So what now?'

'We go back to your place and get a good night's sleep. I think we deserve it.'

'And what then?'

Louise shrugged. 'I can only think of one option left. We go and see Chapel.'

Barry stared at her. 'What? But that's madness!'

She smiled. 'I know. That's why I want to sleep on it.'

The Doctor opened his eyes. And then shut them immediately to keep out the onslaught of light and sound. His most recent memories were disjointed and confused, as if someone had scrambled his synapses. He jumped to his feet and placed his hands on his hips, breathing deeply as he reorientated himself.

The TARDIS sounded in perfect health. To his companions, there was never anything more than a soothing hum, but he was well aware of the choir of harmonies and melodies it contained – a language all of its own. And one glance at the console was enough for the Doctor to assure himself that the ship wasn't under attack.

Whatever had happened, it was gone now, leaving nothing more than a jumble of names and images. But one name suddenly bobbed to the surface: Anne Travers. And that particular train of thought concluded in the appointment they had at Canary Wharf Tower at eleven the next morning. This morning, he corrected, noting from one of the read-outs that it was already eight o'clock.

And Mel had been out all night.

Harker groaned as a bird-like warble impinged upon his dreams. For one, delicious moment he imagined it to be coming through the French windows from the garden. He was chewing on a slice of toast, while the kids were arguing over which channel to watch – the Incredible Death Ghouls or Jolly Jack. And Jean was just waiting for the last drops of fresh coffee to drip through the filter.

Then the birdsong deepened and became the doorbell. Harker got up from the breakfast bar and walked towards the front door, ignoring Jean and Jamie and Edward and their pleas for him to stay but he had to answer the door and it was Chapel and he followed him *and the house wasn't there any more* –

He gave a dry shout and sat upright, realizing that he was in his office and the warbling was his phone. And Jean and the boys were long gone, his family one of the many sacrifices he had made for the man who was now demanding his presence like a king summoning his courtiers.

He swung his legs over the side of the bed and wondered whether it had all been worth it. And then he thought about Chapel's special New Year's Party and smiled. Oh, yes. It would all be worth it in the end. He picked up his telephone.

'Ah, David!' Chapel sounded like he had just eaten a hearty breakfast after a good night's sleep, rather than having spent the night in front of a Tablette. 'I hope you slept well.' Before Harker could reply, Chapel continued. 'I'd like you to pay the university a visit.'

'The university?' Chapel's visions of grandeur were getting worse. Harker was now at the level of a gopher or an office boy, it seemed.

'Yes, the university library, to be precise. I want to borrow someone. And when you've done that, we'll be ready to compile the Codex again.'

As Harker pulled on his suit trousers, he was forced to protest. 'But we ran a compilation last night. Why should this one be any different –' He suddenly understood. 'That Bush woman?'

'Quite. So just run along and get her.'

Harker growled. Soon – so very soon – Chapel would be sorry for treating him like a servant. Extremely sorry. Comforted by warm thoughts of rebellion, Harker started tying up his shoelaces.

From the age of thirteen, Melanie Bush had realized the importance of a healthy body. Much to the chagrin of her parents, she had embraced the doctrine of vegetarianism, forcing her mother to provide her with wholesome meals that didn't depend on animal flesh. At the same time, tea and coffee had become anathema. Herbal drinks only, if you please.

Had she drunk coffee, she might not have fallen asleep over the library's computer. And she might have finished her investigations and returned to the TARDIS without any problems.

This was not to be the case.

Slumped over the Tablette, Mel was completely unaware of the large shadow which fell over her. And completely unprepared for the bear-like paw that clamped itself on her shoulder.

'Melanie Bush?'

The growling inquiry was enough to wake her; the looming presence was more than enough to scare the hell out of her. 'What do you want?' she shrieked, making a futile attempt to squirm free.

The man was massive, massive and grey, with a voice that was deep and extremely threatening. Mel knew immediately that she had no choice but to follow his instructions. 'What do you want?' she repeated. And then she realized that she recognized him.

'David Harker?'

He pulled up the chair from the next terminal and sat down. He stroked his chin and stared at her, a look more of analysis than any kind of threat. Finally he spoke. 'You're a very intelligent young woman, Melanie. Very intelligent.' He reached over and swivelled her Tablette screen round to face him. He obviously recognized the particular module; his eyebrow shot up. 'The C-ASIC routine. Have you debugged that one as well?'

She remained silent, suddenly aware of the copy of Glauss next to the Tablette. Harker also became suddenly aware, and picked the book up, releasing a hacking laugh at the pneumatic blonde adorning the cover. His humour rapidly evaporated, however, when he scanned the indicia a couple of pages in. Mel knew why: © 2023 was enough to make even a seasoned time traveller like herself do a double take.

Rather than ask about the book, Harker took the easy option. He replaced the book on the table and repeated his earlier question. This time, however, Mel decided that honesty was the best policy. Harker obviously knew what she'd been up to all night, and, because of his connection with ACL, Ashley Chapel probably did as well.

'No, I haven't. I fell asleep, I'm afraid.'

'Shame,' he muttered. 'That module has been a pain in the arse since the beginning. I was hoping that you'd spare me the trouble of sorting it out.' He must have noticed Mel's quizzical look, because he elaborated. 'I'm the head of development at ACL, remember. And you've been making my life one hell of a lot easier, Ms Bush. In more ways than one.' He picked up the piece of paper creased up next to Glauss and held it up like a little flag.

'You have me to thank for these protocols. I asked Julia Prince to pass them on to you.' At Mel's frown, he continued. 'I'm also responsible for the lot working here, including Julia.'

'You?' exclaimed Mel. And then realized the significance of his words. 'But why do you want to hack into your own computers? It doesn't make sense.' She eyed him suspiciously. 'You're up to something, aren't you? And I doubt that Ashley Chapel knows about it, does he?'

He stood up, and indicated for her to do the same. 'Now, Melanie, we're off for a little drive.' He started walking towards the doors out of the still busy library. And then he stopped and frowned. 'I think you need a bit of education.'

Six

'Lovely car,' said Mel. 'Is it Mister Chapel's?'

Harker, sitting next to her in the leather and walnut back seat of the Jaguar, nodded. 'We need to talk.' He pressed a button and a glass screen rose between them and the driver.

Mel shook her head. 'If you're planning to enlist my help in your shady business dealings, you've got another think coming,' she stated flatly.

Harker laughed; it did nothing to reassure Mel. 'For Christ's sake, Melanie, you're already involved. Or have you forgotten what you were doing last night?'

Mel felt herself starting to blush. Harker was right. And not only had she illegally hacked into Chapel's files, but she had become so carried away with her own cleverness at interpreting the computer language that she had virtually debugged the whole thing at one sitting, without the faintest idea as to the true nature of the Codex project, or the slightest care as to the circumstances. For all she knew, she might have just helped a couple of mad businessmen in their attempts to defraud the world's banking systems. Considering the circumstances under which she had first met the Doctor, that would be horribly ironic.

'Are you planning a fraud?' she asked meekly.

'What a question,' he responded. And then he shrugged. 'That's what I need you for. Chapel's up to something big, and from what I've been able to find out, he's going to siphon billions out of the stock markets when the year changes over.'

Mel's eyes widened. 'He's going to use the century

change to get into the stock markets? That's, that's outrageous!' And then she frowned. 'And despicable. I won't help you,' she stated, crossing her arms defiantly.

Harker shook his head. 'Either you help me, or I hand you over to the police. The penalty for information incursion is twenty years, remember?'

Mel didn't remember, because that particular piece of legislation hadn't come into force when she had left Pease Pottage. And then something else occurred to her. 'But if you're working for Mister Chapel, why did you want me to break into his files?'

'Because Chapel is deliberately keeping me in the dark,' he barked. 'One research team is working on a totally new computer language, the other is coding up designs that they don't understand.'

'But you're head of development,' she pointed out. 'I thought you were in charge of the programmers?'

'In charge of keeping them working, yes. But Chapel never saw fit to let me in on his plans, and he expects me to follow him blindly!' he spat. 'The only reason I know as much as I do is from the occasional system design that I've come across. And that's where you come in. We're going back to ACL, where Chapel is very keen to meet you. And when he's finished, you're going to carry on where you left off. You're going to dig out everything from that Codex directory that you can find. And then we're going to interpret it.' He held up the slip of paper. 'I mean, if you can crack into one of the most closely guarded program libraries in the whole computing industry, I'm sure deciphering a new language won't be beyond your abilities.'

As the car sped through Chiswick, Mel suddenly glanced at her watch, and realized that it was eleven o'clock. The Doctor and that woman would just have reached Canary Wharf Tower. The rest of the journey would take approximately another three quarters of an hour, just enough time for them to finish their snooping around.

She turned to Harker and smiled. 'Fine. I'll help you.'
But not if we run into the Doctor first.

'Chapel seems to have a very odd view of business,' said the Doctor. After meeting at the railway station within the Tower itself, they had made their way to the red marble foyer and received permission from the security guard to use the lift up to the forty-ninth floor. The floor where Ashley Chapel Marketing was based.

Anne looked away from the lift indicator as it changed from forty-five to forty-six. 'Ashley Chapel has an odd view of everything, Doctor. Is there some particular aspect of his megalomania which worries you?' She knew that her bitterness had spilt over into her reply, but that was unavoidable, really.

He stroked the blue-black cat badge on his lapel. 'He closes the development part of ACL – apart from his advanced research team, of course – and yet the sales force is kept on. Odd, wouldn't you say?'

Anne shrugged. 'Different parts of the great and glorious Ashley Chapel Holdings Corporation. I'm sure he'll dispense with them as soon as they become surplus to requirements.' She calmed down slightly. 'Floors forty-six to fifty house most of his other companies: from the Ashley Chapel Lottery Consortium to the remains of ACL – apparently called FantasyLab Limited now –' At that moment, the lift reached the appointed floor, and the single door opened with a ping, revealing the plushly furnished sales floor. Every single sales person span round and stared at the new arrivals, before looking at one another in mild panic.

'I can't say I'm impressed by their sales technique,' muttered the Doctor archly, before striding from the lift and throwing his arms open. 'Good morning!' he announced. Anne found herself staring at her shoes, hiding her embarrassment from the shocked staff.

'Can, can I help you, sir?' asked a woman in her late twenties, dressed in the blue suit that marked her as a member of Ashley Chapel's uniform public face. She was blonde – dyed blonde, Anne noted – with far too much make-up and a very tarty short skirt.

The Doctor gestured towards the nearest table, a reproduction Chippendale upon which sat a top-of-the-range Tablette, waiting patiently to demonstrate any or all of ACL's software. 'I'm interested in buying something.'

The woman couldn't help pulling an exasperated look, as if to say 'why else would you be here?' But her reply was polite to the point of obsequiousness. 'Of course, sir,' she said through bright red lips. 'Did you have a particular area in mind? Single workstation? Client-server? Local- or Wide-Area-Network?' She fired the jargon words as though she had learnt them by rote, with no idea of the meaning or significance beyond the training manual. Which was probably true, Anne mused. For all the expensive trappings of this prime site sales office, the cheapest part of the operation was the sales staff. Another reason for ACL's decline, she didn't doubt.

The Doctor laid a hand on the Tablette. 'All of it and everything. I'd like to see every bit and byte that Ashley Chapel has to offer.'

Anne caught the smile from the woman and could see her excitement. Given the appalling sales record that ACL software possessed, this was probably the first time she had ever put her training into practice. Anne walked over to the Doctor's side to watch.

Ten minutes later, the sales assistant was enjoying a well-earned cup of coffee in the staff room. Within two minutes, the Doctor's skill with the Tablette, accompanied by his loud, theatrical commentary, had succeeded in totally upsetting the woman. She was on the point of tears before she diplomatically withdrew, suggesting that the Doctor would be better off trying out the software without her interference. He had cracked his knuckles and given a wicked grin. 'Now, we can begin,' he muttered to Anne.

And now she was feeling as left out as the sales woman, as she watched the Doctor's dextrous fingers play the Tablette like a musical instrument. Sometimes he would use both hands on the keyboard and ignore the mouse; on other occasions, he would control the keyboard with one hand and manoeuvre the mouse with the other, tutting over the results on the screen as he did so. And every single one of Anne's inquiries was met with a knowing smile or a secretive tap on his nose as he navigated through the software.

Anne's attentions were wandering – towards the coffee and biscuits provided in the hope of customers that beckoned from a distant table – when the Doctor exhaled a sigh of delight.

'There!' he hissed, pointing at the screen. To Anne, the display of windows was no different from any of the other Tablette monitors placed around the sales floor, but the Doctor's excitement indicated otherwise.

'What am I supposed to be looking at?' she asked, hoping that the Doctor might explain. Despite her grounding as a scientist, she wasn't as up to date with computer technology as she should have been. The Doctor was only too pleased to oblige.

'To anybody lacking my particular talents, the network to which these Tablettes are connected is isolated from both the computers in ACL and the computer systems which control this Tower. But I had my suspicions. The little that you've told me about the esteemed Mister Chapel made it hard for me to believe that he wouldn't have some method of overseeing what happens with these machines –'

'You've found a link?'

'Exactly,' he said proudly, as if Anne were a slow pupil finally getting the correct answer. 'A one-way link between the ACL network and here.'

'But if it's one-way –'

'That's where my genius comes in,' he said proudly; and Anne realized that there was no trace of conceit in his words. He considered his inestimable intelligence as a proven fact, and everything and everyone simply had to operate around it. 'Indeed, reversing the direction of such a link is the key to undermining Chapel's Paradigm operating system.' He tugged on his cravat. 'At least, that's what I told Demeter Glauss when she was writing her book.' Obviously realizing that he had completely lost Anne, he returned to the subject in hand. 'This is what my earlier display of genius has unearthed: this window controls the security systems for the whole of Canary Wharf Tower.'

'Security systems?' she asked. 'Why would you want to tamper with them?'

'Because, Anne, there are limits to even my abilities. The link doesn't have the bandwidth necessary for me to access Chapel's research project.' He indicated a nondescript, grey-bordered window. 'I can see it, but I can't touch it. The link could never carry the amount of information that I want to look at. I need to get into ACL, if I'm to proceed any further.' He started entering data into the security window.

'So what are you doing now?'

'I'm instructing this magnificent glass edifice to let down its drawbridge at three o'clock tomorrow morning, when everything's nice and quiet –'

'No!' Anne's outburst drew alarmed looks from both the staff and the Doctor.

'Anne,' he hissed. 'After all that you've told me about ACL, I can't see that a little breaking and entering would prick your conscience.'

'It's not that. It's just that, well, I think Chapel's going to make his move at midnight. Whatever he's up to, my sources are pretty certain that he's chosen twelve o'clock tonight to make his move. Three o'clock could be too late.' She hoped that that would convince him; she still couldn't bring herself to confess her true fears.

'Midnight, eh? Oh dear. It sounds like Chapel is one of those melodramatic villains, always trying to hog the limelight with their cleverness and theatricality.' He sighed. 'How does twenty-three hundred hours suit you? That gives me an hour to spare, should I need it.' His tone suggested that he wouldn't.

She smiled. 'That sounds fine.'

As the Doctor typed away on the keyboard, something suddenly occurred to Anne. 'Why go to all this bother?' she wondered. 'Why can't you use your TARDIS?'

The Doctor didn't look up from the screen. 'Because there are some odd disturbances in the space-time continuum around here . . .' He trailed off and stared into the distance, and Anne could have sworn that a look of sheer horror flashed across his face. He regained his composure, but a faint flicker of unease was still present. 'Perhaps I might need the extra time,' he murmured.

'You still haven't told me how we're going to get to see Chapel,' said Barry. He and Louise were standing outside Canary Wharf Tower, braving the chilly December morning. Thanks to a temporary power failure on the Docklands Light Railway, they had been forced to take the bus. 'Without our ID cards, the lifts won't work.'

Louise raised a finger. 'That's where my superior intellect comes in!' she said brightly. 'The lift is controlled from the security desk.'

Barry shot her a puzzled frown. 'So? Vincent's hardly going to risk his job to let us back into ACL, is he? He still works for Chapel, remember?'

'And that's where you come in,' she said, waiting for a motorcycle courier to speed past before she crossed the road.

'Me?' Barry hurried to catch up with her. 'What have I got to do with it?'

They reached the glass doors, and Barry realized with a shudder that Vincent had seen them, and was grinning broadly. There was no going back.

'Vincent likes you.'

Barry instantly understood what she meant. 'Oh no!'

he shouted. 'Just because he fancies me, I'm not going to take advantage of him.'

'I'm not asking you to sleep with him,' she protested. 'Just flirt a bit. Say that you've left something behind. That sort of thing.'

'But —'

Louise span round and jabbed him in the chest with a well-aimed finger. 'You bloody hypocrite! It was okay for me to try it on with poor old James, but when it's your turn, ooh, you really get my back up, sometimes.'

Barry refrained from pointing out that 'trying it on with James' had actually been her idea, and that his unfortunate demise had made it rather moot, anyway. Louise was now set on this course of action, and anything he said would only make her more resolute.

'All right, all right. Anything for a quiet life.' He stepped forward, allowing the automatic doors to open.

As they entered the foyer, they didn't notice the dark blue Jaguar driving up Canada Square.

Chapel checked his watch yet again. Harker was taking his time bringing clever Ms Bush back to ACL, and Chapel didn't like his people to slack on the job. Sitting down at his desk, he worked at his Tablette for a few seconds, and then smiled as a video window appeared; the window was tapping into the monitor feed from the foyer of the Tower.

And then his smile vanished, to be replaced by an incredulous stare. After the events of the previous evening, there were two people that Chapel had never expected to see again.

So what the hell were Mason and Brown doing talking to the security guard in the foyer? Either they were extremely brave or extremely stupid. And Chapel was forced to admit that, however badly it reflected on his recruitment process, the latter was probably true.

But the last thing he currently wanted was a personal confrontation with them. So, despite his discomfort, there was only one option open to him. He would have to sit and watch. And hope that the security guard did his job for once.

'Hiya!' said Vincent cheerfully, his pleasure at seeing Barry again written all over his face. 'What brings you back here?'

Barry smiled back. 'It's a bit, well, embarrassing, really. You know how upset I was yesterday?'

'So what?' shrugged Vincent. 'You'd just been made redundant. You were entitled to be a bit down.'

Barry adopted his most persuasive tone. 'Thanks. You've always been so understanding. It's just that I left something in my desk, and I was wondering –'

'Sorry,' Vincent replied curtly. 'No one's allowed back into the ACL Suite apart from Mister Chapel, Mister Harker, and the advanced research team. Not even you.'

Laying it on a bit more heavily, Barry steeled himself and gently brushed Vincent's huge, hairy hand. 'I only want to slip in and slip out,' he whispered, fully intending the double entendre. 'It won't take a second.'

'I'm sorry, Barry, but I've got my instructions. It's my job on the line.' And then he grinned. 'But if you're not busy later, I'm going to a really good party. You could meet some friends of mine –'

Barry snatched his hand away. 'Bloody hell! I only want to pop back to my desk. That doesn't give you the right to make a pass at me!' He immediately realized how hurtful that had sounded, and that Vincent was exactly that. Hurt. And angry.

'Is that what all of this was about?' he shouted. 'Flirt a bit with Vincent and he'll let us back into ACL? You really are a nasty piece of work, aren't you? God knows why I was ever interested.'

'Hold on a minute,' Louise interjected. 'There's no need to get worked up about this.'

'No need? No need? I might be just a security guard,' he replied, 'and I might not have the qualifications necessary to become a programmer or a technical author, but I'm still a person.'

Louise laid her hand on his arm, but Vincent threw it off. 'And you're just as bad as he is.'

'Hang on,' snapped Barry. 'Don't start taking it out on her.'

'I should have guessed,' barked Vincent. 'I should have guessed that you'd stand up for her.' He grabbed Barry by his collar.

'Are you sure that everything's all right?' The look of fear on the Doctor's face was an image that Anne couldn't get out of her mind, even now in the mirrored lift.

'Yes, yes, perfectly,' he replied, but he sounded distracted, worried. 'I wonder how Mel is faring in her investigations,' he added, injecting a note of enthusiasm into his voice. 'Such a headstrong young lady –' He stopped as the lift reached the ground floor and the doors opened.

And Anne stared at the scene in front of them in surprise. A man and a woman were arguing with one of the security guards, drawing everyone's attention away from the external doors opposite the lift, where a blue Jaguar was parked outside.

'Chapel's car!' Anne hissed. 'I can't let him see me here!' She felt the first stirrings of panic and started looking for some means of escape that would avoid the object of her hatred. And then the Doctor's voice cut through her desperation.

'It can't be . . .' he whispered.

Anne recognized the man getting out of the car before she noticed the woman with him. The large, unfriendly shape of David Harker – Chapel's trained gorilla – made her shudder. And then she noticed that one massive hand was grasping the shoulder of somebody else she recognized.

'Of all the infernal cheek!' snapped the Doctor indignantly. 'They've kidnapped Mel!' Almost pulling Anne out of the lift, he strode towards the main doors, obviously intending to confront Harker face to face, but Anne managed to hold him back.

'No, Doctor!' But her words were drowned out by the commotion around the security desk. Raised voices had given way to raised fists, as the man with light brown hair was being held back from hitting the guard by the blonde woman. The few dozen people in the foyer were now gathered round the fracas, blocking the route from the doors to the lift as they tried to see what was going on.

And then Anne realized that the Doctor was no longer standing next to her. He was threading his way through the onlookers, but Anne could see that he wasn't aiming towards the protagonists. Instead, he was heading towards the point where Harker and Mel would come closest to the fracas. As he drew near, he turned to Anne and gestured for her to get away.

The next few seconds were a blur to Anne. As she scurried towards the doors on the other side of the foyer – the other side of the Tower from where Chapel's car was parked – she caught a glimpse of the Doctor elbowing one of the crowd, forcing them to collide with Harker. And then Mel's hair was clearly visible like a red beacon, moving away from Harker and away from the commotion. At the same time, the altercation seemed to peter out, as the blonde woman succeeded in dragging her friend away from the security guard and towards the doors.

Anne left the Tower and hurried round the outside, trying to ignore the cold wind that whipped past her. She waited on the corner, where she had a clear view of Chapel's Jaguar. Moments later, the Doctor and Mel came through the doors and joined her.

'Once again, the Doctor comes to the rescue,' he said proudly.

'That fight had something to do with it, though,' Mel pointed out, unaware of the Doctor's sudden crestfallen expression. 'I wonder what that was all about.'

The very people who had apparently been responsible

for the trouble in the foyer were walking past them, both looking very flustered. They looked over at the Doctor, Anne and Mel, and then made to walk off in the opposite direction.

'Not so fast!' called the Doctor. The words were so intense, so commanding, that the man and the woman stopped and turned round, both looking rather sheepish.

From the antique splendour of his office on the fiftieth floor, Chapel watched the chaos in the foyer on the screen of his Tablette with a sigh of irritation. In just over twelve hours, it would be midnight. A midnight that he had been planning for, preparing for, for nearly twenty years. Two decades of devoting his vast fortune to researches amongst the arcane, buying secrets and people in his quest to create what he now knew as the Millennium Codex. Two decades, inexorably leading up to midnight on 31 December 1999; and yet the Codex was still flawed, still imperfect.

He reached out to the compact, black keyboard and played an elegant sequence, changing the image from the now calm foyer of Canary Wharf Tower to a listing of the one module left in the Codex that was still proving problematic.

In the early hours of that morning, he had watched with anticipation as the serendipitous Ms Bush had turned her attention to the C-ASIC module; thanks to her programming legerdemain, it was the only part of the Codex left to fix. And, three hours later, he had slammed the mahogany table top in frustration as a quick look through the library video feed showed that she had fallen asleep, leaving C-ASIC unfinished.

C-ASIC was the key program: the one whose execution would initiate the cascade through the hundreds of other programs which comprised the Codex, the core of twenty years of research. And with the departure of Ms Bush, Ashley Simon Iolanthe Chapel had just lost the one chance he had of making the deadline.

The knock at the door distracted Chapel from the flawed code. 'Come!' he yelled.

There was an apologetic growl from the doorway.

'Ah, David! Do come in!' Chapel's anger was barely restrained.

'I take it you saw what happened?' muttered the large man.

'That you allowed Ms Bush to escape?' He offhandedly waved at the Tablette. And then his manner changed. 'I had a ringside seat!' he yelled, leaping to his feet. 'That woman was our only hope of completing the Codex within the specified timeframe, David, and you let her slip through your fingers! Thanks to you, the entire project is in jeopardy –' He stopped as something occurred to him, something triggered by both his observation of Mel's techniques in the early hours, and his recent visit to Holborn. When Mel had debugged the C-WSDL module, she had used a very unexpected technique, a technique that might just work on C-ASIC.

Opening a drawer in his desk, he withdrew a large but thin book, bound in faded beige. Thanks to his ownership of the Library of Saint John, the restrictions concerning removal of books didn't apply to him, and he had walked out with two vital volumes. One was an account of the ancient god, Yog-Sothoth; the other purported to be a transcription of writings from the time of Atlantis. He opened it and leafed through the pages, until he found what he wanted, a reproduction of an ancient inscription.

An inscription written in the same language as the Millennium Codex.

Sitting down, he began typing with increasing speed and vigour. Every few seconds, he would stop and stare at the book and the inscription, before returning his attention to the keyboard.

'Ashley?'

Chapel didn't look up, but his anger had dissipated. 'I see it now. I see the problem.' A further minute of quiet keystrokes, and then he leant back in his plush leather chair and placed his hands behind his neck.

'Ashley?' repeated Harker.

Chapel looked at him through his glasses and broke into a broad grin. 'I've done it, David, I've done it,' he whispered, almost afraid to shatter the fragile, exquisite silence. He rose and walked over to the window, savouring the mid-morning view of the capital. A capital that was now ready to accept the word of Saraquazel, and the glory and majesty that would accompany His ascension.

'The Millennium Codex is now complete. And, although it pains me to admit it, the credit rests with our magnificent Ms Bush,' he said, turning from the window. 'She will receive her reward in Heaven.'

Seven

Greenwich seemed far enough away from Canary Wharf and ACL for Louise and Barry to relax, even in the company of strangers. Despite his eccentric clothes and brash nature, the Doctor inspired a trust that made it very easy for both of them to finally unload the horrors and mysteries of the last twenty-four hours. Indeed, as they sat in the small café opposite the park gates and drank endless cups of coffee, it was difficult for either of them to stop. Louise wondered whether it was the very normality of the situation that made it so easy; then she decided that it was simply the chance to tell somebody else about what had happened and get the feeling that they believed her. God knows, she had had enough difficulty stopping herself from telling the policeman about it earlier!

But the best thing about it was that the Doctor, Mel and Dame Anne Travers − how the hell had she got involved, Louise wondered − appeared to believe them. Barry's description of the transformed computer drew an understanding nod from the Doctor, while Louise's account of the death of James Campling was greeted with sympathy, and even elicited a gasp of horror from Mel.

Their story complete, Barry and Louise sat back as the others presented their own findings. Mel described what she had discovered while hacking into Chapel's network − it was Louise's turn to be shocked, since she would have sworn that Chapel's information warehouse was unbreachable. Mel's description of the programming language in which this Codex was written matched that of the module that Barry had stolen, and Louise was impressed — and slightly jealous — when Mel admitted that she had actually understood some of the coding. She then proceeded to write some of it down on a paper napkin. But Louise couldn't help thinking that the effervescent girl was holding back about something. And now the Doctor seemed uneasy.

'Are you absolutely sure this is what you saw?' he asked, holding up the napkin.

Mel looked rather hurt. 'I'm not normally wrong, am I?'

The Doctor shrugged. 'Then things have just gone from bad to worse.'

'What's Chapel up to, then?' muttered Anne Travers, but it seemed to Louise that she was asking the question of herself rather than the others. And she couldn't help suspecting that the woman had an agenda all her own. Louise wasn't looking forward to the time when that agenda clashed with theirs.

'What's the significance of this, then?' She realized that Barry was pointing at the scribbled nonsense words on the napkin.

The Doctor sighed. 'Something that needs considerably more investigation before I can be certain.' He looked under the table at the slim black shape of a Tablette next to Barry's legs. 'That's the Tablette you liberated from Campling's house, I take it?' Barry nodded. 'Then I'd like to borrow it, if I may?'

'Why not?' said Barry, but Louise wasn't quite as sure. 'How do we know that we can trust you?'

Mel giggled. 'If only you could hear yourself, Louise,' she said. 'That's one of the oldest clichés in the book. You've got to trust us, haven't you? I mean, who else would sit here and drink coffee with a couple of people who claim that their colleagues are being turned into drooling monsters?'

Louise had to admit that Mel had a point. 'What are you going to do with it?' she asked the Doctor.

'Examine, investigate, interrogate!' he proclaimed, swinging the Tablette from the floor onto the white tablecloth. 'Although I can't look for skeletons in Chapel's cyberspace cupboard until this evening, I don't doubt that this little marvel can furnish me with a few answers, even if it does throw up a few more questions into the bargain.'

'And what are we going to do while you're playing around with that?' asked Mel.

'Ah. I'm glad you asked that,' he replied, grabbing her left wrist and reading the time from her gaudy watch. 'It's nearly three o'clock now. I need to be at Canary Wharf Tower between eleven and midnight to take advantage of my window of opportunity –'

'And what are we supposed to do until then? Sit and twiddle our thumbs?' Mel sounded very agitated. 'We're all part of this now.'

' "We" do nothing.' The Doctor clasped his hands together and leant his chin on them. 'This situation has now escalated to the point at which I don't want anyone else involved. And that includes you, Mel. I'm not putting any of you at risk, and that's final.'

'But –'

'No buts,' he snapped. 'I have a lot to do, and very little time in which to achieve it. Anne, you have a right to be involved. I'll meet you outside Canary Wharf Tower at 11 p.m. on the dot.'

'That still leaves us at a bit of a loose end,' complained Barry.

The Doctor sighed. 'In the midst of all this ghoulishness, you young people seem to have overlooked two rather salient points.' He pointed out of the café window at the chilly greenery of Greenwich Park. 'We are in London, one of the most cosmopolitan cities in the galaxy. And today is 31 December 1999!' He slammed his fist on the table, knocking over the salt cellar. Louise automatically reached over and righted it, picking up a pinch of the spilt salt and hurling it over her shoulder.

'I'm sure you can find a New Year's Eve party to go to.'

He jumped to his feet. 'Anyway, people to do and things to see. Dame Anne, I'll see you at eleven. And Mel –' He looked a bit puzzled, but Louise was glad to help him out.

'You can come back with us if you want, Mel. I'm sure we can keep ourselves out of trouble while the grown-ups play their games.'

Mel shrugged. 'Well, it's not as if my Filofax is full.' She briefly considered the invitation and then beamed. 'Yes, that would be lovely. Shall we go?'

The five of them left the café and braved the crisp winds on their way to the nearby taxi rank, just next to Greenwich market. As they walked, Mel fell back until she was level with the Doctor. She still wasn't satisfied with his intentions.

'Can't you at least give me some idea as to what you're up to? I don't like the idea of you blundering around without me to look after you.'

He smiled a warm, avuncular smile. 'I'll be fine, Mel. Besides, you were the one who was complaining about missing out on all the fun; Barry and Louise seem nice people, so go and enjoy yourself.'

Admittedly, she was looking forward to spending some more time with them, but she was still suspicious. 'I suppose you're right. But what's really worrying you?' As soon as she had seen the Doctor outside Canary Wharf Tower, she had noticed something different about him, a chilling, disturbing something that lay behind his eyes.

He sighed, and laid a friendly hand on her shoulder. 'There's not much I can hide from you, is there? Very well, I'll tell you. Every instinct in me is crying out that Ashley Chapel is tampering with forces that even the Time Lords fear. I might even have to call them in on this one.'

'That bad?' Her voice was awed. The Doctor's normal

attitude towards his people was one of disdain; to admit that he could be out of his depth was a terrifying prospect.

'Yes, that bad. And I'd feel a lot happier if you were sipping champagne and singing *Auld Lang Syne* this particular midnight.'

'Okay, Doc. For once I'll be a good girl and keep out of your way. If it's as important as you say it is.'

He stopped and stared at the mist- and smog-shrouded monument of Canary Wharf Tower. His voice was sepulchral when he continued. 'It's the Millennium, Mel. The last New Year's Eve of the twentieth century. But it's definitely not party time.' He smiled as he realized that he had been urging Mel to do just that. 'At least for me it isn't.' He stopped and placed his hands on her shoulders. 'And for once, can't you just do as you're told?'

Mel nodded. 'For once, Doctor, nothing would give me greater pleasure.'

With the Codex completed, Chapel had even found time to return to his luxury flat in one of the many Docklands' condominiums for a change of clothes. He was now dressed in an elegant beige suit, the sheen of the fabric rendering it gold. He sipped a glass of mineral water as he surveyed South London, allowing himself to fantasize about the future that lay before that fine city. In eight hours, he would run the most important computer program in history, and become the new Moses, leading London into the third millennium; the era of peace and prosperity that Saraquazel whispered to him in the silent hours.

He turned away from the window as the door opened.

'Can't you knock?'

'Sorry, Ashley.' Harker looked abashed, and so he should. His bungling had almost cost them everything. 'Just thought you ought to know that the research team will be here at ten.'

'Excellent, excellent.'

'I'm still not sure why you need them, though. If the Codex is finished –'

Chapel sat down on his plush leather sofa and picked up the gold figurine of an antelope from the occasional table in front of him. 'David, David, David,' he sighed, studying the figurine without even glancing at his head of development. 'We stand on the ramparts of destiny, and you bother me with trivia and minutiae.' Replacing the antelope, he stood up and walked over to the rear of the office, the wood-panelled and artwork-bedecked wall that hid his secret world.

'You have been with me since the beginning, David. You've travelled with me to Egypt, India, Africa and countries most people haven't even heard of; and stood by and watched, as I've scoured ancient libraries and danced with shamen. While I have wrestled with the greater picture, I have left you to deal with the more irritating aspects of our endeavour, such as people and money. And yet, I have never once taken you into my confidence regarding the true nature of all this, have I?'

Harker coughed, obviously unsure of the correct reply.

'No, David, I haven't. And for good reason.' He laid a hand on one of the panels. 'And, believe it or not, it has very little to do with trust.' He tapped on the panel.

'It mainly concerns your sanity.'

A door-sized portion of the wall vanished, revealing a dark area beyond. Chapel looked back at Harker. The man was agog, his mouth hanging open in shock.

'You seem surprised.' Chapel laughed. 'That was simply the appliance of science. What lies beyond in my sanctum sanctorum could be considered to be magic.' He entered and beckoned for Harker to follow him.

'She's –' Kneeling before the playpen, Mel was at a complete loss as to what to say. Cassandra Mason's face was that of an angel, with hair like spun gold and wide blue eyes that stared through the bars of the playpen with a voracious curiosity. But her problems were obvious at a glance. Her body wasn't just slight, it was withered, with spindly arms and legs attached to a small, doll-like trunk. It looked as if it was an effort for her to support her large head.

Mel had been in this situation once before, back home in Pease Pottage. She had been coming out of the corner shop, when old Mrs Finch had bumped into her, pushing a pram. Mel had immediately peered in, but had been rendered speechless when she had realized that the child was suffering from Down's Syndrome. Being unsure as to whether to ignore the child's condition or make some sort of acknowledgement to it, she had mumbled and muttered and smiled pleasantly, inwardly cringing as she read the awkward, hurt emotions on Mrs Finch's face.

Looking round at Louise, she saw exactly the same expression, but Louise didn't walk off in silence like Mrs Finch had.

'The specialists call it Trainer-Simpson's Malaise.' There was none of the shame, none of the begging for forgiveness, that Mrs Finch had shown, even though everyone had understood that it wasn't her fault. 'A wasting disease. No one's sure, but the general consensus is that it's caused by the rising levels of pollution in the atmosphere.' She dragged on her cigarette.

Mel couldn't stop herself. 'I hope you gave that up while you were pregnant.'

The looks that shot between Barry and Louise indicated that she hadn't just touched on a nerve, she had wired it into the mains. 'I wasn't suggesting –'

Louise cut her short, holding up a hand. 'It's all right, Mel. I didn't give up smoking when I was carrying Cassie, and I'm always going to have to live with the fact that she's like she is. But I'd appreciate it if we dropped the subject, all right?'

Mel paused in the silence, the memory of Mrs Finch vivid in her mind. But Barry came to her rescue.

'Anyone fancy a drink?' he said cheerfully.

'Have you any herbal tea?' As soon as she said it, Mel regretted being so precious, and wondered whether Louise was regretting her earlier invitation. But the reply surprised her.

'My God, it's nice to meet someone with taste.' She accompanied this with a pointed look at Barry. 'Camomile okay, Mel? I've got some pear and blackcurrant if you'd prefer?'

'Camomile would be lovely, thank you.'

Louise turned to Barry. 'Don't worry, I'll make it,' she said and trotted off to the kitchen.

Mel rose from her crouch by the playpen and smiled at Barry. 'This is a lovely house.'

'Lou's very proud of it. Unfortunately, that creature made a bit of a mess.' He nodded at the pile of broken china and glass that had been swept into a pile in the corner.

'You must enjoy living so close to the West End; all the nightlife –'

'I don't live here,' Barry interrupted. 'Lou and I are just friends.'

'You mean you're not Cassie's father?'

Mel felt her cheeks redden at the vehemence of his response. 'Whatever gave you that stupid idea? Cassie's father is Lou's business, and you've got no right poking your nose in!'

'I'm sorry, honestly. I just thought –'

'Well, don't think!' He stormed off and stood by the window.

Mel bit her lip. She knew that she had a habit of speaking her mind, but she was only trying to be friendly. Deciding that Barry and Louise's recent experiences had made them exceptionally touchy, she forgave herself, and followed Barry to the window.

'Lovely view, isn't it?' Whereas the house would have once provided a vista of Battersea Power Station, it now looked out upon the staggered pyramid of the Millennium Hall. Despite Anne Travers's objections – which,

Mel reminded herself, were based upon her hatred of Ashley Chapel – there was a certain grace and elegance in the alternating light and dark brickwork.

'What, that?' Barry seemed to have calmed down since his outburst, but his dislike of the Hall was obvious. 'Monstrous, if you ask me.'

Mel decided that his sense of aesthetics had been clouded by his own dislike of Chapel. 'It's better than a disused power station.'

'That was a work of art.' He scratched his head before pointing at the ziggurat. 'While that's nothing more than a monument to Chapel's ego, if you ask me.'

Mel had a passing interest in architecture. 'Who designed it?'

'That's the most ridiculous part of it. With the millions of quid available from the National Lottery, they could have brought in one of the great architects. But Chapel had a hand in it, didn't he?'

'Anne Travers did mention that the Millennium Fund was running a bit short.'

Barry nodded. 'And Chapel offered his services – and his bank balance – to help out. For the public good, of course,' he added, sarcastically. 'He brought in some pillock who liked ziggurats to design the bloody thing.' He turned away from the window. 'It's marvellous what you can do when you've got the money, isn't it?'

Louise chose that moment to come into the living room with the tea and coffee, setting it down on the coffee table. 'I suppose we ought to work out where we're going tonight.'

Mel picked up her cup and sipped. 'Excellent tea, Louise. What about Stringfellows?'

Barry and Louise looked round in unison.

'That shut down years ago,' said Louise with an odd look on her face. 'I was thinking more along the lines of Barnaby's or the Coliseum.' She caught Barry's surprised look and shrugged. 'It's not as if we can't afford it, Baz.'

Catching Mel's own odd look, Barry explained about

the generous redundancy payment.

Despite her experiences at the hands of David Harker, Mel couldn't help commenting. 'So, he can't be all bad.'

Barry and Louise stared at one another.

'Magic?' Harker began to wonder whether his boss had started celebrating the New Year a bit too early.

Chapel laughed, the sound instantly soaking into the rich fabrics which clung to the walls. 'Call it what you will: magic, dark science, higher powers. For the last twenty years, I have been following a vision, David. A vision of a world where poverty and unhappiness, evil and corruption play no part.' He stepped over to the central cone and stroked its rune-covered surface. 'The twentieth century is considered the age of reason, where the gods of science and technology have usurped their supernatural forebears. But what a simpler world it once was: to achieve a fruitful harvest, one sacrificed a goat or some chickens; to punish an enemy, one stuck pins in an effigy.'

Harker shook his head. 'Superstitious rubbish. What has this got to do with the Codex?' Another laugh from Chapel made him feel decidedly uncomfortable.

'Everything! It lies at the very heart of this entire project and has driven every single step that we have taken over the last two decades.'

'I don't follow –'

Chapel stared at him, transfixed him. 'Oh yes you do, David. That's all you've ever done; follow. I employed you for your tenacity and your greed. For as long as you thought you could wrest control of ACL from me, you were the perfect employee, malleable and obedient, as long as it suited your purpose.

'I've always ensured that the glittering prize of ACL has been just beyond your reach, a lure and a prison that kept you at my side. Did you really think that I wouldn't work out who gave Ms Bush the protocols she needed to access my systems?'

Harker began to feel the first icy fingers of fear. 'The Codex has nothing to do with magic or witchcraft,' he blustered, trying not to get into a conversation about Melanie Bush. 'It's the ultimate computer virus.'

'Really?' sneered Chapel, and Harker could tell that he was toying with him. But why? What the hell was going on? 'A virus. And, at midnight, it will infiltrate all the computer networks and systems across the globe. Am I correct?'

'Of, of course you are.' It was Chapel's plan, how could he not be correct? And although Harker was only aware of the purpose of the Codex through the odd system design and e-mail message that he had managed to intercept, his knowledge about it matched Chapel's description.

'And this oh-so-clever virus. It takes advantage of those poorly maintained software systems whose designers lacked the foresight to ensure that the changeover between centuries was handled seamlessly; systems that cannot distinguish between 1 January 1900 and 1 January 2000?'

Harker nodded. The Codex was designed to enter the great banking systems of the world stock markets, slipping in during the inevitable confusion that would occur at midnight to wait for instructions. Starting with the London stock exchange, the Codex would move around from time zone to time zone, striking at each midnight until it was irrevocably infesting cyberspace.

Chapel sighed. 'Oh my dear David, you have been naïve,' he said, sadly. 'Creating such a system would have been child's play for the talents that I have surrounded myself with. And an unimaginable waste of effort. The Codex is infinitely more than just a virus.

'It is apotheosis!'

Harker backed away from Chapel, whose voice had taken on an almost evangelical tone. 'But the program designs –'

Chapel had moved over to the far side of the room,

where a huge statue of the ACL antelope stood against the blue-black drapes. 'Red herrings. Nothing more than will-o'-the-wisps to keep you from discovering the truth. I permitted you to stumble across the odd memo, the odd page of design, just so that you would think that the Codex was a computer virus.'

'For Christ's sake, Ashley, what the hell are you going on about?' Harker yelled. 'ACL is — was — a software company, a front for the greatest computer fraud in history. The Codex will give us access to every piece of information in any computer across the world. That's what we've been doing.' He shook his head. 'You've really gone off the deep end,' he muttered.

'You're right when you say that ACL is a front. But your limited intellect and even more stunted imagination couldn't even begin to comprehend what I've been doing for the last twenty years. In Africa, I learnt the unspoken truths of the shamen's magic. In Tibet, the secrets of the lamas were revealed to me. In a crypt beneath the Kremlin, the old Russian sigils of power were taken from their silk wrappings and displayed before me.

'And within the august halls of the Library of Saint John the Beheaded, I was privy to the knowledge that now binds all my researches together.'

He turned from the statue with a fire in his eyes. 'I have uncovered all that remains of the dark science of the elder gods, true power that has been buried beneath the relentless flow of science and technology. And that dark science has been converted by the university research team, converted from arcane symbols and whispered truths into algorithms and subroutines, the mundane mathematical building blocks that the advanced research team here has transformed into the programming that comprises the Codex. That is the truth behind Ashley Chapel Logistics, David.'

'You're mad.' It was exactly as Harker had feared. The strain of the Codex project had finally got to Chapel.

'Your eyes are closed to the greater picture, David.' He lay both hands on the cone and closed his eyes in concentration. The runes began to burn with red fire. 'Permit me to open them.'

A scuttling, scraping noise made Harker spin round to face the doorway. And the sight before him drained the blood from his face.

Two creatures, their skin blue-black and inlaid with the same silver and gold pattern as the drapes around the room, were pawing at the floor with the sharp talons on the end of their long, sinewy arms. They looked up at him with slanted, yellow eyes, and simultaneously opened their drooling mouths to show off their fangs, gurgling as they did so.

'Introductions shouldn't be necessary,' said Chapel, walking round the frozen Harker and stroking the distended head of the creature on the left. 'You remember Derek and Ivan?'

'Derek Peartree? Ivan Crystal?' he whispered.

'The very same. Or rather not. As an added bonus to their severance pay, I have used the merest fraction of my discoveries to grant them immortality, in return for their unswerving obedience, of course.'

'What, what are they?'

Chapel shrugged. 'You'd never be able to pronounce the name given to them by the ancient Hyperboreans who first discovered this particular transmogrification. I like to call them cybrids.' And then, with a frisson of menace, he added, 'I hope you like the name.'

'Why?'

'Because I've decided to reward you for your loyal service over the last twenty years, David. I've decided to grant you the same boon of immortality.'

'No!' Harker started backing away.

'Oh, David, I'm hurt. I was sure that you'd prefer it to another of those damned clocks.'

The Doctor sank back into his chair and rubbed the

bridge of his nose, looking around the TARDIS laboratory for inspiration.

When she had first seen the TARDIS laboratory, Mel had described it as a cross between an alchemist's lair and a ransacked electronics factory. And, sitting at a hastily cleared work-bench, the Doctor couldn't really disagree. Especially since the work-bench itself had been a gift from a grateful alchemist. He looked back down at the Tablette and sighed.

Anyone else would have been disappointed by the contents of the Tablette's hard-drive: an accounting program, a spreadsheet, and a small word-processing package. Nothing that even hinted at alien transformations. But the Doctor's search went much deeper, into the operating system itself. And after an intensive few hours spent delving into the system nucleus, the Doctor's persistence had paid off.

Whatever the operating system present on Campling's Tablette, it wasn't Paradigm; at least, not the same Paradigm that could be bought over the counter from any software dealer. A clutch of extra modules lurked amongst the innocuous printer and monitor drivers. Modules that would have been unintelligible to any human computer scientist.

But, of course, the Doctor wasn't human.

The language was so corrupted from the original as to be almost unrecognizable, even to him. But certain elements were extremely familiar: he used the cursor to highlight a block of lines near the top of the module, and felt a wave of emotions crash over him as his suspicions were confirmed. One of the emotions was fear, fear at his recognition of the language. The Doctor brushed the feelings aside and carried on reading what he now realized was the syllabic nucleus of a language that had no place in this universe.

The words were derived from a tongue that had been both ancient and arcane before the first stars had ignited in the cosmic firmament, before the first protons and electrons had combined in the genesis of the first atom of hydrogen. Words that were only whispered in the darkest corners of the darkest worlds, never spoken aloud. Words of power and majesty that could pluck a quark from the heart of a neutron or rend a quasar asunder.

They were words written in a different universe: the cosmos that had existed before the present one, the universe whose death knell had been the birth screams of the here and now. The universe that the Doctor had spoken of to Anne Travers when he had described the origins of the Great Intelligence. And the words were written in that creature's own secret tongue.

The Doctor stood up, feeling the full weight of his nine hundred years. He was used to the Earth being a world of surprises, a backwater planet that would shape the course of empires. But the pure form of the language in which the module was written was one of the most closely guarded secrets of the Time Lord intelligentsia. Indeed, the only reason that the Doctor was aware of the significance of the words was his brief exposure to the Matrix when he had been President of his people.

The most powerful tool developed by the Time Lords was block transfer computation, the ultimate expression of mathematics. With it, one could manipulate matter and energy, time and space, and fold dimensions like so much origami. It was the fundamental basis of the TARDIS technology that surrounded him, and had even been harnessed to bleed off excess entropy from the universe, extending its lifespan by incalculable aeons.

Quantum mnemonics, the dark science of an earlier race of Time Lords, made block transfer computation seem like a conjuring trick. With just a few words, a practitioner of their great art could grasp the basic nature of reality around the throat and shake it into a new configuration. A *bon mot* of quantum mnemonics could bring about a premature death, or a run of good luck. A sentence could transform a planet's history and destiny, changing a world of barbaric war into an elysium.

And a carefully constructed paragraph could rewrite the entire universe. Or destroy it utterly.

So what was Ashley Chapel doing using the deadliest weapon in creation as part of his operating system?

With that frightening thought bright in his mind, the Doctor suddenly became aware of a word in his mind, a name crying out to be listened to. Saraquazel.

And the earlier events in the TARDIS, previously an annoying blank, were instantaneously revealed to him in all their horrifying detail. But this time he was able to look beyond the stark imagery that the TARDIS had pumped into his mind, and register the results of its analysis of the anomaly that he had detected upon his arrival in London.

He left the laboratory at a gallop, running down the white corridors at a speed that would have forced Mel to revise her perception of his fitness level. The readings that the TARDIS had detected earlier indicated that a source of unimaginable energy was hovering above London at a height of approximately three hundred feet. But it was frozen energy, frozen at a precise moment of time relative to the Earth's worldline like a mathematical bell curve. It built up from nothing, before peaking at its temporal anchor point. And then it trailed away. Without any external interference, the energy was sufficiently out of phase with the rest of reality to pose no threat whatsoever, despite the fact that it was equivalent to the detonation of over eighteen billion thermonuclear warheads; it was a phantom, displaced and dispossessed.

But quantum mnemonics was exactly the sort of external interference which could summon the energy, especially if it was used at the moment of the energy's temporal anchor. Which was in four hours' time. Midnight. The time that Ashley Chapel was supposed to pull his masterstroke.

With a quiver of concern, the Doctor realized that the totally alien body of the Great Intelligence – pure consciousness – might very well appear to the TARDIS sensors as a massive quantity of potential energy. It looked like Anne Travers's concerns – and those of her father – really were justified.

Cursing himself for dismissing her fears as paranoia, the Doctor checked the time on the console. It was half past nine, and he was due to meet Anne outside Canary Wharf Tower at eleven. But the discovery that Chapel was almost certainly going to summon the Great Intelligence to Earth meant that the Doctor was going to have to rethink his plan. Rather than fishing around in ACL's computer systems, it was now obvious that he would have to confront Chapel directly.

And, if the Intelligence was coming to Earth, the Doctor needed to defend himself from it. And he knew just the place to find that sort of defence.

As he opened the great doors, he momentarily pondered whether to use the TARDIS to reach his destination. But the knowledge that enough raw power to detonate the Earth's sun was hovering above London was a quite convincing deterrent. The last thing he wanted was for the TARDIS's temporal fields to interact with that.

Despite the advanced technology at his disposal, and his urgent need to prevent even superior scientific techniques from being used, he only had one choice.

Locking the doors of the TARDIS behind him, he hailed a taxi.

'*Chapel!*'

The word was spoken in the form of a blinding gold light that burnt only within his mind. Chapel immediately felt the mixture of immense pleasure and unbearable pain that inevitably accompanied communication with Saraquazel, and concentrated as he tried to make out what was being said.

Slowly, the gold fire turned into a deep roar, and then the roar resolved into words. The words of Saraquazel.

> *We are too close to my epiphany for further cybrids to be created.*
> *Their corruption could endanger my becoming.*
> *Leave this human and destroy the other cybrids in your thrall.*

At least it sounded like 'destroy'. Sometimes, Saraquazel's words were vague and difficult to make out. And then the communication ended, causing Chapel to reel with the emptiness he now felt. Steadying himself against the cone, he pondered the message.

When Saraquazel had first directed him towards the Hyperborean texts that described the transformation of human beings into the demons that Chapel had christened cybrids, it had warned that the technique should be used sparingly, explaining that the fundamental nature of the creatures was at odds with Saraquazel's own. Apparently they were composed of a complex matrix of silicon and spells which could defocus the Millennium Codex if they were present in large numbers. And obviously Harker would have been one too many.

Chapel looked at Harker, his body and mind paralysed by the powers that Chapel could wield. With a brief burst of concentrated thought, he reached into Harker's limited intellect.

And Harker nodded and turned to leave. And then paused. 'Ashley?' he asked, ignoring the outrée trappings of Chapel's sanctum sanctorum.

'Mmm?' Chapel feigned distraction.

'The Codex, it is a computer virus, isn't it?' He sounded uncertain.

Chapel laughed and patted him on the shoulder. 'Why, David, what else could it be?'

After Harker had closed the door, Chapel pondered the cybrids. To assist him in his work, he had created ten of the creatures. But they were all employees who had served him well over the last twenty years – even Peartree, in his own way – and he was loath to kill them like strays.

Better to let them run free, he decided, cutting off his mind from theirs. In only a couple of hours, they would be able to experience the rapture of Saraquazel at first hand.

The creature that had once been Derek Peartree felt the cessation of control like a fire being extinguished in his mind. The shock was sufficient to cause him to drop the dog carcass that had been hanging from his fanged jaws and look around the landscaped gardens of the Millennium Hall in confusion.

The loss of any clear direction was an unbearable thought. For twenty years, he had worked at ACL – although that portion of his life was cloudy and difficult to remember – and while the others had been made redundant, Peartree had been personally approached by Ashley Chapel and offered a change in career, confirming Peartree's importance in the scheme of things. The fact that his new job had resulted in a complete physical transformation hadn't bothered him much at the time. At least, it hadn't after it had happened. But at least there had still been direction in his life.

But now? Peartree reached out with his mind, but he couldn't contact Chapel, and the realization that he had been thrown onto the scrap heap after all these years of service was a very bitter blow. But whereas the old Derek had sat and wept and bemoaned his fate, his cybrid form was powerful enough to exact revenge on the people responsible. Oh no, this excommunication was nothing to do with him. The blame lay with the people who had disrupted his last project, who had made him look foolish in front of Chapel.

That slut, Mason, and her drunken friend, Brown.

Casting his mind across London, Peartree located his colleagues. Ivan was at his usual night-time haunt, London Zoo, while Andrew Palmerstone was prowling the South Bank, probably preying on vagrants again. And there was Dean Mogley, once again visiting the cinemas of Soho and eating the other patrons.

Within seconds he had the precise location of all the other cybrids. And then he told them the situation – not in words, for that was far too clumsy a medium, but in vivid images of pure thought. They too were cut adrift from Chapel, and they too felt the same burning anger. And they were more than happy to assist Derek with his latest business proposal.

From the banks of the Thames to Regent's Park, the cybrids stirred themselves. And set off for Battersea.

Looking at her watch, Anne realized that she was supposed to meet the Doctor in little more than an hour. But then she looked at the two piles of books that sat in front of her, and decided that she would have to stand the Doctor up.

She had spent the entire afternoon and evening in the Library of Saint John. After once again being shown to the annex by Mister Atoz, Anne's first reaction to her discovery had sent her reaching for the drinks cabinet. The book she had found and hidden, *The Many Eyes, Lies and Lives of Yog-Sothoth*, was missing.

At first she had assumed that it was back where she had initially found it, replaced by the efficient librarians. But a few minutes of frantic searching had proved only one thing; it was gone. And since Atoz had told her when she arrived at the library that only one person had visited that particular annex, she had been able to draw only one conclusion.

Ashley Chapel had taken it.

Breathing heavily, she had tried to formulate a course of action. From her informants' communiqués, she knew that Chapel was planning to act at midnight. And now he had stolen a book that confirmed his complicity with the Great Intelligence. After four years of suspicions, after four years of second-guessing Chapel as to why he had destroyed her father's life, she knew the answer.

Chapel was in league with Yog-Sothoth, the Great

Intelligence. And she had only one choice, to repel the Intelligence at the same time. At midnight.

And her handbag had contained the means to accomplish it. Pushing the Doctor's present to one side, she had pulled out her father's stained and crumpled list. And had started gathering the rest of the books that she needed.

Now, seven hours later, she was leafing through one of the books in the pile that was supposed to provide the sixth line of the incantation, but her Latin was far rustier than she would have liked, and her father's instructions as to the location of the precise quote that she required were unusually vague. For a brief moment, a tremor of fear overcame her, undermining her faith in her abilities. And then it was gone, as she cleansed herself with the fire of obsession that had driven her through the last twenty-five years.

But her renewed vigour as she read was disturbed by the sound of approaching footsteps. Her heart pounded as the thought that it might be Chapel occurred to her. Then she realized that Mister Atoz would have warned her if he had entered the library.

So who was it?

Ten seconds later, the heavy red velvet curtain was drawn aside. And Anne was lost for words. It was the Doctor. And he seemed just as surprised. For a few long seconds they simply stared at one another.

'Doctor, I –'

'Anne, what –'

And then they laughed, but it was false laughter, since both of them knew what was going on. Anne nodded at the enormous leather-bound book in front of her, more to lighten the atmosphere than anything. 'I'm catching up on some reading,' she said breezily. It didn't work.

The Doctor's voice was icy cold. 'What are you doing?'

'I told you –'

He strode up to the table and swept the book to the floor. 'Don't come the fool with me, Anne!' he yelled. 'I know what you're doing. And it's going to stop. Now!'

'You hypocritical bastard,' she hissed, standing up and knocking the chair over. 'After all you've done over the years, after all the alien invasions that you've lured to Earth; all I'm trying to do is stop the Intelligence from coming back.'

The Doctor shook his head. 'Anne, you're tampering with forces that mankind is ill-prepared for! To fight Chapel, you're placing this world in even more danger!' He slammed his fist on the table. 'You're playing with a fire so dangerous you could scorch eternity!'

She stared at him. And then laughed bitterly. 'I really can't believe you said that, Doctor. I really can't.' She moved over to the bell-pull that hung next to one of the bookcases. 'And after that particular piece of hyperbole, it's time you left.' She tugged the red silk cord.

The Doctor became even more desperate. 'Anne, you've got to listen to me! It looks like you were right. Chapel is about to summon the Great Intelligence. All I want to do is help you.'

She shook her head. 'You're too late, Doctor. Thanks to you, I can repel the Intelligence all by myself.' She gave her open handbag a nod, and could tell from the Doctor's expression that he had seen what was inside.

'You're wrong, Anne,' he pleaded. 'I've seen what's hanging above this city, I've seen how powerful it is. You aren't aware of all the facts. Please, let me help you.'

'Like you did the last time? My father died because you couldn't get rid of the Great Intelligence after it invaded the Underground. It came back, it wrought havoc. Or have you forgotten what happened?'

The Doctor winced. 'That isn't fair!'

'Isn't it? For all your knowledge and mysterious powers, you seem woefully incapable of preventing the Intelligence from attacking this planet, Doctor.' Her eyes narrowed. 'Or are you and the Intelligence connected in some way? It's funny how you always seem to be lurking around when it decides to visit us.'

Her voice became a venomous whisper. 'I was there in the Underground, when you let the Intelligence escape. And then it came back, and my father died!' Her words rose to a shriek. 'Empty nothings, Doctor, that's all you've got to offer!' She waved her hand around the annex. 'With the information contained in here, I can destroy that vile, murderous creature once and for all. And I don't need you at all.'

'You don't understand –'

She reached into her handbag and pulled out the Yeti sphere that the Doctor had handed to her in the Dorchester. 'As far as I'm concerned, this is the last bit of help I want from you.' She looked over the Doctor's shoulder at the massive librarian standing in the doorway, the sepia light shining off his bald brown head. 'Throw him out,' she ordered.

'But the Doctor is a respected visitor to the library –'

Mister Atoz appeared behind the librarian. 'Is there a problem, Dame Anne?'

A hard aspect entered her voice. 'The Doctor is working for Ashley Chapel, Mister Atoz. And I'd rather he left.'

Atoz turned to the giant and snapped his fingers. 'I think the Doctor was just about to leave, Mister Cornelius. Would you care to escort him to the door?'

'You've got to listen to me!' the Doctor protested. 'You could bring ruin on all of us!'

'Goodbye, Doctor.' Anne turned her back on him and picked the book from the floor. 'It's time that mankind relied on itself, rather than waiting for the Time Lords to get bored and intervene.'

The Doctor struggled, but even his superhuman strength was belittled by Cornelius, whose corded ebony arms pinioned him helplessly. Atoz gave Anne a respectful nod, and vanished through the curtain behind Cornelius and the Doctor, leaving Anne to continue her researches in peace.

* * *

Any thoughts of celebrating the new Millennium at one of the top London nightclubs had evaporated as Louise and Barry realized how exhausted they really were, and Mel – although obviously disappointed – had agreed that a night in front of the television was preferable to Barry or Louise falling asleep in the middle of a club.

Barry had popped out about an hour ago to stock up with drink and nibbles, leaving Mel to keep Cassie entertained while Louise put together some pasta and her extra-spicy tomato sauce.

After Mel's initial reaction to Cassie, Louise had been surprised by her enthusiasm with her daughter. Every game had been played, every story told, and Louise couldn't help smiling as she listened to them while preparing dinner. And Cassie could hardly keep her eyes open as Louise had carried her upstairs at nine o'clock, well after her bedtime, leaving Mel to give the Doctor a call on her mobile.

Indeed, while laying Cassie down in her cot, Louise wondered who had been more disappointed when she had insisted that it was time for bed; Mel or Cassie.

It was as she was about to turn off the main light that she had heard something. A scraping, rustling noise. And a cursory glance out of her bedroom window had made her shudder. She was being watched from the back garden.

At first she had thought that they were cats, their eyes shining in the faint light from the street lights. But how many cats had bright golden eyes? And they were higher and bigger than cats' eyes, and the things to which they belonged cast darker, larger shadows that were more human than feline. Louise had watched them for at least ten minutes, but their unwavering gaze had only confirmed her worries.

It was then that she had crept out onto the landing and called for Mel in a broken, unsteady voice.

'It's them,' Louise whispered, turning back from the window. 'I'm sure of it.'

'Who's them?' asked Mel.

'The thing that Derek became. The demon-things.' Seeing one in Campling's house had been bad enough; the idea that there was a whole pack of them – and prowling round her garden – was more than she could bear.

'Aren't you over-reacting?' said Mel. 'They could be cats,' she said dismissively. 'That is a rather more feasible explanation, don't you think?'

'Is that what you think it is?' Louise snapped. 'That my garden's playing host to a moggies' convention?' She inclined her head towards the window. 'Take a look. Do they look like cats?'

Mel looked out of the window, and then shook her head and gulped. 'We're safe enough here, aren't we?' And then, with a note of panic, 'You did remember to lock the back door, didn't you?'

For one terrifying second Louise couldn't remember. Then she could see herself sliding the bolt across. 'Of course I did,' she snapped.

'We should call the police.'

'After what happened this morning? For Christ's sake, Mel, what would we say? "Excuse me, officer, but I've got demons at the bottom of my garden"? It's New Year's Eve, Mel. They'd assume we were drunk and forget all about it.' She thumped the wall, and then checked Cassie to make sure that she hadn't woken up. 'No, we've got to get out of here.'

They both jumped as a loud banging came from downstairs.

'Oh my God, they're trying to get in!' Louise looked from the window to the stairs in panic.

'It could be Barry,' Mel replied quietly. 'Out there with the creatures.'

That thought was frightening. 'Oh God, I hadn't thought of that.' And then the banging started again. 'We'd better take a look.'

The women tiptoed down the stairs, Louise cursing

herself for never bothering to install a spy-hole or a security chain at the front door. As she passed the hat-stand, she picked up an umbrella and gave Mel a sheepish smile. 'It's better than nothing,' she shrugged.

Mel stepped forward and whispered through the door. 'Who is it?'

'It's me, of course,' came Barry's familiar voice. 'Who else would it be?'

Louise sighed with relief and opened the door.

'Good evening, Miss Mason. I'm so glad to find you at home.' The cybrid grinned malevolently, its spittle dripping onto the welcome mat. 'I've always wanted to be invited home.'

Eight

Mel backed against the hat-stand and screamed, but Louise knew that she had to stop the creature from getting in. She swung the umbrella with all the force she could muster and hit him in the face. With a nauseating wet crack, the Derek-thing tumbled backwards down the front path, and Louise immediately slammed the door and bolted it.

Mel had gone white. 'We're trapped!' she shrieked.

'Not yet,' said Louise, the knowledge that the creatures could be harmed galvanizing her. That's when she heard the explosive tinkle of glass from the back of the house. 'They've broken in through the conservatory,' she yelled. She tried to think. In seconds, they would undoubtedly break down the back door, and if the Derek-demon wasn't too badly injured, he would come in through the front. That left only one alternative; she pointed up the stairs. 'Mel, grab Cassie!'

Mel took the stairs two at a time, while Louise shifted a hall table in front of the kitchen door. And then the back door started to splinter. At least, that's what it sounded like.

When Louise finally reached the top of the stairs, Mel was standing in the doorway of Cassie's room, the child wrapped in her favourite blue blanket. 'She's still asleep,' Mel reassured her.

But Louise wasn't listening. Grabbing the wooden pole that was leaning against the landing wall, she unlatched the loft-hatch and swung the extendible ladder down to the floor.

Mel's eyes widened in disbelief. 'We're going up into the loft? And then what? A roof-top chase across London? This isn't Peter Pan.'

'And I'm not Tinkerbell,' Louise muttered. 'Quickly. I'll explain when we're up there.' She ushered Mel up the ladder, and was impressed by the younger woman's agility. As soon as Mel was through the square hole, Louise followed her, pulling the ladder and the hatch back after her.

The loft had a chipboard floor, but not much of it was visible beneath the boxes and old suitcases full of the accumulated junk of five years.

'Are we going to wait it out up here?' Mel whispered.

Louise shook her head. 'No way. Even if I was sure we could, I'm worried about Barry. He's out there, and so are they. No, we can get out of the house this way.'

'How?' Mel gazed around the loft, but obviously didn't see the escape route.

'Over here,' Louise indicated, gently stepping through the rubbish until she reached the flat wall that the house shared with its neighbour. Lifting up a suitcase, she uncovered a gaping black hole in the wall. 'This leads into next door's loft. And before you ask –' she held up a hand to ward off the inevitable question, 'next door isn't empty. I just hope that they've been celebrating.' Her head jerked round as a scrabble of footsteps could be heard below. 'Come on, quickly,' she urged, heading through the hole.

Gripping Cassie, Mel hesitated for a second, and then vanished into the darkness.

Standing outside the library, the Doctor was well aware of the watching eyes of the two opposing street gangs who were responsible for the institution's security. If he had stolen anything from the ancient shelves, it would have been noticed. And he would have been stopped.

At the turn of the century, they had been cut-throats and vagabonds. In the nineteen sixties they had been mods and rockers. And now? Now they were rival gangs of Yardies and crack-dealers, rivals so that they could keep an eye on each other, as well as visitors to the library.

But they could tell he was innocent – as far as stealing from the library was concerned. But the knowledge that he had given Anne Travers both the motivation and the ability to interfere with Ashley Chapel's plans made him feel far from innocent. Although he was sure that the most that Anne could accomplish using the information in the library was a fairly basic block transfer computation – given the sorts of books that had been sitting on the table – Chapel was wielding something infinitely more powerful. And if Anne's 'spell', for want of a better word, was cast at the same time as Chapel's quantum mnemonic, it would be like sticking a screwdriver in a mains socket.

For one of the few times in his life, the Doctor realized that the situation was possibly too grave for him to handle on his own. Perhaps it was time to call for some help. And then he checked his watch; it was already half past ten. Given the traffic situation – it was New Year's Eve, after all – it would take him at least an hour to reach the TARDIS, and, given the build-up of energy hovering above London, he doubted that he could get a message through to the Time Lords even if he could reach it.

There was only one option. Visiting Canary Wharf Tower had been his original plan, but that had been to investigate the Codex more fully. The Doctor now knew all he needed to about the mysterious piece of software.

No, it was time to confront Ashley Chapel himself. If he could switch the power off at the mains, Anne's screwdriver should be harmless. Hopefully.

With that cheering thought, he hurried out of the St Gile's Rookery and away from the watchful gaze of the gangs, and started looking for a taxi.

Compared with the mess in Louise's loft, next door's was a picture of order. At least, that's what Louise remembered when she had been up here with a flashlight. She reached out and located Mel's arm, and gently pulled her towards her. 'I think the hatch is around here.'

'Have you been in here before?'

'Once,' admitted Louise. And then, realizing how awful that sounded, she elaborated. 'I was curious.' She sank to her knees, and fumbled around in the dark for a few seconds before she found the hatch. Carefully, she found the catch and released it. Light burst in from the landing.

'This is all wrong,' Mel complained. 'We're not meant to be up here.'

'You're the one who hacked into Chapel's computers,' Louise snapped, more to shut Mel up than to be hurtful. And then she pushed the ladder through the hole, relieved when it obediently extended to reach the floor. 'Now get a move on. And be quiet.'

Louise held out her arms and grabbed Cassie as Mel descended the ladder. All she could hear was the television, blaring out from downstairs. Hopefully it would drown them out as they left the house. And they could blame the ladder's appearance on the crate of spirits that Louise had seen them buy in Safeway's the other day.

'Hello.' The voice was quiet, but it still made Louise jump. Her neighbours' little girl, five-year-old Mandy, was standing at the top of the stairs. 'What are you doing in here?'

Mel kneeled down in front of her. 'We're here because your mummy and daddy asked us to their party.'

'So why did you come through the ceiling, then?' asked Mandy with that wonderful logic that children seem to possess.

'Because it's a secret,' Mel explained. 'So don't tell mummy and daddy, will you?'

The girl nodded, and strolled into the bathroom regardless. Louise sighed. Mel would have made a brilliant baby-sitter. But it was time to take advantage of their escape route. She tiptoed down the stairs, Mel behind her. This was so easy, she decided.

'Mummy!' came the scream from above. 'There are monsters!'

Louise froze. Should she go back and rescue the girl, or should she, Mel and Cassie get away?

'They're coming up the plughole! The plughole monsters!'

Louise sighed. She remembered telling Cassie about the plughole monsters, who would crawl into the bath if a certain little madam wouldn't consent to having her hair washed.

The living room door opened, and Mister Pettinger emerged. 'Ms Mason?' he asked incredulously.

Before Louise could come up with a convincing excuse, another voice entered the discussion. From the top of the stairs, two golden eyes observed her. 'Going so soon?' it gurgled.

Louise clutched Cassie closer to her and opened the door, running into the freezing night air, and hoping that her daughter was sufficiently wrapped up.

Anne rubbed her eyes and yawned. It was nearly eleven o'clock. Only an hour remained until Chapel summoned the Intelligence, and her counter-measures were still not complete. Her father's instructions, which had been so detailed early on, had become obscure and fragmented towards the end. Anne assumed that this was due to his mental collapse rather than any desire to be obtuse, and the memory of the once proud professor as a blind, broken man, brought a lump to her throat. But then the knowledge that what she was doing that night would give her vengeance against the man responsible – and would vindicate her father's career – stoked her flagging enthusiasm.

She opened the next volume in the final pile of books which may or may not have been the ones her father's legacy indicated, and started scanning the pages for the line which matched her father's cryptic clue. The final line.

The Doctor tapped his pockets and then growled. 'It's times like this when I really miss my sonic screwdriver. I should have sued the Terileptils for criminal damage.' But he had gone some way to replace his beloved device. He plucked a small sonic probe from within his jacket and let it loose on the locked metal door near the eastern corner of Canary Wharf Tower. Within seconds, there was a plaintive click from the lock, and the door opened enough for the Doctor to prise his fingers into the gap and pull it open.

Stepping into the pitch-black room within, he pulled out a pencil torch and looked around. According to the computer systems, he was just in front of one of the emergency stairwells. And he smiled when he saw the door – with handle – opposite him. Mel might go on about her eidetic memory, but the Doctor's was just as exact; the only problem was, he put the photographs in the album in a more random way than she did. But he did know that the door led directly to the service staircase, and therefore the fiftieth floor.

The only problem was that it meant fifty floors to climb. Making a note to tell Mel about it – unfit indeed! – he walked over to the door and opened it.

'I've got to stop for a moment,' Louise panted, adjusting Cassie in her arms. 'I'm out of breath.'

'You should give up smoking,' chastized Mel.

Louise looked at her in annoyance. Didn't this woman have any faults? 'I hardly think that matters at the moment, Mel. We've got to find Barry, and then get to the Doctor.' She was beyond panic. All she wanted was to see was Barry, walking towards them on his way back from Safeway's.

'There!' Mel pointed over Louise's shoulder at a distant figure shambling towards them, swaying from side to side under the weight of two full carrier bags. They started running.

Barry was obviously drunk. Very drunk. And it was a miracle that he still had the shopping. Then again, thought Louise, it's not exactly as if we need it anymore.

'Met Eddie and Mike,' he slurred. 'Went for a drink in the Anchor.'

'That's all well and good, Baz, but those things are after us!' Louise yelled. 'We've got to find the Doctor!'

'Things,' he muttered. And then the threat finally took root in his mind. 'You mean –'

'Yes!' screamed Louise. 'Things!'

Mel joined in screaming 'things!' as well. And then Louise realized that she was pointing down the road. Six dark, crouched figures were shambling towards them.

'This way!' Louise pointed beyond Barry, only to see four more of them heading towards them from the opposite direction. 'Oh my God, we're cut off from the train station,' she shouted, having just realized that that was their best chance of reaching Canary Wharf Tower.

'The Millennium Hall!' Barry drunkenly gestured towards the stepped pyramid that lay in the distance. 'Loads and loads of people there. They won't come near us.'

'Good idea,' said Louise tersely, adjusting the still sleeping Cassie in her arms. 'But how do we get there?'

'Taxi!' screamed Mel. The large black car came to a halt just next to them, and Louise waited for Mel to enter before shoving Barry inside, leaving the shopping behind.

As she got in and slammed the door behind her, she leaned forward to the driver. 'The Millennium Hall, please.'

The creatures might be willing to murder James in his own home, but she doubted that they would attack them if the celebrations in front of the Hall were being televised. Especially since Noel Edmonds was master of ceremonies.

She looked out of the rear window and swallowed. The cybrids were eating the shopping.

Chapel decided that it was about time he broke his most cherished resolution. Opening the antique cabinet that stood beneath his office window, he withdrew a bottle of 1935 Crozes Hermitage and set it on top. If there had ever been a time to celebrate, this was it. The Codex would run in less than twenty minutes, and then paradise would reign supreme. With the will of Saraquazel – moderated through him, of course – controlling first London, and then the world, a new age of harmony would hold sway.

And, after the Earth, there were other worlds that desperately needed the word of Saraquazel: Skaro; Telos – home of the creatures who had killed his mentor, Tobias Vaughn; Sontara; Polymos; they would be the next to hear the word.

He reached down and went to grab a glass from the cabinet. And then, deciding that he really ought to have company on such an auspicious occasion, he took out two and reached for the phone.

'Ah, Gillian, could you ask David Harker to join me in my office? Thank you.' He replaced the phone and smiled. Whether David was with the advanced research team or with him in his office, the result would be the same. They would all become servants of Saraquazel. The only difference would be David's memory of the excellent wine.

Chapel poured two glasses.

Anne slammed the final book shut and checked her watch. 11.45. She had finished compiling the incantation with fifteen minutes to spare, and walked over to the drinks cabinet to pour herself a drink in celebration. In fifteen scant minutes, Chapel's life would be in ruins, and she – and her father – would have satisfaction.

She sipped the sweet sherry and smiled. She was sorry

that she had been so rude to the Doctor, but at least this way she would live to regret it.

The taxi stopped. 'Sorry,' the driver called back without apology. 'Can't get any further because of the crowds.'

Mel looked beyond the driver and saw the people, milling around in front of the pyramidal Millennium Hall. Now that she was closer to it, she regretted her comments to Barry earlier. The staggered, sloping sides of the pyramid were a chaotic mess of blue, grey and beige tiles arranged in abstract patterns. Quite frankly, it was horrid. And then she looked behind, and could see the group of golden eyes, running towards them. 'We should get out here,' she insisted.

As Louise shoved a ten-pound note into the driver's hand, Mel opened the door and helped Barry out. And then waited as Louise clambered out with Cassie in her arms. 'Come on!' Mel urged.

As the taxi did a three-point turn and sped off down Battersea Park Road, Mel looked to their right and realized that they were standing next to the wall that acted as a boundary between the Millennium Hall and the road. She stared behind her and saw the demonic figures running towards them, only five hundred yards away.

'Over the top!' screamed Louise, nodding at the wall. 'We can do it!'

It only took thirty seconds, but by the time that Mel – leaving herself to last so that she could pass Cassie over her head and into Louise's arms once again – had clambered over the wall, the creatures were snapping at her heels. She righted herself and pointed towards the Hall. 'You get over there – I'm going to call the Doctor!' It was something that she should have done ages ago.

As Barry stumbled away with Louise's support, Mel took out her portable phone and dialled the Doctor's number, extremely grateful that she had persuaded him to move with the times.

* * *

'Ah, David!' Chapel ushered him into the office and handed him a glass of wine. 'I'm so glad that you could make it.' He made to close the door behind him, but an odd noise made Chapel stare out into the office area. It sounded like a phone, but that wasn't possible. And then he remembered an earlier warning from Saraquazel. About the man responsible for the death of Tobias Vaughn.

Chapel bolted out of his office towards the source of the noise, stopping in front of a concealed door that led to the emergency stairs. Pulling it open, he clicked his fingers at Harker, who was just behind him. Harker went in and pulled out the brightly coloured intruder.

Chapel smiled. 'Ah, Doctor, just in time for the final act.' He nodded towards his office. 'David, Could you escort our visitor to my office?'

Mel gave up on the tenth ring, and the sight of a drooling mouth and evil eyes that suddenly appeared over the top of the wall made her glad that she had. She hurled herself away and ran after Barry and Louise as the creature pulled itself over.

'They're coming over the wall,' she screamed ahead of her. 'Keep going!' She pointed towards the Hall, and the side doors that were now close enough to be seen. 'It's our only hope,' she implored.

'You were expecting me?' asked the Doctor with a raised eyebrow.

Chapel sank back into his chair and steepled his fingers in front of his face. 'In a manner of speaking. Saraquazel warned me that you were on Earth. Given your track record in interference – and your association with that paranoid hag, Travers – it was only a matter of time before you made your move.' He laughed. 'Then again, it's all a matter of time, isn't it? Especially for a Time Lord.'

The Doctor stepped forward, but Harker immediately

put his arm out to restrain him. 'You really do have me at a disadvantage, Mister Chapel.'

'I know.' He looked at the antique clock on his desk. 'Ten minutes, Doctor. Ten minutes until the appointed hour.'

'So, Anne was right. You're going to run the Codex at midnight.'

'For such a dreary, used-up woman, she can be so perceptive.' He stood and walked over to the far wall. 'But the true nature of the Codex has constantly eluded her, hasn't it?' He opened his hidden door and stepped through, indicating for the Doctor and Harker to follow.

The Doctor looked around the blue-draped room and gave an appreciative nod. 'Solid holography, Mister Chapel. Very clever.'

'A conjuring trick, Doctor, nothing more. This is the real magic.'

'Magic? Is that what this is to you?' His voice rose. 'There's enough potential energy hanging over this benighted city to split the sun in two. And you are tampering with –'

'With forces beyond my comprehension?' He completed. 'I've heard it all before, you know.'

'From Professor Travers? He tried to warn you, but you destroyed him. You should have listened, Chapel, you really should. When you summon the Great Intelligence, it will consume you, before turning its attention to the rest of the planet.'

Chapel turned from examining the rune cone with a puzzled expression on his face. 'The Great Intelligence? My dear Doctor, whatever gave you that idea?' He tutted. 'I knew that Anne Travers and that crackpot father of hers were obsessed by the Intelligence, but I would never have expected you to join in. Do you really think I want hordes of Yeti roaming around London? Terribly bad for business,' he laughed. 'I can assure you, Doctor, Saraquazel hasn't anything to do with the Great Intelligence.'

'It hasn't?' It was the Doctor's turn to look puzzled. 'Then what is it?'

'I've told you, Doctor; Saraquazel. He who will usher in a new age of harmony and prosperity.'

Anne checked her watch: 11.50. After hours of research and preparation, she was certain that everything was ready. Sitting on the carpeted floor of the library annex with the scribbled incantation in front of her, she clutched the Yeti sphere tightly in both hands.

It was time to begin.

In a hushed yet expectant voice, she started to cast the incantation.

Louise slid the bolt across the heavy metal door that was presumably the loading bay for the Hall, and stepped back. Until they had actually reached the inset door at the side of the pyramid, she hadn't been sure whether they would be able to get in or not. Thankfully, it seemed that any security that the Millennium Hall possessed was mingling with the crowds at the front; not only had the door been unguarded, it had also been open.

And then she jumped as something hurled itself against the door from the outside. And she didn't need three guesses to work out what it was.

'That won't hold them for long,' she said. And then, Cassie — who had taken everything up till now in her stride, with wide-eyed wonderment and silence — started wailing. 'That's all I need,' Louise sighed, trying to calm her.

She looked around. The loading bay was large and empty, without any obvious places to hide. And thanks to the huge banks of fluorescent lighting, there weren't any dark corners to protect them either.

'Look around for some way out!' she ordered. Barry — the excitement having gone some way in sobering him up — ran over to the left, while Mel took the opposite side.

'This one's locked!' Barry called over, pointing at the door next to him. Mel's shrug opposite indicated that she had discovered the same thing.

'We're trapped!' she screamed, making Louise wince. Then the thumping grew much louder, and Louise suddenly realized that the hinges were giving way.

'They're almost through!' she yelled, causing Cassie to scream even louder. Deciding that the door was not the most sensible place to stand, she ran over to Barry, who had picked up a large piece of wood and was weighing it up in his hands.

'What good will that do?' asked Mel.

'That umbrella had quite an effect on Derek,' Louise pointed out as she joined them.

'But it didn't last long, did it?' yelled Barry as the door caved in, hitting the floor with a deafening slap. The cybrids were through.

'Group together!' Mel instructed. 'And pick up something to defend yourself with,' she added, hefting up a two-foot long piece of discarded scaffolding.

Louise looked around, but immediately realized that she was hardly in a position to start swinging pieces of wood or scaffolding around while holding Cassie.

The lead cybrid stopped about ten feet away from them. From the almost healed scar across its face, it was obviously Derek.

'You've led us a merry dance, children,' he hissed. 'But it stops, now.' His mouth opened, and a flickering tongue licked the razor-sharp teeth. 'All that exercise has made me and my colleagues rather hungry.'

The others began to approach.

The Doctor's mind was in turmoil. He had come to ACL to stop Chapel from summoning the Great Intelligence, only to discover that the Intelligence wasn't even involved. At least according to Chapel, and he seemed pretty convinced. But the fact remained that Chapel was about to summon something, and that something was hovering over London with the power of nearly twenty billion nuclear bombs.

Chapel had moved over to the golden antelope statue.

'Since I'm going to die anyway, perhaps you'd care to tell me who Saraquazel really is,' asked the Doctor nonchalantly. He knew it was a cliché, but his options did appear rather limited.

'Die?' repeated Chapel. 'No, Doctor, I have no intention of starting the new millennium with bloodshed. After the Codex has run, your eyes will be opened to the new glories –'

'Cut the evangelism, Chapel, and just tell me what's going on!' the Doctor shouted.

'Very well,' replied Chapel, the irritation at being interrupted clear in his voice. 'Saraquazel is displaced from his own universe, just as Anne's precious Intelligence is. The difference between them is simple, however. While the Intelligence is a revenant from the previous universe, Saraquazel's pedigree is far more impressive.

He comes from the universe that will be born from the ashes of this one.'

The Doctor's eyes widened. In all his years, with all his experience, he had never encountered anything that had made the leap back across the Big Crunch that would wipe away the current cosmos in untold billions of years' time. To find one hanging above the Earth . . . He shuddered.

'The Codex is a collection of powerful incantations which will alter the laws of physics around us, changing them so that Saraquazel can manifest himself among us.'

The meaning behind the words hit home. 'No, Chapel. You can't do that. Introducing these alien physical laws will destroy the universe!' He jumped towards Chapel, but Harker grabbed him in an unbreakable grip. The Doctor suspected that his strength was being augmented by another of Chapel's 'spells'.

The very fact that Chapel was able to wield quantum mnemonics – even if he was being directed by this mysterious Saraquazel – made him a formidable enemy.

'Empty rhetoric from a defeated adversary, Doctor. And so unnecessary. I've been planning this for twenty years, ever since I first contacted Saraquazel.' He looked at his watch and obviously decided that he had time to gloat. Which was exactly what the Doctor wanted, because that was when they tended to make mistakes.

With a tap on the cone, a ghostly image appeared against one of the drapes. A map of London. And Canary Wharf Tower, the Millennium Hall in Battersea, and a point in Holborn were glowing. With a rising feeling of horror, the Doctor realized that it was the Library of Saint John the Beheaded.

'Thanks to my foresight – and my fortune – these three buildings all belong to me. And when the Codex is run –' The points of light were suddenly joined in a lop-sided triangle. 'A barrier, formulated by Saraquazel himself, to limit the effects of the Codex.' A distant, terrifying smile crossed Chapel's face. 'Until the time comes to spread the word further afield, of course.'

'You have no idea what you're doing!' the Doctor bellowed. 'You mustn't run the Codex!'

'You killed Tobias Vaughn, didn't you?' said Chapel quietly.

The Doctor frowned at the non sequitur. And then shook his head. 'He was killed by the Cybermen. After he had seen the error of his ways, that is.'

'The error of his methods, perhaps. In the five years that I was Vaughn's personal assistant, I learnt a lot of his vision for mankind. He knew that mankind was weak, disorganized, but his mistake was to enlist the help of creatures whose only aim was conquest. My vision is the same, but I have allied myself with a being whose power is incalculable, even compared with the Cybermen.' He nodded at the antelope.

'Saraquazel understands my vision, he understands

that humanity needs strength and foresight in its leadership. And when the Codex is run, I shall be that leader, bringing the word of Saraquazel to the poor and the homeless, the hungry and the needy. The dirt and the darkness will be swept away, and a new paradise will be born in its stead.' And then he looked at his watch once more.

'And I'm afraid we've run out of time, Doctor.' He turned off the map and opened the antelope statue's chest. A solid gold Tablette lay inside a cavity which was lined with blue silk. Chapel placed his fingers on the keyboard and closed his eyes, a beatific smile on his face.

'No, Chapel, no!' He struggled desperately, but Harker wouldn't let him move.

Chapel's fingers began to play the keyboard with an almost musical finesse. 'By the way, Doctor,' he cheerfully announced over his shoulder.

'Happy New Year.'

Anne held the Yeti sphere aloft as she read out the final line of the incantation. It was five seconds to midnight, and the feeling of satisfaction that swept over her was like nothing she had ever felt before. She could feel the tears beginning, but she kept her voice steady.

And then the words were spoken, the incantation complete. There was only one thing left to do. 'This is for you, father,' she said through her tears, now flowing freely.

And then she dashed the sphere to the floor, watching as its silver surface shattered like glass and a cloud of emerald light burst from within.

The Peartree cybrid leapt at Mel with outstretched talons. Instinctively, she hoisted the scaffolding, and the cybrid impaled himself on it. She jumped back as he exploded soundlessly, his blue-black body evaporating into a swirling miasma of azure, silver and gold.

* * *

Chapel stepped back from the gold Tablette, rubbing his hands together. 'Behold, the Codex!' he screamed, the dedication clear in his voice. 'Behold, Saraquazel!' A deep heartbeat began to echo around the chamber, resonating as it increased in both volume and pitch. It grew and grew until the very walls began to vibrate. At the same time, the circuit patterns in the drapes began to burn with red fire.

The Doctor winced. 'Whatever this Saraquazel is, Chapel, you'll never control it!' he shouted over the noise. 'Stop it, stop it now. While there's still time, man!'

Chapel shrugged, and his voice was distant when he replied. 'But I don't want to control him, Doctor. I only wish to serve –' He stopped as the heartbeat became irregular, out of kilter. 'I, I don't understand . . .' The noise had been disturbing; now it was discordant. And it didn't take a Time Lord to realize that something was going terribly wrong.

The Doctor struggled against Harker. 'Is there a problem?'

'I don't understand,' whispered Chapel, staring at the screen of the Tablette. 'Other forces are interfering with the Codex.' The noise was now a warbling screech, wavering up and down the register like an undisciplined opera singer.

A rogue quantum mnemonic. Just the sort of thing that he wanted to deal with, thought the Doctor. 'You must let me help!' he implored.

'I am the servant of Saraquazel, Doctor: he needs no other.' But Chapel's face betrayed his own concerns.

'Somehow,' said the Doctor, 'I don't think that's particularly relevant at the moment, do you?'

Chapel was standing over the rune cone, his face rapt with effort. 'There has to be an explanation. There has to be a reason. Saraquazel's ascendancy must be assured –'

The Doctor had given up struggling. He could only stand and watch as the cone's red glow grew brighter and brighter, and his thoughts went out to Mel, unaware of what was going on. He sighed, preparing himself to die but knowing that too many other people would share his fate.

The light from the cone became incandescent, filling Chapel's office with blinding, tearing forces that seemed to reach into the very fabric of time and space, twisting, bending, rearranging.

Trafalgar Square was packed with revellers – hardly surprising given the circumstances. But they were quiet, their attention aimed at the nearby Palace of Westminster and the imminent chimes of Big Ben. And then the chimes began, and an air of anticipation swept over the crowd. They were moving into the new millennium, with all the hope that it promised.

The first chime rang, its tocsin singing through the cold night air of London. The crowd began to roar.

And across the world, in places that were also celebrating the millennium as well as in places still waiting for it to occur, those whose senses were attuned to disturbances in the ether were suddenly distracted.

In an old brownstone in New York, a thoughtful man levitating in a voluminous blue cloak cocked his head to one side, attempting to interpret the warnings that the spirits were screaming at him. And in a Dublin bar, a blond-haired man in a dirty beige trenchcoat looked up from his Guinness, but dismissed the odd sensations as a result of the previous fifteen pints.

But those willing to listen to and understand the psychic maelstrom emanating from London could only come up with a single answer.

The Universe had stopped.

And then, just as suddenly, it restarted. But nothing would ever be the same again.

Magic had returned to the Earth.

Part Two

Millennium

Nine

The Technomancer staggered backwards as if she had been struck. Which she had, although it hadn't been a physical attack; it had been far more insidious than that.

Her heart racing, she grabbed one arm of her massive sapphire throne for support and tried to catch her breath. For the briefest of moments, bizarre, alien images had flooded her mind, visions of the Great Kingdom so warped and twisted as to be almost unrecognizable. But, most frightening of all, had been a fragmented picture of her, divested of both her royal armour and her air of imperious dignity, more like a child than the Technomancer, dynastic ruler of one third of the Great Kingdom.

'Majestrix?' Addressing her in the formal way, the Chancellor rushed forward to help, but the Technomancer waved her away.

'Do not concern yourself, Louella, it was nothing. A brief malaise, no more.' She gazed out of the enormous window opposite at the panoramic view of the Great Kingdom. The window – nothing more than a giant rectangle cut into the staggered side of the Ziggurat of Sciosophy – afforded an ideal view of the other two seats of power with which the Ziggurat shared the Kingdom: the shining gold Tower of Abraxas, its pyramidal roof reflecting the energy discharges which rent the sky above; and the pattern of low flat squares that marked the underground warren that was the Labyrinth of Thaumaturgy.

The Technomancer snapped her fingers and mentally

directed an order at one of her cybrids: within seconds, he scuttled up to her, holding a blue-black goblet. She plucked it from his talon and thanked him, watching with a maternal smile as he bounded back to the side of the throne room. And why not? Was she not mother to the cybrids, as the Archimage was father to the auriks? And of course, that hag, the Hierophant, was she not mother – or grandmother, rather – to her twittering, fussing thaumaturgs?

Sipping the sweet, heady wine, she continued to stare through the window. It had been countless millennia since the Great Kingdom had been created by the Three Gods of Past, Present and Future. They had sealed the Kingdom behind the electric-blue waterfall of their tears to keep out the barbarians, and placed the three citadels to rule in their stead. From the gilded edifice of the Tower, the Archimage governed his auriks, while the Hierophant skulked in her Labyrinth with her thaumaturgs. And the Technomancer attended to the needs of her cybrids from the grand palace of her Ziggurat. All was as it had been, and would be always.

Until now.

The Technomancer closed her eyes, and remembered the unprecedented events of the previous day. Not with the blurred inexactitudes of others, but with the vivid accuracy that her royal blood granted her, she could see the visitor to the Ziggurat standing before her.

'I bring you proof that my words are true, Majestrix.' The figure – stooped, cloaked and hooded – had reached into his cloak. Two of her personal guard of cybrids had leapt forward, but the Technomancer had held up her hand to stay them, watching as the stranger held out an object wrapped in white silk. And she had taken it and opened its wrapping, gasping as she did so.

Then she had dismissed everyone from the throne room: cybrids, her Chancellor Louella, and Bartholemew, whose role was a unique mix of court jester and major-domo. And as soon as she was alone, she had cast a spell of wards to shield the room from unwanted attention, before ordering the stranger to disrobe.

Casting off his grey cloak, he had straightened up to reveal his true nature – the nature indicated by the platinum sigil he had presented. He was thin to the point of emaciation, but that was his natural state. And he was tall, at least seven feet in height, with grey skin, silver hair swept back in a floor-length ponytail, and silver-grey eyes; bulbous eyes suited to a nocturnal creature. But the most disturbing feature was his complete inability to stay still. His eyes darted around the throne room, while his long, spindly fingers twitched like spiders.

It was a thaumaturg, an emissary from the Hierophant.

'Your mistress dares the wrath of the Three Gods, thaumaturg,' the Technomancer had whispered. 'The last time one of your kind entered the Ziggurat of Sciosophy unbidden, the Gods went to war and almost destroyed the Kingdom.'

'Then that should be further proof of my mistress's urgency, Majestrix,' he had trilled in his reedy voice. 'She desires that you pluck an image from my mind.'

'Does she now?' The Technomancer had laughed, a light, bubbly laugh. And then her voice had hardened. 'And what happens when I reach into your pitiful mind, eh? Has your mistress planted a psychic bomb that will detonate at my touch?' She had shaken her head, perhaps just a little too theatrically. 'Her great-grandfather's reign as Hierophant was renowned for the convenient deaths of the lesser princes. Perhaps he passed on some of his secrets to her?'

The thaumaturg had twittered even more. 'But, Majestrix; you dismissed your guards and courtesans. If you feared an attack –'

'Silence, fool! I am the Technomancer, and my powers are without compare.' She had snapped her fingers, and the thaumaturg had reached for his throat, trying to catch a breath while her incantation slowly strangled him. And then the torment had ended, and he had fallen to his knees.

'Very well, creature of the shadows, I shall trust that your mistress possesses the meagre intelligence with which I credit her, and has not planned to assassinate me, thus urging the anger of the Gods. Open your mind so that I can understand "your mistress's urgency".'

With that, she had reached out and touched the thaumaturg's mind.

And then she had understood.

That was yesterday.

'You look troubled, Majestrix,' said the Chancellor with concern. 'If there's anything I can do –'

Startled, the Technomancer grasped her advisor's hands in her own and smiled. 'Oh, Louella, you have always been more a friend than a servant. And yes, there are matters of state which weigh heavy on the mind – on the soul, even. But they cannot be discussed, even with a true and trusted friend such as you.' She sighed. 'Leave me, Louella. Leave me alone with my matters of state.'

'But Majestrix –'

'Leave, Louella!' the Technomancer snapped. But she immediately regretted her outburst and laid a hand on her Chancellor's shoulder. 'Please? I'm sure that you want to look in on Cassandra, don't you?'

'Thank you, Majestrix.' Louella bowed before leaving the throne room.

And the Technomancer stared at her reflection in the window, wondering whether her mother, Hypatia – the previous Technomancer – would have been proud of her. Like her mother, she wore the blue-black armour that signified her position. Over a form-fitting blue fabric undergarment that covered arms, legs and body and reached up to just under her chin; the armour was carved and contoured in an unbreakable material, reinforced by mystic wards, that was patterned in thin lines of gold and silver, and fanned up and out behind her head in a high collar.

But unlike her mother – a stout, dour woman with jet black hair – she was petite, with a mouth that easily formed a toothy smile, and red hair piled up above her head. Gold and silver streaks – an inheritance from her paternal grandmother – crept up from her temples, adding a dignity that befitted her position and belied her youth.

She had been Technomancer for three years, and her reign had been a prosperous and peaceful one. But yesterday's news from the Hierophant suggested that this would soon come to a bitter and violent end, and not just for her. Abraxas and Thaumaturgy would also fall, and the Great Kingdom would be engulfed in chaos.

The Dark One was now among them, He Whose Name Dare Not Be Mentioned. His arrival had always been foretold, but the Technomancer had never imagined that that day would be during her tenure. She turned from the window, intending to retire for the evening.

And then the vision returned. The vision of her as a mere mortal. Steadying herself against the wall, she studied the images and shook her head in incomprehension. Her given name was Melaphyre. Who would dare to address her as 'Mel'?

The Doctor slipped from Harker's bear hug and stared around the room in disbelief.

It was now shining gold, and much, much larger. The internal walls that separated Chapel's sanctum sanctorum from his office, and his office from the desks and partitions of ACL, had vanished, creating an enormous golden chamber with a strip of window all the way round, with smooth walls and no furnishings, save the giant antelope that seemed to have survived the transition and a heavy throne – gold, of course – in front of it.

The Doctor blinked rapidly, but it wasn't an hallucination. Everything had been transformed. Chapel was now dressed in a high-collared robe of shining gold, while Harker . . . Harker's grey suit was now gold as well, but more like armour than anything else. And although his skin was still ashen, his hair and eyes were of the same, ubiquitous gold. He released the Doctor and started looking around the room in confusion.

The Doctor ran for the stairs, only to pause as he realized that he had no idea of their location. And then he saw what appeared to be a lift, its door open and inviting. Looking back, he saw Chapel and Harker regaining their composure, and realized that he had very little time and even fewer options.

He ran.

A second after he entered the lift, the door closed, leaving him trapped in the mirrored cubbyhole. But despite the barrel-load of uncertainties that surrounded him, the Doctor sighed with relief – at least the lift appeared unchanged. And then he jumped as the lift spoke to him.

'Going down?' it asked in a deep but cheery voice.

'What?' The Doctor looked around for a loudspeaker grille, but quickly came to the conclusion that the lift really was talking to him. It just seemed the sort of thing that would happen.

'I presume you came in here to go somewhere?'

Might as well humour it, he decided. 'Ah, yes. Ground floor, if you please.'

'Had enough of the Archimage and his warlord, have you?' asked the lift as it started to descend rather more rapidly than the Doctor's still queasy stomach would have liked.

'Archimage?' The Doctor shook his head. The last thing he remembered was Chapel cackling over his gold Tablette, preparing to run the Millennium Codex. Was this Saraquazel's age of peace and harmony? Something told him that it wasn't, and he frowned. That's the problem with quantum mnemonics, he decided. One can never be sure of the end result. Chapel had miscalculated and curdled reality, and now the Doctor was going to have to sort it all out. He just hoped that the triangular barrier had held: if the mnemonic had spread, well, there was no telling the damage that could have been caused.

Deciding that his first priority was to reach the sanctuary of the TARDIS and assess the extent of the problem, he suddenly realized that the lift was talking to him again.

'The Archimage; glorious leader of the auriks. Okay, okay, I'll be blunt. He's that bloke with the grey hair and the gold cloak up on the top floor. His warlord is the thug in the armour,' added the lift as it passed the twentieth floor, according to the gothic numerals which appeared in the mirrored surface.

Deciding that deception was the better part of valour, the Doctor agreed. 'Yes, yes, yes. But it didn't go very well, so I thought it best if I left.'

'Sound move,' agreed the lift. 'But where are you going? Are you one of the Technomancer's lot, or are you working for the Hierophant?'

'Neither. I'm –'

The lift stopped with a jolt. 'I know you!' it said. 'You're the Dark One, aren't you? It's about time you arrived. That'll shake 'em up a bit.'

The Doctor frowned. 'I'm sorry, but I'm no such thing. I'm –'

'I see, travelling incognito. No problem.' It restarted its descent.

I should have called the Time Lords in when I first detected Saraquazel, the Doctor decided, and let them deal with it. Now it's up to me, and I'm not sure that I can handle it.

'Ground floor, He Whose Name Dare Not Be Mentioned.' The doors opened.

'What?'

'Sorry, was that a bit formal? I'll stick to Dark One if you want.'

The Doctor stepped through the door. 'Doctor, if you don't mind.'

'Fine, Doc, whatever you say.' The doors closed behind him.

'Doc?' the Doctor muttered. 'Doc? Doc!' And then he

remembered who else kept on calling him that, and looked around what had been the foyer with alarm. Where was Mel in all of this?

The Archimage leant against the wall, trying to quell the nausea. He was a rational man, dismissive of the superstitions that the Technomancer and the Hierophant embraced. But omens were omens, and he remembered his great-great-grandfather's vision of cataclysm should the rulers of the Great Kingdom ignore the rules and strictures. They had been ignored, and then the Gods had taken up arms against one another and come close to laying waste to the entire Kingdom. All because the Hierophant and Technomancer of the time had broken the sacred laws.

'Did you sense the Gods' anger, Harklaane?' he asked his warlord. 'Did you?'

Harklaane shrugged. 'There was something, a spasm, a tremor. But you are the lord here, Archimage –'

'Of course I am. Who else?' But as the Archimage stared out of the window, his eyes were drawn to the blinding light that burned from the geometric centre of the Great Kingdom: the Tabernacle, home of the Gods. To approach the Tabernacle was the greatest crime in the Kingdom, upheld by all three states; the last recorded incursion was over ten generations ago, when a warrior aurik had led his tribe to confront the Gods. No punishment at earthly hands had been necessary, however, since the Gods themselves were more than capable of defending themselves. The foolhardy auriks had burnt in supernal fire, a terrifying lesson to would-be heretics.

But the Archimage knew far more than he had told his duplicitous warlord. His spies and eaves-droppers about the Great Kingdom had informed him of the Hierophant's blasphemous contact with the Technomancer, and the thaumaturg in question had been apprehended leaving the Ziggurat. The interrogation had been a short-lived but satisfying pleasure – for the

Archimage, not the thaumaturg — and the information he had provided had been well worth the messy inconvenience.

He Whose Name Dare Not Be Mentioned was abroad in the Kingdom, and, if the ancient tomes were to be believed, this was the first sign of the impending War of the Gods. But the Dark One was claimed to be a man of great power. If his powers could disrupt the Kingdom, who could say what would happen if he allied himself with one of the Lords of that Kingdom?

Turning from the window, the Archimage approached his throne. He had every intention of being that Lord; because only he had the strength and vision to unite the Kingdom as it had never been united before. And he was sure that his God, Saraquazel, would look upon his plans with beneficence.

So why did the Archimage shudder when he looked at the Tabernacle?

The gold and marble splendour of the foyer had been one thing. What passed for London was another.

Standing in front of what had been Number One, Canada Square — virtually unchanged, save its unsurprising golden sheen and incandescent light atop the pyramidal roof — the Doctor placed his hands on his hips and surveyed the landscape. He had already analysed the blindingly azure sky, alive with silent electric storms, and decided that he was looking at the physical manifestation of Chapel's mnemonic barrier. In front of him, Old Father Thames flowed with its usual sluggishness, but the waters were full of dark shapes that were definitely not salmon. As he watched, a dragon-like head cleared the surface, bellowing plaintively before diving below. The Doctor frowned. The last time anything like that had been swimming in the Thames, it had been the Zygons' bio-engineered Skarasen.

And then a screech from above drew his attention. Craning his neck, he could just make out a flock of birds.

But then he realized that they weren't birds; cast in gold, with bat-like wings and devil's tails, they were airborne bipeds. He shuddered. Was he the only person in London unaffected by the transformation?

He looked at his immediate surroundings. Strangely enough, the pavement and its associated furnishings were physically unchanged. Lamp-posts, litter bins, parking meters; but they were a curious translucent grey, as if the life had been sucked out of them, leaving only husks. Even the boats moored in the stretch of the Thames opposite the Tower were the same, desiccated grey, bobbing on top of the monster-filled waters. Quantum mnemonics was a subject about which he was woefully ignorant – along with virtually everyone else in the cosmos, he reassured himself – but the Doctor wondered whether the peculiar transformation of the Tower's surroundings was due to their proximity to the source of the Codex.

Deciding that this was a trite and simplistic answer, he filed the problem away for future analysis. It was time to find the TARDIS and, hopefully, a way out of this nightmare. And then he thought about Mel again, and wondered what had happened to her in this new reality.

Leaning back in her throne, Melaphyre sent out a mental summons for her confidantes. What she was about to do was both heretical and extremely dangerous, and she needed the counsel of her friends.

'Majestrix?' The chorus of voices interrupted her.

'Ah, my Chancellor and Major-domo. Please, approach the throne.' She watched them as they walked towards her. Blonde Louella, always a rich source of gossip about the private lives of the cybrids, and Bartholomew. Ah, dear Bartholomew, she thought warmly.

Once Louella had been made human, the Technomancer had soon realized that her newly inaugurated Chancellor needed a suitable companion. Knowing that her Chancellor had a fondness for the tubby cybrid who waited on table, Melaphyre had elevated him to humanity, and his gift of humour had been a welcome addition to a court that had for so long been arid of mirth – save the tired old jokes of General Gargil, commander of Melaphyre's cybrid army. And any laughter he elicited was more due to respect than amusement.

Melaphyre had turned a blind eye to both of her courtiers' indulgences. Louella enjoyed breathing the noxious fumes produced by burning the leaves of the plants that flourished on the banks of the Great River, as did Bartholemew, who also drank far too deeply – and frequently – of the royal cellars. But these indiscretions were soon overshadowed by a far greater crime.

Louella had become with child.

The laws of the Great Kingdom were strict upon this point. The only humans permitted to breed were the members of the First Families, whose humanity could be traced back to the formation of the Kingdom; elevated creatures were forbidden to procreate.

The penalty was death.

And so the Technomancer had spent countless hours in silent meditation with her Goddess, the Lady Tardis, before deciding their fate. And that fate was a merciful one, for the Lady Tardis had told her – in a vision, as is the way of these things – that the child must live, for it would play a role in the days to come.

She stared into her courtiers' eyes with a final doubt as to whether she could trust them. But if she couldn't trust them, who could she trust? The Dark One? She laughed, and was forced to ignore the quizzical look from Bartholemew and Louella.

'As you are both aware, I had a visitor yesterday.' They nodded. 'That visitor was an emissary from the Hierophant.'

'A thaumaturg!' gasped Louella. 'But the Laws of the Kingdom –'

The Technomancer raised her hand. 'I am familiar with the laws, Louella. I am also familiar with the legends of the Kingdom. The thaumaturg informed me that the Dark One, He Whose Name Dare Not Be Mentioned, is abroad in the Kingdom.'

Bartholemew's eyes widened. 'The end of the world,' he muttered. 'The Wall of Tears will crumble, and the barbarians will invade.'

'Well quoted, my Major-domo,' said Melaphyre. 'The Kingdom faces its greatest crisis, and, in times such as these, I am forced to consider actions that would once have been unthinkable.

'I must speak to the Hierophant.' She observed the horrified reactions with not a little satisfaction. If she was going to commit blasphemy, she would rather it felt like she was going to commit blasphemy. And their shocked looks did exactly that.

'But that means going into the Labyrinth!' Louella exclaimed. 'The Laws –'

'The Laws are an artifice to bind the Kingdom in peace, my Chancellor. If the Kingdom is to stave off destruction, the Laws must be bent, broken even.' She gestured towards the view of the Kingdom. 'I depart for the Labyrinth within the hour. And I would be grateful of companionship.'

She waited as her words sank in. And the result was hardly unexpected.

'If the Majestrix wants companionship, then we will be honoured,' stated Bartholemew.

'Honoured,' repeated Louella.

'Then it is settled,' said the Technomancer, rising from the throne. 'Change into your travelling clothes and meet me at the Great Doors in thirty minutes.'

They reached the doors of the throne room before Melaphyre could humble herself sufficiently to say her next words.

'Thank you.'

They were embarking upon a journey with deadly ramifications. It was the least she could say.

* * *

The Archimage stared out of the window at the shining heart of the Great Kingdom and frowned.

Beyond the confines of the Tower, the Dark One roamed the Kingdom, and the Archimage needed to find him before the others did. His usual techniques were useless. The Dark One was shielded from the gaze of the Archimage's auriks, including the winged ones who wheeled about the sky. The Dark One could even breach the walls of the Tower before the Archimage sensed him, and that would be far too late.

He needed an advantage, and the only one that he could think of lay within the Tabernacle. He needed to consult Saraquazel.

His mind reached out to the aurik that tended his meagre library — if only he could access the great works within the Labyrinth as easily, he thought wistfully — and directed it to a beige-bound volume. The volume had been written by the vizier to the Archimage's great-great-grandfather — who had transcribed it from tablets of stone that were purported to have come from the other Great Kingdom, the one that fell beneath the sea — and apparently contained an incantation capable of protecting one from the wrath of the Gods, dare they approach the Tabernacle.

The Archimage just hoped that it worked as well as the legends claimed.

The more the Doctor saw, the more worried he became. From his brief observations, what had been London was now a triangle about a mile on each side, bounded by a golden Canary Wharf Tower, a blue, silver and gold ziggurat that was presumably once the Millennium Hall, and grey flats that could only be what remained of the Library of Saint John the Beheaded.

Within the triangle, he could see three separate encampments with three contrasting building styles: little blue-black pyramids; gold blocks, and flat grey constructs suggesting underground dwellings. All well and good, but there was a problem. The closer the Doctor looked, the more of each type he could see. It was as if the mnemonic had made up for the lack of three-dimensional space in the new London by fractalling reality, folding and cracking space to fit more in.

The Doctor turned away. The artificial city of Castrovalva, with its complete lack of internal logic, had been bad enough, when only the laws of distance and perspective had been shattered. But Castrovalva had been created by the Master using block transfer computations; this farrago was the direct consequence of Chapel's quantum mnemonic, and far more sinister. As for the shining white light that stood at the heart of the three encampments, well; the closer he had looked at that, the larger and more awesome it had become. Shivering, he turned his back on it to face the outer reaches of the new London.

The last time he had seen the TARDIS, it had been in the shadow of Nelson's Column. And while Trafalgar Square had originally lain within the triangle that Chapel's barrier had enclosed, the Codex had turned everything inside out. The buildings that had once been tourist landmarks now filled the space between the triangle and the scintillating energy barrier.

But they hadn't escaped the transformation either. Saint Paul's Cathedral, Telecom Tower, Big Ben, and, of course, Nelson's Column. All were dark and distorted, nightmare mirror images designed by architects from the depths of Bedlam, their silhouettes clear against the actinic blue of the barrier. Saint Paul's dome was lopsided and melted, with twisted, fungal growths reaching up from the top of the dome to the bright blue sky. The regular spires of the Palace of Westminster were now bent corkscrews, pointing in every direction. And Telecom Tower was now a pinnacle of darkened deformity, like a decaying asparagus spear.

As for Nelson's Column, instead of the Doctor's old friend, a vile representation of the human figure surmounted the pillar, a distillation of corruption that leered at the horrific transformation of London.

The Doctor shuddered, and immediately wondered why such immature imagery was occurring to him; this was all in a day's work, surely? And then a gnawing doubt surfaced. Had he really ridden the mnemonic unscathed?

He quelled the worry and set off for the warped version of Nelson's Column. He would soon be back in the TARDIS, where he would get some answers. But another worry immediately surfaced to replace it. For the first time in ages, he couldn't sense the TARDIS in his mind.

'They're coming.' The Hierophant tapped her hand on the wooden desk and looked up at Atoz, the thaumaturg that attended her.

In the past, she had considered raising both Atoz and her warlord Alane to humanity, in the same way that the Archimage and the Technomancer had with their chosen ones, but had dismissed it as a wasteful indulgence. But during the dark hours of the previous day, freshly burdened with the knowledge that He Whose Name Dare Not Be Mentioned was stalking the Kingdom, she had pondered the wisdom of her decision, desperately yearning for an intellectual equal with whom she could discuss the situation.

'What of the Archimage, oh Bibliotrix?' asked Atoz in his thin, uncertain voice.

'His presence is unnecessary. The Technomancer and myself can deal with the danger that threatens the Kingdom.'

The thaumaturg simply nodded, and the Hierophant again wondered what it would be like to have some intelligent conversation for a change. 'I'll find out soon,' she said aloud, prompting – and ignoring – a strange look from the thaumaturg. And then she thought about the Technomancer's ungrounded hatred of her – information passed along through her network of informants – and sighed. Such emotions would have to be overcome if they were to stand any hope of saving the Kingdom.

'Leave me,' she ordered, and watched as Atoz nervously tottered towards the door. Maybe a confidante would have been a good idea, but could she have spoken of the deeper fears that concerned her? Could she have told them of her conviction that she had brought the disaster upon them all? She rose and stared at her reflection in the polished table top. As hard as it was to admit, age had not given her dignity, only hardness, emphasized by her severely back-combed grey hair. All the warmth and love that she had possessed in her youth was gone, spent on her ungrateful children, leaving only bitterness and regrets. And her subterranean Labyrinth of Thaumaturgy.

And if the prophecies concerning the Dark One were to be believed, even that would soon be taken from her.

Louella and Bartholemew were dressed in only marginally less grand versions of the blue armour that the Technomancer wore. Armour that would expand to cover and protect them at a single mental command. Such measures were necessary when leaving the sanctuary of the Ziggurat and braving the Great Kingdom. Even the cybrids could be vicious if caught unawares.

'Are you both sure of this endeavour?' asked Melaphyre. They were standing on the steps that led from the Ziggurat into the world of the cybrids, with their pyramid dwellings and camp fires and primitive ways. Her Chancellor and her major-domo had family in the dwellings, but now was not the time to visit them; Melaphyre had another route in mind.

'Majestrix, you cannot travel abroad without protection,' stated Bartholemew. 'As we said earlier, it is an honour to serve.'

According to the ancient rites, General Gargil should have been sufficient as her honour guard, but Melaphyre had decided that she didn't really have the stomach for his blood and thunder approach. Louella and Bartholemew were infinitely better company.

Yet the old doubts were still there. She had raised them to humanity. Was their obedience true, or was it nothing more than a legacy of their transformation? Then again, given the current circumstances, any loyalty was better than nothing.

'Very well,' she announced, 'we proceed towards the Labyrinth. But I suggest we travel via the Wretched Wastes. If my people see that the Technomancer has left the Ziggurat, they will draw their own conclusions. And I cannot afford for unrest to foment. When the Dark Times are upon us, we shall need our unity.'

She looked beyond the simplistic dwellings of her cybrids, towards the grey, melted buildings that lay between the Great Kingdom and the Wall of Tears. The region was swarming with renegades of all three castes, but their violence was mollified by the fact that they were forced to live together. And besides, the Technomancer wielded enough power to vanquish any foe.

Melaphyre set off down the steps – Louella and Bartholemew a respectful distance behind – and turned to face the thin, foggy barrier that separated her realm from the Wastes. Legend had it that the Wretched Wastes were all that remained of the civilization that had lived before the Gods had created the Kingdom. Passing through it would be a fortifying reminder of the horrors that would descend should the Dark One succeed.

The Doctor stopped in his tracks. Within seconds of turning his back on the settlement area, he had passed through a wall of light mist, only to discover that the entire environment had altered. The azure glow of the energy barrier had darkened to virtually purple, casting sinister shadows off the deformed buildings and making the hairs on the back of his neck stand on end.

He shook his head. The mnemonic had well and truly altered the local properties of the space-time continuum, and the rational part of his mind wondered how stable it all was. The way things were currently going, it wouldn't have surprised him if the whole lot collapsed on top of him – in a metaphysical sense, of course – and then it would take a lot more than a respiratory bypass system to save him.

He stroked the surface of the building alongside him; warm to the touch, it resembled crumbling grey marble. Whereas the area surrounding Canary Wharf Tower looked as if the life had been sucked out of it, the desolation of these Wretched Wastes suggested that decay had set in.

The Doctor froze. How had he known that the borders of the Great Kingdom were called the Wretched Wastes? How had he known it was called the Great Kingdom, come to that? Shaking his head, he filed it away alongside the ever-increasing number of questions that he wanted answers for.

Continuing his stroll, he peered up at the looming grey edifices, trying to keep track of Nelson's Column. Of course, he thought worriedly, there was no guarantee that the TARDIS was still in the same relative location, but without his usual instinct, it was all he had to go on. The idea that the Millennium Codex had affected it was too terrifying to contemplate unless absolutely necessary.

He stopped again. Although his Time Lord senses might be dulled, his more pedestrian ones were as keen as ever, and the irregular scuttling noise behind him was undeniably the sound of being followed. He increased his pace through the meandering alleyways, but heard his pursuer speed up accordingly.

His brisk walk became a run. His multicoloured coat flapping behind him, he swerved down a tiny turning, hoping that it wasn't a dead end.

It wasn't.

He was in an open courtyard, flanked on both sides by dark stone griffins – this London's Landseer lions, he guessed. And, directly in front of him, the base of an enormous pillar thrust from the ground, its surface encrusted with what looked like stone fungus. But it was the object next to it that cheered the Doctor's heart: the resolute blue shape of the TARDIS, apparently unchanged by the mnemonic.

His relief was knocked out of him by whatever leapt onto his back. From the dark blue talons that were reaching for his face, the Doctor assumed that it was one of Louise's demons – a cybrid, he knew with certainty. He struggled, but the cybrid was tenacious and preternaturally strong, and its arms slowly but unbreakably reached round his shoulders. The glistening tips of the talons were only inches from his face when he threw himself backwards onto the courtyard floor; the impact dislodged the cybrid, and the Doctor jumped to his feet, realizing that the loud crack he had heard must have been the creature's back breaking.

As he reached the doors of the TARDIS and fumbled for the key, he realized that there was silence behind him. Turning, he was relieved to see that the cybrid was unmoving, but the faint noises from just down the alleyway indicated that it hadn't been alone. Still, he'd be safe enough in the TARDIS, he reminded himself, inserting the key.

Nothing happened. The key refused to turn. He remembered the countless defences that he had installed over the centuries to prevent unauthorized entry: the twenty-two tumbler lock; the metabolism sensor, the isomorphic controls. None of them would have proved a barrier to him! He tried again, but it was as if the lock had been changed. Could the quantum mnemonic have warped the block transfer computations that drove the TARDIS's police-box shell, effectively jamming the doors? The scraping and scuttling was getting closer, and he turned the key again in desperation.

As he prepared to attempt direct communication with the TARDIS telepathic circuits by laying his hands on the doors, a booming concussion made him step back. In time with the pulsing roof light, a trumpeting roar began to echo around the courtyard.

'No!' he screamed, banging on the doors which were rapidly becoming insubstantial. 'You can't leave me!' But his next impact never connected; he sprawled forward into the space where the TARDIS had once been.

But was no longer.

As his bewilderment turned into panic, he suddenly saw that he had a more immediate problem. Five more cybrids were crouched in front of him, chewing on the lumps of meat that hung from their drooling mouths. But their slitted amber eyes were focused on him. And beyond them lay the half-eaten carcass of their colleague, its face a rictus of posthumous satisfaction.

Ten

Melaphyre paused and held up her hand. They had been skirting round the Great Kingdom for an age, along the winding lanes and through the great empty courtyards of the Wretched Wastes, but they had remained completely unmolested. And that worried her.

'Is something wrong, Majestrix?' asked Louella, moving to her side.

'We should have drawn attention to ourselves by now,' she murmured, 'and yet we stroll through the Wastes as though it were part of my domain.'

'Surely that's something to be grateful for?' asked Bartholemew.

The Technomancer smiled. 'Dear Bartholemew, your innocence is refreshing. The Wastes are notorious for their roving bands of renegades – auriks, thaumaturgs and cybrids –'

'A renegade thaumaturg,' laughed Bartholemew. 'That I'd like to see.'

Melaphyre fixed him with an impatient stare. Despite his position at the bosom of her household, she really did not like to be interrupted. 'In a killing frenzy, a thaumaturg can rip the living heart from a cybrid,' she said coldly. 'And this is the region of the rogue cybrids, yet they do not approach.'

'Would they dare attack their own queen?' whispered Louella.

'Do not delude yourself,' Melaphyre chastised. 'The cybrid that claims my severed head as its prize can take my mantle from the Gods themselves, or have you forgotten the myths of our forebears concerning the genesis of the First Families? No, we should have been attacked by now.' Do I sound disappointed, she wondered? Because I am. It had been far too long since she had honed her skills in true combat. 'I can only assume that they are otherwise engaged –'

An ululating cry rose from the distance; the death rattle of a cybrid.

'And that would appear to confirm my assumptions!' she whooped. 'Protect yourselves and follow me!' Within half a second, her armour expanded, extending from her arms and legs to create invulnerable gauntlets and boots, while the high collar grew up and round to cover her head with a high-domed helmet with a pointed top and a fluted front.

Once Bartholemew and Louella were similarly protected, the three ran towards the source of the noise; the Courtyard of Griffins, unless her senses deceived her.

The Technomancer stopped as they entered the Courtyard. A human figure, dressed in brightly – and tastelessly – coloured raiments and with a thatch of curly blond hair, was poised like a cat on the far side of the yard, the mutilated bodies of five cybrids lying broken around him. Even as Melaphyre watched, the remaining cybrid – a violent youth that she herself had exiled from the realm of Sciosophy – threw himself at the stranger.

The cybrid exploded like a melon shot with an arrow, his remains dropping to the ground with a sickening plop. For a moment, the man looked at the bloody mess with an expression of both puzzlement and disgust. And then he appeared to notice the Technomancer and her aides, and stepped forward.

Melaphyre was proud of Bartholemew's reaction.

'Halt! Approach the Majestrix at your peril, stranger.'

The man shrugged. 'Very well. Is it all right if I stay here, or is this too close for the Majestrix?'

'Do not mock!' snapped Louella.

'I wouldn't dream of it,' he shrugged. 'I'm the Doctor, and I seem to be lost.'

'Lost in the Wretched Wastes,' tutted the Technomancer, deciding that it was now safe enough to order her armour to stand down. 'Not very wise.' She wasn't prepared for the look of happiness on the stranger's face. Ignoring Bartholemew and Louella, he jumped forward and grabbed Melaphyre's hands in a warm grip.

'My dear Mel, you can't imagine how glad I am to see a friendly face in this, this travesty!' He laughed, looking her armour up and down. 'Although I can't say that your dress sense has improved.'

The Technomancer snatched her hands away. But her anger was moderated by this madman's odd familiarity – his with her, and hers with him. And the fact that he used the name that had been in her vision. Once again, Melaphyre was forced to ask herself, who in the Great Kingdom was this Mel?

According to the Archimage's flight of airborne auriks, Harklaane was busy in the depths of the aurik encampment, ordering his toy armies into neat little rows and staging bloodthirsty little wars. The Archimage smiled. If his warlord's previous games of conflict were anything to go by, he would be piling up the bodies for many hours to come. Which suited the Archimage's purposes perfectly.

He was standing inside the glittering pyramid that surmounted his Tower, in a room that no one dare enter, save himself. He knew for a fact that Harklaane had made many an attempt to pry open the door to the stairwell that ascended to this, the Archimage's armoury, but the mystic wards that protected the door would have needed a grand master's abilities to unravel, and Harklaane fell far short of that.

As he lifted each weapon in turn from its rack, he wondered whether any of his illustrious ancestors had ever had a warlord that they could trust. He knew that his own lineage was descended from a warlord who had successfully wrested the title from his master; only his own mystical abilities kept the rapacious Harklaane at bay. And if Harklaane knew that the Archimage planned a visit to the Tabernacle; well, in the magick-shrouded corridors of that shining palace, the Archimage would find it difficult to even summon up a spell to repel a simple sword.

Best that he travel alone. And through the thaumaturg settlement. If he travelled through his own realm, there was a danger he might run into Harklaane. A final reason confirmed his decision; the other routes were either the cybrid realm or the Wretched Wastes, and the Archimage's spies had warned him that the Technomancer was abroad in the Wastes. Either route would reveal his destination to the prattling Melaphyre.

Returning to his choice of weapons, he chose a small silver dagger as his only armament. The Stiletto of Vaux, an elegant weapon whose impressive pedigree of bloodletting was less likely to enrage the Gods. He left the armoury and headed towards the lift, hoping that – for once – it wasn't in a garrulous mood. He needed to collect his thoughts, and the last thing he wanted was that damned elevator trying to be friendly.

'I ask again, stranger. Who is this Mel?'

'Well –' But even as he began, the Doctor could see that his companion had been altered by the Codex. Physically, she was the same – although the Bride of Frankenstein hairstyle was a striking improvement – but she had a presence, a regal bearing and an overpowering dignity, that was almost tangible. And something else. The Doctor didn't doubt for one moment that the Majestrix Melaphyre possessed the raw power to destroy him, as she must have destroyed the cybrids. All he could remember was watching them as they exploded, one by one.

And then he put his hand to his head. Where were these names coming from? How did he know so much about the alien environment that surrounded him? The answer was obvious: the Codex had affected him. Indeed, he had been right next to its point of detonation, so how could it not have done?

'Majestrix, I apologize,' he said chivalrously and bowing deeply. 'My conflict with the cybrids must have unsettled my mind.'

She laughed. 'I'm not surprised. To destroy six of the rogues, you must be an adept, Doctor, at least. Perhaps even a grand master?'

He smiled. 'Chess was my fourth incarnation's strong point, but I have been known to play a mean opening gambit –' He trailed off as the meaning behind her words sank in. 'You mean, I destroyed them?'

'You're too modest, Doctor.' She snapped her fingers and gestured for him to take her arm. 'Walk with me awhile, stranger. Tell me of whence you come?'

Still reeling from the knowledge that he had murdered the cybrids, he had to do a double take as he linked his arm round the Technomancer's. Was it his imagination, or was his jacket a shade darker? Filing it away with all of his other questions, he began to explain about his abortive attempt to enter the TARDIS. In the minutes since its disappearance, the Doctor had come to the conclusion that the Hostile Action Displacement System – the HADS – had been activated, but an attack by cybrids wouldn't have been sufficient grounds for it to abandon him. He froze, well aware of the concerned looks from the Majestrix and her two colleagues, both now unarmoured.

The TARDIS hadn't abandoned him.

It simply hadn't recognized him.

'Doctor – are you unwell?' asked the Technomancer.

He held up his free hand. 'No, no, I'm fine.' He gave a reassuring laugh, but he wasn't sure who he was supposed to be reassuring.

'You were telling us about yourself,' prompted Louella. The Doctor hadn't paid her any attention until now, but the face, the voice, the wavy blonde hair; it was

Louise Mason. And the stocky man with collar length brown hair was her friend Barry. It was all too much of a coincidence. He decided to continue, mainly as a means of establishing at least one set of facts.

'I tried to open the door of my, ah, cabinet –'

'A magic cabinet?' asked the man who had once been Barry.

'In a manner of speaking, yes. But the key wouldn't turn. And then my, erm, cabinet dematerialized, and then the cybrids attacked. I take it that they weren't loyal to you, Majestrix?' Another new concept that had popped into his mind, the knowledge that the majority of cybrids were loyal to Melaphyre.

She shook her head. 'No. Renegades and exiles who lurk in the Wretched Wastes. What did this cabinet look like, Doctor?'

'It's about ten feet tall and six feet wide, blue with panelled sides and a light on its roof. It's called –'

'The Lady Tardis!' she gasped pulling free of his grip.

He smiled. Obviously this version of Mel remembered something. 'Exactly –'

She raised both hands and snapped her fingers. 'Louella, Bartholemew, protect yourselves!' The Technomancer's own armour engulfed her.

'Listen, there really is no need for this, you know.' The Doctor started backing away.

' "And the Dark One shall walk the Great Kingdom. And his first encounter shall be with the Lady Tardis, the Goddess in Absence from the Tabernacle," ' quoted Louella, slightly muffled through her helmet. It made her words sound like a heavenly pronouncement. Which it probably was, the Doctor decided. ' "And he shall attempt to breach the Lady Tardis's being, upon which the Goddess shall retrench to the Tabernacle." '

'Exactly!' snapped the Technomancer. 'You may call yourself the Doctor, but we know you by another name. A name that dare not be mentioned!'

The Doctor shrugged. 'I know that my real name is a

little difficult to get your tongue round, but isn't that taking it a bit far?'

'Louella, Bartholemew. Return to the Ziggurat at once,' Melaphyre ordered.

'But the Dark One —' Louella protested mutely through her helmet.

'I am the Majestrix Melaphyre, Technomancer of the Great Kingdom,' she hissed. 'The coming of the Dark One is my responsibility, and mine alone. Now go!'

As soon as they had vanished down one of the alleyways off the Courtyard, the Technomancer's armour returned to normal and her expression changed to a welcoming smile. 'Matters of state are not for underlings, Dark One, and you and I have many things to discuss, do we not?'

The Doctor sighed. The alternative set of memories that was blossoming in his mind indicated that the Technomancer was a leading figure in the balance of power in what now passed for London. It wouldn't do any harm to play her along, he decided.

'Well that wasn't very nice, was it?' said Louella, hurt by the Technomancer's brusque dismissal. 'We're her trusted confidantes —'

'Face it, Lou,' snapped Bartholemew, 'at the end of the day we're nothing more than servants; cybrids that the Technomancer elevated to humanity to keep her company.' Louella started to protest, but Bartholemew silenced her with a raised hand. 'She keeps us around for amusement, nothing more. We're not in the same league as her, and you know it!' His tone was a clear indication that he was as upset as she was.

'So,' she shrugged. 'Back to the Ziggurat, I suppose.' She placed a finger to her lips and looked around their surroundings. 'Although I'm not really sure where we are —'

'Perhaps I can help,' said Bartholemew brightly. 'We're in the rogue cybrid section of the Wastes. If we keep walking in this direction, we should eventually reach the cybrid settlement.'

She cocked an eyebrow. 'I'm impressed.'

He grinned. 'Come on, Lou, I've always been able to find my way home. A vital skill for a piss-head like me.'

Louella stared at him in confusion. 'I'm sorry, Bart, but I didn't understand a word of that. What's a "piss-head"?'

'I don't know,' he whispered. He sounded frightened. 'I just don't know where the words came from.' He shook his head and pointed towards the grey building with the domed roof – the Cathedral of Lost Souls. 'Forget it. There's a passageway behind there that leads to the Steps of Nostalgia. From there we're home and dry.'

They headed towards the Cathedral in silence.

The Tabernacle. The Archimage threw his head back and drank in the glory and the majesty of the heavenly palace before him. The dimensions of the Tabernacle were impossible to ascertain. He would stare at a single tower for a second, only to realize that he was looking at a cluster of hundreds of minarets; a small courtyard would become an auditorium upon further inspection. Such are the mysteries of the Gods, he decided humbly.

The one constant was the material from which the Tabernacle was constructed, although the Archimage doubted that the Gods had used the artisans and labourers that had been responsible for the Tower of Abraxas: theirs was the ultimate magic.

Everything was built from tessellated panes of glass in all the colours of the spectrum, and more besides. And each pane was shining with the light of the Gods, casting thousands of shadows and offering millions of reflections. The Archimage took a deep breath, and looked for an entrance. And yes, there it was. Beyond the reality of a carved buttress was a deeper truth, an arched doorway that shone with the pure illumination of the Gods.

In his long life, the Archimage had faced countless horrors and fought endless foes. He had killed a thousand cybrids in one night with a single blade; he had stood back to back with his warlord as they defended Abraxas from a renegade army of auriks, and finally vanquished them, knee deep in their golden blood. Throughout all of it, he had never flinched, never wavered.

Passing through the archway into the Home of the Gods, he freely admitted that he was terrified.

By rights, she should have destroyed the Doctor on the spot.

'So, you think I'm the Dark One, do you?' he asked.

The Technomancer laughed, a rich giggle. 'You arrive in the Great Kingdom and fulfil the first part of the prophecy. What else am I supposed to think?'

'And the name Mel means nothing to you?' he asked.

She stopped, withdrew her arm, and turned to look at him. 'We are alone, here, Dar – Doctor. We can talk freely without being overheard. The name does mean something, but I'm not sure what. I saw a vision, scarcely hours ago. A vision of the Great Kingdom, but not as it is –'

'But as it could be?' he interrupted.

'Indeed. And wrapped inside that vision was a young woman of my own aspect. A woman called Mel. Is she known to you, Dark One?'

The Doctor smiled. 'Mel is a good friend, Majestrix – hence my lèse-majesté upon meeting you. But I must insist that I am not the Dark One.'

She shrugged. 'Doctor or Dark One, you are a stranger in the Great Kingdom, and that is unheard of.' Turning her back on him, she continued. 'I am due to meet with the Hierophant – indeed, I am now overdue. Her request to see me is also unheard of.' She span round. 'So many unheard ofs, eh, Doctor? Something is terribly amiss in the Kingdom, and so far the prophecies would appear to be coming true. If I stand back and let destiny take its course, the Kingdom will be consumed in chaos, and the Wall of Gods' Tears will fall, releasing the barbarians to ravage the land.'

'Colourful but probably accurate. I have the most horrible feeling that this entire situation is dynamically unstable. It's tempting to let destiny take its course, but I doubt that everything will fall back in place without a little assistance.'

'Your words mean little, Dark One, but I do not believe that you are as evil as the legends portray.' There was something about the stranger, something that invited trust. She pointed towards the black shape of the Pinnacle of Tongues, with its mysterious covering of dishes. 'If we head in that direction, we come out close to the Labyrinth of Thaumaturgy. The Hierophant is waiting for me.'

'And me?' The Doctor frowned. 'Hang on one second. Is the Hierophant a middle-aged woman with greying hair? Quite severe?'

'An apt description, Doctor,' said the Technomancer with a smile. 'Do you know her?'

'In a manner of speaking, yes. And I doubt very much that she will be overjoyed to see me.' He took her arm. 'But needs must when the devil drives, eh, Me –, erm, Majestrix?' He nodded towards the Pinnacle. 'Shall we go?'

Louella tapped Bartholemew on the shoulder. 'Where are we going, Bart? Why are we in the encampment?'

He ignored her and carried on, knowing exactly where to go. It was no different from any of the other dwellings, but he knew. Despite his elevation to humanity, despite the ten years that he had been away, he knew exactly where he was headed. And, a few seconds later, he was there.

'Is this where I think it is?' asked Louella.

He nodded. 'It's about time, don't you think? Especially if the world is about to come to an end.' He knocked on the square doorway of the turquoise pyramid.

As far as Bartholemew was concerned, the wait for the

door to open could have been an eternity. And then it opened a crack, and an old cybrid, her eyes rheumy, peered from the darkness.

'Yes?' And then she stepped back, throwing open the door. 'It can't be —'

Bartholemew leant forward and grabbed the cybrid in a tight hug. 'It is, it is. I've come home, mother.' He was crying. 'I'm home.'

It was an effort to walk down the vast glass corridor without stopping and staring at the iridescent walls. It was so very tempting, but after less than a second the surface realities would unfurl, revealing deeper and more terrifying secrets beyond. The Archimage knew that even his great intellect would crumble if he peered too deeply into unspoken truths that no mortal mind could comprehend.

The path to the heart of the Tabernacle was well known to him, but only in the form of ancient writings in dark tomes. No one had approached this close since the foundation of the Great Kingdom, when each of the Gods had chosen a breeding couple from their respective peoples and elevated them to form the First Families. The first Archimage had sketched the plans of the Palace in his journal, a journal which had passed from father to eldest son across the generations, but no one had ever put them to practical use.

Until now. And the very fact that the Archimage had been able to enter the Palace suggested that there was a holy purpose to his journey, a purpose sanctioned by the Gods.

The corridor came to an abrupt halt with a shimmering wall of multicoloured glass, and a fainter heart might have turned back. But the first Archimage's journal warned of the wall, and explained that it was only a barrier to the weak and faithless.

Bolstering his faith and taking a deep breath, the Archimage stepped decisively through the crystal wall —

— and was in the presence of the Gods.

Calming himself, the Archimage pronounced the ritual words that would introduce him to the Gods, the rich phrases echoing from the walls and ceiling of the awesome chamber in a tinkling mockery. At no time did he look up. To gaze upon the countenances of the Gods was heresy.

'I, Magnus Ashmael, Archimage of Abraxas, do present myself before the three Gods of the Great Kingdom, and await your indulgence.' Words written when the Kingdom was young, but never used before.

The silence that erupted after the echoes died away was initially reassuring to the Archimage. At least he hadn't been struck down by a bolt of lightning. But as the minutes dragged by, he began to suspect that something was wrong. Steeling himself, he raised his head. And felt the breath freeze in his throat.

The first thing he noticed was that the throne of the Lady Tardis, the Goddess in Absence, was occupied; the blue double-cube rested upon her crystal plinth for the first time since the Kingdom had been created. This was disturbing enough – why was the Lady Tardis back in the Tabernacle?

But when the Archimage saw that the throne belonging to the Lord Yog-Sothoth was empty, he looked around for some explanation. And found it on the throne of Saraquazel.

Although possession of a graven image was heresy to the extreme, the images of the three Gods were known to everyone in the Great Kingdom, from the lowliest aurik serf upwards. So the Archimage knew that the figure on the throne of his own God was terribly, unimaginably wrong.

Saraquazel's imposing bulk, a golden humanoid with the head of an antelope, writhed on his throne in obvious agony, and the reason for his pain was clear. The emerald green tetrahedron of Yog-Sothoth was imbedded in his body, the two Gods fused in an unholy union that beggared the imagination. And there were words, whispered words.

His fear counteracted by curiosity, the Archimage ran to the throne to hear what his God was saying, and brought his hands to his head when he realized that it was a stream of gibberish and nonsense words.

He stepped back from the throne in mute horror. There was but one explanation.

The Gods were mad.

Eleven

Having reached the Pinnacle, the Technomancer stopped to check her bearings. Although they were close to the Labyrinth of Thaumaturgy, they weren't as close as she would have liked. She looked at the gaudy figure of the Dark One. How would he fare in combat? she mused. And then she remembered how he had fought the rogue cybrids.

'Since we are late, I suggest we cut across the settlement of the auriks,' she muttered. 'There may be dangers, but we are very late, and the Hierophant's summons was of the utmost urgency.'

The Doctor shrugged. 'Since this Great Kingdom business is all new to me, I'll respect your judgement. These auriks, are they Ashley Chapel's creatures?'

'If you mean Ashmael, the Archimage, then yes. But in the settlements, their loyalty is to their fellows. Any treaty of alliance that you have with the Archimage may not be respected.'

'Treaty?' laughed the Doctor. 'I wouldn't exactly call it that. The last time I saw the Archimage, he was, erm, not himself, shall we say.'

'None of us have been ourselves since the visions came,' she said, pointing towards a fog-bank of golden mist. 'Hence my unprecedented audience with Anastasia.'

'Might I enquire as to the purpose of the mist?' asked the Doctor, squinting at it suspiciously.

An odd question, but Melaphyre was happy to answer it. 'The mists divide the three realms of the Kingdom,

Doctor; both from each other and from the Tabernacle of the Gods at its heart. Only the rulers of the Kingdom and their chosen ones may pass through the mists; strays or people of dishonourable intent all suffer the same, horrifying fate.'

'Far more effective than checking passports,' muttered the Doctor. 'And since you're a ruler and I appear to be your chosen one, I suggest we get a move on.' They walked towards the mist.

The sky immediately changed the moment they passed through the fog, a golden glow that instantly banished the chill of the Wastes. Melaphyre answered yet another question from the Doctor, explaining that even dusk was different from realm to realm. The depressing and ominous twilight of the Wastes, the indigo of the realm of Sciosophy, and the burnished bronze of Abraxas.

'The auriks are not known for their ferocity, Doctor. If we ignore them, our passage should be unhindered. Should they attack, however —' she grabbed the Doctor's bicep. 'A man of strength such as yourself should have nothing to fear.'

'Now I know you're not Mel!' he said with amusement.

The aurik settlement was unnaturally quiet, the Technomancer decided. Although her visits to the realm of the Archimage had been rare, she always remembered it as being noisy, with auriks carrying out their business with raucous good humour. But the tall thin dwellings with their pyramidal roofs were silent, the huge square debating fora empty. A light breeze stirred up the yellow sand, but that was the only life in the realm of Abraxas.

'This is disquieting, Doctor.'

'The lack of attention, you mean?' He nodded. 'Abraxas is well-known for the rowdiness of its inhabitants.' He stopped. 'Now how did I know that?'

'You are the Dark One and your secrets are your own,' she stated. 'Hurry, now. The boundaries of Thaumaturgy lie ahead.'

'Well, well, well. The Majestrix honours us with her presence,' boomed a growling voice from behind them. And Melaphyre didn't need to turn round to recognize the person responsible.

'Harklaane,' she said dismissively. 'What ails you, warlord of Abraxas; is the rarefied atmosphere of the Tower too much for you?'

He was crouched on a small hillock, his body encased in the smooth golden armour of his rank. One hand was resting on his right thigh, the other was stroking his chin. 'My movements are none of your concern, cybrid witch. But yours . . . What are you doing in Abraxas?'

Melaphyre turned her back on him. 'Leave him, Doctor. The Archimage's dog poses no threat.'

As they walked away, Harklaane jumped from the hillock and snapped his fingers. A number of heavy footsteps could be heard behind him.

Three auriks appeared from the rear of one of the dwellings. Each was about six feet tall, and their skin resembled the armour worn by Harklaane: a golden carapace with curved spikes at each joint. Their faces were carved masks with blank black eyeslits and a dark gash for a mouth, while ram-like horns swept and curled from their temples.

'Armour yourself, Doctor,' the Technomancer advised, as her suit flowed to cover her.

'I'm afraid that isn't an option, Majestrix,' he said, tugging on the lapels of his jacket.

'Then prepare for battle, man!' she hissed, assuming a cat-like stance as one of the auriks strode towards her. Behind it, Harklaane smirked.

The aurik jumped forward and slashed out with his arm, obviously trying to wound Melaphyre with his barbs. She parried the blow with her own arm, but his greater weight caused her to stagger back. She glanced at the Doctor. He had removed his jacket and was holding it out in front of him like a coloured sail. And, to her astonishment, he seemed to be urging the auriks to attack him.

Rolling to one side to avoid her own attacker, she suddenly understood the Doctor's actions. As the aurik lunged, the Doctor stepped adroitly to one side, and the aurik charged through his jacket and tripped. Stunned, he just lay there. Standing back, the Doctor bowed to Melaphyre. He was unaware that the third aurik was right behind him.

'Look out!' she yelled, simultaneously throwing a burst of scalding light into the face of the aurik that loomed over her.

The Doctor turned, but it was too late; the aurik grabbed him by the shoulders and dropped his head, preparing to spear him with its horns.

Without a word, the aurik exploded, shards of fractured armour spinning outwards. The Technomancer got to her feet and grabbed the Doctor, who was staring blankly at the pile of golden armour that remained.

'Quickly, before the others recover!' she shouted, pulling him away.

Behind them, Harklaane looked at the remains of his aurik with an unfathomable expression. And then he looked up.

'If you have allied yourself with the Dark One, Melaphyre, then may the Gods have mercy on your soul,' he yelled after them. And then smiled. The threat that the two now posed to the balance of the Kingdom would occupy the Archimage. And that would make it so much easier to wrest control of Abraxas.

Satisfied, Harklaane set off for home.

Night was falling fast over the Great Kingdom. In the cybrid realm, the azure light was darkening to indigo, while the thaumaturgs, safe in their warrens, sensed the silver sky turning grey. Walking hurriedly through the aurik settlement, the Archimage shivered as the golden fog above him began to tarnish to bronze. But it wasn't only the drop in temperature that was to blame. The horror in the Tabernacle was mainly responsible.

As he walked, his mind kept dwelling on the image of Saraquazel and Yog-Sothoth fused together in mutual insanity. Perhaps that crone in the Labyrinth had been right; the severity of the situation demanded a cessation in the aeons-old conflict between the three great powers. He made up his mind to send runners to both the Ziggurat and the Labyrinth as soon as he got back to the Tower. If the Gods were mad, it would need all their combined strength to save the Kingdom.

His thoughts were interrupted by the realization that he wasn't alone. He was being shadowed, but his pursuer was not an aurik: he sensed a higher intellect at work.

The situation was far too grave for a game of cat-and-mouse, the Archimage decided; it was time to confront whoever it was. Stopping, he turned in the direction that his senses indicated; the only thing in his line of sight was a desiccated copse of bronze-coloured shrubs.

'Show yourself!' he bellowed, but only silence greeted his words. So, his assailant lacked even the courage to identify himself, preferring to hide behind trees. That was easily solved.

Muttering some minor words of power under his breath, the Archimage pointed a finger at the copse, and smiled as it erupted into purple fire. Moments later, a figure rose from behind the flames, a large figure with a bemused look upon his face.

'Harklaane!' snapped the Archimage. 'Why were you lurking in the copse like a rogue aurik?'

His warlord looked from left to right in panic.

'I am your Archimage, Harklaane. And yet you hide yourself from me.' He fingered his chin. 'And I can't help asking, why?' Something told the Archimage that this was only the beginning of a difficult situation; he had always known that Harklaane harboured deep ambitions that would one day pose a threat to his position, and the uncertainty that hung over the Kingdom would seem an ideal opportunity.

'I sensed a person of power –'

'Really? A person of power, eh? And you didn't realize that it was me. I find that very difficult to believe, Harklaane.'

Harklaane walked up to him. 'I've just run into the Technomancer. She's with the Dark One!'

'Really?' He was being sarcastic, but the Archimage could read the images from his warlord's mind as easily as scooping the froth off a tankard of ale, and realized that he was telling the truth. And there was something about the person who claimed to be the Dark One which was familiar.

'They were travelling to the Labyrinth. The Dark One destroyed an aurik with a single thought.'

'The Dark One's actions were unremarkable for a man of his dark design, and do not explain your clandestine behaviour.' He pointed a finger at the man's chest, a finger burning with power. 'So tell me the truth or I will dissect your mind!'

Harklaane summoned and fired a bolt of psychic energy, obviously using up most of his life-force to create it. The Archimage deflected it; not easily, for Harklaane's powers were base yet strong, but the bolt ricocheted off his defensive wards and exploded on the ground.

Harklaane was barely standing, his now emaciated form a testament to the effort he had exerted. 'For twenty years, you have humiliated me, Ashmael. For twenty years I have pandered to your every whim, your every caprice. And you have never given me even the slightest sliver of your power!'

The Archimage laughed. 'And why should I? You were an aurik that I raised to humanity for amusement, and for those tasks over which I chose not to dirty my hands. For two decades, I ignored your rapacious appetite for power. But no more, Harklaane, no more. The Kingdom is entering the darkest age in its history, and your support is a hindrance more than an asset.'

Harklaane fell to his knees. 'I have always supported you, my lord. Always!' he insisted.

'Your lies are as transparent as a windrider's wings, oh warlord. But death is too easy an option.' He reached out to Harklaane, who started crawling backwards in the dust. A simple mantra of immobilization rooted him to the spot. 'In the coming crisis, I cannot afford to waste the vitality that you embody. So I shall absorb you into myself.'

'No!' screamed Harklaane. 'Spare me!'

The Archimage placed both hands on Harklaane's head. 'This is far more than you deserve. It will be a painful process – for that I apologize. But you have the consolation that your essence will become part of me; and you shall share in the epiphany that I shall bring to the Kingdom.' And then he reached into Harklaane, touching, stroking the furious vitality; and then he wrenched his warlord's essence from his struggling body, drinking the ambition, the hatred, the strength.

Something was wrong. The Archimage tried to break free, but the flow of energy was more than he could handle. All he could do was accept the life-force that was enervating and tainting every cell of his being. And as it did so, the Archimage could feel his values and ethics becoming tainted with those of his servant. He tried to fight the influx, but suddenly realized that he didn't want it to stop. He bathed, he luxuriated in its cold radiance. And then the transfer was complete.

The Archimage rose uncertainly, allowing the husk of his former warlord to fall to the ground, where it rapidly crystallized and crumbled to dust, before a silent wind blew the remains away. Time was short, the Archimage realized, and if he was to wrest control away from the Gods, he would have to act quickly. A tiny portion of his mind suggested that he join forces with the Technomancer and the Hierophant, for the good of the Kingdom. He laughed. The only good would be attained by seizing control of the Kingdom. And by destroying those who opposed him.

Such as the Technomancer and the Hierophant.

* * *

It was almost dark by the time that the Doctor and the Technomancer reached the Labyrinth. At least, the Doctor assumed it was the Labyrinth. The only indication that there was anything out of the ordinary about the area of scrubland around them, was the pattern of slate slabs faintly visible under the grey dust beneath their feet.

'This is it?' he asked, kicking at the dust. 'Not exactly an awe-inspiring edifice, is it?' Then again, he remembered, the original Library of Saint John was hardly known for advertising its presence.

'The Hierophant and her thaumaturgs scorn both the surface and the daylight, Doctor.' Her tone suggested that the Hierophant herself was victim of some scorn from Melaphyre.

'Do I take it that you and the Hierophant don't exactly see eye to eye?'

'None of the three rulers of the Kingdom see "eye to eye", Doctor. Such is the way of these things.' She looked around. 'Indeed, Anastasia hasn't even the good grace to receive us into her warren,' she added venomously.

'I'm glad to see that even the Majestrix Melaphyre can occasionally be wrong,' came a dry voice from behind. The Doctor span round – almost losing his footing on the dusty roof of the Labyrinth – and came face to face with the Hierophant.

The last time the Doctor had seen Anne Travers, she had been consumed with the imminent destruction of the Great Intelligence. Hatred had burnt behind her eyes, a hatred that had swept away the bitterness, and replaced it with a self-destructive yet strangely invigorating strength. None of that was visible in the grey, thin woman in the plain silver toga, only a sad and barren emptiness that the Doctor found both sad and disturbing.

'Still we must observe the formalities, Majestrix.' Anastasia nodded at the ground, and a square hole materialized at her command. Steps were visible within, descending into the darkness of the Hierophant's Labyrinth. She looked round and nodded at the Doctor.

'And who is this handsome stranger, Melaphyre?' she said wistfully. 'One of your elevated cybrids? If it is, your magicks are improving.'

Melaphyre fixed her rival with an arch look full of playful mischief, and the Doctor couldn't really blame her. 'No, Bibliotrix, he is no cybrid. You can call him the Dark One.' Clearly revelling in the Hierophant's growing horror, she added, 'but if you're feeling particularly pious, He Whose Name Dare Not Be Mentioned will do just as well.'

The Hierophant moved to bar the entrance to the Labyrinth. 'You are a fool, Melaphyre!' she hissed. 'Whatever possessed you to bring him here? Or has he possessed you?' She glanced at the Doctor, who attempted to smile; the terrified look in the Hierophant's eyes suggested that this was not a good idea. He turned to the Technomancer, who assumed a very sincere expression.

'Since the arrival of the Dark One was the reason for this meeting, I thought it best if I brought him with me.'

The Hierophant contemplated this for a moment. And then she stepped aside from the entrance. 'These are grave times, and I have already broken the ancient covenants by inviting you here. One more heresy cannot damn us further.' She gestured at the stairs. 'Please, I bid you enter.'

Pleased by the relative smoothness of their arrival, the Doctor was in fairly good spirits as he descended the stairs. Until he heard the muttered words of the Hierophant as she closed the entrance behind them.

'And so the Kingdom falls.'

With those reassuring words fresh in his mind, the Doctor entered the oil-lit corridors of the Labyrinth of Thaumaturgy.

Mixed feelings greeted Bartholemew as he and Louella emerged from the cybrid settlement and saw the blue, silver and gold Ziggurat of Sciosophy.

For the last decade, he had become accustomed to the silks and satins with which the Technomancer had furnished the Ziggurat. At dawn, he would throw off the perfumed sheets, perform his toilet in the marble and gold bathroom, and then take a leisurely stroll to the kitchens, where the cybrid staff were preparing breakfast. After eating, he would inspect every room in the Ziggurat, before returning to the kitchens to supervise luncheon.

The afternoon would be his to fill – lately, he had spent the time with Louella and their daughter Cassandra – while the evenings would require more supervision in the kitchens, as the Technomancer's latest banquet pushed the chef's culinary skills to their limit. And then he would entertain Melaphyre and her entourage with bawdy stories and racy anecdotes while crossing verbal swords with Gargil, as they sat and drank wine, laughing and crying, heckling and bantering.

But a single meal of plain vegetable stew with his mother had shown the transparency of his life. A routine that had seemed so important, so vital, to the smooth running of the Ziggurat – of the Kingdom itself – had been exposed as an empty and decadent travesty that betrayed his birthright.

As he mounted the steps to the Ziggurat, he began to wonder whether the end of the Kingdom wasn't such a bad thing after all.

It made Melaphyre's skin crawl. Narrow, chilly corridors lined with books, gloomy yellow oil lamps – surely the Hierophant still possessed enough of her gifts to light the Labyrinth with fluoromancy? – and those dreadful twittering thaumaturgs, hiding in the shadows with their whispering voices.

Her dislike of the current Hierophant was hereditary. Since time began, all three rulers had coexisted in their animosity. But Melaphyre's spies and runners had painted a picture that she found both distressing and repugnant. The woman was eaten away with the emptiness of her life. She had never dared raise any of her thaumaturgs to humanity, preferring to hide alone in the darkness of the Labyrinth, and her instinctive dislike of both the Technomancer and the Archimage was reinforced with a jealousy and resentment that was overpowering.

'This is remarkable!' exclaimed the Doctor suddenly. 'These books are unaltered, unchanged.' He grabbed a volume from the shelves and waved it under her nose. 'This book is by Bertrand Russell. Have you heard of him?'

'Should I have? Some thaumaturg nonsense, no doubt.'

'No, Mel,' he insisted. 'This book was written by a philosopher on Earth in the twentieth century. Does that ring a bell? He was one of Mel's favourites.'

The Doctor's rantings were becoming an irritation, talking of this 'Earth' and this frightening creature, 'Mel'. 'Please, Doctor, cease these prattlings. We are here to meet with the Hierophant, not to indulge your fantasies.' She started to continue, and then stopped. 'And kindly desist from calling me Mel!'

He shrugged. 'Whatever you say. But can you grant me a favour in return?'

'Which is?' she asked in exasperation.

'Kindly desist from calling me "Dark One"!' he bellowed. 'It's hardly befitting my outfit is it?'

She tugged his jacket. 'Your outfit obviously has other ideas, Doctor.'

He frowned, and opened his mouth to protest. And then he looked down to where she was holding his lapel, and fell silent. But his eyes proclaimed his sheer horror.

The reds and oranges and yellows were dulled and darkened, and the patchwork was losing its definition. Even the cut was different. The lapels were much wider, and it hung behind him more as a cloak than a jacket.

'Is this some sort of camouflage, Doctor? Or are you summoning body armour to protect you from the Hierophant's bile?'

His voice was almost a whisper. 'As you said,

Melaphyre, seeing the Hierophant is more pressing than my sartorial elegance.' But the voice was shot through with a primal terror that disturbed her.

They carried on down the dim corridor in strained silence.

Saraquazel tried to scream, but his mind wouldn't connect with his mouth; in fact, he wasn't even sure that he still had a mouth. He wasn't even sure whether he was a he or not.

His emergence should have been a smooth transition between the half-life of imprisonment in the interstitial void, and the vitality of the universe-within-a-universe that he had instructed the Chapel entity to create for him.

Instead, he was wracked with exquisite agonies that seared every element of his being, as if he was constantly being torn apart then smashed together, particle by particle, wave form by wave form. He wasn't even sure where he was: any visual or physic input was scrambled and distorted well before his mind had a chance to interpret it. Saraquazel was deaf, dumb and blind. And quite probably mad, he decided in one of his brief moments of lucidity.

Along with everything else, his memories were fractured and fragmented, but the knowledge of his arrival in this alien dimension was strangely vivid, as if some part of his mind was clinging to the recollection in a vain attempt to remain sane. Clasping hold of the memory, he lived it yet again –

The journey was a routine one, the direct route through the underspace tunnel from his home world to the next star system. Gathering his energies, he launched himself through the rainbow atmosphere of his home world into the pink void of his native universe, sweeping past the green mists of orbiting plankton and narrowly avoiding a herd of mindless grazers, their eyeclusters turning in his direction through instinct.

Extending his senses, he was pleased at the lack of turbulence between his home and underspace tunnel which led to the location of his brood-siblings. He would probably arrive early, which would certainly surprise them! He wrapped his iridescent rudders around his tessellated mid-carapace and sped ever faster, past the triple helices of the void-drifters and the clicking, clacking constructs in which the function-breeders nested.

As he accelerated towards the purple entrance to the tunnel, he was faintly aware of a slight flicker to one side of his route. Dismissing it as a phenomenon of no consequence, he was concerned when he realized that he was being drawn towards it, slowly yet inexorably. And no amount of rudder-flexing or quantum-peristalsis would shake off its grip.

As it grew closer, Saraquazel felt his first stirrings of alarm bloom into sheer panic. The region of space that he was heading towards appeared to have been curdled, the regular structure of the continuum torn and frayed in twisted strands of pink and magenta.

And then he recognized it with a jolt of horror that shocked his neural filaments: a pan-dimensional vacuum emboitement, a hole in the fabric of reality that tore into underspace and beyond. Such things were known to Saraquazel's people, but were considered to be both rare, and – when they did occur – confined to the turbulent, jagged reaches of cosmic oblivion.

So when he was dragged into the maelstrom, Saraquazel hadn't the faintest idea how to escape its unbreakable pull. All he could do was scream for help, not even sure if his psychic powers could break free of the emboitement. And then his mind had cut out, unable to cope with the influx of incomprehensible images and feelings.

Consciousness had returned piecemeal, a jumble of confused impressions and garbled sensations that dripped into Saraquazel's waking mind. The first thing that he noticed was an inability to move, but any concerns that this might have caused were immediately overridden by the awareness that he no longer possessed a body. The journey through the emboitement had transformed his natural form — a comfortable flux of matter and energy that lapped backwards and forwards across all of the twenty-seven dimensions around him — into a rigid lattice of mental energy served by a paltry eleven. He was capable of a tortured awareness, but was unable to physically influence the world around him.

And then he began to interpret the images that assaulted him, images of the environment in which he was trapped, and was shocked by the greatest revelation yet. He was locked in a frozen moment of time, his awareness coming in fits and starts when the quantum-drifts permitted.

He was able to understand the problem in an instant: the physical laws of his native universe were totally incompatible with those of the dimension in which he was now stranded. And the new universe, unsure of what to do with him, had anchored him to a single moment of time, smearing probabilistic echoes of himself backwards and forwards through time until they died away in whispers. Indeed, he theorized that the only reason why he still possessed self-awareness was that an infinitesimal bubble of his own space-time was trapped there with him.

Panic overwhelmed him for meaningless aeons, his mind thrashing across his new timeline in desperation. But when he had calmed down, he realized that escape, although difficult, was possible.

While casting his consciousness over the ball of cold, solid matter that he was trapped above, he had sensed fragments of the higher science which his own people used to manipulate reality. The fragments were incomplete, corrupted almost to the point of uselessness; but with Saraquazel's great intellect, it would be possible to derive an equation which would recreate a limited region of his own physical laws. And then he could look for the way home.

To do this, however, would necessitate physical interaction with the cold sphere beneath him, and Saraquazel's telekinetic abilities were stunted in this reality. He needed another agency to assist him, one of the limited yet resourceful intelligences that swarmed over the planet. And his earlier panic had brought him into contact with the perfect vessel for his purposes: a being whose mind was, in some basic, instinctive way, sympathetic to Saraquazel's vast mentality.

Time meant nothing to Saraquazel, trapped as he was in a standing wave that bounced back and forth over a period of fifty years, as the Chapel-entity measured time. But the task of gathering the pieces of the equation would be a lengthy one for Chapel, so Saraquazel focused his awareness on the earliest point in Chapel's life that he could reach.

For twenty years he had urged and cajoled, directed and instructed, watching as Chapel collected the brief snatches of that higher science from every region of the planet. To assist Chapel, Saraquazel provided him with the means of creating obedient servants in the cybrids, although this was not without risk. The cybrids embodied the essence of this alien universe, and might pose a danger when the time came to use the equation. The last thing Saraquazel wanted was to damage the universe that was currently playing host to him.

Once he had initially contacted Chapel, Saraquazel was forced to follow Chapel's own timeline. Although it would have been easier to jump forward and check and recheck Chapel's progress, and then travel back along the standing wave to adjust and correct Chapel's actions, Saraquazel was well aware of the harm that this could inflict on this space-time continuum.

And so he had waited. Waited until Chapel had completed what he now called the Millennium Codex: a reference that Saraquazel understood to refer to his own temporal anchor point. In the hours that remained, Saraquazel prepared for his release; the moment that he was once more immersed in the laws and rules of his own universe, he would be able to locate the exit point of the emboitement, and return to his own cosmos, dragging the bubble of his own reality behind him.

But it had all gone horribly wrong. Rather than turn the cybrids back into their original forms, Chapel had simply released them. Saraquazel could probably have coped with that, but his attention was grabbed by the approach of something far more devastating.

While he had concerned himself with Chapel's incantation, he had overlooked a more minor one being put together in one of the node points that Saraquazel had created to limit the spread of his own reality any further than necessary. This incantation was considerably less powerful than the Codex, but it was performing a far simpler task. It was summoning an entity to Earth. An entity whose physical nature embodied yet another set of physical laws, Saraquazel realized incredulously.

The Codex, designed and written with irreverent speed, possessed none of the contingency measures that Saraquazel would have included, had he had the time. And it was woefully inadequate for the ensuing catastrophe.

Three totally incompatible universes clashed. With Saraquazel in the middle of the collision.

And now that particular memory was the only coherent part of his mind. He was still trapped, but everything else was different. And, more distastefully, another intelligence was occupying the same space as him. By an effort of concentration, Saraquazel was just able to make the briefest of mental contacts: the creature called itself Yog-Sothoth. And it was totally and utterly mad.

As am I, Saraquazel realized. As am I. And started his soundless screaming once again.

Anastasia gestured towards the two leather armchairs with a flick of her fingers. 'Please, make yourself comfortable,' she said, sitting at her table and feeling anything but comfortable. Never in her wildest fantasies had she ever imagined that she would be engaging in small talk with the Technomancer and the Dark One in the heart of her Labyrinth.

'If I've understood the situation correctly, Hierophant, I'm the reason for this unprecedented summit meeting,' said the Doctor, accepting a small glass of sherry from Cornelius. Anastasia dismissed her servant with a curt mental order before continuing.

'In a manner of speaking, yes,' she replied, sipping her own drink. 'Yesterday, I saw a vision –'

'As did I,' the Technomancer interrupted. 'I saw the Great Kingdom, but it wasn't the Great Kingdom. Everything and everyone was seen through a dark glass, including myself.'

'That's what I've been trying to tell you,' sighed the Doctor.

'Be quiet,' the Hierophant snapped. 'Were you able to learn much about this alternate version of yourself?' she asked the Technomancer.

'Only a name.' She glanced at the Doctor. 'Mel.'

'My powers are superior to yours, Melaphyre,' Anastasia stated without a trace of conceit. 'So I was able to see further. My alternate life was spent in the guise of Anne Travers. A familiar name, Doctor?'

'Only too familiar.'

'A fruitful woman who lived life to the full, I imagine,' she said wistfully.

'That's one way of putting it, I suppose.' He stood up and started examining the nearest bookshelf. 'Have you ever wondered who wrote these books? Have you ever wondered what most of them are about, come to that?'

With the fate of the Kingdom at stake, the Dark One was more interested in books! But her voice was calm as she continued. 'They date from the old times, before the formation of the Kingdom. It is said that the heresies that were committed by the savages almost brought the Gods to war, before the Gods' tears sealed the Kingdom from the barbarians and their unholy ways.'

She wasn't prepared for the Doctor's laughter. 'You find the situation amusing, Dark One?'

'Don't you?' he announced. 'This set-up is a preposterous farrago of half-baked myths and legends, hiding the truth behind an enormous conjuring trick! There is no Great Kingdom, can't you see that?' he implored.

Anastasia smiled at the Technomancer. 'I see that the stories of the Dark One's poisoned tongue were true, Melaphyre.'

'So how do you explain your visions, eh?' the Doctor protested.

'Fantasies, sent to unsettle the Kingdom prior to your arrival.' And yet she had seen this alter-ego, this Anne Travers.

'Oh, very neat and tidy. And just the sort of narrow-minded thinking I'd expect.' He walked up to her table and leant over it, his face only inches away from hers. 'This Great Kingdom is the result of a very dangerous experiment performed by a man called Ashley Chapel. At least, that's what he was called in the real universe – to you he's the Archimage. He unleashed a force which proceeded to distort his surroundings, although how it went so catastrophically awry is still a mystery to me.' He picked up Anastasia's favourite paperweight, an emerald green pyramid.

'Everything and everyone, apart from me, it seems, has been caught up in this, this reality warp.' He waved a hand in the air. 'Don't you see. This is all an illusion! A solid, three-dimensional illusion, I'll grant you, but an illusion all the same.'

Anastasia was about to deliver another scorching put-down, but then her memories of Anne Travers surfaced once more. 'This Anne Travers, was she aware of something called "The Great Intelligence"?'

'Oh yes,' the Doctor agreed. And then his eyes widened. 'Great Intelligence? Great Intelligence?' He slapped himself across the forehead. 'Of course, the answer was staring me in the face all the time, and I've been too blind to realize.' He slumped into the chair.

'Is this significant?' asked the Technomancer.

'Vitally!' he announced. 'The last time I saw Anne, she was preparing a block trans – a spell! – to banish the Great Intelligence from Earth. At the time, the full ramifications of her actions escaped me,' he raised an eyebrow at the Hierophant. 'It was a very short meeting. But the Intelligence wasn't on Earth; it wasn't even coming to Earth. And Anne's rudimentary knowledge of the power she was playing with was sadly limited. Instead of banishing the Intelligence, she must have summoned it. And when Chapel ran the Millennium Codex, the Intelligence was caught up in it.'

Anastasia stood up, her voice thoughtful. 'This Anne was convinced that she had made a heinous error and brought this Intelligence to the Great Kingdom –'

'No, Bibliotrix,' said the Doctor. 'She brought the Intelligence to Earth. And that was what formed the Great Kingdom.' He looked behind him at the door that led to the corridors of the Labyrinth. 'If I'm to stand any chance of setting this sorry situation right, I've got to disentangle the three sets of physical laws.' He suddenly stared at the Technomancer. 'What did you call your particular God?'

'The Lady Tardis,' she replied.

'And yours, Bibliotrix?'

The Dark One was testing her. But he would not find her wanting. 'Yog-Sothoth, the key and the guardian of the gate.'

'Exactly. That's the real name of the Great Intelligence.' He rubbed his chin. 'And somewhere in this Labyrinth is the means to banish Yog-Sothoth and get things back to normal.'

The meaning of his words took time to sink in, but when it did, Anastasia's course of action was clear.

The door to her inner sanctum was flung open, and two thaumaturgs entered. They grabbed the Doctor, pinioning his arms behind his back.

'What are you doing?' he cried.

'As Hierophant of the Great Kingdom, I am sworn to uphold the laws that bind us. What you are suggesting is deicide, Dark One, and there can be only one penalty for such an act.'

She nodded at the thaumaturgs.

'Kill him.'

Twelve

The Technomancer stepped back, her mind torn between helping the Doctor or allowing the Hierophant's state execution, an execution that the laws of the Kingdom demanded.

It wasn't a choice that she was forced to make. With a whoosh, the two thaumaturgs burst into flame; their grey skin shrivelled instantly, the bones igniting moments later in the cold, yellow flame. Within seconds, all that remained were two pools of grease on the dark carpet. Melaphyre was taken aback, but the oddest thing of all was the Doctor's reaction. He seemed even more surprised than Anastasia.

Her surprise didn't last long. Her voice a furious scream, she stabbed the Doctor with an outstretched finger. Blue sparks shot across his chest, forcing him to the floor. 'Do you think you can defeat all my thaumaturgs, Dark One?'

'No, Hierophant!' the Technomancer shouted, hurling a bolt of lightning at her rival and knocking her against a bookcase. Steadying herself, the Hierophant aimed a finger at the Technomancer –

'Ladies, please!' bellowed the Doctor, standing between them with a hand raised against each. 'This is not doing anybody any good, least of all me.' He looked at the oily stains on the carpet with a distant expression, before continuing. 'That was unforgivable,' he whispered. 'It seems that I've not been as unaffected by this transformation as I thought,' he admitted quietly. Melaphyre could see that the deaths of the thaumaturgs had affected him badly. 'But this situation cannot be allowed to continue. Anne – Anastasia, look deep inside yourself. You claimed that your superior powers gave you a glimpse at Anne Travers; look deeper, and see the truth of my words.'

His words were persuasive, Melaphyre had to admit. And their effect on the Hierophant was profound. She turned her back on the Doctor and leant on her table. For what seemed like an age, a brittle silence filled the oil-lit room. And then the Hierophant looked round.

'Perhaps you speak the truth, Doctor. You claim that the Great Kingdom is nothing more than a living myth, perpetuated by the false beliefs of myself, the Majestrix here, and Magnus Ashmael. I remain . . . uncertain.' She nodded over his shoulder. 'You also claim that the Labyrinth contains the accumulated knowledge of this other kingdom you call Earth. Use it wisely, Doctor.' With that, she fell back against her desk, all her strength drained from her.

The Technomancer moved over to her and did the unthinkable. She flung her arms around her and hugged the woman that the Laws of the Kingdom – artificial laws designed to support an artificial existence, according to the Doctor – decreed was her bitter enemy. And, like the Hierophant, she too started to cry.

Behind them, the Doctor put his hands on his hips and smiled, completely unaware that his jacket and trousers were now a uniform dark grey. Almost black, in fact.

'She's fine,' said Louella, coming out of Cassandra's bedroom into the chamber that she and Bartholemew shared. Her daughter had been asleep in her little bed, her cherubic face nestling against the satin pillow. Everything was perfectly normal, just as it had been before they had left that afternoon. So why did Louella feel that everything about her daughter was terribly, terribly wrong?

Bartholemew was staring out of the window at the night-time view of the Kingdom. The sky was deep blue, the blue-black of the cybrids, constantly on fire with the energy discharges from the Wall of Tears, but his eyes were drawn to the gilded Tower of Abraxas, its roof ablaze like a furnace. Louella came up behind him and wrapped her arms around his waist.

'Beautiful, isn't it?' she whispered in his ear.

'Beautiful?' he sneered. 'It's evil; soulless and evil, that's what it is. Our daughter's lying in there, suffering with her withered limbs –'

'Barry!' she screamed. 'Why are you saying things like that?'

He slipped from her arms and frowned at her. 'Why did you call me "Barry"?'

'I, I don't know,' she murmured. 'But what you said about Cassie, I mean Cassandra –' A look of terror crossed her face. 'What's happening? Where are these words coming from?' It was as if she was seeing somebody else's memories, overlaid upon her own.

Bartholemew pointed out of the window, towards the faintly visible plains of the Labyrinth. 'Get Cassie. We're going out for the night.'

Louella hardly noticed the strangeness of her partner's words. 'The Labyrinth?'

He nodded. 'At best, Melaphyre will know what's going on. At the very worst, it'll be more evidence for her claims that the Kingdom is coming to an end.' He sighed. 'Unless you fancy waiting here for the end of the world?'

She shivered. 'You're right. I'll get Cassandra ready.'

As she re-entered the bedroom, Bartholemew's comment about their daughter's withered limbs echoed in her ears. Louella gently lifted her from the bed. Her beautiful, perfectly formed daughter. So why did Bartholemew's words ring true?

The Archimage caught his reflection in the coloured glass of the Tabernacle, and was momentarily taken aback by how tarnished his armour appeared. Nothing that a good polish wouldn't sort out, he decided, before heading back towards the inner chamber of the palace.

Since his fateful encounter with Harklaane, the Archimage's understanding of what he had seen earlier had grown. Along with Harklaane's strength, he seemed to have absorbed an instinct that he never knew his warlord possessed. And that instinct had driven him back to the Tabernacle.

Without a trace of the apprehension that he had originally felt, the Archimage strode into the chamber with the arrogance and confidence of a conquering hero. Nothing had changed. The Lady Tardis sat silently upon her jade and sapphire plinth, while the fusion of Saraquazel and Yog-Sothoth still writhed on its golden throne.

Stepping up to the throne, the Archimage inclined his head to hear the whispered mutterings. For ten minutes, he stood immobile, listening and interpreting. And then he took a step backwards. Power was flowing into him, enormous power that belittled the influx from Harklaane.

The Archimage was drinking from the fountain of the Gods, Saraquazel's majesty washing over and into him in a torrent of irresistible might. Was this the Archimage's doing, or was Harklaane reaching out from beyond the grave? Somehow, he was drawing the power of Saraquazel into himself. Why?

He staggered as the infinite and eternal glory of Saraquazel fulfilled every cell of his being. Who cared who was responsible?

'What precisely are we looking for?' asked the Technomancer, trying not to breathe too deeply. The musty smell of ancient books was overpowering, and so unlike the clean, fresh air of her beloved Ziggurat.

The Doctor peered over the top of the green-bound book he was reading as he climbed down the steps of the sliding ladder. 'When I was last here – or rather, the other-dimensional analogue of here – Anne was poring over a collection of esoteric volumes relating to the banishment of the Great Intelligence.'

'Can you map the layout of the Labyrinth onto the Library of Saint John the Beheaded, Doctor? Topologically, I mean,' she asked, examining one of the bookcases. If a one-to-one mapping existed, it would make their search considerably simpler.

'Probably. I haven't,' he paused, staring at her.

'What's wrong?' she asked.

He raised an eyebrow. 'Quite a number of things, actually. But two of them come immediately to mind. Firstly, your manner of speech is becoming less formal. And secondly, well, I never told you that the analogue of this place was called the Library of Saint John the Beheaded.'

Melaphyre began to feel nervous. The Doctor was right, but she had no idea why. 'Can you explain it?'

He shrugged. 'Not yet, no. But I could hazard a guess,' he said enigmatically, opening the books and then resting them on the desk in a series of upright V's.

'Come on, Doc, spill the beans!' she exclaimed. And then it registered. 'Did I say that?' The words had seemed so natural, so her, and yet so wrong for Melaphyre to utter them.

The Doctor was placing some more books horizontally on top of the others. He looked up at her and grinned. 'Yet another symptom, I'm afraid. This reality is fundamentally unstable, and the persona of your other self – Melanie Bush – is bleeding into this pocket universe.'

She returned his grin. 'She must have been a good friend of yours, Doctor, for you to risk so much to get her back.'

He started another line of upturned books on top of the first. 'There's a lot more at stake than just Mel, but, yes, she does mean a lot to me. We've been together for a considerable time, and, despite her constant lambasting, I'm very fond of her.'

'I'm glad. She sounds like me – a me without the

constant weight of responsibility on her shoulders.' She shrugged those shoulders. 'But I'm not real, so what does it matter?'

At that, the Doctor jumped up from the table and placed his hands on her shoulders. 'Melaphyre, you must believe me when I tell you that I wish there was another way. But you, and Anastasia – even the Archimage, who's responsible for all of this – have other lives, and this is nothing more than an elaborate fiction, written using techniques that have no place in any universe.' He sat down again and continued, his tone softer. 'How long have you known your Chancellor and major-domo?'

That was an odd question. Then again, these were odd times. 'I've known Louella and Bartholemew since they were 'bridlings. We played together on the banks of the Great River.' She frowned. 'What are you implying, Doctor?'

'I just wanted to point out that Louise Mason and Barry Brown worked for Ashley Chapel – the man you know as the Archimage. Mel only met them a day ago.'

She knotted her brows. 'And yet I have my memories; rich and varied. Truly an incantation worthy of the Gods, Doctor.' And then something occurred to her. 'What about their daughter? Does Cassandra exist in your version of events?'

He nodded. 'Sadly, she was a victim of the chemical pollution which covers the analogue of the Great Kingdom. Her body is atrophied, and her life will always be difficult.'

Melaphyre closed her eyes. 'Then there is an injustice, Doctor. In this world, the child is an angel in both body and soul.'

He sighed. And then sat bolt upright, his expression earnest. 'We're trying to put things right, Melaphyre,' he said urgently. 'Meanwhile, the Kingdom is being flooded by images from the real world.'

'But if the original reality is already filtering through, why can we not wait for it to happen naturally?'

He shook his head, and placed one last book on the top of his tower. 'I can't guarantee that the cards will fall in the correct order, Melaphyre.' As he spoke, the precisely balanced construction toppled, and the books crashed onto the polished wood of the desk. He shrugged. 'Or the books, come to that. This entire reality may very well become an even worse nightmare, and I can't stand by and let that happen.'

'This way,' whispered Bartholemew, nodding towards the gap between two of the golden dwellings with their pointed roofs. They had been lucky so far: the auriks were asleep, and their journey had been uninterrupted. But he doubted that their luck would hold out much longer. They were only half-way through the settlement, and it was inevitable that Cassie would soon wake up.

'This is wrong, isn't it?' said Louella, cradling Cassie in her arms.

He shrugged. 'You think it is, I think it is. And Melaphyre obviously thinks it is. Why else did she vanish off with the Dark One?'

'But this other reality . . .' She stroked her daughter's blonde hair. 'Cassie isn't, she isn't right, is she? In this other universe, I mean.'

Bartholemew darted between the gap, gesturing for Louella to follow him. Once she had caught up, he put his hand on her shoulder. 'No, I don't think she is.'

Louella looked down at her daughter, and imagined her as the spavined creature that she and Bartholemew had seen in their fleeting visions. And then she started to cry, racking sobs that drew him over to her in a familial hug.

'It won't come to that, Lou,' he whispered insistently. 'I'll make sure that Cassie is okay, I promise you. We'll find the Technomancer –'

'The Technomancer?' she yelled. 'The Technomancer? For the Gods' sake, Barry, she's as much of a fake as we are. What can she do to help?'

He closed his eyes and shook his head. 'I'll even ask the Dark One for help –' He stopped when he sensed that they weren't alone. Three auriks were standing no more than ten feet away, their ridged horns glinting in the electric bursts from the Wall of Gods' Tears. Bartholemew gulped. They didn't stand a chance.

The Archimage looked down, kicking away some of the grey dust to reveal the sparkling slate roof of the Labyrinth. Had it been normal stone, nothing more trying than a simple hex would have been required to create a hole in it, but the Archimage knew very well that it was almost certainly reinforced by the Hierophant's considerable powers. And to overcome her mystic wards by the brute force of his magicks would alert her without doubt. No, his entrance to the Labyrinth demanded stealth and cunning, and, thanks to Harklaane, he now possessed those attributes in abundance. As well as a measure of the might of the Gods.

His arrival in the region of Thaumaturgy had been cloaked by wards no less powerful than those protecting the Labyrinth, rendering him undetectable to the dormant thaumaturgs that dwelt underground. With the merest effort, he suddenly weakened his defences, making himself known to any of the creatures that lurked nearby. Not that they would realize that the Archimage of Abraxas was there; they would only suspect an unwelcome presence, too insignificant to bother the Hierophant about.

He didn't have long to wait. Within minutes, a lone thaumaturg rose from the dust, its hand resting on a spiked mace attached to a belt around its waist. One of the Hierophant's personal guard, decided the Archimage, not moving from his position.

The thaumaturg was clearly suspicious: its movements were slow and calculated as it approached. The Archimage remained still, enticing it closer and closer with the subtlest of mental urges.

And then he effortlessly infiltrated the creature's mind, overlaying its thoughts with his own. The takeover was so smooth, so practised, that the thaumaturg didn't even realize that its actions were no longer its own. And if that were the case, then neither did the Hierophant.

The thaumaturg's mind was simple in comparison to the Archimage's, but he was careful not to rush his explorations. The Hierophant was a wily old bird, and it would be just like her to rig her creatures with psychic tripwires in case such a takeover were ever attempted. He probed with a lover's touch, stroking the thought processes and caressing the memories, until he located the images he was seeking; the images that represented the simple yet secret incantation which would open the Labyrinth to him.

Moments later, the Archimage descended the dark stairs into the Hierophant's warren. He didn't give the smoking husk of the thaumaturg a backwards glance.

'Would this be of any use?'

Both the Doctor and the Technomancer looked round with a start. Anastasia was standing next to the curtained doorway, pulling at a heavy silk sheet that was draped over a table in the corner. The Doctor wasn't sure what surprised him most: the fact that she was offering to help them; or the serene majesty that she radiated, in total contrast to the anger and bitterness that she had previously wrapped around herself. And then he recognized the artifact that she had revealed. Despite its wooden exterior, the keyboard and monitor identified it as some sort of computer terminal.

'Fascinating!' exclaimed Melaphyre, hurrying over to it and sitting down. 'Where did it come from?'

'Come from?' The Hierophant laughed. 'It didn't come from anywhere, Melaphyre. The computer system has been here since the creation of the Great Kingdom.'

'Oh, very convenient,' muttered the Doctor. 'The haphazard logic that holds this pantechnicon of cozenage together would try the patience of a saint.' He started to smile, but a wave a dizziness overcame him. Unseen by either of the women, he supported himself against the nearest bookshelf, hoping that the effect would soon pass.

It didn't. The room started to spin around him, accompanied by waves of nausea, nausea with a smiling face and engulfing black wings.

'Doctor, look at this!' Melaphyre's shrill voice brought him to his senses, but he still felt odd; detached, distant, as if his body were nothing more than an ill-fitting space suit with him inside it. Shoving this worrying allusion to one side, he obeyed Melaphyre's irritating summons and walked over to her. But he still needed the desk to provide surreptitious support.

'This system indexes the entire Labyrinth!' she gushed, her fingers moving from keyboard to mouse and back in a dazzling blur. Although that could be an after-effect of his earlier malaise, the Doctor ruefully admitted to himself. 'And the index itself is a relational database with over thirty dimensions!'

Melaphyre's enthusiasm was sickening, but she was evidently skilled in the use of such technology. Not surprising, he decided, given the nature of her original template. 'The information we need is, is . . .' He lurched against the desk.

'Are you all right, Doctor?' asked the Hierophant, coming to his aid. He waved her away, shocked by how dark his sleeve appeared in the gloomy light that the desiccated Hierophant favoured.

'I'll be fine if you just leave me alone,' he snapped. 'No wonder the three great rulers don't talk to one another. You'd be climbing up the walls after five minutes of what passes for meaningful discussion around here.'

Melaphyre looked up from the computer. 'Doctor? What's wrong? Why are you being so, so horrid?'

'Horrid?' he repeated. 'Horrid? Horrid? Now I know you're Mel. Insipid words from an insipid person. Now move aside and let a real genius have a look.' With a violent push, he knocked her chair aside, throwing the Technomancer to the floor.

'Now, if this database is designed along the Darwen model –' He navigated through the thirty-dimensional web of the database at breakneck speed, ignoring the Technomancer who was now standing behind him, her anger tangible. And there it was, the book that he needed. Only a couple of shelves away, according to its database record.

'How dare you!' screamed the Technomancer. 'I am –'

'Yes, yes, yes,' he muttered, rising from the computer. 'Your empty posturing is beginning to bore me.' With that, he walked briskly into the dark recesses of the annex.

Melaphyre turned to the Hierophant. 'What's got into him?'

Anastasia shook her head. 'Whatever it is, it justifies the name "Dark One".' She pointed at the computer. 'From my vision, I have a vague idea as to the books that Anne Travers had concerned herself with. Can you locate a book from a fragment of its name?'

Melaphyre cracked her knuckles and leant over the keyboard. 'Just you watch me,' she said proudly.

The corridors of the Labyrinth were exactly as the Archimage had imagined them to be: narrow and dark, their antiquity hanging in the air like an invisible, yet cloying, fog. The only light came from the meagre oil-lamps affixed to the walls, a sepia tint that glinted off the worn leather and gold leaf of the books that were shelved on either side.

The whole place was dead, he decided. Dead and decaying. It just didn't realize it yet. When he seized the total power of the Gods, he would take immense pleasure in seeing the entire Labyrinth burn, a funeral pyre to the Hierophant and her incessant complaints about her lot in life. That particular bonfire would give her something to moan about.

He stopped as he reached a red velvet drape. If his senses were correct, the prize that he sought lay just beyond, in one of the innumerable annexes dotted about the Labyrinth. He took a deep breath and centred himself. Despite his new-found strength, he would need his wits about him if he was to withstand an all-out assault from both the Hierophant and the Technomancer. Despite his disdain for both of them, they were formidable adversaries; and to attack them here, in the Hierophant's own domain, would have been unthinkable until hours ago.

But that was before the secrets of the Gods were revealed to him. The fusion of Saraquazel and Yog-Sothoth had imparted some of its dark wisdom in his soul, and now he was invulnerable.

With that reassuring thought, he pulled the drape open, and smiled at the shocked expressions on the women's faces.

'Good evening, Majestrix, good evening, Bibliotrix,' he said politely. As he expected, they reacted swiftly. The Technomancer flung a bolt of concussive force at him, while the Hierophant attacked with her usual insidiousness, her mind trying to seize control with all the subtlety of a charging aurik.

With the faintest of efforts, he deflected the force bolt; the crackling sphere went wide, breaking an oil lamp and releasing its contents. Burning oil dripped down onto the bookcase below; within seconds, it was on fire, the flames threatening to make the short jump to the drapes. The Archimage quickly generated a razor-sharp mantric spear, and hurled it at the Technomancer. With a gasp, she toppled backwards into the desk and slid onto the floor.

As for the Hierophant; he allowed her mental talons to grip his mind, and then sent a surge of hatred through them. Screaming, she fell to the floor, her face in her hands, but she was unharmed. Which was showing her far more mercy than she deserved.

'Very, very foolish,' he announced, waving away the

smoke from the burning bookcase. It would only take a minor incantation to extinguish it, but his earlier thoughts of a funeral pyre persuaded him to let it burn. 'I won't detain you. I'll take what I want and then leave.'

'I won't let you steal a single book from the Labyrinth,' hissed the Hierophant. 'You'll have to kill me first.'

'Nothing would give me greater pleasure, Anastasia, but I don't want any of your dull and dreary books.' He pursed his lips. 'I've come for a much greater prize.' He looked over her shoulder, caused her to glance behind. She gasped.

Standing in the shadows, the Doctor's face was cruel and hate-filled, a vicious light shining in his eyes. His once brilliant jacket was now a jet-black robe that reached down to the floor, with a huge, silver-trimmed black collar which covered his shoulders.

'He Whose Name Dare Not Be Mentioned,' whispered the Technomancer, obviously recognizing the clothing from the secret myths of the Kingdom.

The Archimage threw back his head and laughed. 'My dear Melaphyre, there is nothing I wouldn't dare.' He held out his hand in greeting, and the Doctor stepped forward.

'An unexpected pleasure, Magnus Ashmael,' he said, taking the open hand in a firm grasp.

'The time has come to brazen the wrath of the Gods,' pronounced the Archimage, 'and to laugh in the face of the ancient strictures. Welcome to my side, Valeyard.'

Thirteen

Melaphyre tried to stand, but a single glance from the Dark One — she could no longer think of the black-robed man with his malevolent expression as the Doctor — froze every muscle in her body. Immobile, she could only watch as the Archimage committed the ultimate heresy. He had uttered the forbidden name.

'Your arrival is most timely,' the Dark One told the Archimage. 'Indeed, I doubt that I could have stood much more of these prattling women.'

The Archimage smiled, and glanced at the inferno that was raging next to them, its effects held at bay by a sparkling barrier of protection. 'Our departure is also timely, Valeyard. Let us leave Melaphyre and Anastasia to the flames. An apt fate for a brace of witches, don't you think?'

They strode from the annexe in a flurry of gold and black cloaks. Melaphyre was immediately released from her paralysis, and leapt to her feet.

'The fire!' screamed the Hierophant, panic in her voice. 'My powers are still depleted from the Archimage's attack —'

'Calm yourself.' The Technomancer held her hands out in front of her, and muttered a brief incantation. The wall of flame froze, and then evaporated like a spent cloud. Melaphyre sighed. 'I'm sorry about the damage; molecular regeneration isn't one of my fortes.'

The Hierophant used the desk to lever herself to her feet. 'The damage is irrelevant. A few scorched books mean little if the Great Kingdom is in danger. And what we have just seen in this annexe did nothing to reassure me.'

The Technomancer nodded. Until the Doctor's terrifying transformation, she simply didn't believe that he was the Dark One of the prophecies, but now . . . The costume had been exactly as described in the eldritch texts, and hadn't he answered to the darkest of dark names, that of Valeyard? Given that evidence, there was no reason to doubt that he also possessed the power to topple the Kingdom and bring chaos down on them all. She began to wonder whether she should ever have trusted him in the first place.

'There was something else –' The Hierophant broke off and frowned. 'Did you notice anything odd about Ashmael?'

'No –' And then Melaphyre realized that there had been something not quite right about him. 'His garments were darker, more warlike in their cut, and his attitude was more belligerent than my cybrid spies have indicated.'

The Hierophant nodded. 'And there's more. I am attuned to every aspect of the Labyrinth and the thaumaturg settlements. But I didn't detect the Archimage's arrival until he entered the annexe.'

The Technomancer shrugged. 'He is a ruler of the Great Kingdom –'

'As are you, Melaphyre,' she interrupted, 'but every step of your journey here was observed by my thaumaturgs.' She closed her eyes, and the Technomancer could feel the psychic communication spreading throughout and beyond the Labyrinth. And then a swirl of astral energy materialized in the centre of the annexe, a whirling vortex of greens and golds.

'What are you doing?'

'Ashmael attacked and murdered one of my thaumaturgs. I want to know what happened to it.' Even as she spoke, the energy resolved into the spindly figure of a thaumaturg, translucent but stable.

Melaphyre was amazed. Although she knew that it was possible to reach beyond the veil of death, she had thought that such knowledge had been lost after the last war of the Gods. In spite of her resentment towards the Hierophant, she was impressed by the older woman's abilities. If she could conquer death, what else was she capable of? For the first time since the arrival of the thaumaturg emissary, she felt a glimmer of hope. She suddenly realized that the Hierophant was addressing the spirit.

'What transpired, shade?'

'The Archimage was shielded by wards of great power, Bibliotrix,' it explained in a tremulous voice. 'He passed through the settlement without alerting anyone. Only when he reached the roof of the Labyrinth did he allow himself to be detected. I prepared to attack him, but he –' It fell silent, an expression of shame on its puckered, grey face.

'Continue!' commanded the Hierophant.

'Then the Archimage possessed me, Bibliotrix! He reached into my mind, and forced me to unlock the mystic wards that guard you!' The creature was positively babbling.

The Hierophant raised an eyebrow. 'Such abilities are unheard of. The Archimage should be incapable of controlling a thaumaturg, just as I cannot ensorcell one of his auriks. Unless –' She dismissed the ghostly image with a wave of her hand, and watched as its translucent form faded into nothing.

'How has he gained such powers?' asked the Technomancer urgently. 'How has he done this?'

The Hierophant sighed. 'Such things are possible, but never spoken of.' She walked over to the burnt bookcase and ran a finger through the charred remains. 'The Magnus Ashmael, Archimage of Abraxas, has stolen a fraction of the power of the Gods. And by doing that, he is a greater threat to the Kingdom than the Dark One ever was.'

* * *

Once again shielded by unbreachable wards, the Archimage strode through the darkness of the thaumaturg settlement, the Valeyard at his side. Although the settlement was bustling with the nocturnal activities of the thaumaturgs, their passage went unnoticed.

'Such power, Ashmael,' commented the Valeyard. 'I begin to wonder why you need me.'

'I was already mighty, Valeyard –' the vicarious thrill he received just saying the forbidden name was intoxicating – 'but with you by my side, I shall be omnipotent.'

The Valeyard stopped and looked at him, an unfathomable look in his eyes. 'Omnipotence is a relative term, Ashmael. How great is your ambition? Will you settle for control of the Great Kingdom? Or do you desire the enslavement of the Gods themselves? Or –' His voice lowered. 'Or do you thirst for the world beyond the Wall of Tears, the universe that can be yours if you grasp the wider picture?'

The Archimage allowed the Valeyard's words to sink in. Until now, he had not thought beyond control of the Kingdom. But the universe beyond the electric blue barrier, the universe that the Gods had denied them so long ago. He narrowed his eyes. 'Such power, you could help me in this?'

'Oh yes,' said the Valeyard seductively. 'Yours is the power, but mine is the vision.' He reached into his cloak and withdrew a thin black book. 'Since the foundation of the Kingdom, the Hierophant has always had the potential to be the greatest of the three rulers. The Labyrinth contains the sum total of the knowledge of the Gods, scattered throughout the bookshelves. Only the blinkered minds of the Hierophant and her ancestors have prevented them from seizing total control of the Kingdom.'

'Then we should return to the Labyrinth,' the Archimage said urgently. 'Even together, the Hierophant and the Technomancer are no match for our combined might. We can wrest the power of the Gods from under their very noses.'

'No, no, no, Ashmael,' the Valeyard chided. 'Now is not the time for knee-jerk demonstrations of brute force.'

'But you saw how easily she fell —'

The Valeyard held a hand up to silence him. 'She was unprepared. She has since had time to garner her defenses, and I doubt that a rematch would have the same result, especially with that vixen Melaphyre at her side. No, our course must be more subtle, more, insidious.' He waved the book in the Archimage's face. 'This book contains the Black Scrolls of Cardinal Leofrique DeSable, a powerful sorcerer from the universe beyond the Wall.'

The Archimage was puzzled. 'But the Gods say that magic does not exist beyond the Wall.'

'Another of their lies. Throughout the centuries, there have been a few mortals who have recognized the dark science, and DeSable was one of them. He spent his life collecting multifarious incantations and words of power, and, despite the fact that he understood nothing of the ancient language and knew even less about its correct use, he succeeded in compiling this single volume.'

The Archimage snorted with derision. 'One little pamphlet, compared with the corridors of books in the Labyrinth —'

'If you would cease your constant interruptions, I'll explain!' bellowed the Valeyard. 'This one book is more powerful than the rest of the Hierophant's library put together. With this "little pamphlet", Ashmael, we can breach the Wall of Tears, and be the first to gaze on the outer world since the formation of the Kingdom.'

The Archimage smiled broadly at the image. 'To breach the Wall of Tears; and this book of DeSable's is all we need?'

It was the Valeyard's turn to smile. 'Not exactly, no. But I'll explain in greater detail after we have reached the Tower.' He wrapped his ebony cloak around him. 'This cool night air might be agreeable to the thaumaturgs, but I find it most unpleasant.' He gestured towards the misty wall that separated the thaumaturg settlement from that of the auriks. 'Shall we go?'

'I hated you.' The words were clear and crisp in the still air of the staircase that descended into the depths of the Labyrinth. 'Ever since I was old enough to reason, I hated you from the depths of my soul.'

'And now?'

Melaphyre shrugged. 'I was wrong. I was told by my mother that you and the entire dynasty of Hierophants were responsible for the evil that beset the Kingdom. That you would bring the Dark One amongst us and rain destruction upon us all.'

The Hierophant chuckled coldly. 'And have I not done that? According to the Doctor, this entire illusion – the Great Kingdom – has resulted from Anne Travers's interference. And who am I but Anne Travers under another guise?'

Melaphyre stopped and placed a comforting hand on her shoulder. 'No, Anastasia, you are not. You are the Hierophant of the Great Kingdom, and you are no more Anne Travers than I am the Doctor's friend Mel. Whatever magicks were used to create the Kingdom were far beyond our comprehension, let alone our abilities. All we can do now is ally our forces, and try to bring the Doctor back to us.'

The Hierophant smiled. 'You are a good woman, Melaphyre. And if it has taken the threat of total annihilation for me to recognize that, then I am glad.'

The Technomancer returned the smile, just as warmly. 'So am I, Anastasia, so am I. And if the Doctor's soothsaying is proved wrong, and the Kingdom survives, it will be a new era of co-operation between our two houses.'

'Then let us start that co-operation now,' said the Hierophant. 'How easy would it be . . .'

They walked down the staircase, deep in discussion.

Bartholemew looked up as the giant crystal doors of

the Tower swung open, allowing two figures to enter. Unbelievably, the auriks hadn't killed them; he, Louella and Cassandra had been escorted back to the vestibule of the Tower of Abraxas. And, for the last hour, they had been waiting for some unspecified fate and guarded by two auriks. It just didn't make sense. And then he realized that he recognized who was coming through the doors.

One was obvious. The Archimage in all his golden glory, although Bartholemew would have sworn that his armour was duller than normal. As for the other . . .

The outfit was totally different, but horrifyingly familiar – the legendary garb of the Dark One – and the arrogant good humour of the face was twisted into a cruel sneer. It was the Doctor, obviously embracing his dark heritage with a vengeance.

The Archimage waved a gauntleted hand around the vestibule. 'Welcome to Abraxas, Valeyard!' he announced, and Bartholemew and Louella shot horrified looks at one another: the Archimage was hurling around the forbidden name as if it meant nothing.

'Who are the two humans?' asked the Dark One, approaching them with measured strides. 'Ah, yes, Melaphyre's elevated cybrids and their bastard whelp.' He looked round. 'What is their purpose here, Ashmael?'

The Archimage nodded at the aurik guards, and even Bartholemew felt the intensity of the telepathic command. Immediately, the horned creatures grabbed them.

'They were roaming the aurik settlement. Since they are the Technomancer's closest confidantes, I wondered whether they might be useful.'

He raised an eyebrow at the Dark One, who withdrew a small black book from his robes and leafed through the contents, before looking up with a malicious grin. 'Oh yes, Ashmael. I can definitely find a use for one of them.' And then he stared at Cassie.

Bartholemew shuddered.

* * *

'What you propose, is, of course, heresy,' said the Technomancer wearily.

'Of course,' laughed the Hierophant. 'But when the old truths crumble to dust, heresy is often the only thing left.' She strained at a heavy grey volume, easing it from the shelves of the endless corridor that they had arrived in. 'And this is probably the greatest heresy contained within the Labyrinth.' She handed the book to Melaphyre, who read the faded gold lettering from the cover.

' "The Architecture of Pelli." An odd title.' But also an oddly familiar one, she realized.

'Indeed. But the knowledge of this book has been passed down from Hierophant to Hierophant since the foundation of the Kingdom.' She retrieved the book and opened it. 'It details the nature and the structure of the Tower of Abraxas, Melaphyre. And will tell us the best way to lay siege to it with our combined army of thaumaturgs and cybrids.'

'Ah,' the Technomancer sighed, understanding why the Hierophant had asked her whether her cybrid troops could fight alongside thaumaturgs. 'I take it we storm the Tower and rescue the Doctor?'

The Hierophant shook her head violently. 'Oh no, Majestrix. We storm the Tower and execute the Dark One. That is the only way.'

'Your throne room does you justice, Ashmael,' muttered the Valeyard, running his fingers over the golden window ledge. In truth, he found the man's obsession with gold irritating, to say the least. 'But we are not here to exchange pleasantries. We are here to breach the Wall of Tears.' He watched the horrified reaction of the cybrid-things in the corner of the room with satisfaction. 'Tell me more of what you saw in the Tabernacle.'

The Archimage mounted his throne. 'A nightmare, Valeyard. The Goddess in Absence, the Lady Tardis, was on her plinth, while the forms of Saraquazel and Yog-Sothoth were joined in an unholy alliance.'

The Valeyard rubbed his chin in contemplation. 'The quantum mnemonic and that hag Travers' block transfer computation must have interacted, merging the two creatures in the process.' His eyes glinted. 'Very, very unpleasant.'

He walked over to the window. 'And I suppose you should know this as well. The superstrings which support the pocket of reality that comprises the Great Kingdom are unravelling. I can feel it. This pocket dimension is fundamentally unstable.' He held up his hands. 'And before you bombard me with yet another question, Ashmael, I will explain it in words of less than one syllable: if the unravelling is not stopped, the Great Kingdom will dissolve into tiny, tiny particles that will be blown away on the time winds like so much flotsam.' He raised a finger. 'The effects of the unravelling are already making themselves felt. Both Melaphyre and Anastasia remember shards of their other lives.'

'Can your magicks prevent this destruction?'

The Valeyard nodded. 'Yes, they can. In fact, it is a necessity. If I were to breach the Wall of Tears without stabilizing the space-time continuum, it would endanger the entire universe. And I doubt that all the power of the Gods could contain that.' He withdrew the book from his cloak once more and held it up.

'Within this, DeSable has recounted both the incantations which will halt the unravelling, and those which will open a door in the Wall. All that is needed is the life-force of an innocent human to catalyse the release of the Gods' own power.'

The Archimage stood from his throne. 'But that is impossible, Valeyard. The only humans in the Kingdom are the members of the three ruling families, and those creatures that we have elevated.' He nodded at Bartholemew and Louella. 'But it is written that none of us is innocent, for we all share the blame for the evil that was the original sin.'

The Valeyard went over to the elevated cybrids and

snatched the child from Louella's arms, holding Cassandra up in triumph. 'But this infant is innocent, Archimage. Born of elevated cybrids, she is both truly human and truly innocent – the only such being in the Kingdom. And her sacrifice will provide the means of accomplishing our goal.'

Bartholemew leapt forward and tried to wrest Cassandra from his hands. The Valeyard knocked him unconscious with a single thought, and then smiled. 'Have you a table and a knife, Archimage?'

Melaphyre looked up from the book. Once she had deciphered the odd language, she had begun the search for a weak spot in the strength of Abraxas; and that had proved to be simplicity itself. She pointed a finger at a line-drawing of the building. 'This side entrance to the Tower offers us the best chance, Anastasia.'

'But what of the Archimage's auriks, Melaphyre?' she countered. 'They will be ever vigilant.' But the question was asked with a playful mischief.

'Why do I get the feeling that you have the answer to that one?' said the Technomancer with a chuckle.

'Indeed I have,' replied the Hierophant, holding up a tiny blue book. 'With this – and our powers combined – we can erect wards over our army, shielding it from observation so that we can approach the Tower without detection. Have you summoned your cybrids?'

The Technomancer nodded. 'They are already massing on the Plains of Despair. But I still insist that we try to save the Doctor, rather than kill him.'

'I have considered your proposal, Melaphyre,' said the Hierophant. 'And I have discovered an incantation that might, possibly, bring the Doctor's personality back to the surface.'

'That's wonderful!' she exclaimed.

'But –' The Hierophant's voice was stern. 'The moment that I suspect that he is beyond redemption, I will kill him myself. Is that understood?'

Melaphyre nodded. 'Let's get on with it, then.'

The Hierophant gestured towards the stairs. 'My thaumaturgs await, Majestrix. Shall we go?' They ascended the book-lined staircase with urgent steps, rapidly reaching the final flight of silvered slate. With a muttered incantation the Hierophant opened the Labyrinth to the ghostly dawn light, and walked out onto the surface.

The combined might of the thaumaturg and cybrid armies had never before been seen under the azure sky of the Great Kingdom. The cybrids were all dressed in simpler versions of the Technomancer's blue armour, while the thaumaturgs wore heavy silver chain-mail, secured at the waist with dark grey belts.

'A glorious sight,' muttered the Hierophant. She was also armoured; a delicate chain-mail tunic, and a skirt composed of strips of heavy silver. She was leaning on a dark steel staff.

'Truly a miracle,' agreed the Technomancer. They had reached a high promontory that overlooked the plains of the thaumaturg settlement, a point which offered a perfect view of the armies.

'Ready?' asked the Hierophant.

'Try and stop me!' the Technomancer squealed, before giggling nervously. 'A bit of Mel slipping through, no doubt.'

The Hierophant smiled, and raised her staff. 'Advance!' she commanded, watching as the thaumaturgs marched forward. Simultaneously, the Technomancer held up her hand and reached out mentally to her cybrids, urging them to march in step with their silver colleagues.

Melaphyre was close enough to Hierophant to hear her murmured prayer. 'And may the Gods have mercy on all our souls.'

Bartholemew woke up to find himself propped up against a wall of the Archimage's throne room, his head throbbing. Slowly and painfully, Louella's face resolved out of the blur. And then he corrected himself. She wasn't Louella – Louella was part of another world. The woman leaning over him was Louise Mason. Mother of his daughter.

'Thank God you're all right, Barry,' she said urgently. 'They've got Cassie!'

Barry – because he was Barry – Barry Lawrence Brown of Catford in London, not that phantom Bartholemew, struggled to his feet. On the far side of the room, the Doctor was leaning over a massive golden table, a knife glinting in his hand. For some reason, he was wearing long black robes.

And Cassie's prone form was lying on the table.

Barry's heart raced, and he ran over to rescue her. At least he tried to. An invisible barrier had been erected around them, and he smashed into it with a shocking coruscation of light. Winded, he stepped back. 'Let me out of here!' he screamed, banging on the transparent wall and getting only golden sparks in return.

Beyond the barrier, the Doctor looked round from his unholy pursuits. 'Ah, woken up, have we?' He grinned. 'Please try to be quiet, will you. I'm about to cut your mewling 'bridling's throat, and I'll make a cleaner cut without your irritating disturbances.'

'That's my daughter you've got out there, you bastard!' There was only one thought in Barry's mind, and that was to get out and hug the child that had been denied a real part of his real life.

The Doctor was positioning the knife against Cassie's bare throat. He ignored Barry and turned to the Archimage. 'Once the jugular is cut, the life-force will ebb rapidly. You must recite the incantation when I give you the signal.' The Archimage nodded and picked up the open book.

And the knife sliced downwards.

Fourteen

The Stiletto of Vaux clattered off the nearest wall and skittered across the floor. The Doctor, having thrown it away from him – and Cassie's throat – with a furious roar, had then dropped to his knees, his head clutched in his hands. And then he started rocking backwards and forwards making odd mewing noises.

It took Barry a couple of seconds to register that the barrier was no longer there. It had collapsed at the same time that the Doctor had. And it took him less than a second to cover the few yards to the table, where he snatched Cassie and ran back to Louise before the Archimage could work out what was going on.

'Take her!' Barry snapped at Louise, looking round the throne room for some means of escape. The doors that they had originally come through were gone, and Barry had a vague recollection of them vanishing after the Archimage had cast an incantation. He shook his head. He was still carrying two sets of memories around in his head, although those of Barry Brown seemed to be taking precedence.

He looked back at the Archimage; but he was more concerned with the Doctor's condition than that of his prisoners, though that wasn't much help if he, Louise and Cassie were trapped in the throne room, was it? And then he saw it; another door, immediately behind them – and it was sliding open like a lift.

Grabbing Louise's arm, Barry pulled her and the baby through the door, and held his breath as he saw the Archimage look up and stare straight at him. But then the door slid shut, and the little room started to descend. With a sigh of relief, Barry realized that it was a lift, although its complicity in their escape was a mystery to him.

'Bet you're glad to be out of there!' came the cheery – and oddly familiar – voice. Barry looked around the lift with a mixture of panic and bewilderment, but he, Louise and Cassie were the only people in sight.

'Don't bother looking for me; I'm all around you – I'm the lift!' the voice continued. 'I gathered that you were having problems, so I thought I'd give you a hand. Not that I have any hands,' it babbled, 'but you know what I mean.'

'Where are we going?' asked Louise.

'Well, I'd take you down to the foyer, but I really don't think that you want to go down there at the moment.'

'Why the hell not?' barked Barry, still uneasy about the idea of a sentient lift.

'Because there's an army of thaumaturgs and cybrids – commanded by the Hierophant and the Technomancer, I might add – advancing on the Tower of Abraxas, that's why. And despite the fact that two of you are elevated cybrids, you might be torn from limb to limb in the confusion.'

'Why the concern?' asked Louise.

There was a significant pause before the lift replied. 'I'm a decent lift, that's why. Now, what if I drop you off on the first floor? You can wait there for the fisticuffs to finish.'

'Okay –' Barry paused, weighing up a question in his mind. 'Okay, but do me a favour.'

'If I can.'

'Go back to the Archimage's throne room. I think the Doctor might need you.'

The lift shuddered to a halt. 'The Doctor? Oh, you mean the Dark One.'

'Don't you mean the Valeyard?' corrected Louise.

'Oi!' chastised the lift, 'Don't use that sort of language

in here, if you don't mind.' It opened its door. 'As soon as you get out, I'll go back for the Dar– the Doctor. Just get a move on!' it urged. 'Things are going to get nasty, and I want to be as far from the ground floor as I can.'

Stepping out of the lift, Barry looked back into its mirrored interior. 'Why did you help us? Really?'

The lift closed its door, but not before it muttered something which took Barry a few seconds to understand. And when he did so, he smiled.

'What is it?' asked Louise.

'The lift, Lou, the lift. It was Vincent.' He shrugged, and looked around the transformed first floor. It was empty, a great golden void with windows everywhere. He ran over to one of the windows, and the view took his breath.

'Look!' he urged. And as soon as Louise and Cassie joined him, he allowed himself to fully appreciate what was happening outside the Tower.

Hundreds of cybrids and thaumaturgs were waiting impatiently around the base of the Tower, all dressed in their battle armour and wielding staves and battle whips. And behind them in the distance, as still as statues, were the Hierophant and the Technomancer, tiny figures brimming with barely restrained power. Barry shuddered. The Great Kingdom was at war, and the remaining part of his Bartholemew persona was shouting one thing.

They were facing armageddon.

The Doctor opened his eyes to see the Archimage standing over him with a concerned expression. But what were they doing in his throne room, he wondered. The last thing he remembered was feeling faint, but that had been in the Labyrinth of Thaumaturgy. And why had he changed out of his wonderful jacket, only to put on this ridiculous garb? As he considered the black robes, a terrifying thought entered his head. And the Archimage's next question confirmed his worst nightmares.

'Are you recovered, Valeyard?'

'Vale—?' The force of the memories almost made the Doctor vomit. In his arrogance, he had assumed that his Time Lord nature had rendered him immune to the quantum mnemonic of the Millennium Codex. In truth, it had worked its magic in a far more sinister and insidious way, and he had ignored all the clues, such as the gradual transformation of his clothing.

And that arrogance had left him completely unprepared when the final metamorphosis had overcome him, the quintessence of his darker nature, erupting from the hidden recesses of his soul and dressing his mind and body in its foul garments. For the last few hours, he had become the one thing he feared and despised above all else. Forget the Daleks or the Cybermen; the most dangerous force in the universe was a creature possessing all of the Doctor's intellect and abilities, but with none of his moral scruples.

Facing such a being across a Time Lord courtroom had been bad enough, especially with the Master tittering over the situation from the depths of the Matrix. But to know that he had lived the life of that monster made the Doctor feel unclean to the core of his Gallifreyan soul. And that was a long way down indeed.

He rose unsteadily, trying not to flinch at the Archimage's helping hand. His main priority now was to return to the Labyrinth and undo this abortion of reality, before he reached the point where his subconscious could no longer free him from the clutches of the Valeyard.

'Valeyard?' the Archimage repeated.

'The forces we were unleashing are cruel and wishful, Magnus Ashmael,' the Doctor replied, trying very hard to impersonate the sneering pretension of his alter-ego. 'I was momentarily overcome by them.'

The Archimage frowned. 'But you are the Valeyard; there is no force in the Great Kingdom that can stand against you.'

'I was unprepared. It will be different the next time.'

'Next time? We have lost the child, Valeyard.' The

Archimage wandered to the window and looked out. And then bellowed, 'By the Gods!'

The Doctor joined him and saw the reason for the Archimage's distress. An army of cybrids and thaumaturgs was surrounding the Tower of Abraxas. And, even as they watched, the army started to advance.

'How could they have approached so close without my being warned? Unless Anastasia and Melaphyre have united to erect unyielding wards.' He waved his hand. 'But that is irrelevant now. We must defend ourselves.' He squeezed his eyes shut and started muttering under his breath; the Doctor guessed that he was ordering his own aurik forces to attack the armies. With a shudder, he realized that the carnage would be unthinkable. And, despite the alien appearance of the protagonists, they were all human beings; people who had been milling around the streets of London innocently preparing to celebrate the new millennium.

He had to get through to the remnants of Mel and Anne and try to persuade them to call off their attack, before things got really unpleasant.

'They've come for me,' he stated.

'How did you come to that conclusion?'

'Because the Hierophant has just communicated with me,' he lied. 'She will call off her army if I am delivered to her.' There, he thought smugly, that should do it.

'Really?' asked the Archimage, raising an eyebrow. 'Despite the Hierophant's great powers,' he sneered, 'she could never breach the Tower's four walls with her mind. That is one of the fundamental laws of the Great Kingdom. So why did you lie to me, Valeyard, unless –' He nodded in realization. 'Unless you aren't the Valeyard. That's it, isn't it? You've reverted to that self-righteous Doctor.' He snapped his fingers, and two auriks entered the throne room.

'I watched you destroy two of my auriks earlier, Doctor. I watched through their eyes, I felt their deaths. And yet I wonder whether victory will be so assured against auriks who have drunk deep of my power?' And it did seem that these brutes were larger than their fellows, with a faint golden aura surrounding their bodies.

'And once you are defeated, I shall continue from where we left off. I will retrieve the child and confront the Gods in the Tabernacle, and watch as they beg for mercy while their very life-blood is drained from them.'

While the Archimage continued his dreams of glory, a small voice in the Doctor's mind started whispering to him, telling him that a simple incantation would leave the auriks burning cadavers on the floor, but he was well aware of the consequences of that course of action. Any use of the powers that had been granted him by the Millennium Codex would guarantee his transformation into the Valeyard.

A massive explosion rendered such considerations irrelevant. Both the Doctor and the Archimage were knocked off their feet by the blast, which the Doctor estimated came from the very base of the Tower. With a sinking feeling, he realized that the battle – and the bloodshed – had begun.

Scrambling to his feet, the Doctor glanced at the Archimage, but he was too preoccupied with his incantations to pay him any attention. And then something else caught the Doctor's eye: the sleeve of his robe was lighter, the patterns of his jacket visible. Perhaps his transformation into the Valeyard was avoidable, after all! He skirted round the two dazed auriks and tried to locate the lift that had come to his aid the last time he had escaped from the Archimage's clutches, but the walls were a uniform gold. Even the doors through which he and the Archimage had entered were gone, their absence the result of some spell or other.

'Of course!' he exclaimed. Using his borrowed powers to destroy an aurik was one thing, but a simple incantation of egress wouldn't damn him, would it? He concentrated and muttered a short sentence that his brain told him would work. To his relief, a set of gilded double doors faded into existence in the featureless wall.

Running from the throne room, he was too busy with his escape to notice that his robes were once again a featureless jet black.

Louise sat up and rubbed the back of Cassie's head to quieten her. The explosion had thrown them both to the floor, and she had only just managed to protect her daughter from the impact. 'This is it, Barry,' she whispered. 'We're going to die.'

'Be quiet!' he snapped. 'I don't understand what's going on any more than you do, but there's got to be a way out of this situation. I mean, look at you and me: it's Barry and Louise, not Bartholemew and Louella. Perhaps everything will just revert back to normal, and we can get on with our lives. I just wish we could pick and choose what changed.'

Louise stroked the back of his hand. 'You're thinking about your real mother, aren't you?'

He laughed. 'That's very selfless of you, Lou, but no, I was thinking about Cassie.' He nodded at the sleeping child. 'I always suspected that I was her father, you know. Why didn't you tell me? Why did you always claim that it was that ex of yours, the one who moved up to York, never to be seen again?'

'Because of the way she is – was, that's why.' And then she sighed. The lies that she had told over the years, she thought, all because of her headstrong determination to prove to people like her father that she could stand on her own two feet. Given their current predicament, what was the point of lying any more? 'No, there's more to it than that. I just wanted to prove to everybody that I could cope on my own, that I didn't need a man to support me. That was when I first got pregnant. And then, when I saw Cassie's deformities, well, I didn't love her any less. In fact, it made her even more special. But I didn't want to burden you with any guilt or blame.'

'Burden? How could I ever think of Cassie as a

burden?' he said in a shocked tone. 'Even before I realized that I was her dad, I loved her. Why the hell did you think I kept coming round? Not your cooking, that's for sure.' He winced as she kicked his leg. 'I've always loved Cassie, and I've always loved you. And even if she does change back, I'll never stop feeling that way.' He swallowed, and Louise understood the pain that he was going through. 'I was adopted, Lou. I never knew my real parents, never had any sense of belonging, of continuity. I don't want Cassie to go through what I went through.' He looked away in embarrassment as his voice filled with emotion.

Louise could feel the tears welling up in her eyes. It was something she had considered before she had even become pregnant, but her stubbornness had always stood in the way, backed up by her internal justification that marriage wouldn't change the relationship that she and Barry had. But now she wanted commitment; not from Barry – she already had that. It was commitment from herself that she needed. She looked him in the eyes through the blur of tears. 'Barry, when this is all over, why don't we, well, get married?'

He threw back his head and roared. 'That'll be one to tell Cassie when she's older, won't it? I can see it now. When she asks about how we got married, we can tell her that mummy proposed to daddy in a building with talking lifts, while goblins and demons fought a pitched battle outside!' And then he reached out and hugged both Louise and Cassie, tears in his eyes now. 'But yes, Lou, yes. Of course I'll marry you.'

The voice that boomed out from behind them was rich and fruity. 'Wonderful; I do so love a good wedding.' The Doctor – still in the disturbing black robes – was standing behind them, hands on hips. Instinctively, Louise stepped back, but he threw his arms open. 'You have nothing to worry about, I assure you. That side of my nature is locked away, and that's where it's going to stay. He inclined his head towards the central pillars which housed the lift shafts. 'Now, we've got to get out of here, but somehow we must avoid being torn apart in the altercation one floor below us.' Louise shuddered. The last time she had seen the Doctor, he had been preparing to sacrifice her daughter. But the cruelty and malice that had coloured his voice and nature had been replaced by the trusting tones that had won her over in that café in Greenwich. Something that seemed centuries ago.

'The lift told us to wait here until the battle was over,' offered Barry.

'That's all well and good,' countered the Doctor, 'but by then, hundreds of people will have died.'

'But they're goblins!'

'As were you, Louise,' replied the Doctor. 'You two remember your previous existence, don't you?' They nodded. 'The cybrids, thaumaturgs and auriks preparing to tear one another limb from limb out there are probably poor unfortunates who were revelling in Trafalgar Square. The entire population of the Great Kingdom comprises the human beings trapped in the triangle Ashley Chapel set up between the Millennium Hall, the Library of Saint John in Holborn, and here, in Canary Wharf.'

'You mean they're all real? Like us?' asked Barry. 'But why aren't they remembering what everything is supposed to be like? I mean, we are.'

The Doctor shrugged. 'Perhaps it has something to do with your proximity to the Millennium Ziggurat when the Codex was run. Or maybe it was something else.' He shook his head. 'I'll be honest with you. Whatever transformed London is as much a mystery to me as it is to you. All I do know is, I don't want even more bloodshed on my hands.'

'They've already started fighting, Doctor,' said Barry.

'No. They've stormed the entrance, but the auriks haven't engaged them yet. It's me that Anastasia and Melaphyre want, and as soon as I make my grand entrance, this senseless carnage can be avoided.'

* * *

The first wave of the unprecedented cybrid-thaumaturg alliance broke through the glass boundaries of the Tower of Abraxas with surprising ease. Their mantric grenades had cut through the Tower's wards, taking out the physical barriers with an explosion which had nearly knocked them off their feet. But finally the vestibule was theirs to command, its few aurik defendants ripped to shreds by thaumaturgs in their mindless fighting frenzy.

And then nothing. No more auriks, no sudden attacks by the expected guardian spirits, nothing. The general of the cybrid forces turned to his silvered equivalent.

'This is wrong, Alane. The Tower is virtually open to attack.' General Gargil scratched his blunt blue nose with a taloned hand. 'I expected far more resistance than this.'

The thaumaturg nodded. 'As did I, Gargil, as did I. Where are the auriks, spoiling for blood?' He shook his head. 'I had hoped for a valiant battle, my friend, not an empty victory amongst these deserted halls.'

'Patience, Alane.' The cybrid pointed towards the thick columns of gold and marble in the centre of the vestibule. 'The lift shafts are there,' he announced, 'but I am unsure as to whether that would be the best route of assault. The Archimage is probably holding the Dark One in his throne room, and to use the lift would announce our presence.'

Alane smiled, revealing pointed golden teeth. 'Agreed, friend Gargil. I suggest –' He broke off as a familiar but exhilarating noise filtered through from outside the Tower. The flapping, screeching cacophany could only be one thing: the anticipated attack by the auriks, the only inhabitants of the Great Kingdom capable of airborne assault.

'We must stand at the head of our armies, Gargil!' shouted Alane. 'We must fight –'

'No!' snapped the cybrid, clamping his sharp claws around the thaumaturg's stick-like upper arm. 'Our priority is to rescue the Dark One, not engage in battle with the auriks.'

'But the laws of the Kingdom –'

'To perdition with the laws. We have our orders from both the Hierophant and the Technomancer. We are inside the Tower. I suggest that we make the best use of that fact and storm the throne room.' A sudden mental image from the Technomancer filled his mind. Although the Archimage's mystic defences interfered with the vision, the intention was clear; there was a stairwell in the corner of the vestibule, a stairwell which led eventually to the throne room.

'But there are only two of us,' argued Gargil.

'We are warriors of the Great Kingdom, my friend. And we fight for the good of that Kingdom. I can think of no better cause, can you?'

They reached the hidden door to the staircase and hurried inside.

* * *

'This is carnage!' screamed the Technomancer as she ignited a swooping aurik with a mantric torpedo. The Hierophant was on her knees, her stave fending off another of the horned creatures. For a second, Melaphyre wondered why her peer was resorting to such direct tactics, but quickly decided that Anastasia was actually enjoying the action.

'We must hope that Gargil and Alane locate the Dark One quickly,' she called, just before she beheaded the aurik. Its decapitated torso fell heavily to the beige sand, and vanished in the purple flame that issued from the Hierophant's hands. 'The auriks may have taken their time in arriving, but they are certainly making up for it.' She pointed towards the battleground, where the auriks were attacking with unprecedented ferocity. The Archimage was undoubtedly behind their magnified strength and bloodlust, and that left her with only one option.

With a muttered incantation, she granted her army a portion of her power.

* * *

Louise pointed as the door handle to the first floor – gold, in keeping with all of the Tower's fixtures and fittings – turned downwards.

'Back to the other side of the room!' the Doctor ordered, as the door was flung open to reveal the incongruous sight of a cybrid and a thaumaturg together.

With instincts honed in a different reality, Barry and Louise triggered the transformation of their blue armour to cover them. But the cybrid stepped forward with his taloned hands outstretched in a gesture of peace.

'Bartholemew, Louella, surely you recognize Gargil, warlord to the Technomancer?' he asked in a gruff voice.

Louise's brow furrowed as she tried to remember her other life as a member of Melaphyre's court. And yes, the cybrid in front of her was the same Gargil that had bored them all during countless banquets with his endless tales of war and battle. 'Of course, Gargil. What are you doing here?'

He nodded over her shoulder. 'The Dark One; we're here to rescue him.'

'Me?' asked the Doctor. 'I'm honoured –'

'Don't be,' whispered the thaumaturg in his sibilant tones. 'My mistress wanted you dead. Only the Technomancer's intercession saved you.'

The Doctor raised an eyebrow. 'Good old Mel,' he muttered. 'Anyway, I suppose we should be off. I take it that this bloodshed will cease as soon as we're clear of the Tower?'

'Of course,' Gargil answered. 'The entire campaign was engineered to liberate you from the Archimage. And I admit to being disappointed that you managed that feat without our assistance. I was looking forward to testing the Archimage in combat.'

'Can we stop this bloodthirsty conversation and get out of here?' snapped the Doctor irritably. 'The sooner this senseless conflict is over, the better.'

'Very well,' said Gargil, pointing at the door. A sudden noise drew their attention; the lift door was opening.

'All aboard who's coming aboard!' came Vincent's cheery voice.

'After you,' said the Doctor, bowing and holding out his arm for Louise.

She smiled. Perhaps they would get out of this nightmare after all.

From her position on the promontory, the Hierophant reached out with her mystic senses in an attempt to contact her warlord. For long moments there was nothing, but then.

'They have the Doctor!' she shouted. 'I can see through Alane's eyes; they are bringing him out – and your elevated cybrids are with them.' She span round as an aurik dropped from the sky towards her. With a sharp flick of her wrist, it exploded in a ball of purple fire.

'Bartholomew and Louella?' The Technomancer frowned; she hadn't even been aware that her chancellor and her major-domo were absent from the Ziggurat. What were they doing in the Archimage's lair? 'I'll tell my cybrids to fall back as soon as they're clear of the Tower. I suggest that you order your thaumaturgs to do the same.'

'My dear Melaphyre, do not presume to question my skills in warfare,' she snapped. 'I was waging war in the Kingdom when you were a suckling at your mother's teat. The moment that they are away from the Tower, this skirmish will end. I do not relish bloodshed, any more than you do.'

Reassuring words. But Melaphyre wasn't completely satisfied that she believed the Hierophant's peaceful intentions; the chance to engage in conflict after years of isolation in the Labyrinth was frighteningly alluring. And as she destroyed the aurik that was running towards her, she realized just how alluring.

The vestibule of the Tower was disturbingly peaceful, the heavy crystal doors keeping the noise of the conflict at bay. Alane and Gargil stepped out of the stairwell, looking around the red-gold chamber for any signs of ambush, followed up the rear by Barry, Louise and the Doctor.

'The vestibule is clear,' growled Gargil. 'We must make haste before the auriks sense our presence. Alane and I will defend you through the battlefield. The Technomancer and Hierophant are waiting on a hillock overlooking the Tower.'

'How's Cassie holding up?' asked Barry.

'Better than I am,' Louise quipped. 'She's fast asleep.' And perfectly normal, she reminded herself. A sudden pang reminded her of something more mundane. 'You know, I'd kill for a cigarette right now.'

He nodded. 'A ciggie and a pint of lager – sounds like paradise.' He grinned. 'As soon as this is over, I'm going to take you to the White Lion and we're both going to get totally plastered.'

Further musing over the future ended abruptly.

'Leaving so soon?' The voice was rich and resonant, and came from a spot between them and the huge doors. Half a second later, a burst of amber light exploded in front of them, fading to reveal the Archimage in his tarnished battle armour. 'I'm hurt by your rejection of my hospitality.'

'It's over, Ashmael!' shouted the Doctor. 'As soon as we're back in the Labyrinth, I fully intend to put an end to this charade.'

'Really? And how do you propose to return to the Labyrinth, eh? I fully intend to keep you here until you fulfil your earlier promise and breach the Wall of Tears.'

The Doctor shook his head. 'Never. The Great Kingdom is an abomination which must be stopped before any more lives are lost.'

'Like this, you mean?' The Archimage stabbed a finger at Gargil, who sank to his knees in obvious agony, crackling electricity surrounding him in a vicious aura.

'Stop that!' ordered the Doctor.

'Why don't you make me?' laughed the Archimage.

'Or do you fear your powers that much?' Gargil was choking, his talons clutching at his throat. If the assault continued much longer, the cybrid would most certainly die.

The Doctor's face was a mask of horror. His earlier statement about not using his powers was clearly tearing him apart. Was he that frightened of what might happen that he would stand by and let Gargil die?

Louise caught a movement beside her, and was horrified to see Barry launching himself at the Archimage. Ignoring her shouts to stay back, Barry threw a heavy punch at the Archimage's unprotected face. As the Archimage stumbled backwards, momentarily stunned, he ceased his attack on Gargil.

'Run!' screamed Barry, rubbing his bruised fist. Alane helped Gargil to his feet and headed towards the door, but Louise's fear paralysed her. And then she realized that the Archimage was getting up.

'Barry, look out!' she bellowed, realizing that he hadn't spotted the Archimage's recovery.

'You presumptuous insect!' snarled the Archimage, his eyes ablaze with anger. 'You dare to attack the Archimage of Abraxas?' He raised his fist, burning with supernal fire.

'No!' screamed Louise. She tried to run over to him, but the Doctor restrained her.

'You'll get yourself killed!' he yelled. 'We've got to get out of here!'

'I'm not leaving Barry!' With a tug, she pulled herself clear of the Doctor's grasp, only to stumble over her own feet. To her horror, she lost hold of Cassie, who slid across the floor in the direction of the Archimage. And then she banged her head on the cool marble floor.

'A gift,' he muttered, pulling the child towards him in a telekinetic grip. 'How kind.' And then he unleashed his full power at Barry.

The last thing Louise saw before she lost consciousness was Barry, her friend, her confidant, her lover and the father of her child, vanish in a blinding conflagration.

And, standing behind the flames with an expression of triumph etched into his features, was the Archimage, a screaming Cassie in his arms.

And then merciful blackness overcame her.

Fifteen

Saraquazel shuddered as another brief spell of lucidity overcame him. And then realized that — for the first time since it had become trapped in this madness — the other intelligence that shared its physical space was also momentarily sane.

'Who are you, Yog-Sothoth?' he demanded in over a thousand methods of communication. 'What are you doing here?'

The answer came back as a series of mental images, tinged with confusion and anger. 'I do not know, Saraquazel. After my last visit to this planet, I was flung into the void, where I waited, recovering from the damage inflicted on my being. And then a compulsion overcame me, dragging me back here in an unbreakable thrall. Since then, I have been barely conscious.'

'A familiar tale. All I can recall —'

'I have no interest in your personal history.'

Saraquazel was surprised by Yog-Sothoth's brusque dismissal. 'If we pool our resources —'

'I neither crave nor need your assistance to free myself: I still possess enough of my power and intellect to find my own way out. I simply warn you to beware the duplicity of the humans who infest this world.' And then the Intelligence lapsed into silence, but Saraquazel could detect it marshalling its considerable mental powers, drawing matter from the material form of the Tabernacle and moulding it into new designs. Dark shadows began to materialize around the central chamber.

Resigned to the fact that help would not be forthcoming from that particular quarter, Saraquazel decided that it was time to put its new-found sanity to good use. Reaching out, it tried to locate the psychic patterns that belonged to the human being who had helped create this situation in the first place: Ashley Chapel.

It took but a few instants, but Saraquazel was puzzled by what he found. Patterns resembling those of Chapel were approaching the Tabernacle even now, but there was a strength behind them that was both unexpected and strangely familiar.

And then Saraquazel realized what he was sensing. Chapel – or whatever Chapel had become – was host to a portion of his own powers, a portion that he had either stolen or, more worrying, he had been given by Saraquazel during his madness. Deciding that further speculation was pointless, Saraquazel waited for Chapel to arrive. Besides, he was fascinated by the entities that the Intelligence was creating.

'They're free!' exclaimed the Technomancer triumphantly, watching as Gargil and Alane escorted the Doctor and Louella from the Tower. 'Order your thaumaturgs to protect them from the auriks, and then withdraw.'

The Hierophant nodded, barely able to contain her anger at Melaphyre's presumption and arrogance. But she decided that silence was the better course of action, given the urgency of their current situation, and did as she had been told.

'You said that Bartholemew was among them,' said the Technomancer, pointing towards the little group that was wending its way towards them. 'But –' And then she gasped; Gargil had obviously given her the same bad news that Alane had given his mistress.

Anastasia placed a comforting hand on Melaphyre's arm. 'I grieve with you, Majestrix. Bartholemew's name will forever be venerated as a hero of the Labyrinth of Thaumaturgy.'

'A hero? A hero?' The Technomancer span round, her

face contorted in anger. 'Barry never asked to be any part of all this. You wanted one last chance to prove yourself in battle, and look at the cost, eh? All because one bitter and twisted old spinster wanted to justify her empty and sterile life!' She turned away and began crying with deep, uncontrollable sobs.

Anastasia watched the display of emotions with conflicting reactions. The other woman's words had cut deep, but she was sure it was Melanie, not Melaphyre, who was saying them. Then again, that didn't detract from the truth that lay behind them. She had craved excitement, she had wanted to do something that would make Anne Travers proud of her. And all she had done was lead countless innocents to their deaths. And, despite the fact that the conflict had only been partly responsible for Bartholemew's death, the guilt cut deeply.

Part of her defended her actions. The thaumaturgs, cybrids and auriks that had laid down their lives were servants of the Great Kingdom, nothing more, and their very souls were foresworn to its service. But the Doctor had convinced her that the very notion of the Kingdom was nothing more than a fallacy; if she and the Technomancer had other lives, lives that were free from servitude to the Gods, then it stood to reason that every other living being that existed in the shadow of the Wall of Gods' Tears had such a life as well.

Her need to prove herself had condemned those people to death, and even her abilities to reach beyond mortality and communicate with their shades couldn't give them that life back.

'You're right. This carnage was not worth the cost.' She looked at the joint army as it retreated away from the Tower of Abraxas, the Doctor and the others protected at its centre. 'And I shall carry the blood of those who have fallen to satisfy my folly to my grave, Melanie.' Because the frightened girl in front of her was exactly that. The magicks that had created the Great Kingdom had worn off, leaving a distraught young woman in the armour of the Technomancer.

Mel smiled bravely. 'That was unkind of me, Anastasia. No – it was downright horrible. Things are bad enough round here, without my hurling insults at you. I just hope that the Doctor can find a way of getting everything back to normal.'

'So do I,' sighed the Hierophant. 'So do I.' *And may souls of the dead forgive me for my hubris*, she prayed.

Surrounded by packed throngs of thaumaturgs and cybrids, the Doctor carried Louise's limp body, flanked by Alane and Gargil.

'How is she?' hissed Alane.

'She's still unconscious,' the Doctor replied, 'but that's not such a bad thing at the moment. She's just seen her boyfriend incinerated and her daughter abducted. I doubt that she could handle it.'

'Why did you refrain from fighting, Dark One?' asked Gargil, the suspicion clear in his voice. The Doctor sighed; he had been expecting that particular question from the moment that they had escaped from the Tower.

'Because, Gargil, I am not the Dark One; not at the moment. But if I use these powers that I have been cursed with, that's exactly what I will become.' He ran a hand through his curly hair. 'And then nobody in the Great Kingdom will be safe.'

Gargil nodded his blue-black head. 'I see. And I apologize for considering that it was cowardice that stayed your hand.'

'Thank you, warlord,' said the Doctor, his voice weary. 'But I wonder whether the cost of my inaction has been too great this time.' But when he looked down at the prone figure in his eyes, he knew, with a stabbing pain in his hearts, that he could never have willingly donned the Valeyard's mantle, even to save Louise's agony.

'Doctor!' screeched Mel, running over to him and hugging him as he turned from handing Louise to one of the cybrids. 'You can't believe how pleased I am to see you!'

He gently pulled away from her and smoothed down his robes, and Mel was pleased to see that their black sheen was giving way to the normal, clashing colours of his jacket. As the joint army surrounded them and escorted them back to the Labyrinth, she hung back to talk to him out of earshot of the Hierophant.

'I take it that Melaphyre is no more?' he asked with quizzically raised eyebrows. 'I can't say I'm disappointed.'

Mel giggled. 'I still seem to have all her memories,' she said, tapping her piled-up red hair, 'but not her disposition.' And then her voice dropped, as she indicated the unconscious Louise. 'What happened? How did Barry –' She swallowed, temporarily overcome with emotion.

'The Archimage must be stopped at all costs, Mel. He has Cassie, and he's quite prepared to sacrifice her to achieve his unholy ends.'

Raising her hands to her mouth, Mel gave a horrified gasp. 'Cassie?'

'And she'd be the first. Unless I can find a way to return this all to normal, he'll breach the Wall of Tears, and then the warped reality of the Great Kingdom will spill outwards, consuming the rest of Britain, and then . . .' He shrugged. 'I can't say whether there'd ever be an end to it. And since this altered state is fundamentally unstable, the whole universe is in danger of dissolving into chaos, aeons before its time.'

'The whole universe?' said Mel. The concept was mind-boggling, and, to be honest, incomprehensible. London was one thing, the whole world was another, but at least the human mind could feel the scale of the threat. But the whole universe . . .

Mel shuddered.

The unravelling of the Kingdom had definitely affected the structure of the Tabernacle. Instead of the intricate but self-consistent geometry of the stained-glass palace, the angles were twisted and skewed to the point where it made the Archimage feel queasy if he stared at it for too long. He just hoped that he could find his way back to the domain of the Gods.

The child had stopped crying, and he checked to see whether it was still alive; its pulse confirmed that it was. Excellent, he thought; the baby would be useless to him dead.

And then a wave of dizziness overcame him, and he had to put the baby on the floor in case he dropped it. No, not an it, he corrected himself, a she. Cassandra Mason, daughter of Louise Mason, once an employee of Ashley Chapel Logistics; he was Ashley Chapel, he realized.

Standing unsteadily, he looked down at the dull bronze armour that he was wearing with a mixture of uncertainty and disbelief. The last thing he remembered was being in his office with Chapel and that Doctor fellow, running the Millennium Codex. He stared at his current environment – the dusty beige soil, the walls of mist in the distance, the sapphire blue sky with its silent electric storms, the impossibly shaped palace of coloured glass – and felt his heart race. Was this the paradise promised by Saraquazel? If so, what was he planning to do with Mason's child?

The memories evaporated as quickly as they had invaded his mind. Picking up the child, the Archimage braved the nauseating sight of the Tabernacle and located the entrance. Nothing would stop his domination of the Great Kingdom. And the universe beyond.

'I'm worried about Louise,' said Mel. Louise was lying on a makeshift bed – actually one of the library tables – covered by a thin sheet of grey silk, but she hadn't moved or spoken since she had collapsed.

The Doctor, half-way up one of the bookcase ladders and half-way down the corridor, was reaching for yet another tome to add to the ever-increasing pile that was weighing down poor old Gargil. 'Hardly surprising,' he called out. 'The shock of what happened in the Tower, coupled with the dual personalities that plague nearly all of us, has almost certainly shaken up the synapses. She's healing naturally at the moment — or what passes for natural in this place — and I think we should just let her be.' He jumped down from the ladder and extracted one of the books from Gargil's pile, threatening to unbalance the whole lot.

'Read this, and look for anything about the polarity of magic.' He hurled the book down the corridor like a square discus, and Mel could only assume that it was Melaphyre's instincts that enabled her to catch it without thinking.

'Polarity of magic?' It sounded like gibberish to her.

'Don't argue, Mel. You have a photographic memory and can read faster than a spielsnape being chased by a rabid dog,' he snapped. 'We have very little time left, what with the Archimage's mad dreams of glory and the unravelling of reality. Somewhere in here' — he threw out his arms to encompass the entire library — 'lies the answer to all our problems. So get reading.'

Mel sat down with a sigh, only to jump up again when her armour jabbed her in the back. Earlier, she had asked the Doctor whether she could take it off, but he had insisted that she continue wearing it for protection. Sitting down more gingerly this time, she opened the massive book and started to absorb its contents, occasionally glancing up to see what the Doctor was up to.

Thankfully, all traces of the Valeyard's costume were almost completely gone; that was something that Mel was especially grateful for. Although Mel didn't really understand who this 'Valeyard' was, the Melaphyre portion of her mind told her that he represented the ultimate pinnacle of evil. The thought of *that*, housed in and abusing the Doctor's body, was almost more than she could bear. She shuddered and returned to her studies.

She was half-way through the book — which did seem

to concern 'polarity of magic' after all — when a cry disturbed her. Looking up, she saw that Louise was thrashing around on the table.

'Cassie!' she was screaming, her eyes darting around the library annexe in sheer panic. Mel ran over and grabbed her hand, squeezing it tightly and — she hoped — reassuringly.

'It's all right, Louise. You're safe here.'

Louise seemed to calm down, but her eyes were empty and cold.

'They've gone, haven't they? Barry and Cassie, they're gone.'

Mel swallowed. Her entire life had been spent bubbling along, looking for the best out of every person and situation that she encountered. But part of the trade off for a life of eternal optimism was a complete lack of exposure to displays of deep emotions, and she realized that she was completely incapable of dealing with Louise's grief. 'They, they . . .' she mumbled.

'Cassie is still alive. You can be sure of that,' stated the Doctor flatly. Mel hadn't even heard him approach. 'If she weren't, this whole *son et lumière* performance would have come crumbling down around us.'

If the Doctor's words were meant to be a comfort, they were a failure. Louise swung her legs off the table and stood in front of him.

Then she slapped him round the face. 'You bastard! You could have saved them, you could have saved both of them! But no, you were too frightened to use your powers. So, thanks to your selfishness, Barry is dead and Cassie is in the hands of that maniac!' She went to slap him again, but the Doctor grasped her wrist.

'I made a decision, Louise, the consequences of which you and I will have to live with for the rest of our lives. And believe me, that could be a very long time in my case. But Cassie is still alive; help me to find some way to defeat the Archimage, and we might stand a chance of saving her life.' Mel had never heard the Doctor sound so full of guilt and self-recrimination, and her heart went out to him.

Louise nodded, and then started to sob quietly. But it was clear that the Doctor's words had sunk in. Mel leaned over to him and whispered: 'How are you feeling?'

He smiled wearily. 'I've been better.' Then he nodded at the book. 'Find anything?'

'There's a small section on polarity –'

'Excellent. Mark it up and give it to Alane.' He indicated the thaumaturg in the shadows, carrying a similar pile of books to Gargil.

'It might help if I knew what was going on,' she complained. This wasn't an uncommon occurrence – the Doctor holding all the cards to his chest – but it still annoyed her.

'All right, all right,' he said, holding his hands up. 'Very quickly, though. This Great Kingdom is based on three very different laws of physics: those indigenous to this universe; those of Saraquazel who hails from the universe that follows this one, and those of Yog-Sothoth – the Great Intelligence – who is a survivor of the cosmos that existed before the Big Bang. Thanks to Chapel and Anne's meddlings in forces beyond their comprehension, all three sets of laws are fused into an unstable equilibrium. I've got to unbalance that equilibrium, but, at the same time, ensure that all the pieces fall back into the same place that they were to begin with.' He huffed. 'Satisfied?'

'All the pieces?' She cocked her head at Louise.

The Doctor lowered his voice. 'I'm afraid not. Although it is possible to use quantum mnemonics to manipulate individual strands of reality, that would demand a far greater knowledge of the subject than I possess. And if I tried, I might make matters incalculably worse.' He laid a hand on her shoulder. 'I'm sorry, Mel, but Barry – and all the other poor unfortunates who've perished during this sorry incident – are dead. And Cassie, well, she'll revert to her original physical form.'

Mel shook her head sadly. 'That just isn't fair,' she muttered.

'The universe rarely is,' he whispered. 'That's why I'm here.' He paused for a moment, an indecipherable look on his face. And then he smiled. 'Now, carry on reading. We've got a lot to do, and very little time left.'

The Archimage stopped at a crossroads and tried to get his bearings. It seemed like hours since he had entered the Tabernacle, but there was still no sign of the central chamber of the Gods. Whatever Saraquazel was doing, it had completely rearranged the internal architecture of the Tabernacle.

Hoping that a direct route to the chamber still existed, the Archimage chose one of the routes on offer and set off down it.

'Is this it, Doctor?' asked Mel wryly, looking at the huge pile of books that Alane was placing on the table. 'Are you sure that you've got enough there?' Then again, to her credit, she had read all of them from cover to cover, and each one was carefully bookmarked to indicate the sections covering 'the polarity of magic'.

The Doctor nodded his thanks to Alane and sat at the table. 'Thanks to your skilful use of the Labyrinth's indexing database, yes, I think it is.'

'So what now?' Hours of reading and research, she guessed.

'We storm the Tabernacle,' he said curtly, 'and confront the Archimage.'

'Direct action? It's about time,' she muttered. But there was one question that she really wanted an answer to. 'I know this sounds, well, morbid, but why hasn't he killed Cassie yet? If he needs her life-force to do the dirty, I mean.'

The Doctor rubbed his eyes with his palms. 'While I was, not quite myself, I told the Archimage how to stabilize this reality and then breach the Wall of Tears. But to start the ball rolling, he needs to sacrifice Cassie. The release of her life-force will catalyse an artron energy transfer into the Archimage, which he can then use to achieve his ambitions.'

Mel suddenly saw what the Doctor was getting at. 'He's going to steal the power of those creatures in the Tabernacle, isn't he?'

The Doctor nodded. 'And siphon off the TARDIS's artron energy, while he's at it.'

'But that still doesn't explain why he hasn't done it yet.'

'The Archimage could have initiated the transfer from within the Tower of Abraxas, but his conceit is such that he wants to do it in the presence of the Gods. And the Tabernacle is holding him back from the central chamber until we arrive,' he said smugly. He picked up a single book from the top of the pile and started scribbling in the margin. 'Or had you forgotten the identity of your Goddess in Absence? Anyway, go and gather Anastasia, Louise, Gargil and Alane, and then you can all meet me at the foot of the stairs to the surface in about ten minutes.'

Mel reached the curtained doorway of the annexe, but turned back. 'And what are you doing?'

The Doctor smiled as he looked up from the book. 'A little homework.'

Dawn was breaking over the whole of the Great Kingdom. Standing on the grey roof of the Labyrinth, Louise decided that there was something refreshing about the cool wind that whipped through her blonde hair. She still felt sick, sick to the stomach, and knew that most of the pain that she was due hadn't even hit her yet, but there was still a chance that they could save Cassie. And she owed it to Barry to do everything in her power to do just that.

'Ready for the off?' announced the Doctor cheerfully, his multicoloured jacket flapping in the breeze.

'But won't the Tabernacle be defended?' asked Gargil.

'The legends state that the will of the Gods shrouds the palace, and that it is heresy to approach.'

'Trust me, Gargil,' said the Doctor, 'the Gods have got a lot on their minds at the moment. A few more interlopers won't exactly be at the top of their agenda.'

The Hierophant raised a finger. 'Our best route is directly through the settlement –'

'No need, Anastasia,' the Doctor interrupted. 'I have a far more direct route in mind.' At her puzzled expression, he smiled. 'I'll teleport us.'

'What?' snapped Louise.

'It's perfectly possible, Louise, I assure you.'

Her voice was icy as she replied. 'That's not what I meant, Doctor. What was all that crap about not being able to use your powers, eh?' She stabbed him in the chest with a finger. 'You stood by and let Barry die, and let that bastard Chapel take Cassie, because you didn't want to risk using your powers. But now, well! Don't fancy the walk, so you'll teleport us there. You make me sick,' she spat, walking away from him.

'She's right,' added Mel. 'Why is it okay to use them now?'

'Mel, Mel, Mel – trust me. I know what I'm doing.' He handed her a book. 'In case anything should happen to me, I want you to follow the instructions I've scribbled in the margin.'

'You're up to something, aren't you?'

He leant down and whispered in her ear. 'I am, and it's extremely dangerous. But it's the only way to get close to the Archimage and keep him occupied. Now –' He held his hands in the air. 'Time to leave, everybody.'

'Will it hurt?' asked Mel.

He shrugged. 'Don't know. I've never teleported anyone before. Well, not without technological support, at any rate.' He frowned. 'Here goes. Next stop, the Tabernacle of the Gods.'

Louise blinked as the grey landscape of the thaumaturg settlement sparkled and fragmented around her, breaking down into a featureless void. For endless, timeless moments, she was surrounded by total nothingness. And then the sparkling began again, this time a multicoloured kaleidoscope that rapidly resolved into, well, a multicoloured kaleidoscope.

The Louella personality which still nestled inside her recognized the palace of stained glass as the Tabernacle, the home of the Gods. But to Louise it was a nightmare of odd angles and broken reflections, a bit like one of those three-dimensional illusions that had been popular about five years ago, except that the only result of closer inspection was the beginnings of a blinding headache.

'Are you all right?' asked Mel. The Doctor was leaning against one of the walls of the little room, clutching his head with his hands. Once again, he was wearing the long black robes of the Dark One.

'The strain was a little unexpected, that's all.' He straightened up and sniffed the air. And then slammed the wall angrily. 'Damn!'

'What's wrong?' asked the Hierophant.

'I've lost contact with the TARDIS again. I don't know where the central chamber — and therefore Chapel — is any more. Damn — I should have anticipated something like this.'

Both Mel and the Hierophant pointed towards the doorway opposite them. 'That way,' they said simultaneously. 'Just ask a ruler of the Great Kingdom,' added Mel.

'Come on then,' said the Doctor impatiently. 'There's no time to lose —'

A gurgling roar echoed around the room.

'I thought you said that the Tabernacle would be unguarded?' growled Gargil.

'That's because it should be!' barked the Doctor, struggling to make himself heard over another roar. 'Unfortunately, it sounds like whatever it is stands between us and the Gods.'

'Alane!' ordered the Hierophant. 'Defend us!' She

turned to Mel. 'What about Gargil?'

Mel frowned, clearly unsure as to what to do.

'Worry not, Majestrix,' said the cybrid, stepping forward to join Alane. 'My oath as your warlord compels me to protect you.'

The roaring drew closer, and Louise suddenly realized with a feeling of rising horror that it was coming from more than one source. 'They're all around us!' she shouted.

'What are they?' yelled Mel. And then she screamed as the doorway in front of them was filled by a monstrous shape. Eight feet tall, its body was covered with matted red-brown fur. Two circular eyes glared at them malevolently as it lurched towards them, its clawed hands reaching out.

'A Yeti,' hissed the Doctor. 'I should have guessed.'

Sixteen

The Doctor looked around the small room, and quickly realized that all three escape routes were blocked by Yeti. And, despite the fighting prowess of both Gargil and Alane, he doubted that they would stand a chance against the sheer ferocity of the Great Intelligence's creatures.

The teleportation had been a deliberate act, designed to push him closer to becoming the Valeyard in order to convince the Archimage of his loyalty, and therefore buy his friends the time they needed. But another display of his abilities would undoubtedly push him too close; and then he would become a liability – if not an out and out threat – to his friends. A sudden movement made him look round.

Gargil leapt at the nearest Yeti, his talons outstretched. He clung onto its neck, attempting to dig his sharp claws into any weak spot. But before he could do it, the Yeti bucked beneath him. He was flung across the room, hitting the crystal wall with a sickening crack.

With resignation, the Doctor knew that, once again, it was up to him to save the day. He just hoped that the side-effects didn't make matters worse. Summoning the powers that he now possessed, he reached out with his mind, touching all three of the Yeti. And then he struck.

The last thing that he saw were the three Yeti, burning like giant candles. And then he felt himself slipping down a long black tunnel, cackling laughter propelling him into oblivion.

* * *

The Archimage's patience was wearing very thin. The child had started screaming again, and the chamber of the Gods didn't appear to be any closer.

He started as the wall in front of him suddenly seemed to unfold like glass origami. And then he realized what was behind it: the chamber of the Gods!

'Welcome, Ashley Chapel!' the voice boomed in his mind. 'Behold your God, Saraquazel!'

The words were odd and confusing, but the meaning was clear. The Archimage stepped into the chamber, noting that everything looked exactly the same as it had done the last time he had been there. The Goddess Tardis rested on her plinth, while the forms of Saraquazel and Yog-Sothoth were still inexplicably merged as one. But the clarity of his God's words suggested that the madness was no longer afflicting him.

'Have you come to free us from our thrall?' came the words.

The Archimage frowned. How could he separate the Gods? But Saraquazel seemed certain that he could. Then he remembered the child in his arms, and the book in his pouch. He had come to the chamber to steal the sum total of the Gods' might, in preparation for breaching the Wall of Tears and conquering the universe beyond.

'I have no time to engage in debate, Saraquazel,' he muttered, laying the child on Yog-Sothoth's empty throne. 'I have work to do.'

'He plans to siphon off our artron energy and use it for his own ends,' came an unfamiliar voice. 'I warned you of the duplicity of these material beings, Saraquazel, but you wouldn't listen. Now I suppose I'll have to deal with matters in my own way.'

Figures started to shamble out of the shadowed corners of the chamber, huge furry beasts with outstretched claws.

The Archimage laughed. 'Are these the best that you can do, Yog-Sothoth? Then again, given the sterile imagination of the Hierophant, it doesn't surprise me.' He snapped his fingers, and the creatures suddenly found themselves entangled in sparkling nets of spells, glittering mesh that constricted around them. After a few moments of flailing, they toppled onto the floor as Yog-Sothoth withdrew his control.

The Archimage reached into his pouch and took out the black book of Cardinal DeSable. And the Stiletto of Vaux, stained with ancient blood.

Mel tried to ignore the stench of the burning Yeti as she tended to the fallen Doctor. His breathing was shallow, but both heartbeats were strong and regular. Even as she watched, he opened his eyes and smiled wearily.

'Doctor?' she asked uncertainly.

'Expecting someone else?' he muttered, and then frowned. 'Now that sounded familiar.' He jumped to his feet. 'To tell you the truth, that was a close one. The Valeyard almost got his hooks into me. Anyway, time to press on, don't you think?' But Mel was aware of the suspicious looks from the others, especially Louise.

'Gargil is . . .' The Hierophant looked at the floor. 'I mourn with you, Majestrix.'

It took Mel a few seconds to understand what the Hierophant was saying. She looked over to the prone figure of the cybrid, and could sense that he was dead, his back having broken when he hit the wall. 'He was trying to save us,' she muttered, feeling tears in her eyes. The Hierophant put a comforting arm around Mel's shoulders.

'Let us hope that your warlord will be the last to fall,' she said softly, but Mel could detect the doubt and fear in her voice. And then the Doctor was talking.

'Come along!' he insisted, walking through the doorway that led to the chamber of the Gods. 'We've got a sacrifice to prevent.'

The Archimage rubbed his hand across his forehead as the words on the page blurred and swam. He tried to focus on the incantation that the Valeyard's book indicated would leech the Gods' powers, but it was difficult.

When the Valeyard had explained the procedure to him, back in the throne room of Abraxas, it had seemed simplicity itself. Recite the incantation, and, at the climax, slit the child's throat. As its life-force seeped away, it would act as the catalyst for the release of the Gods' powers. And those powers would then flow into the Archimage, giving him total, ultimate control over the Great Kingdom.

He allowed himself a moment to wallow in his imminent apotheosis. When he replaced the Gods in the pantheon, he would wipe the Tabernacle from the face of the land, and build another, greater Tower of Abraxas. A Tower that would afford him a view of the universe that would be his, once the Wall of Tears fell. And all it would take was the blood of an innocent. The blood of Cassandra Mason.

He steadied himself against the plinth and breathed deeply. For the briefest of moments, it was as if someone else's life had been overlaid on his. But he wasn't Ashley Chapel, he was the Magnus Ashmael, Archimage of Abraxas, and soon, so very soon, he would be Archimage of the Great – no, Greater – Kingdom.

'It's over, Ashmael. Drop the dagger and step back from Cassie.'

The Archimage span round to see the Doctor standing in the recently created doorway, flanked by the Hierophant, her general, Alane, the Technomancer and her Chancellor. Quite a blasphemous little gathering, when all was said and done.

'I don't think so, Valeyard,' he spat, emphasizing the last word. 'And your antagonism surprises me. I mean, all of us have played our parts in this, this situation, haven't we?' He pointed at the Technomancer.

'You, for example. As Melaphyre, you allowed your elevated cybrids to breed, which brought the innocent Cassandra into the world. But as Melanie Bush, you completed the Codex for my alter-ego, Chapel. Without you, Majestrix, the Great Kingdom would never have existed. Then again,' he continued, 'more thanks must go to the dreary Anastasia's even more dreary counterpart, Anne Travers.' He laughed cruelly. 'Don't look so surprised, Anastasia. Compared with Anne Travers, you are the most fruitful and fulfilled woman in the Kingdom! And if she hadn't summoned the Great Intelligence to Earth, Saraquazel's paradise – the paradise that I worked towards for twenty years – would have come into existence, rather than this sword-and-sorcery fiasco.'

'Ashley Chapel, I presume?' asked the Doctor, stepping forward into the chamber. 'I wondered when you would regain your senses. Can't you see that all of this has to stop. Now?'

'I am many things,' the Archimage replied. 'Ashley Chapel, the Magnus Ashmael, and Haarklane.'

'Also known as David Harker?' The Doctor shook his head. 'And that gives you the right to be ruthless, without compassion?'

'Being me gives the right!' he shouted. 'And, very soon, being me will be the most important position in the universe!'

'You don't know what you're dealing with here, Chapel! If you try to take the powers of the Gods, they will consume you.' He pointed at the blue box on her plinth.

'The entity you call the Goddess Tardis is a space-time machine created by beings who were ancient when the human race was counting its cells in single figures. It draws its energies from the primal forces of a black hole – think you can handle that? And the other "Gods"? Yog-Sothoth, a malevolent creature from an earlier universe that has tried to conquer the Earth on at least three occasions. And Saraquazel; a throwback from a time that hasn't even happened yet!' He stepped up to the Archimage.

'A time machine and two time-lost energy creatures; those are your gods, Chapel. And if you steal their powers, you will very probably die; at the very least, you certainly won't be human any more.'

'Maybe not, *Valeyard*, but I'll be a god in my own right. A god with the power to control the entire universe –'

'Listen to me, Chapel, or Harker, or whatever is currently sitting up there –' he pointed at the Archimage's head. 'That unravelling I told you about when I was, ah, unbalanced, is still going on. You may be able to steal the Gods' powers, but you haven't the ability to wield them properly. The unravelling will spread out; across London, across the Earth, and finally to the stars. Your universal empire will consist of nothing but random cosmic strings and a lot of hard radiation. Is that the destiny of the Great Kingdom, Archimage?'

'Ah, but you do have that ability, don't you, *Valeyard*? With you at my side, nothing would be impossible.'

'Me? At your side? You must be joking, Chapel.'

'You may wear the countenance of the Doctor, but your attire suggests otherwise. Doesn't it?' Before the Doctor could react, the Archimage hurled a mantric spear at his heart.

And the Doctor deflected it instinctively with a wave of his hand. Which was exactly what the Archimage had wanted.

Mel gasped as the Doctor collapsed. The Archimage's attack seemed to have been deflected, but the Doctor had fallen, nonetheless.

'We've got to help him!' she said to the Hierophant.

'It is too late child. We must attack. Now! Alane, destroy the Archimage!' Anastasia ordered, but her thaumaturg's advance was brought to a premature end by the force field that appeared around them.

'You shall play no part in this,' stated the Archimage. 'I have the only ally I shall ever need.' He indicated the prone form of the Doctor, but he was no longer unconscious; he was rising to his feet. And there was a worse shock in store.

The man standing next to the Archimage wasn't just wearing the Valeyard's costume; he was the Valeyard. The Doctor's entire physical appearance had changed, leaving a man with slicked back black hair and a cruel, hawk-like face in his place, a man that Mel recognized from Melaphyre's arcane knowledge. A man with no redeeming features whatsoever, virtually radiating malevolence.

Mel turned to the Hierophant. 'That really is the Valeyard, Anastasia! We've got to stop him!'

'Child, we cannot.' She gestured towards the hazy barrier that had suddenly materialized. 'The Archimage has sealed us behind his wall of force –'

'You're a ruler of the Great Kingdom, aren't you? Surely you can do something?'

Anastasia raised an eyebrow. 'You too are a ruler, Melaphyre. Perhaps together?'

Mel considered the Hierophant's words. The Technomancer's psyche was still with her, but buried, contained. Dare she unleash it? But the Doctor was gone, replaced by his dark side. And her guilt – hadn't she completed the Codex? – supplied the final shove. Reaching into herself, she grabbed Melaphyre's personality and dragged it to the surface.

And the Majestrix Melaphyre, Technomancer of Sciosophy, turned to the Hierophant. 'The Doctor gave me a book; it contains instructions on how to turn everything back.'

'Then we withdraw and recamp,' stated the Hierophant. 'The rear is unguarded; we must leave.'

With a final backwards glance at the Archimage and the Valeyard, the Majestrix Melaphyre left the chamber of the Gods.

'Valeyard?' asked the Archimage.

'Do not concern yourself, Magnus Ashmael. I am both the Valeyard and your ally. And finally I have shrouded myself in the physical form in which I feel most comfortable.' He nodded at the child. 'You were about to utter the incantation to seize the power of the Gods, were you not?'

The Archimage nodded. 'Together, we shall rule infinity.' His stratagem had worked. One last display of power had pushed the Doctor over the edge and turned him into the Dark One permanently. Now they could begin his ascension. 'I'll read the incantation, you can slit the 'bridling's throat.'

The Valeyard shook his head. 'I have a better idea. Quantum mnemonics are difficult beasts to tame, Archimage. But that –' He pointed towards the Goddess Tardis. 'That can do all the hard work for us.'

'But –'

'No buts. You may view it as a Goddess, but I know it as a faithful and loyal vessel, mine to command. With its help, we can reverse the effects of the Millennium Codex, and then recreate reality in our own image.' The Valeyard reached into his robes, and extracted a key. 'The universe will be ours, Archimage. How does that feel?'

The Archimage smiled. Despite the interference of the other rulers, he had finally succeeded. The Great Kingdom – and beyond – would be his. 'After you, Valeyard, after you.'

Far enough away from the chamber of the Gods to feel relatively safe, Louise watched as the Technomancer leafed through the small book. The difference between Melaphyre and Mel was obvious: the latter's infectious enthusiasm had been replaced by a dignity and hauteur befitting a ruler of the Great Kingdom. And the Louella that watched through her eyes knew what that meant, even if Louise herself was unsure.

'What are you looking for?' she asked hesitantly.

'Ah, dear, faithful Louella,' Melaphyre replied. 'I too mourn the loss of Bartholemew.' She fell respectfully silent for a second before continuing. 'The Doctor indicated that this book contains the solution to this problem;

a means of wiping the Great Kingdom from existence and replacing it with the truth.' She gave a fruity laugh, and turned to the Hierophant.

'Although the idea that we are but phantoms, twisted reflections of other lives is difficult to believe, my heart knows it to be true.' She turned another page and gave a screech of triumph. 'There!'

'What is it?' said Louise.

'The solution, my dear Chancellor. As the Doctor said in the Labyrinth, the answer to this lies with the polarity of the magicks which underpin the Kingdom. Three distinct flavours of magick, all incompatible.' She steepled her fingers. 'The Doctor has bought us the time needed to accomplish this – and paid the highest price for his purchase – and it falls to us to make similar sacrifices.'

'Is it dangerous, Melaphyre?' asked the Hierophant, and Louise could detect true concern in her voice.

The Technomancer was quiet as she replied. 'My cybrids are unique in the Kingdom, Anastasia, since they possess the capability to conduct and focus magick. And as their Technomancer, they will obey my commands without question.

'I shall order them to form a living chain, joining the Ziggurat of Sciosophy, the Tower of Abraxas, and the Labyrinth of Thaumaturgy together –'

'Blasphemy,' hissed the Hierophant. 'Heresy! But I admire your audacity, Melaphyre. How can I help?'

'By commanding your thaumaturgs to protect my people from the auriks while the chain is being constructed. The operation should take no more than half an hour.'

'But is it dangerous?' repeated Louise.

Melaphyre laid her hand on Louise's shoulder. 'I could never lie to you, sweet Louella. There is a final chain needed to complete this sorcery. A chain connecting the three seats of power to the Tabernacle, and to the Gods. I shall have to direct that chain, marching at its head. But the book implies . . .' she fell silent.

'You're going to die, aren't you?' Louise regretted saying the words the moment she spoke them, but there was no recrimination in the Technomancer's reply.

'A small price to pay to end this horror, and to give the people trapped in the Kingdom their lives back. And for Melanie Bush, it will be a chance to make amends for her complicity in this matter.' She stepped back. 'Now, I will require solitude to arrange this, so I ask that you do not disturb me.' With that, she turned and left them.

'I can't believe that the Doctor would order her to her death,' Louise muttered. 'She's his friend.'

The Hierophant placed a hand on her shoulder. 'The Doctor willingly gave up his life to grant us this opportunity, Louise. We can do nothing less.'

The Archimage looked around the huge room in disbelief. The idea that he was inside the Goddess Tardis was mind-boggling enough; the discovery that the interior of the small blue box was yet another cathedral, probably no smaller than the Tabernacle itself, was yet another example of the miracles of the Gods.

The walls were blue marble, shot through with veins of silver and gold. But they weren't smooth; roundelled indentations were carved at regular intervals. The floor was of a much darker marble, and in the very centre of the room was a large blue altar, hexagonal in shape, with a cylindrical column of gold and silver rising from the middle. And then the Archimage realized that it wasn't an altar. The six surfaces of the object were carved and studded with almost invisible controls. Buttons, levers, screens and dials, all crafted from the same blue stone.

Then Ashley Chapel's consciousness took over, and rationalized the TARDIS as nothing more than a technologically advanced machine, the product of a race of alien life forms who regarded mankind on a par with insects and amoebas.

'What do you think, Magnus Ashmael? Impressive, is it not?' The Valeyard was hunched over the hexagonal console, studying the readouts and screens with intense concentration.

'This is your ship?'

'Not exactly, but it will do for the time being. And it seems like the Millennium Codex has prompted a little redecorating.' He gave a short chuckle. 'I'm sure that the Doctor would have hated it.' And then he pointed at one of the monitors set into the console. 'Now, time to get things going, don't you think? According to the instrumentation, the unravelling is continuing, but at a much reduced rate. If I can staunch that particular flow of chaos, we'll be in a perfect position to undo the Millennium Codex, and start again.' His hands flew over the controls like a virtuoso musician. Seconds later, the silver and gold pillar in the centre of the console started to rise and fall.

'What are you doing?' asked the Archimage suspiciously.

'Cycling energy through the TARDIS systems,' he muttered. 'Shouldn't take more than a few hours.'

'Really?' The Archimage stepped forward. 'Stand away from the console, *Doctor*.'

'What are you babbling on about?' snapped the other. 'I'm trying to help you.'

'I should have realized that your transformation into the Dark One was too fortuitous. This is all a ruse, a means of keeping me away from the Gods, isn't it?'

'Don't be so ridiculous –'

The Archimage held up his fist, which was crackling with barely restrained power. 'Open the doors, Doctor. Or I'll take your TARDIS apart, piece by piece.'

Anastasia stood alone, her mind wandering between the solitary figure of the Technomancer, and her thaumaturgs in the Great Kingdom. Through their eyes, she could see the unprecedented feat that Melaphyre was orchestrating: thousands of cybrids scampering around, forming a vast living chain.

But another part of her mind was focused on Anne Travers, the woman she had envied since learning of her existence, only to learn that she was as unfulfilled and barren as the Hierophant. Despite the Archimage's evil intent, she didn't doubt his words for a second. In all possible alternatives, she was a failure, someone who had squandered her life on a vain crusade of revenge and bitterness.

Perhaps she could still salvage something from the situation.

'You came very close, Chapel,' said the Doctor, still playing for as much time as possible. With the Valeyard's persona once more under lock and key in his mind, the Doctor's physical appearance had reverted to normal, although he still wore the black robes of a Gallifreyan court prosecutor. 'I was already close to the transformation; defending myself from your attack really did push me over the edge.'

'So why did you change back?' asked the Archimage. 'The last time, it was your compassion for the child, wasn't it?'

The Doctor noted with satisfaction that the Archimage was clearly being drawn into the conversation, and was hopefully unaware of what Mel and the others were up to.

'I imagine so, yes,' he explained. 'When I entered the TARDIS, the Valeyard was definitely in control of every aspect of my mind and body. He was even able to couple the unique physics of the Great Kingdom with my natural regenerative abilities to affect a physical transformation. It seems that I have the TARDIS to thank this time. When I operated the controls, the telepathic circuits detected the hostile takeover and helped me to regain control.' The Doctor couldn't help looking down at the console and glancing at a monitor; it showed the cybrid chain stretching away from the Ziggurat of Sciosophy.

The Archimage must have followed his gaze. 'Open the doors now, Doctor!' he yelled. 'Now!'

The Doctor stepped back from the console. 'Do what you want, Chapel. But I warn you: I certainly wouldn't like to be inside a TARDIS when its owner is killed. Very nasty.' Actually, the Doctor wasn't really sure what would happen to the TARDIS if he died, but it sounded quite threatening.

'A risk I am prepared to take, Doctor.' The Archimage smiled. 'Indeed, there is nothing I would not risk to seize the power of the Gods.' And he hurled the spear of psychic energy straight at the Doctor's chest.

Louise wandered the silent corridors of the Tabernacle, unable to concentrate on anything for more than a fleeting moment. Her daughter was lying on a sacrificial altar in the chamber of the Gods, while two madmen decided her fate. And all she could do was wait, and rely on her colleagues to save the day.

She thought of Barry, and another twist of pain hit her in the stomach. For three years, she had kept him in the dark about his fatherhood – despite his own deep-seated insecurities about not knowing his natural parents – and she realized now that that was probably the cruellest thing that she had ever done to anyone. And Barry had been her best friend ever: friend, lover, everything.

As she started crying, she prayed. Prayed to whatever God or Gods were listening, begging them to bring Barry back to her. If the whole of London could be transformed into a world of Technomancers and Hierophants, surely the life of one man was trivial. And then there was Cassie, hale and hearty in this Great Kingdom, but severely handicapped in the real world.

She stopped herself. It didn't matter what Cassie looked like, it didn't matter what illnesses or handicaps she suffered from. She was their daughter, hers and Barry's, and no little girl could ever hope for more love. All Louise cared about was making sure that she was going to be safe, safe from whatever Ashley Chapel had become.

She just hoped that Mel, or Melaphyre – whoever was currently playing the part of the Technomancer – got it right. Looking around, she could see her standing in the distance. Louise decided to see whether she could give her a hand.

'I'm so sorry,' said the Doctor. 'Didn't I warn you that psychic attacks don't work inside the TARDIS? It must have slipped my mind.'

The Archimage didn't reply. The Doctor's cleverness was infuriating, but he couldn't allow his anger to cloud his judgement. The Hierophant and the Technomancer were obviously up to something – something designed to thwart his ascension – and he needed to be in the chamber of the Gods, not stuck with some time-travelling buffoon and his parlour tricks. He turned his attention to the control console, and tried to understand the controls. Stupidly, he had failed to observe the Valeyard when he had closed the door. But, since the Doctor could not harm him without turning into the Valeyard – his ally – he seemed to be in a win-win situation.

'Try all the controls you like, Mister Chapel,' said the Doctor smugly. 'It won't do you any good. Whether you like it or not, we're both stuck here.'

'That's what you think,' the Archimage called over his shoulder, flicking switches and pressing keys at random. 'Aren't you a little worried that I might trigger the self-destruct, or something unhealthy like that?'

'Not at all, Magnus Ashmael, not at all. It appears that my darker half was far more untrusting than you suspected. The Valeyard activated the isomorphic subroutines when he entered the TARDIS.'

'Meaning?' snapped the Archimage, getting extremely tired of the Doctor's prattling.

'And I thought that you were a genius. Oh, I'm sorry, I suppose the Chapel portion of your personality is getting rather lost in that mind of yours, what with all the others running around. Isomorphic means one-to-one.

The Valeyard arranged matters so that only he – or I, of course – can operate the controls. And since your psychic abilities are rather pointless given the console room's state of temporal grace, it seems that we find ourselves at an impasse, don't you think?' The Doctor stepped over to the console and flicked a switch. A blue curtain drew back in one of the roundelled walls, revealing a scanner screen – and the chamber of the Gods.

'There,' said the Doctor. 'A ringside view of the end of the Great Kingdom. Why don't you pull up a chair?'

Melaphyre observed the progress of the cybrid chain with satisfaction. The main linkages would be complete within minutes, and the final chain would arrive at the doors of the Tabernacle a moment later. And then she would lead that chain deep in the palace, into the chamber of the Gods.

The fact that she would be caught in the centre of the maelstrom as the three magicks shorted out was unimportant: it was the right thing to do, and even Melanie Bush agreed with that. If Mel hadn't completed the Codex, Chapel could never have effected the changes. It was only fitting that she should be the one to put matters right.

A sudden noise behind her shattered her reverie.

'Have you come to wish me good fortune?' she asked.

The chop to the neck was as painful as it was unexpected. Thankfully, the pain didn't last long. Unconsciousness came rather quickly.

'Doesn't it worry you?'

The Doctor started. 'Doesn't what worry me?'

'That your dark side can be brought to the surface so easily.' The Archimage held a finger in the air. 'I was led to believe that you were a force for good in the universe, a crusader for justice and morality. I find it hard to reconcile that with your dual existence as the Valeyard.'

The Doctor frowned. 'I don't have a dual existence. The Valeyard is yet another aberration caused by the quantum mnemonic that you let loose.'

'Really? That's not what he told me. He told me that he was the amalgamation of the darker side of your nature. All your evil, all your malice, all of the things that you try to keep buried; and he seemed convinced that you and he went back a long way.'

'Nonsense!' snapped the Doctor. Although his mind had still been present on both occasions when the Valeyard had assumed control, he hadn't been privy to much of what had transpired. Only the sheer horror of the attempted murder of the child and the reassuring force of the TARDIS had managed to reach down into the depths in which he had been abandoned. It was quite possible that the Valeyard had told Chapel everything, and yet –

Surely, the Valeyard that he had become was a different person from the one that he had faced in the Celestial Intervention Agency's courtroom?

The Master had claimed that the Valeyard came into being somewhere between the Doctor's twelfth and final, thirteenth, incarnation, and hopefully that was a very long time in the future. But the Doctor's recent preoccupation with his alter-ego had definitely been the seed for the Valeyard's presence in the artificial world of the Great Kingdom, surely?

The Doctor was convinced that there were two different Valeyards: one drawn out of him in the far future, and one extracted when the Millennium Codex had been run. He felt a deep sense of relief. There was nothing to worry about. This Valeyard was nothing more than his fears made real, a two-dimensional copy of his memories of the arrogant, sneering figure that had tried to steal the rest of his life from him. It didn't bear any relation to what he might or might not become.

'He was extremely frank with me, Doctor,' the Archimage continued, 'and his account of his creation was fascinating. Have you any idea what your twelfth incarnation will be like?'

'That's enough, Archimage!' yelled the Doctor. 'The Valeyard you spoke to was an illusion, a phantom of my mind. I don't have a dark side capable of creating such a monster, and I never will. The true Valeyard, the one I faced during that drumhead trial, was the result of something that might or might not happen centuries in the future!'

'Really?' said the Archimage quietly. 'All I know is that you gave Melanie Bush the means of cancelling out the Millennium Codex, but at the cost of her life. True?'

The Doctor looked at the scanner, but there was still no sign of Mel. But it was true; he had worked out how to short-circuit the three laws of magick, and he had known that the person who led the final strand into the central chamber of the Tabernacle would die. The trouble was, he had intended that he would be there to sort matters out, without any need for self-sacrifice. Now, he was stuck in the TARDIS, babysitting a bloodthirsty maniac whose intentions were even worse than letting the Kingdom continue. Somehow, he needed to get out of the corner he had painted himself into, and rescue Mel.

He froze. Was the creature he had become an illusion, or did he really carry the seeds of the Valeyard inside him? The same Valeyard that was the quintessence of all that the Doctor feared inside his soul. The same Valeyard that would willingly allow a companion to die.

Without a moment's hesitation, the Doctor turned to the console.

'Changed your mind?' asked the Archimage smugly.

'I've got to save Mel. I never intended it to get this far!' With a chilling realization, the Doctor turned to the scanner. The armoured form of the Technomancer was entering the chamber, marching at the head of a chain of cybrids, each one holding the clawed hand of the one in front.

'The road to hell is paved with good intentions, Doctor,' mocked the Archimage. 'And we all know your personal definition of hell, don't we?'

'Shut up!' The Doctor pulled the door lever, but nothing happened. He tried again, but the result was the same. 'I don't understand . . .' he muttered.

And then he did understand. The Valeyard had rigged the isomorphic defences. Rigged them so that only the Valeyard could open the doors. Either he forced the transformation – and accepted the consequences – or stood and watched as his companion sacrificed her life.

He was damned either way.

The magicks that flowed through the Technomancer armour made it heavy and sluggish, but salvation was only a few feet away. The cybrid chains crossed the Great Kingdom, joining elemental forces that should never have been joined, and she was the spearhead of those forces, a living, breathing avatar of Sciosophy, Thaumaturgy and Abraxas, three-in-one.

In a few moments, the travesty that she and Ashley Chapel had created would be wiped away, replaced by a reality that deserved to exist. Through the helmet of her armour, she could see Louise, tears streaming down her face, watching and waiting with her beautiful daughter in her arms. Poor Louise, who had suffered so much, who had watched her lover burn before her eyes.

As she reached the plinths and thrones of the Gods, her gauntleted hands outstretched, she remembered the Hierophant's dominance over the veil of mortality, and wondered.

Her hands touched the fusion-body of Saraquazel and the Great Intelligence –

– and the fundamental nature of the Great Kingdom flooded through her body, a blinding, scorching energy that burnt around her and through her and into her. She braced herself against the torrent, but quickly realized that something was wrong. She could tear down the

Kingdom, wipe its abomination from the face of the Earth, but she suddenly doubted that her mind was strong enough to ensure that the true reality replaced it.

She began to panic as the primal forces threatened to overwhelm her.

The Doctor closed his eyes, shutting out the image of the Technomancer on the scanner and shutting in his emotions. Mel's sacrifice was necessary, whispered the dark voice from the depths of his mind. Only she could control the cybrids, only she could lead them into the Tabernacle. The Doctor had taken the only decision possible, hadn't he?

But cold hard rationalizations had never been the Doctor's prime motivation. Melanie was an innocent, one of the countless innocents that he had drawn into his schemes and stratagems. Time and again, the Doctor had laughed at death, mocked it, as he righted wrongs and battled injustice in his endless crusade through time and space. After Katarina and Sara's deaths, he had sworn that he would never again place one of his companions in danger; only to stand helpless, his hands tied by the Laws of Time, as Adric plummeted to his death above prehistoric Earth. And then there was Kamelion, who had perished at the Doctor's own hands. And now Mel was giving her life. He glanced at the screen, and knew with conviction that she was running into difficulties.

He had no choice.

Reaching deep into his soul, the Doctor found the cancer that lurked within, waiting like a trap-door spider, waiting until it could consume him utterly, corrupting and perverting everything that he had ever believed in.

He embraced it.

One half of his mind devoted itself to the Valeyard, allowing just enough of his existence to filter through so that the isomorphic locks were released. The other half focused on the now free telepathic circuits, reaching out and adding the power of the TARDIS to the

Technomancer's efforts. If he could transfer enough artron energy into the blue armour, he could bolster her abilities and ensure that reality would reassert itself correctly. And hopefully protect Mel from the full force of the realignment into the bargain.

As he lent his support to the Technomancer, the Doctor knew that it was time to deal with the horror that lurked inside, the persona that was now blossoming within his soul.

A final, inevitable confrontation . . .

'At last, Doctor. I was beginning to fear you had lost yourself.'

The Doctor repressed a shudder. Those were the exact words which had greeted him at his so-called 'impartial inquiry', all those years ago on the Celestial Intervention Agency's station. And the figure standing before him was just as he remembered: the same slicked-back dark hair, the same sneering, condescending expression, the same superior tone. The quintessence and personification of all that rotted and festered in the Doctor's soul, wrapped in the silver and black robes of a learned Gallifreyan court prosecutor: the Valeyard.

A single pool of light was the only illumination in the ebony void; other than that, they were alone in the night, a night that existed solely in the endless, timeless depths of the Doctor's subconscious.

'On the contrary,' the Doctor replied, matching his alter ego's arrogance. 'I'm just beginning to find myself.'

The Valeyard gave a spiteful laugh. 'Excellent. I knew it was only a matter of time.'

The Doctor frowned. 'You've lost me.'

'Found, lost . . . your indecision will be the death of you,' the Valeyard uttered scornfully. 'Melanie Bush, Doctor: the companion that your actions have placed at risk. Her death is the only way to save this situation, and you made that decision, fully aware of the consequences. Is that not true?'

'Unless it's escaped your notice, I'm saving her life as we speak.'

'This time, yes,' said the Valeyard. 'But what of the future?' He turned his back on the Doctor and continued. 'There is a violent storm approaching, Doctor. A storm that will consume time and space — unless Time has a champion, someone with the strength of his convictions, the courage to make the difficult decisions and carry them through. Even if those decisions demand the greatest of sacrifices.' He faced the Doctor once more. 'And Time's Champion will also require an intimate familiarity with the undiscovered country, for Death will have his own avatar.'

The Doctor pondered the Valeyard's words. Over the last few years, he had heard whispers on the galactic grapevine, hushed and frightened predictions that suggested that the Valeyard's prophecy was far more than empty rhetoric. A major shift was occurring at the very pinnacle of reality, and its effects would be felt by everyone throughout the cosmos.

' "Things fall apart; the centre cannot hold . . ." ' the Doctor muttered. 'So, Time needs a champion to defend herself, does she? Let me guess: you want to apply for the job.'

'And why not? I would not flinch from carrying out my duties, Doctor. If a companion's death were the only way to salvage a situation, I would willingly accept that. I do not fear that undiscovered country; I do not fear death.'

The Doctor snorted in derision. 'And that's what this whole thing boils down to, isn't it? It isn't the act of sacrifice at all — it's because you want to revel in the carnage and chaos that your actions would cause.' He stabbed an accusatory finger. 'That's the fundamental difference between us, Valeyard: I'm learning to make those sorts of choices, those sorts of decisions, but I know with a certainty that I can make them without succumbing to the evil and corruption that you represent.' He shook his head. 'You, as Time's Champion? I'd have more faith in the Black Guardian!'

'Mock away,' replied the Valeyard with an arched eyebrow, his voice dropping. 'But remember this: of all your incarnations, your sixth is the weakest link, the one most likely to succumb. Beware your hubris, Doctor: it will be your undoing.'

Weakest? Weakest? The Doctor dismissed the Valeyard's words as a parting shot from a vanquished foe. Another part of his mind told him that Mel was succeeding in her efforts; his task here was at an end. Concentrating, he willed the other figure away, consigning it to the locked and bolted vaults of his deepest subconscious . . .

The Valeyard remained.

'Having difficulty, Doctor?' he asked mockingly. 'Perhaps I'm already too much a part of you to be dismissed so —'

He was gone. Finally. For the briefest of moments, the Doctor studied the infinite darkness, and had the most disturbing feeling that the abyss was looking right back at him.

And then he was in the console room, his hands clutching the telepathic circuits. Releasing them, he turned and focused on the scanner and the scene in the Tabernacle: the brilliance surrounding Mel was both breathtaking and terrifying, her armoured figure the dark heart of an incandescent sun. He squinted against the radiance, but the light from the scanner suddenly burst through his eyelids and into his mind, searing and cleansing and

Louise hugged Cassie even tighter as the radiance from the centre of the chamber burnt like a star. Even if the Doctor's plan worked, Mel would be dead, Barry would *still* be dead, and Cassie . . . She sighed. Cassie would be Cassie. Her daughter. The little girl that she loved.

Stroking Cassie's blonde hair, Louise stared into the

heart of the incandescence as it expanded to consume them all. As the fringes of the transformation washed over her, a single thought crossed her mind. If this was the face of God, she just hoped He could hear her prayer. And then the light

Part Three

Epiphany

Seventeen

The Doctor opened his eyes and winced as the brilliant lighting assailed his vision. As he scrambled to his feet, he noticed a few things immediately. He was wearing his usual jacket once more, Ashley Chapel was dressed in a beige suit, and the interior of the TARDIS was once more white. And then he looked at the scanner and swallowed. What had happened? The TARDIS was still surrounded by the multicoloured crystal of the Tabernacle. Had the Great Kingdom survived, despite all their efforts? Or had it been transformed into something far, far worse?

'Do not worry, Doctor. All is as it was.' The voice, resonant yet kindly, rang in his mind like a bell. And he recognized it.

'Saraquazel?'

'I have very little time left, so please: join me.'

Opening the doors of the TARDIS, the Doctor stepped out into the brightly coloured, brightly lit interior of the Tabernacle. 'I don't understand,' he muttered. And then he saw the prone form of the Technomancer, collapsed in front of Saraquazel's throne. The giant golden figure, man-shaped with the head of an antelope, was staring down at her.

'Her life ebbs, Doctor. But her sacrifice was a valiant one.'

'Was it?' he spat bitterly, kneeling down beside her. 'Mel? Mel, can you hear me?' He noticed a small catch on the neck of the helmet, and tugged it. The face plate came free. And the Doctor gasped.

'Anastasia?' he whispered.

The woman smiled. 'It's Anne, Doctor. Anne Travers.'

'Don't move, Anne. I'll get some help –'

She shook her head. 'It's too late, Doctor. I'm dying. But everything's going to be all right, isn't it?'

He shot a questioning look at Saraquazel.

'I am maintaining the Tabernacle. The shock of the final realignment would rob her of her last moments.'

The Doctor nodded and returned his attention to Anne. 'Why did you do it?'

'I couldn't let Mel die, Doctor. She didn't deserve to sacrifice herself. She's young, she's got so much to look forward to. I squandered my life, spent it on bitterness, regrets and revenge. Perhaps this one act goes some way towards making up for that.' She smiled. 'What do you think?'

'Oh Anne,' he sighed.

'And the Intelligence. It won't be bothering the Earth again.'

'You destroyed it?'

'No –' She started coughing.

'Easy now.'

She caught her breath and continued. 'No. I could have done. The power that I controlled – it would have been easy. But that would have made me as bad as the Intelligence. No, I banished it. It's stranded on the edges of the universe, riding the blue shift outwards into infinity. Poetic justice, don't you think?'

'Rest now, Anne –'

She smiled weakly. 'Thank you, Doctor. It wouldn't have worked without your help. That extra strength . . . and the fact that Saraquazel lent his own abilities . . .' She grabbed the Doctor's hand and squeezed it. 'I was even able to undo a little of the damage . . .' Another spasm of coughing began.

'What do you mean?' asked the Doctor, but Anne's eyes were unfocused, distant.

'Father, I did it for you,' she muttered. And then she died.

The Doctor closed her eyes and stood up. 'She's gone,' he stated flatly.

'I mourn her passing, Doctor,' intoned Saraquazel. 'The others are waiting for you.'

The Doctor turned – and saw Mel running towards him with her arms outstretched. A moment later, she was hugging him warmly. 'Oh, Doctor – I thought you'd become that, that thing.'

'No, Mel. The Valeyard is gone.' He just hoped that she was convinced, because he wasn't sure that he was. Would the bars of the Valeyard's prison contain him? And then he returned to the here and now. 'Where are the others?'

'Here, Doctor.' Louise appeared from the doorway, cradling Cassie in her arms. Sadly, the Doctor noted that the little girl's condition had returned. Louise must have seen his expression.

'It's all right, Doctor. She's got us to look after her.'

'Us?' And then the Doctor realized what she meant, as Barry appeared next to her, smiling broadly.

'I'm not sure I understand.'

'It was the Hierophant,' Mel explained. 'She stole my armour, but remained in touch with me telepathically – she needed my help to control the cybrids. Just as the transformation began, she attempted to "reach beyond the veil of mortality", she called it.' Mel shrugged. 'It was something that the Hierophant could do.'

Louise put her arm around Barry and squeezed his waist. 'However she did it, I'm not complaining.'

'Saraquazel?' The voice came from the open doorway of the TARDIS. It was Chapel.

'Ah, Ashley Chapel,' came the reply. 'The cause of my imprisonment.'

Chapel approached the golden figure. 'I did it for you, Saraquazel. You were going to usher in a new age of harmony, of humanity –'

'You superimposed your own desires and caprices, Chapel. I begged you to set me free; you sought to control me.'

'Give me another chance, Saraquazel.' It was obvious that he just wasn't listening. Or didn't want to hear, the Doctor decided.

'It is time for me to complete the transformation and leave this world.'

'How will you get home?' asked the Doctor. 'I'd offer to help, but the TARDIS isn't really designed to travel that far into the future. Some minor Law of Time or other.'

'My imprisonment gave me time to study the alien physical laws which govern your universe, Doctor. There are many routes back to my home: wormholes, temporal rifts, even another pan-dimensional vacuum emboitement. It may take me a long time, but at least I shall have company.'

'What do you mean?'

'I desire a companion, someone to share the wonders of your cosmos.' Saraquazel pointed at Chapel. 'He shall join me.'

'No!' he screamed. 'You can't –' But the plea was never completed. Chapel faded away in a sparkle of golden light.

'He is with me now,' said Saraquazel. 'I will show him the glories of the universe, and he will teach me humanity.'

'I wouldn't be so sure about that,' muttered the Doctor. But Saraquazel never heard: he stood from his throne and crossed his arms over his chest.

'Goodbye. All of you.' And then the antelope's mouth formed a smile. 'The last of the Gods leaves the Great Kingdom.'

And then he was gone, in a fountain of light.

'What happens now?' asked Mel, looking around the Tabernacle. 'I thought everything was supposed to return to normal?'

'Some residual effect, perhaps?' replied the Doctor.

And then the Tabernacle vanished around them. One

second, they had been in the middle of a stained glass cathedral, the next, they were –

'Tooting Bec!' yelled Barry. 'We're in Tooting Bec!'

Mel frowned, and noticed the building they were standing next to. 'You mean the Tabernacle was a, a public convenience in Tooting Bec?' She giggled.

The Doctor raised an eyebrow. 'Yetis on the toilet in Tooting Bec; now there's a thought.' He linked arms with Mel and smiled at the others, noticing the tall man with curly hair standing behind Louise, looking around in confusion before slipping into the crowd around them. 'Alane, I presume,' said the Doctor. 'Anyway, does anybody fancy a glass of champagne?'

'Champagne?' asked Louise. 'Why?'

'Because it's New Year's Day – the millennium, Mel. And it definitely is party time.' He nodded at the clock above a nearby jeweller's: 12.10.

'That all took place in ten minutes? I don't believe it,' laughed Louise.

'Quantum mnemonics are powerful things, Louise – not to be trifled with,' replied the Doctor.

'And everything's back to normal?' asked Barry. 'Just as it was before it all happened?'

The Doctor frowned. 'That remains to be seen. But I suggest we make the most of what's left of the evening. Eat, drink and be merry, for tomorrow –' He stopped himself. Hardly the sentiments for the start of a new millennium, were they? In spite of the painful truths he had learnt about himself, they all deserved some downtime.

To the strains of Auld Lang Syne, the Doctor, Mel, Louise and Barry introduced Cassandra to the twenty-first century.

Breakfast in Louise's house was both very late and very subdued, but subdued in a pleasant, slightly hungover sort of way. Mel had complained about feeling under the weather, but had soon shut up when Louise reminded her about the bottle of champagne that she had appropriated, before vanishing into a dark corner with a very handsome young man.

' "Police are baffled by the unusually high number of deaths that occurred during the New Year's celebrations in Central London last night",' Louise read out from the teletext news. ' "Fifteen revellers died from heart attacks, according to Scotland Yard." Fifteen people,' she repeated.

'Anne saved as many as she could,' explained Mel. 'If it hadn't been for her bringing them back, the numbers would have been astronomical.' She smiled. 'She even managed to save Gargil.'

'Er, I think this is even more worrying,' said Louise, beckoning the others over. She could see the words on the screen, but wasn't sure whether she believed it or not.

'How did that happen?' asked Barry, and then smiled. 'I know, I know. Quantum mnemonics are not to be trifled with, eh Doctor?'

The Doctor nodded. 'Still, if those are the only two side-effects of the Millennium Codex, the Earth has come off lightly.' And then he left the room.

In London's Docklands, Cesar Pelli's magnificent feat of architecture, Number One, Canada Square, had apparently changed shape: its trademark roof was a pyramid no longer. It was now a huge golden spire.

And, further up the Thames, the monstrous Millennium Hall, Ashley Chapel's gift to the nation, was gone. In its place, Battersea Power Station had apparently risen from the ashes.

Barry leapt from the sofa and threw open the curtains. And laughed at the view of the four tall pillars he had thought were gone forever. 'Poetic justice,' he sighed. 'Come and take a look.'

Louise stood beside him and nodded. 'Now that's what I call a view.' And then she looked downwards. The Doctor was walking down the street. 'Where's he off to?'

Mel shrugged. 'Probably gone to fetch the TARDIS

from Tooting. I wouldn't worry about it. Now, is there any more coffee?'

Barry nodded. 'I'll do it. And then I think I'll pay my mother a visit.'

The streets were cold and empty, but that matched the Doctor's mood precisely. Although catastrophe had been averted, he had been given a glimpse of a much darker future. His own, personal future.

Then he smiled, and allowed himself a brief laugh. He knew himself, he knew the most distant recesses of his own mind. And the Valeyard was safely under lock and key.

He shook his head. The Doctor, grandmaster of chess on a thousand boards, with his companions as sacrificial pawns?

That would be the day.

Craig's Bit – The Return

Hello there. Did you enjoy that?

I'd like to thank the following people, who greased the path, oiled the wheels, made the coffee and poured the Carlsberg. So, in no particular order . . .

The people I forgot the last time round: Eddie Thornley, Tim Parker, Dave Richards, Chris West, Jim Mortimore.

The people who suggested, proofread, commented etc: Paul Leonard, Andy Lane, Andrew Hair, Justin Richards, Rebecca Levene, Andy Bodle.

The people who provided inspiration: Lindsey Ashworth, Adrian Middleton, Neil Gaiman, Alex Musson, Chris Claremont, Peter David.

The editors who put up with missed deadlines: David Richardson, Gary Russell, Gary Gillatt.

The people who made it possible simply by being there: Christine Hinton (my Mum!), Peter Ashworth, Kevin Gibbs, the ever-mysterious Mister J, Troy Turner, Mike Ramsay, John Pearson, James Lynch (especially!).

And yet again I'd like to prostrate myself before the artistic genius of Alister Pearson for the quite breathtaking cover – can you imagine Bonnie Langford wearing *that*? Then again, I'd give my eye teeth to have seen the Sixth Doctor in the Valeyard's robes . . .

Not last and not least, Marc Platt for allowing me a sneak preview of *Downtime* – the third invasion by the Great Intelligence – and Steve Lyons, for tying *Head Games* into *Millennial Rites*.

Finally, I doff my hat to the Internet crew, and – most

importantly — to all of my erstwhile colleagues at the Warwick Software Development Laboratory. This one's for you. Can you guess why?

That was the dedication I originally wrote, months and months ago. But now I'm going to go all deep and meaningful for a moment.

Five minutes after I completed draft one of *Millennial Rites* (back in April 1995) I got a phone call, informing me that my ex-lodger and old friend Ian Clarke had died of cancer the previous day. Ian was only thirty-seven, but he packed more into those years than most people pack into a full lifetime. For those who are interested, Ian was the role model for the Maitre D' in *The Crystal Bucephalus*, and he really was just like that — only far more fun.

I shall miss him terribly, and the least I can do is dedicate this book to his memory.

Goodbye, Ian.

Available in the *Doctor Who – New Adventures* series:

TIMEWYRM: GENESYS by John Peel
TIMEWYRM: EXODUS by Terrance Dicks
TIMEWYRM: APOCALYPSE by Nigel Robinson
TIMEWYRM: REVELATION by Paul Cornell
CAT'S CRADLE: TIME'S CRUCIBLE by Marc Platt
CAT'S CRADLE: WARHEAD by Andrew Cartmel
CAT'S CRADLE: WITCH MARK by Andrew Hunt
NIGHTSHADE by Mark Gatiss
LOVE AND WAR by Paul Cornell
TRANSIT by Ben Aaronovitch
THE HIGHEST SCIENCE by Gareth Roberts
THE PIT by Neil Penswick
DECEIT by Peter Darvill-Evans
LUCIFER RISING by Jim Mortimore and Andy Lane
WHITE DARKNESS by David A. McIntee
SHADOWMIND by Christopher Bulis
BIRTHRIGHT by Nigel Robinson
ICEBERG by David Banks
BLOOD HEAT by Jim Mortimore
THE DIMENSION RIDERS by Daniel Blythe
THE LEFT-HANDED HUMMINGBIRD by Kate Orman
CONUNDRUM by Steve Lyons
NO FUTURE by Paul Cornell
TRAGEDY DAY by Gareth Roberts
LEGACY by Gary Russell
THEATRE OF WAR by Justin Richards
ALL-CONSUMING FIRE by Andy Lane
BLOOD HARVEST by Terrance Dicks
STRANGE ENGLAND by Simon Messingham
FIRST FRONTIER by David A. McIntee
ST ANTHONY'S FIRE by Mark Gatiss
FALLS THE SHADOW by Daniel O'Mahony
PARASITE by Jim Mortimore
WARLOCK by Andrew Cartmel
SET PIECE by Kate Orman
INFINITE REQUIEM by Daniel Blythe
SANCTUARY by David A. McIntee
HUMAN NATURE by Paul Cornell
ORIGINAL SIN by Andy Lane
SKY PIRATES! by Dave Stone
ZAMPER by Gareth Roberts
TOY SOLDIERS by Paul Leonard
HEAD GAMES by Steve Lyons

The next Missing Adventure is *The Empire of Glass* by Andy Lane, featuring the first Doctor, Steven and Vicki.

Available in the *Doctor Who – New Adventures* series:
TIMEWYRM: GENESYS by John Peel
TIMEWYRM: EXODUS by Terrance Dicks
TIMEWYRM: APOCALYPSE by Nigel Robinson
TIMEWYRM: REVELATION by Paul Cornell
CAT'S CRADLE: TIME'S CRUCIBLE by Marc Platt
CAT'S CRADLE: WARHEAD by Andrew Cartmel
CAT'S CRADLE: WITCH MARK by Andrew Hunt
NIGHTSHADE by Mark Gatiss
LOVE AND WAR by Paul Cornell
TRANSIT by Ben Aaronovitch
THE HIGHEST SCIENCE by Gareth Roberts
THE PIT by Neil Penswick
DECEIT by Peter Darvill-Evans
LUCIFER RISING by Jim Mortimore and Andy Lane
WHITE DARKNESS by David A. McIntee
SHADOWMIND by Christopher Bulis
BIRTHRIGHT by Nigel Robinson
ICEBERG by David Banks
BLOOD HEAT by Jim Mortimore
THE DIMENSION RIDERS by Daniel Blythe
THE LEFT-HANDED HUMMINGBIRD by Kate Orman
CONUNDRUM by Steve Lyons
NO FUTURE by Paul Cornell
TRAGEDY DAY by Gareth Roberts
LEGACY by Gary Russell
THEATRE OF WAR by Justin Richards
ALL-CONSUMING FIRE by Andy Lane
BLOOD HARVEST by Terrance Dicks
STRANGE ENGLAND by Simon Messingham
FIRST FRONTIER by David A. McIntee
ST ANTHONY'S FIRE by Mark Gatiss
FALLS THE SHADOW by Daniel O'Mahony
PARASITE by Jim Mortimore
WARLOCK by Andrew Cartmel
SET PIECE by Kate Orman
INFINITE REQUIEM by Daniel Blythe
SANCTUARY by David A. McIntee
HUMAN NATURE by Paul Cornell
ORIGINAL SIN by Andy Lane
SKY PIRATES! by Dave Stone
ZAMPER by Gareth Roberts
TOY SOLDIERS by Paul Leonard
HEAD GAMES by Steve Lyons

The next Missing Adventure is *The Empire of Glass* by Andy Lane, featuring the first Doctor, Steven and Vicki.